A River of Magic

Ashuan Greed 2

Janna Ruth

First published in New Zealand in 2022

Copyright © 2022 by Janna Ruth

www.janna-ruth.com

ISBN-13: 978-1-99-117291-4

also available as ebook: 978-1-99-117292-1

ASHUAN GREED BOOK 2

A RIVER OF MAGIC

JANNA RUTH

A note about sensitive topics

There is a lot of magic and fantastical creatures in this book, but the teenagers at the core of this story are just that: they are teenagers. And as such they deal with a number of very real issues on top of the magical ones.

If you don't like spoilers and you're cool with anything, skip this note and start the book. If you like to be prepared, keep reading. I'm writing this because reading should be fun, not a bad surprise.

While this series starts out as a YA fantasy, there are mentions of sex, drugs and sadly no rock'n'roll. There will be no graphic sex scenes. In this book, there is a plot around (magical) drug abuse. You will also encounter teenagers and adults drinking alcohol, including an alcoholic mother who is neglectful to her children. As for the underage characters: the age of drinking beer and wine without adult supervision in Germany is 16. For drinking spirits and cocktails, it is 18.

As fun as it sounds, hunting monsters and wielding magic is dangerous. People will be hurt in this series and some will die. That includes characters who you got to know well. Their deaths will not be meaningless, though it might feel like that to the surviving characters. Because I'm a big fan of consequences, that means you will see depictions of grief in various stages.

In this book in particular, you will encounter a demon that murders several people while also getting hurt badly. There are consequences about this and the character won't get away with a slap on the hand.

Last but not least, there are instances of bullying, mostly verbal, by other teenagers. These scenes are few in between and our affected characters will rise above that.

The characters live in a dangerous world, but it's also beautiful. For every dark spot, there will be light and humour. And of course magic. Lots and lots of magic.

Enjoy!

Love, Janna

Part 1
Drugs & Romance

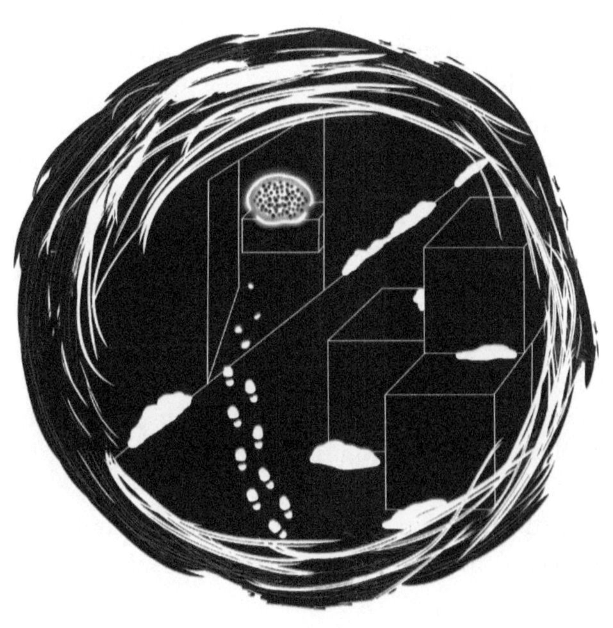

Rachel

Nico's favourite music flowed softly from his stereo, filling the room with its dark and sultry notes. Posters of his beloved football and soccer teams adorned the wall, some of them taped multiple times to extend their lifespan. The plants on his windowsill remained green and luscious, alive in a way that he no longer was.

Rachel had taken it upon herself to care for them, just as she cared for his room. The bed was neatly made, the shelves wiped clean, and the carpet vacuumed. Each time she cleaned, however, it felt like a piece of Nico was lost, and the room became just that—a room. No amount of posters or gentle music could bring him back.

Finally, Rachel made the decision to go through his belongings, continuing what her mother had started before Rachel had so rudely told her to stop. Since then, her mother hadn't dared enter Nico's room. In the house, they tiptoed around each other, never spending too much time together in one room.

Nico had accumulated a lot of stuff. Some of the clothes in the wardrobe were likely from five years ago, but he'd never got rid of them. Now, Rachel sorted them into piles, with most of them destined for donation, some for a second-hand shop, and a few select pieces she would keep to remember him by, such as his favourite T-shirt.

Once she finished with the clothes, Rachel moved on to the desk, where Nico's half-done math homework still lay. Rachel solved the equations in her mind until the page became blurred, and she had to wipe away her tears.

Shaking her head, her gaze fell upon two presents—one slender, the other cube-shaped. The memory resurfaced from the haze of the funeral, and Rachel realised they were the birthday presents her father had left with her. One for Nico and one for her.

Should she open Nico's present? Or should she leave it wrapped for forever? Maybe she should place it at his grave?

Annoyed, Rachel shook her head. Leaving it there would only invite theft from opportunists. Instead, she grabbed the gift and tore the wrapping paper open, curious about what her father had chosen for Nico, and what she should do with it now.

A watch.

Her father had given Nico a watch. Sure, it looked fancy and all, but it also felt terribly impersonal. Or so it seemed. When Rachel turned it around, she noticed it was engraved *from Warren to Nicholas*, and from *Nicholas to Michael*—though her father was known as Mick by everyone—and from *Mick to Nico*. This watch had been passed down to three generations of Hadden men, and now it had reached its final destination.

No. Rachel wouldn't let it end here. Her father had given it to her to keep, so she would wear it, whether her name was engraved on the back or not.

After fastening it around her wrist, she opened her own present, wondering what family heirloom awaited her. The gift was a bit boxier, about two hands wide and tall. Rachel tore off the wrapping paper and lifted the lid of the box, revealing pink gauze.

Frowning at the colour her father had chosen for her, Rachel reached for the hidden object and placed it on her lap. It was surprisingly light for its size. Carefully, she unwrapped the gauze, being cautious not to tear it. As the first beechwood twig came into view, Rachel gasped.

Three intertwined circles formed a sphere. The wood was completely covered in soft white strings as delicate as silk, which led to an intricate woven web between the circles. As Rachel moved it, the spheres moved in and out of each other like a perpetuum mobile, giving the impression that the intricate web was a living, breathing entity. Five elegant white feathers hung from the bottom node point as she lifted it from the gauze. It was like a dreamcatcher.

No, not a dreamcatcher. A dreamweb.

The dreamweb.

Rachel's mouth went dry. Could it be? She thought she felt a connection to it, but how did her father come across an Emblem of Power? He was a Maths professor. True, he had some roots in New Orleans, which might explain Rachel's affinity for ghosts. However, she was convinced that the dreams came from her mother's side. It was Annette she saw in the dreamworld, not her father.

Had it come to her in the same mysterious way that Shitaten's Feather had found its way to Fabian? But who could have known? Who could have convinced her father to give her this for her birthday if he had no choice in the matter?

Rachel knew she could ask him. He would be awake soon, although he rarely had time for a chat on a weekday. But Rachel couldn't wait. The answers she sought would not be provided by her father.

She needed to find them for herself.

As soon as Rachel's head hit the pillow, she fell asleep. If that wasn't a sign of the dreamweb's power, then the sight that awaited her in the dreamworld surely was. She'd hung the dreamweb above her bed, where it swayed gently in a soft breeze. The moment she awoke in the dream, she felt invigorated. Her vision was sharper, her touch more sensitive, and her awareness seemed to stretch endlessly.

There was a path in between her dreams, one she'd never walked before. Rachel willed herself along this path, watching as the meadow transformed into a grassland and then into a desert. The wind blew the sand, but in her dream, Rachel was untouchable, never straying from her chosen path.

Night had fallen in the desert, or perhaps it was always night in this part of the dreamworld. The wind died down, revealing a house nestled among the dunes. Several trees stood around a shimmering silver pool in the moonlight. The house itself was made of red sandstone, with small, round windows and a flat rooftop that appeared easily climbable.

On the roof stood an old man, his blind eyes gazing at the moon, forever lost in his dreams. But he wasn't the one Rachel had come to find. She entered the house, its rooms separated by colourful curtains. A woman sat humming in a chair, diligently writing down dreams.

Rachel couldn't explain how she knew, but she did. The woman hadn't dreamed the dreams herself; she merely transcribed them, taking great care to capture each and every detail she was told. And when she wasn't writing, she would cook, clean, and sell the dreamwebs that adorned the opposite wall. She kept the house running while her husband dreamed, and her son assisted.

It was the son Rachel had come to see, the one who'd crafted this dream, because this was where it had all started. But as she slipped through the curtains, she found Nico sitting in his room, his back hunched over a dreamweb—*her* dreamweb.

He held it up for her to see and squinted in the moonlight. "Do you think this will satisfy him?"

"Satisfy whom?" Though Nico had said him, she instantly thought of her own mother, whom she'd spent years trying to impress.

"The dreamer," he relied, a hint of annoyance in his voice that was so reminiscent of Nico it took her breath away.

"Are you dreaming?" Rachel asked. "Or are you what I'm dreaming of?"

Nico set down the dreamweb and blinked. "One could say you're in my dream since you've ventured here."

"Can ghosts dream?" Her voice trembled with emotion. Nico hadn't become a ghost. He hadn't stayed behind to keep her company. What if this was truly him? What if he now resided in the dreamworld?

"I'm not the one your heart desires," Nico replied, dashing her hopes. "Though I will not force you to change the dream you long for. Comfort is good. It keeps us safe on these dream roads."

So, he only wore Nico's face—or rather, Rachel had given it to him because that was the face she understood. The face she trusted. And she wanted to trust this stranger, needed to trust him, because he'd crafted the Emblem of Power—her dreamweb.

"Ah, yes. My finest creation. It was the last one I crafted before the moon visited me."

"The moon visited you?" Rachel peered through the tiny window at the night sky. The moon was full and more silvery than Earth's.

Nico—since she had no other name for him, she might as well keep calling him that—stepped closer. As he looked up at the moon, his face bathed in its silver shine, she glimpsed an eternal love.

"She's beautiful, isn't she?" Nico asked, then shook his head. "There is such beauty in this world that my father is blind to. He lives only in his dreams. Reality doesn't matter to him." Although he didn't voice his pain aloud, Rachel could hear it clearly: *I don't matter to him.*

Her heart ached for the boy, and she knew they were connected in more ways than just their dreams.

"It's an old pain, ancient, really," Nico said. "It repeats itself. From dreamer to dreamer."

His words struck a chord, piercing Rachel's heart as she thought of her mother, seemingly lost in her dream, oblivious to reality. "I understand. So, this is where it all started?"

"Oh, no. The neglect is pretty much ingrained in dreamers as long as dreams existed. But this is where you began."

"Where I began?" The concept was so complex that the dreamworld blurred at the edges. Rachel's mind couldn't fully comprehend what Nico meant, and she felt herself being pulled back to the waking world, where thoughts were clearer.

But Nico took her hand, keeping her in the dream. "The dreamweb," he said softly, nodding towards the unfinished object on the bed. "Here in this dream, it's merely that. When the moon kisses it, it will become something so much more. The Power of Devotion flows through it as it has flowed through my family."

Rachel turned to look at him, searching his face for the parts that weren't Nico. "Who are you?"

"Your brother." Then he sighed, and some of his edges frayed until he was Nico and not quite Nico. His voice deepened. "The eternal dreamer. The one who never woke from the dream." He chuckled, and it was as if the world righted itself. His demeanour, so strikingly similar to her brother's, cleared the image again. "Not in this memory, but soon." Although his words were foreign, he was once again Nico.

"We could've dreamed together," Rachel said wistfully, longing to share the dreamworld with her brother.

"We're together now."

Rachel squeezed his hand, overwhelmed with sadness. She missed him so much. "Now, we're together." This was her world—*their* world. Their reality.

Nico shook his head. "Now that you have arrived in this place—let's call it *'the before'*—you must understand, Rachel. The dreamworld is intoxicating. It is filled with fantasies fuelled by longing. It can reveal hidden truths. But it's not reality. Don't be like my father. Or your mother."

"What do you mean?" The pain that united them resurfaced.

"Don't close your eyes to the beauty of the real world just yet, Rachel. You are alive. So live. Create your own dreams. The fate of the future will be in your hands soon enough."

And with that, the sand swirled until Rachel could no longer see her own hand before her eyes. When it settled, she found herself back in the meadow. Alone.

Live.

Nico was gone. The person the dream had shown her wasn't truly him. As much as she wished it were. Living without her brother was difficult, but Rachel knew he would want her to carry on. So, as challenging as it was, that was exactly what she would have to do.

Jan

"... has the ability to store vibrations and transform..."

The tablet balanced against his knees, Jan lay on the bed, watching the YouTuber go through their collection of crystals.

Half-dozing, Jan had seen many videos like this before. By now, there was hardly anything new to learn. His own collection of gems and crystals far surpassed that of the YouTuber. Thanks to Caroline and Samantha, he'd verified his collection, separating the genuine magical gems from the fake ones.

Through the wall next to him, the same K-Pop album played he'd been hearing for the last five weeks. If Anne didn't stop listening to it soon, he'd be able to sing along, Korean or not.

But that wasn't the only sound he heard from next door. Far louder than the music were the sudden and prolonged outbursts of giggling. Jan would've been annoyed, wondering what could possibly be so funny, but instead, his ears strained to pick up the distinct sound of Meg within Anne's deeper laughter.

As was often the case on a Friday night, Meg was sleeping over. Although, in Jan's opinion, she'd chosen the wrong room to do so. Probably because, so far, Meg hadn't told Anne about their brand-new relationship and didn't want to neglect her friendship by hanging out with him.

They had officially started dating the day they encountered the demon. Meg had taken his hand and led him into the guest room she slept in whenever she visited her grandma. Under the pretence of dressing his wounds—which were really just a slightly rolled ankle and some scratches—she'd touched him, until he ended the charade by kissing her.

That had been three weeks ago, and so far, their relationship consisted of stolen kisses and naughty text messages. Nothing more.

Annoyingly, Matt had been right. On the night they watched Nico, Jan had proudly proclaimed that he would wait for the girl to be ready. But that was before he'd even had a girlfriend. Now he had Meg, and she wouldn't even be his official girlfriend. Instead, she seemed to enjoy the stolen moments far too much for his liking.

The door creaked open, and Jan decided that he actually liked those stolen moments more than he would openly admit. Pretending not to have noticed her, he kept his eyes fixed on the tablet, although he hadn't been listening to what the YouTuber had been prattling on about for quite some time.

Next to him, a weight settled on the bed, and then Meg's warmth pressed against his arm. For at least half a minute, she didn't say a word, although Jan could see her glancing back and forth between his face and the tablet from the corner of his eye.

Finally, she groaned. "Do you really believe all this nonsense?"

"You'd be surprised how much of it is true." While he suspected she wasn't quite as averse to magic as she pretended to be, they hadn't had an open conversation about monsters and magic. Not even when she tended to his hellhound wounds.

"Now you sound like Sam."

Jan chuckled. He paused the tablet and set it aside, leaning slightly into her. "What's the matter? Did you finally realise how boring Anne is?"

Meg grinned, no longer taking offence when he teased his sister. "She has to help your mum with something. I didn't feel like joining them."

He leaned back and raised an eyebrow. "Is that so? What do you feel like then?"

A wicked little smile appeared on her lips, setting Jan's insides on fire. Still, he patiently waited for her to make the first move. He didn't want to take control of the situation too early.

The smile disappeared, and Meg licked her lips instead. Then, she leaned forward agonisingly slowly and cupped his face with her hands.

Her lips came closer, hesitated for a second, before barely brushing against his, as if she expected him to pull away.

Jan patiently waited for her to show a little more courage and was rewarded when the pressure increased slightly. It was a nice kiss, but not quite what he yearned for.

Before Meg could pull away, he slipped his hand around her back and flipped her so that she lay beneath him. Meg squealed in surprise, but her eyes sparkled. It was enough to spur him on.

"This is a kiss."

With a hand on her neck, he leaned down and pressed his lips firmly against hers. His tongue darted out, seeking entrance, which she granted almost instantly. As soon as their tongues met, the heat in Jan's stomach intensified. He kissed her more passionately, relishing the feeling of her beneath him.

"Jan, do you—?"

Dammit! Anne had entered the room, looking for Meg. Now, his little sister stood in the doorway, her eyes as wide as saucers. "What are you doing with Meg?"

"What does it look like?" Jan quipped, his blood still rushing through his head—and other body parts.

He glanced down at Meg, her cheeks flushed as she gasped for air. It was such a lovely sight that he wanted to kiss her again, Anne or no Anne. But Meg wriggled out from under him and stood up so fast she must've felt dizzy for a moment. "Are you done, Anne?" Her voice sounded a bit squeaky.

She quickly regained her composure, however, and as she left his room, she swung her backside in a way that could only be meant as a tease.

Jan found himself grinning until he noticed Anne's glare. She *hadn't* left his room. Instead, she leaned forward and hissed, "I told you not to hit on my friends!"

"Then maybe you should tell your girlfriends not to hit on me. Meg came into *my* room."

Anne grunted in unspoken fury. "As if!"

Losing interest in her teenage tantrum, Jan grabbed his tablet again and pressed play. "Ask her yourself."

"You... you're such an idiot!" Anne exclaimed before storming out of the room.

Jan grinned as his door slammed shut. He'd kissed Meg and annoyed his sister. It was a good score for the evening. Too bad that was all that was going to happen. With the secret out in the open, he doubted Meg would come into his room again. She and Anne would probably have a long girl talk with lots of tears, hugs, and silly promises. In the end, Meg might not even be his girlfriend anymore, not that he thought she would be that stupid.

But girlfriend or not, the rest of the night promised only boredom. This video was definitely dull.

Annoyed, Jan turned it off, got up, and grabbed his jacket. Patting his pocket to ensure he still had some cigarettes, he went out into the corridor and put on his shoes. From Anne's room, he could hear agitated whispers and sniffles.

Jan rolled his eyes. "I'm going out," he called to no one in particular.

One thing was certain: he wasn't going to stick around for teenage girl drama.

His breath rose in white clouds from his lips. It had snowed a couple of days ago, and then again yesterday. Jan pushed his hands deep into his pockets, rolling the lighter between his fingers.

Down at the docks, the snow had been ploughed aside, leaving behind the slushy grey of concrete. Further down, between the storage units, Jan saw a fire flicker, and his lips stretched into a grin.

He rubbed his hands for warmth and approached the group huddled around the burning garbage can. "Hey guys, what's cooking?"

The others greeted his arrival with loud cheers, hand clasping, and fist bumps. "We were wondering if you got lost in some ditch, man," his friend Felix said.

"Nah, couldn't decide whether I wanted to stay warm and cosy or hang out in the cold with you guys."

Felix laughed, grabbed Jan's jacket by the arm, and pulled him closer to the fire. "Some vodka to warm you up?"

"Did you raid your dad's pantry?" Jan asked, before nodding enthusiastically. "Yes, please."

The alcohol was just the thing he needed. First, it burnt his throat, and then it ignited a fire in the pit of his stomach, warming him.

Meanwhile, he noticed Lutz rubbing his nose as if he had a cold, his eyes darting back and forth. After a while, Lutz shuffled closer to Felix and nudged his elbow. "Can I have the money now?"

Jan would've had to be an idiot not to notice the signs of withdrawal. "Did your parents cut you off again?"

"It's more that Lutz is craving the expensive stuff now," Felix drawled, not reaching into his pocket at all. "Why do I always have to give you money?"

Lutz huffed. "Not everyone has parents who shower them with money the moment they feel a little bad."

Felix laughed, and Jan joined in. Like Lutz, Jan didn't have a huge allowance. And like him, he had his way of getting the extra money he needed. Their first step was always to bug Felix. His parents paid pretty well for his happiness, something Felix took full advantage of.

"How much?" Felix asked, finally taking out his wallet.

"Eighty for ten."

"Eighty euro for ten?" Felix started to put the wallet back. "Are you mad?"

Lutz's eyes bulged. "It's magic stuff." His tongue pushed between his teeth. "Literally magic."

"All drugs are magic." While Jan had tried one or two things, he wasn't too keen on the harder stuff.

"No! M-A-G-I-C!" Lutz bared his teeth in frustration. "I don't know what it's short for, but the stuff is magic. If I had some, I'd show you."

"I've got some," a guy from the opposite side of the trash can, Kevin, called out.

Instantly, Lutz was by his side. "Give it to me."

Kevin snorted. "What was the price? Ten for a pill, right?"

"Felix!" Lutz barked.

Felix exchanged a look with Jan. "What do you think?"

"It's probably the same old thing with a different name." But Jan couldn't help being curious. "Give him the money."

"All right. Hey, Kev, three pills for twenty-seven," Felix called.

A minute later, the exchange was made. Jan held the innocuous-looking pill between his fingers and watched it as the flicker of the flames painted it orange. Lutz had already swallowed his, finally calming down. Felix shrugged and swallowed his.

"And?" Jan asked.

"I don't notice anything different," Felix muttered.

Just then, the flames in the trash can shot higher and turned purple. To Jan's horror, Lutz stuck his hand into the flames and pulled them into the air as if they had substance. He balanced the fire between his hands, making it dance between his fingers like a magician with a coin. His eyes were glowing green with fervour.

"Well, fancy that," Jan mumbled. "It is magic."

Samantha

As was so often these days, the six of them had their own table in the school hall. Jan was sleeping with his head on his arms, while Lucille was eye-flirting with a Year 13 student across the hall. Fabian and Rachel were eating, but they were keeping their hands suspiciously under the table, and Samantha was sure that if she checked, she would find their fingers intertwined.

Not that she was interested enough to check, as she was too busy conversing with Matt. This morning, Rachel had told them about the dreamweb, and Matt seemed to be the only one she hadn't exhausted the topic with.

"You can't tell me it's coincidence that these emblems keep turning up."

"I'm not," Matt replied, amused. "Actually, I know for a fact it's not."

Samantha felt the excitement rise like bubbles in her stomach. "For a fact? Tell me more!"

Instead, Matt grinned at her, his eyes locked on a spot next to her mouth, as if he'd forgotten how to speak.

Self-conscious, Samantha rubbed her chin. "Do I have dirt on my cheek?"

Matt blinked. "What?" A gleam entered his eyes as he leaned forward. "Maybe."

Samantha found herself entirely captivated by the finger he extended excruciatingly slowly. It came closer and closer until she began to see it in double, and still, it hadn't touched her skin. Just then, Matt moved forward and lightly tapped the tip of her nose. "All clean."

Annoyed, she clicked her tongue and batted his hand away. "Stop being silly."

Matt's wide grin, however, was simply enchanting, and she forgave him immediately. Recently, the two of them had started to tease each other constantly. It was a game, nothing serious, just two friends fooling around.

But that didn't mean Samantha was about to be completely sidetracked. "So, tell me what's with the fact?"

Matt leaned back, folding his arms behind his head as he stretched out his legs, accidentally bumping into hers. "Well, think about it. That's the, what? Fourth Emblem of Power that's turned up? Most of the Emblems in the book haven't even been described well enough. Now we've got four in one place. It means something." He sounded uncharacteristically serious about it. His tongue flicked over his lips as if he was a little nervous. "Have you read the whole book yet?"

Samantha shook her head. "Didn't have any time, there's too much schoolwork. But I've decided to devote my Christmas holidays to the cause."

"You can't," Matt replied with a straight face.

"Why not?"

The corners of his mouth twitched again, unable to contain the grin. "Well, because you need to celebrate my birthday, of course."

It wasn't what Samantha had expected. "Your birthday is during the holidays?"

"New Year's Day, I'm told."

"You're told?" Once in a while, Matt said the most awkward things that made her wonder if he truly was a normal teenager. As normal as each of them could be called. But today, she only chuckled about it. "You're messing with me. It's not really New Year's Day."

"Sure is. And I've never had a birthday party." He scrunched up his face. "Well, that I remember." The grin returned to his face. "So, you need to help me organise it."

Samantha's heart skipped a beat. She didn't quite know why, and so she huffed, which came out as a half-choked giggle. There was so much hidden in his few words. The fact that he'd never had a birthday party. That apparently, besides living with his mother and a bunch of older siblings, they'd never once celebrated the day of his birth. It was so sad. If he wasn't messing with her, which was still quite the possibility.

But the one thing she zoned in on was: "You want *me* to organise the birthday party?"

"Well, you're the most organised person I know, and..."

She would never hear what else qualified her as his party planner because at that moment, the cafeteria owner shuffled close and kicked Jan's chair.

Jan shot up and looked around wildly. "What's happening?"

"This isn't an inn!" the cafeteria owner snarled. "If you want to sleep here, you have to pay for the night." He extended his hand, as if he truly expected Jan to pay up.

But Jan only stared at him, dumbfounded. Instead, Fabian asked. "There are overnight charges?"

"There are now," the cafeteria owner bellowed.

"What kind of weirdo are you?" Jan asked, showing not the slightest respect for the adult.

"I watched you. You've been sleeping here for two hours."

Matt clicked his tongue, entirely unaffected by the power battle. "So, that's why you missed Geography."

"Why should I go if you're already there?" Jan asked. "I'll just copy your notes as always."

"Perhaps I should charge for that," Matt quipped.

Samantha elbowed him, and he smiled in return. The cafeteria owner regarded them both with an ugly glance before focusing on Jan again. "If I see you sleeping here again, I'll charge you by the hour."

Jan shot up, screwing up his face in anger. "Who do you think you—"

"There you are!" To Samantha's dismay, her little sister came running towards them, Anne trailing behind her.

Meg ignored the cafeteria owner and threw her arms around Jan's neck. "You were supposed to meet me at the table tennis tables outside."

"I was?" Jan asked confused.

Meg planted a kiss on Jan's lips, which was apparently too much affection for the cafeteria owner. He turned around and yelled at some other student who wasn't using the school hall as he thought fit.

"And you didn't come home until long after I fell asleep."

Jan let himself fall back into the chair and pulled Meg onto his lap. "Were you planning to sneak into my room again?" He completely ignored his little sister who seemed not enthused in the slightest.

Neither was Samantha. It had been three weeks since Jan and Meg had started dating, and her sister was head over heels for her first boyfriend.

"Your sister and Jan?" Matt mouthed.

She rolled her eyes at him. "Don't ask."

Meg had been nearly insufferable ever since, strutting around with a haughty look as if she knew all the secrets of the world now.

"You need to make up for it," Meg said and jabbed Jan's chest, not shy at all. "Now that Anne knows about us, we're going to have a real date. Tonight. My parents are out."

"Meg!" Samantha flushed, wishing for the ground to swallow them all up. She'd promised her parents she'd take care of herself and Meg tonight, and Meg went and invited her boyfriend over.

Her little sister ignored her completely. "What do you say?"

Jan flicked a nervous glance at Samantha—at least one of them showed a modicum of decency. "I'm actually already meeting the guys at the docks."

"The bell's going to ring soon," Anne interjected softly.

None of them moved. Apart from Lucille, whose attention was still on her latest flirt, everyone was watching Jan and Meg with bated breath.

"So, tell them you've got a date." Meg drew her brows together, completely oblivious to the fact that Jan was trying not to have a date right now.

"I can't," he said. "I've already promised them, and if I start cancelling for a girl, I'm out. Bro Code, and such things."

Pouting, Meg crossed her arms. "You find me embarrassing?"

Samantha had to bite her tongue to keep from saying that Meg was acting quite embarrassing right now.

"No, no, I don't." Jan grabbed her arms. "It's just our thing."

"It could be my thing, too." Meg was almost begging.

Jan paused. "You want to join us?"

"Meg, please." Samantha had no idea what exactly happened down at the docks, just that it was an area she would rather avoid at night. "Mum—"

"Unless you tattle to her, she won't know," Meg hissed. "Just because you're a bore doesn't mean I have to be one." She grinned at Jan. "Sounds like fun."

Jan didn't have to look so pleased about it, in Samantha's opinion. "Great, I'll pick you up at seven, then."

"No, you can't!" Samantha protested, but Matt drew her to her feet. "We need to go to class."

The bell rang a second later, and mortification grabbed hold of Samantha. She hated being late to class—or anywhere, really. "Meg!"

Her sister was busy kissing Jan, as if to demonstrate a point, before Anne pulled her away and hissed that they had to go to class as well.

"I don't think you're a bore at all," Matt whispered as they strode swiftly out of the hall.

Jan remained behind, already resting his head on his arms again, which made Samantha feel utterly disgusted with him. The feeling deepened when she heard the cafeteria owner clear his throat, prompting Jan to flip him the finger.

"Why does it need to be him?" Samantha moaned, unable to think of a worse boyfriend for her barely sixteen-year-old sister.

Rachel

Since Samantha's parents were away for the night, she had organised a girl's slumber party. Rachel had brought her dreamweb for two reasons. First, because she didn't trust leaving it at home where her mother might find it, and second, to show it to the others.

However, the Emblems of Power seemed to be far from anyone's mind tonight because Lucille and Samantha had launched into boy talk the moment they arrived. And for some reason, Rachel found herself in the middle of it.

"So, how is it going with Fabian?" Lucille asked, her eyes gleaming with anticipation.

Unfortunately for Rachel, Samantha chimed in, "You two are holding hands an awful lot."

Rachel felt her cheeks flush with heat. "And that's about it," she muttered.

"What do you mean?" Lucille had already changed into her pyjama, a cute two-piece set that was prettier than anything in Rachel's wardrobe.

Rachel sighed as she thought about Fabian. Ever since they'd defeated the demon, they'd developed a strange connection. They hadn't talked about it, but their hands would find each other whenever it felt right. And that was the extent of their relationship.

"We haven't kissed or... or anything, really." She blushed. "I'm not saying it hasn't been nice," she hurried to add. "I like it. It's definitely nice." She stopped when she saw Lucille trying to suppress her giggles. "What?"

Lucille composed herself. "You're among friends, Rachel. You can tell us that you want him to sweep you off your feet and kiss you passionately."

Now it was Samantha who burst into giggles, while Rachel was convinced steam must be coming out of her ears from the heat in her face.

"Sorry." Samantha tried to stifle her laughter. "It's just that... that's not Fabian." Her eyes bored on Rachel. "You know he can be a bit of an idiot."

"Which I find endearing," Rachel whispered.

Samantha frowned. "Yeah, well. Sure, it can be endearing when it's not annoying. What I mean is that he probably misses all the obvious signs you're sending him."

"I'm sending him obvious signs?"

She looked back and forth between Samantha and Lucille, who also exchanged glances. Then Lucille leaned forward, her face suddenly serious. "Well, you did let him know that you'd like him to kiss you, right? Maybe not explicitly, but..."

"You've been on a date?" Samantha asked, her face equally serious.

"With just the two of us?" Rachel asked, feeling foolish only a moment later. "No, not yet."

Once again, the other two shared a knowing look. To make matters worse, they nodded at each other. Lucille turned back around. "You two are going to the cinema on Saturday night."

"Expect an invitation," Samantha added.

Rachel wasn't sure whether to be annoyed they were meddling, or whether she was relieved she didn't have to take matters into her own hands. What had the dreamer said? *Live?* Living in reality was much harder than he thought.

But if it included Fabian, she was willing to try. "Okay. I mean, thanks."

"You and I will go shopping together on Saturday, while Samantha works on Fabian," Lucille declared. "And I'll teach you some of those obvious signs. Fabian won't miss these."

"Can we change the topic now?" Rachel asked, feeling like she'd die of embarrassment any moment. She needed another fixation fast. Luckily, she had one ready to go. "What's going on with you and Matt, Sam?"

Samantha looked as if she'd swallowed a frog, her eyes widening. To Rachel's surprise, Lucille hadn't picked up on it yet and seemed to be equally as shocked. "You and Matt?"

"There is no Matt and me!" Samantha said a little too quickly. "Why would you think there is?" It was almost convincing, if not for the slight pitch in her voice.

Glad that the attention was off her, Rachel pointed out, "Well, the two of you are always on top of each other, teasing and joking, and you can't keep your hands off each other." It was true. Just today, Matt had gone out of his way to touch Samantha—all hidden behind jokes, for sure, but obvious, nonetheless.

"We do not have our hands all over each other!" Samantha huffed, her cheeks definitely reddening now.

Rachel stared at her with what she hoped was a no-nonsense glare. She distinctly remembered a playful slap and an elbow jab earlier.

Samantha wasn't giving in so easily, though. "You're imagining things, Rachel. Yes, we've become close friends over the last few weeks, but that's all. You know how I am with Fabian. It's the same thing."

Truth be told, Rachel envied Samantha the level of comfort she displayed around male friends. Maybe that was why the words slipped from her mouth without thinking. "Who you slept with."

Now Samantha truly turned red. "Rachel! That's..." She took a deep breath, trying to calm herself down. "You know that's ancient history."

"Yes," Rachel blurted. But the realisation remained that Fabian hadn't needed obvious signs from Samantha to kiss her in the rain. Or perhaps all those playful jabs Samantha did were the kind of signs she should be sending.

"Either way, I'm not planning to sleep with Matt," Samantha said with an indignant huff.

Lucille, who had remained surprisingly quiet throughout, picked up the conversation now. "Why not?" Rachel could hear the slight challenge in her words. This was about more than just curiosity. Not too long ago, Lucille had been infatuated with Matt. And quickly burnt by him.

"You know how he is. This is all fun and games to him. Honestly, if he were interested in me, don't you think he'd actually flirt with me?"

Rachel thought to herself that what she witnessed each day looked an awful lot like flirting to her. But obviously, she wasn't the resident expert here.

Lucille sighed and twirled a lock of her hair. "Isn't every interaction with him a flirt?"

"We're really just friends," Samantha stressed, now quite serious.

"I wouldn't mind," Lucille clearly forced herself to say. Her shoulders deflated a little. "It's really stupid of me. I've actually got my eyes on someone. So, even if there was more between you and Matt, it would be okay."

Samantha put her hand on Lucille's and looked deeply into her eyes. "I don't have any interest in becoming the next person on his list. And you should be glad you weren't either."

"Only because I blew all chances of that," Lucille said, then rolled her eyes. "You're probably right. However, he doesn't act like he only has sex on his mind when he's with you. He looks like he enjoys spending time with you. It's a talent. Getting along with boys, that is. I wish I found it as easy."

Rachel was just about to say that she wished for the same thing when they heard a loud thud from next door, followed by a fit of giggles and another bump. "What's going on there?"

Samantha paled. She jumped up and was out of the room before they could stop her. Rachel and Lucille shared a glance and followed her into Meg's room.

When Rachel saw what was going on in there, she froze. Meg wasn't alone. Jan was with her, and by the looks of it, they both seemed intoxicated.

Meg's top was already on the floor as she stumbled onto the bed, dragging Jan down with her. His hands reached for her pants, but they never made it there, because Samantha grabbed his arm and hauled him back. Unsteady as he was, Jan landed hard on his backside.

"What the hell?" he hollered, too drunk to get up right away.

Samantha put her hands on her hips and glared at him. "Yes, what the hell, Jan? Get out of here before I forget myself!"

Rachel had rarely seen Samantha this furious. When she was, she looked downright frightening, her eyes blazing. Unfortunately, Jan was too intoxicated to grasp the situation. "Why? In case you haven't noticed, Meg's my girlfriend."

"Yes, your sixteen-year-old girlfriend who's apparently drunk for the first time in her life," Samantha hissed. "So, you will leave her alone and walk out of here."

Jan scrunched up his face and looked at Meg. "Do you want me to go?"

Meg had sat up, but she was swaying dangerously. "Of course not," she managed to slur. A second later, she doubled over and vomited on the carpet and Jan's shoes.

"That should be answer enough." With surprising strength, Samantha pulled Jan to his feet and pushed him towards the door.

Rachel sidestepped him while Lucille took hold of Jan's arm. "I'll make sure he leaves."

"And I'll get something to clean this up." Rachel ducked out of the room to search for some cleaning supplies.

When she returned, Samantha had moved Meg to the bathroom, holding her younger sister's hair back as she hurled into the toilet bowl and cried some nonsense about how Jan would surely hate her now.

Judging by Samantha's expression, Meg should be more concerned for Jan's well-being than his reaction.

Matt

It was already pitch dark outside when Matt returned from his walk with Crumbs, the golden retriever puppy René had adopted for him. It had been drizzling for the last half hour, leaving them both covered in a fine mist, but Matt couldn't have been happier. His cheeks were flushed, warm compared to the rest of his ice-cold skin. And Crumbs loved it too. Even though he was exhausted, his tail waggled wildly as they walked up the stairs and opened the door.

Once inside, the dog continued to scurry around Matt's legs, urging him to move. Matt laughed as he rubbed him off, taking great care to ensure that his little dog didn't catch a cold. The puppy tried to climb onto his knee. "Just a moment, Crumbs. I'll get you food in a minute."

As soon as the feeding bowl was filled, the dog pounced on it. Only then did Matt consider drying himself off.

"How much are you feeding him?" Chay asked. For the past couple of weeks, he had been staying with them, which was highly unusual for the seer.

Matt knew that he spoiled the dog a little too much, but one look into those glossy brown eyes and he couldn't find the strength to refuse him. "He gets plenty of exercise."

Chay chuckled. "I never saw you with a dog."

For a moment, Matt held his breath. Considering Chay could see the future, he immediately worried about Crumbs. "Nothing's going to happen to him, will it?"

"You're not asking me to see the dog's future, are you? Dogs have even shorter lifespans than humans." Whenever possible, Chay refrained from looking at individual fates, precisely because every life, even the near eternal ones of demons, eventually ended in death.

"I'm fine. And Crumbs will be too," Matt emphasised. One would think that as a half-demon he would be accustomed to death. After all, demons fought and killed each other constantly. But the concept of mortality was different in Ashuan, and he wasn't sure he liked it. Crumbs had already grown so much in these few weeks and would continue to do so until he grew old. It wasn't a concept Matt was terribly familiar or comfortable with.

He let go of Crumbs and sat down at the table with Chay. His father had left a plate of food out for him, and Matt realised he was as hungry as Crumbs.

"Why are you here, Chay?" he asked after devouring several spoonfuls of hearty stew. He had avoided the topic for weeks, enjoying Chay's presence far too much. The seer was usually off saving some poor world, a hobby he'd picked up over a hundred years ago. He didn't have the time to look after young half-demons. Unless... "Does Ashuan need saving?"

Chay raised an eyebrow. "All worlds need saving eventually."

Matt rolled his eyes. "Would it kill you to give a straight answer once in a while?"

"Possibly. I haven't tried it," Chay said, his humour so dry Matt felt his toes curl.

It was a lie. Matt knew Chay well enough to assume he had tried every strategy possible to save a world, even a plain-as-day prophecy. It was a trait inherited from his human side, Chay would probably say. But Matt knew better than to press the matter. Chay would give him precisely the amount of knowledge he needed, and nothing more.

Which brought Matt back to his original question. "So, why are you here?"

"The Emblems of Power, of course. They're coming together."

"Rachel found the dreamweb last night. She dreamed of... Nico, but not really Nico." Matt tried to recall her exact wording.

"Did she now?" When Matt glared at him, Chay chuckled. "The powers of this particular emblem are quite peculiar. At least half of it resides in the dreamworld, and it's said to absorb energies and reflect them. Not the most elegant weapon, but useful."

"Right." It wasn't lost on Matt that Chay hadn't elaborated on Nico's dream appearance. "And the other two? Will they also miraculously appear as well?" Matt had a suspicion that Chay had orchestrated their discovery but, of course, he would never get confirmation.

"I imagine so," Chay said. "Though the paths of the emblems are difficult to trace. I'm afraid they choose their own way."

"You gave me the sword," Matt pointed out. While it was true that the sword had possessed some peculiar powers, such as being hidden in some unknown dimension until the moment he drew it, he couldn't quite believe it was sentient.

Chay shrugged. "And it found its way into my hands before that. Likely because it knew I would be in a position to give it to you when the time came."

"When the time came? You mean when I'd proved my proficiency?"

"I found that sword over forty years ago," Chay said nonchalantly. "But it wasn't until I held you in my arms nearly eighteen years ago that I realised to whom it belonged."

Eighteen years—that's how long Chay had been preparing him. All this time, Matt had thought of him as a friend, a trusted adviser, an elder half-demon among all those he'd grown up with. The fact that their friendship was only facilitated by whatever Chay had seen when he picked Matt up as a baby was a bitter truth to swallow.

"Do you actually care about me or just the sword?" he asked, seeing no point in dwelling on the question any longer.

Chay's gaze softened considerably. "I wouldn't be here if I didn't care about you."

And that, Matt realised, only left him with even more questions than before.

Fabian

Fifty euros. Fifty euros. Fabian repeated the amount in his mind as he worked under the body of a car. It was Saturday, and he should be out with his friends. The Christmas market downtown had opened, and he needed a break after another terrible week at school with Mr Herbert pressuring him. But the Christmas market required money, as did all the Christmas presents he planned to buy. So, instead, he wasted his Saturday helping his dad in the workshop.

Mr Herbert may have cruelly joked that Fabian wanted to join his father's business as soon as he graduated from school, but that couldn't be further from the truth. Sure, he knew his way around cars, and there was something immensely satisfying about being able to fix them or doing his own builds. Apart from that, though, he considered the workshop rather unglamourous. And with both parents juggling their own businesses, he was well aware of the constant struggles and fears of self-employment.

No, Fabian wanted a more stable career. Something fulfilling that he could leave behind when he went home. Something that wouldn't require him to rope in his children. And if Mr Herbert didn't extinguish all the joy in him before graduation, he wanted to give science a try. He hadn't decided yet whether to pursue Physics or Biology—though Biology seemed much more promising simply because it was taught by the slightly kooky, but infinitely nicer, Mrs Brandt. Luckily, he still had a year and a half to figure it out.

"I'm done," Fabian said with a huff as he rolled out from under the car.

His father leaned against the nearby pillar, holding a clipboard. As usual, his clothes were smeared with oil. Not that Fabian's own clothes looked any better after spending most of the morning under the car. Unlike Fabian and his mother, his father had plain brown hair streaked with the first signs of silver.

"Very well. Let's see if we need to order in a replacement car," his father joked. Praise didn't come easily to him, but Fabian could hear the subtle pride in his words. "You can clean up and watch the phone in the office."

"Watch the phone or answer it?" Fabian asked.

His father snorted. "You think you're very clever, huh? Sam's in the office. Let her handle the calls."

"She is?" Fabian asked. He didn't get an answer as his father took over the rolling board and disappeared under the body of the car to check his work.

Fabian shrugged and made his way to the office. He got the hint that his work for the day was done, which was more than fine with him. "Hey, Sam. Dad said you've got the phone under control?"

As usual, she was busy with the filing system. But now she looked up with a groan. "Man, I thought you'd never finish. Was it a challenging fix?"

"No, not really. I just didn't feel like rushing through it." He never did, a fact his father frequently commented on. "Are you earning some money as well?" He gestured towards the files.

"Well, now that I'm doing the work, I might as well cash in on it." She grinned. "I *do* need some extra for Christmas."

Fabian found himself mirroring her grin. "Same."

"It's not why I came, though." Samantha, setting the files aside. "I wanted to talk to you."

If that didn't sound ominous, Fabian didn't know what did. "Am I in trouble?" She had a tendency to scold him quite often.

Samantha only laughed at that. "That, my dear, depends entirely on you."

"My dear? I *am* in trouble." He plopped himself down on the desk. "What did I do wrong this time?"

"It's not so much what you did wrong, but more what you haven't done." When he raised an eyebrow, she took a deep breath and continued. "Don't you want to do something with Rachel?"

The sudden change of topic confused Fabian. "What do you mean? Should we all go to the Christmas market together?"

"No!" Samantha shook her head, a sure sign that she was starting to get irritated with him. And he still had no idea what he'd done wrong—or failed to do.

"What do you want from me?"

Samantha took another deep breath. When she spoke again, her voice carried a slightly condescending tone, as if speaking to a toddler. "Don't you want to spend some alone time with your *girlfriend?*"

"I'm not sure..." Was Rachel his girlfriend? They'd never discussed it. To be honest, he had no idea *what* they were.

Naturally, Samantha seized on his uncertainty. "Not sure about what? Not sure if you want to be alone with her?"

"Not sure if she wants me to be alone with her," Fabian replied before he could think about it. Surprisingly, it was the truth. After everything the others had said, he wanted to give Rachel a chance. But ever since he'd made the first move, they'd been stuck. She'd accepted him but never pushed for more or really made any clear indication that she *wanted* more. Could Jan and Matt have been wrong when they said she was desperately in love with him?

For some reason, Samantha's face softened. "Oh, Fabian. Yes, she wants that. Very much, I'd say."

Now Samantha couldn't be wrong, could she? She never was. "So, you want me to invite just her to the Christmas market?" He always did the first stroll with Samantha. It was *their* tradition.

"How about a movie and the Christmas market afterwards?" Her eyes gleamed as if she held a secret. "Rachel mentioned a movie she wanted to see. I don't remember which one it was, but..." She leaned forwards. "It's dark and cosy in the cinema. You can put your arm around her shoulders."

Fabian tried to imagine himself in the cinema with Rachel. It wouldn't be the first time they'd done that, but usually Samantha sat between them. Just the two of them in the dark, his arm around Rachel... He rubbed the back of his neck. "Isn't that a bit cliché?"

Samantha slapped his knee. "Fabian! Do you want to be with Rachel or not?"

How was he supposed to answer that? Of course, he wanted to be with her. Or at least, he wanted to see if there truly was something between them, which he couldn't admit to Samantha because she would give him a hard time. Then again, who else but his best friend could he talk to about this dilemma? "Sam..."

"Yes?" The change in his tone caught her attention. She seemed to be expecting the worst.

And he truly was the worst, wasn't he? Who dated someone just to see if it could work? If Rachel was truly in love with him—and he still doubted that—he'd break her heart. Fabian would never forgive himself if that happened. And yet, here he was, stringing Rachel along by just holding her hand and nothing more. And he still hadn't figured out whether he was genuinely interested in her or not.

Fabian took a deep breath. He would probably make a fool out of himself, but Samantha should be used to that. "I don't know if I want that. It's just... When you and I were together—" He paused when her eyes practically begged him not to declare his feelings for her. Not that he had intended to do so. Quickly, he cleared his throat and avoided her gaze. "It was so easy between us. Maybe too easy. I don't know. With Rachel, nothing is easy. I don't get the impression that she loves me. Half the time, I'm not even sure she likes me. She's just too hard to read, and I never know where I stand. How am I supposed to know when it's okay to kiss her or not?"

There! He'd said his piece, and he felt rather relieved. A bit flushed, but that was because he had practically vomited out his feelings and insecurities all at once.

Samantha had a contemplative look on her face. She leaned back and tapped her chin. "How about you just try and see where it gets you?"

"Sam!" he groaned. "Girls are complicated."

"And boys aren't?" She chuckled softly. "Okay, here's the thing, Fabi. Rachel wants to be kissed. By you. Trust me."

Fabian thought he'd better hold his tongue now. And truly, giving it a try seemed like be the sensible thing to do. He wasn't being fair to Rachel or himself if he didn't take the next step. They could hardly hold hands for the rest of their lives. "So, the cinema?"

Samantha clapped her hands. "She's expecting your call."

He should've known the whole thing had been orchestrated from the start.

Samantha

Samantha thought that the meeting with Fabian had gone splendidly. She'd heard the doubts in his voice. She would've had to be deaf in order not to, but she fully believed that once both Rachel and Fabian got over themselves, they would have a lovely relationship. Rachel deserved someone good, and though he was a bit dense sometimes, Fabian was a good guy. Maybe not the most exciting, but certainly the most steadfast.

And he deserved someone like Rachel as well. Someone who adored him for all his little quirks, who truly, deeply loved him. It had been six months since Samantha had realised how perfect they would be for each other, and she was glad that they'd finally started to see that as well.

Still in a good mood, Samantha rushed up the stairs to her room when she heard a soft sniffle. Meg was crying in her room, and Samantha had a sinking feeling she knew who was to blame for that.

It still filled her with fury when she thought about Jan. He'd got her little sister drunk! And then he'd tried to have his way with her. It didn't matter that he'd been just as wasted and possibly barely remembered a thing today. Samantha's problem was that it was a situation that had been bound to happen.

Jan didn't have a bad reputation because he was terribly misunderstood. He seemed hell-bent on making sure his parents lost all their hair before they turned sixty. He got into fights, took illegal substances, stole, and hung out in the worst parts of town.

In the last few months, she'd gotten to know him a bit better, and it was true that there was more to him than he let on. He may have been dependable in a fight, but the one thing he wasn't was a dependable boyfriend.

Samantha knew she had to let Meg make her own experiences. Yet, she wished they wouldn't have to be with Jan of all people.

Normally, she gave her sister a wide berth. The two of them had next to nothing in common. Meg prided herself on how many friends she had and how many parties she was invited to, usually when Samantha had excelled again at school. Their parents didn't treat them any differently. They were just as proud of Samantha's good grades as they were of Meg's tennis successes, but her sister was still jealous. Ever since she'd entered puberty, Samantha had the feeling that Meg needed to show her up. Needed to show the world that what she lacked academically was more than made up for with what Meg had termed as "having an actual life".

And while it was true that Meg was popular and had a lot of friends, Samantha could never muster the energy to compare herself. She was happy with what she had, her few but true friends, her schoolwork, and her magic. She didn't want what Meg had, and she felt far too mature for sisterly envy. So, she usually endured Meg's moods stoically, and tried not to spend too much time with her.

But this time, she couldn't do that. Not after what she'd seen last night. Meg needed her. There was no way in hell she'd told their mother—or father, for that matter. And her best friend Anne happened to be Jan's little sister. How much could Meg truly vent to her about her older brother?

Samantha took a deep breath, then knocked on the door. The crying stopped, and Samantha was sure she could hear a couple of slow, steady breaths. Meg was apparently trying to stay as quiet as possible and pretend she wasn't home. Well, tough luck.

She pressed down the handle, slipped into the room, and softly closed the door behind her. Meg was on her bed, dabbing her tear-stained cheeks as if she hoped no one would notice. "Hey, Meg."

"What do you want?"

Samantha took another step, then sat down on the far corner of Meg's bed. "I wanted to check on you after last night."

"The night you ruined?" Meg barked. Her hostility lasted for barely a second. "He's angry," she said while pushing her phone towards Samantha.

Tentatively, Samantha took it. She wasn't normally allowed to read Meg's messages. And she wasn't quite sure she wanted to.

Jan: I went back to the guys. Call me once you're old enough to make your own decisions.

Samantha's fingers tightened around the phone. He was obviously less angry at Meg and more at Samantha's meddling. Though she wouldn't call it meddling but protecting her little sister from making a terrible mistake.

"You weren't sober enough to make your own decisions," she said in a soft whisper, but quite determined.

Meg blanched. "You didn't tell anyone, did you?" Her eyes flickered to the door and then down to the floor, where her mother was likely sitting in the living room.

Samantha stretched out her hand and brushed Meg's knuckles. "No, I didn't. Contrary to what Jan thinks of me, I don't tattle." The way Meg bit down on her bottom lip told her that Meg also thought she'd tattle on her. "Meg, I know you hate every word that comes out of my mouth. I'm not fun enough, too serious, and too responsible." She couldn't help her eyes rolling in her head. "But what Jan did last night was not okay. If you want to have a relationship with him, that's your decision, but he got you drunk."

"I chose to drink."

Biting down on her tongue, Samantha swallowed her initial reply. She was about to tell Meg that she was too young, that it had been a stupid decision, but Meg would only fly into a rage. She wouldn't trust her older sister if Samantha tried to give her life advice. Not if Samantha was so unsuccessful in her own life, as Meg saw it. And Samantha had never been drunk before.

"You did. But did you also choose to have sex with him?" Meg's silence was answer enough. "If you wanted to have sex, I guess that's okay. Though in my mind, you're still playing with dolls." Samantha had been a few months younger when she'd had her first time with Fabian.

Meg swatted at her and crossed her arms. "I'm sixteen."

"I know. But there's no need to hurry, and I personally believe that the first time should be nice. Not a quick thing you can't even remember the next day." Samantha didn't even want to consider whether Jan would've been aware enough to use protection.

To her surprise, Meg didn't protest. In fact, she looked as if she was about to cry again. She stared at Samantha, her big blue eyes blinking fast. "You're worried about me?"

Samantha laughed a little. "*Of course* I am. I know you don't like me much, but you're still my little sister."

"I *do* like you. A lot at this moment, actually."

"Aww." Samantha couldn't help the sudden warmth rising in her stomach. She slipped closer to Meg and wrapped her into her arms. "I like you too."

Meg sobbed into her shoulder, unable to contain her tears any longer. For a while, Samantha held her, enjoying this rare sisterly moment, even if the cause for it was anything but beautiful.

"Hey, how about we both take a trip to the Christmas market in town?" she said, after allowing Meg to cry for a couple of minutes.

Her little sister's head shot up immediately. "Oh, I'd love that! We could pick what we're getting Mum and Dad. Imagine that, having their presents ready a month before Christmas."

Samantha laughed. "That would be something indeed." She pulled Meg up with her. "Alright, let's do this then."

The Greenvalley Christmas market may not have been able to compete with the big city ones, but what it lacked in flashy rides and size, it made up for with charm. The entire pedestrian zone was decked out with snow-covered little huts that offered all kinds of food, drinks, and trinkets. A number of them had artisan crafts you could only find in the Harz region, and around the fountain on the marketplace, a little stage had been erected. Each weekend day, there were two big fairy-tale performances by the local theatre for the children.

Samantha and Meg had bought presents for their parents and some of their friends. They'd tried this year's stollen and picked up a bag of candied almonds each. Now, Samantha warmed her hands on a hot cocoa while Meg checked out a jewellery stand. Samantha had no affinity for jewellery, and so she watched the play instead.

The minutes passed, and Meg still hadn't made her choice. Slightly annoyed, Samantha turned to her. "What's taking so—" Her breath caught in her throat when she saw the knotted bracelet Meg had in her hand. Or rather, she saw it in double.

There was the bracelet in Meg's hand, yet it was overlain by fine threads of magic that were intricately woven in a pattern Samantha couldn't even begin to understand. It wasn't just the green threads of magic she knew but other colours, most notably, a single strand of gold.

Samantha blinked. Golden magic. In a simple bracelet found at the Christmas market in Greenvalley, amongst hundreds of non-magical bracelets.

"Can I take a look at that?" she asked, her voice full of awe.

"It's pretty, isn't it?" Meg asked, turning to her.

Samantha barely nodded before running her finger over the bracelet. It was electrifying. The magic rippled over her finger, eager to do her bidding. Instead, she got her phone out, in which she had saved scans of the *Circle of Magic* book, and flicked through them until she landed on the section "The Bond of Levante". There was a sketch, which suggested it was a simple knotted bracelet, though the Seer hadn't got the shapes on it right. If it truly was the Emblem of Love.

At the centre of the powerful nation of Levante stood the Golden Tower. It is the only tower that has been completely lost to us since the breaking of the Old World. It fell like all the others when Draken's armies descended on Levante, but the Hunters of the Golden Tower didn't budge easily. Herne, the only one of the Twelve who never made it to the Black Tower, died with his back to the wall, his blood seeping into the magic and sealing it forever. There is only one thread of golden magic still in existence, the one Vesta, Herne's wife, wove into the Bond of Levante.

"I've got to have this!" Samantha exclaimed.

As soon as the words were out of her mouth, she knew she'd made a mistake. Meg's eyes narrowed with suspicion. "No, I saw it first. You don't even wear bracelets." As a precaution, she snatched the bracelet back.

"This is different." Samantha roamed the rest of the table, then pointed to a green bracelet that was just as pretty, though decidedly unmagical. "Why don't you take this one? Green's your favourite colour."

"Why don't you take it?" Meg huffed and turned to the salesperson. "I'll have this one."

For a powerful magical artefact, Meg only paid a pittance—which was fair, since neither Meg nor the salesperson could feel the magic emanating from it.

"It's brimming with magic," Samantha pointed out when Meg pocketed the bracelet. She was internally shaking in her effort not to assault Meg in order to get her hands on it. The Emblem of Power couldn't end up as a piece of jewellery for Meg to parade around. It was obviously meant for her with its patterns and thread of magic.

Meg only rolled her eyes and quickened her step. "You're mad."

Samantha hurried after her. "Meg, please. What you just bought is a powerful piece of magic. It is called the Bond of Levante, carrying the Power of Love."

"Oh my god, you're so embarrassing!" Meg cried, then quickly looked around in panic, if anyone had heard them.

It was the kind of thing Cheryl would say to her in front of everyone. Needles of shame pricked Samantha's skin as the painful memory washed through her. It only fuelled her anger now. "See! You hate magic. You don't believe in magic. So, what do you need a magical bracelet for? You don't even get it."

"Are you saying that I don't get love?" Meg was just as furious now. "Newsflash, Sam, I'm the one with a boyfriend, while you're alone."

The jab took Samantha's breath away. Meg wanted to compare herself? Well, here was what she thought of that. "Oh, you mean that drinking, smoking, unreliable gem of a boyfriend you managed to score? You're right, last night was pure love."

Tears shone in Meg's eyes as she was reminded of last night's disaster. But before Samantha could feel sorry for her words, Meg lashed out right back at her. "You don't understand love. You threw it away and for what? Nothing! Jan is so much cooler than you think, but of course you wouldn't get him. Since we all know you're Little Miss Perfect."

There it was again, the same old drama with Meg. "Great, now it's my fault you're only getting threes at school. It's always my fault, never yours. No wonder you're so enamoured with Jan."

Meg's eyes narrowed even further. "There are more important things in life than good grades."

"What a wise thing to say!" Samantha replied in pure sarcasm. "You've got it all figured out, huh? Three weeks with Jan and you're already taking him as a role model. Mum and Dad will be delighted."

"I knew you were going to tell them everything!" Meg spat at her. "So much for caring for me, right? Admit it, you're secretly glad Jan's probably going to break up with me!" And with that, Meg stomped off, tears flying from her eyes.

Samantha didn't follow her. She was too busy *not* admitting how happy she'd be if Jan were to break up with her little sister after what happened last night. But Meg had hurt her when she questioned her sisterly care. More than when she'd ridiculed her for her good grades and passion for magic.

And Samantha probably had hurt her just as badly. And all for the stupid Emblem of Power, which was now firmly in Meg's possession, where it had no business to be.

Frustrated, Samantha grunted. Then she hurried after Meg.

Jan

MAGIC was the good stuff. Expensive, yes, but totally worth it. The effects held for about three to four hours, and while Jan was high, he was able to do things others could only dream of. He felt stronger, more invigorated, and... creative. Creative was a good word because the magic came out of him in countless different ways. Last night, he'd been able to pull electricity from the power poles and turn it into firecrackers. Today, he opened the locked apartment door just by hovering his hand over the lock.

A million ideas floated into his head of what he might do with the power that let him open every door in the city. "This is so rad," he muttered.

He pushed against the door and found himself face to face with his little sister, Anne. For someone half his size—well, one-and-a-half heads smaller—she looked downright frightening. It was almost cute. "Hey, Annie. Missed me?" Jan couldn't help but tease.

Anne's eyes narrowed. "No, but Meg did. You ignored her all day."

Jan shrugged off his jacket and kicked off his shoes. "Well, she should complain to her sister. Sam was the one who threw me out last night." Technically, it had been Lu, but she'd only done what Samantha had told her to do.

"For good reason, I've heard," Anne retorted.

"What's your problem?" Jan pushed past her and went into his room.

Of course, Anne had to follow him there. "You can't make a move on her and then shut her out completely."

"Her stupid sister threw me out of the house! How many times do I need to tell you?" Jan turned around, positive he was going to wring his little sister's neck if she didn't stop bothering him soon.

"And that means you stop calling her altogether and ignore her?" Anne was shaking with anger, her eyes filling with tears. "Meg was crying her eyes out because of you!" she shouted.

Yep, he was definitely going to strangle her. "Be quiet, for god's sake!" he hissed, but it was already too late.

Their mother appeared in the doorway, a worried look on her face. "What did you do to Meg?"

"He tried to sleep with her!" Anne cried out, crossing her arms in a defiant gesture.

Jan stilled. Anne never ratted him out. She was his good little sister who loved him even if he was a mess. Apparently, that love had hit its limits today.

His mother's face had gone white. "What? Jan, what's got into you? That girl is fifteen."

"Sixteen," Jan shot back. "And you wouldn't know from the way she's throwing herself at me."

Anne gasped, but before she voiced her protest, his father joined them, making the disaster complete. "What's going on here?"

"Great, someone else to butt in," Jan muttered.

"You lose that tone right away!" His father pointed his index finger to stress his words.

Meanwhile, his mother had caught herself. "Jan is sleeping with Meg."

"What?" Jan turned to her, barely keeping up with the pace of events. "I tried to sleep with her. That's quite a difference." Yes, it hadn't been his finest moment, drunk as he'd been, but she was his girlfriend, and she'd wanted it as much as he had.

Needless to say, the difference didn't matter to his father. His face grew beet-red, and he raised his voice. "Are you mad? She's a child!"

"No, she's not. She's sixteen." There was a three-year difference between them, hardly the cause for such outrage.

"You could go to prison for that."

Jan rolled his eyes. As if he was the first boyfriend who had already passed the magical barrier of eighteen in a teenage relationship. "Yeah, but only if she really, really hates me and complains about that. Or maybe Anne will, since she loves to tattle." He snarled at his sister for good measure.

Anne burst into tears. "You're treating her like shit!" She turned around and ran from the room.

His mother gave him one evil glare before following Anne, leaving him alone with his father, who promptly crossed his arms and shook his head. "I really don't know what to do with you anymore. You're out of control. Out of..." He snuffed.

"Do you want me to leave? Then you won't have to do anything with me," Jan shot back. Last night was a low point for sure, but he didn't deserve this amount of flack. And surely not from his father, who'd leapt at every chance to scold him.

Now his father snorted. "Where would *you* go?"

"Does it matter?" Jan shrugged. "Somewhere I don't have to deal with this shit anymore."

Smack!

One second, Jan had been fine, the next his cheek burnt viciously. For a moment, he couldn't quite believe it. His father had never slapped him before.

"Are we stopping you from becoming a complete asshole?" his father asked darkly.

Jan felt his jaw muscles tighten. Until then, he'd only boasted of leaving. Now his mind was made up. Without another word, he turned around and stuffed his soccer bag with whatever caught his eye and seemed useful in the moment.

"What are you doing?" his father sounded slightly unsure all of a sudden.

Good. He deserved every guilty conscience in the world. "I'm leaving," Jan said, not granting him a glance. "I'm sick of listening to that broken record about how disappointing I am."

"Of course." The insecurity must've been imagination because his father's voice was back to its usual condescending tone. "It's always someone else's fault. Never yours. You're without fault."

Jan's blood was boiling. Couldn't his father just shut up and let him go? "I got it!" he shot back. "I'm not amazing like Anne. But you know what?" He rose his gaze until he locked eyes with his father. "You and Mum aren't the greatest parents in the world either."

His father's index finger rose again. "Don't use that tone with me or—"

"You'll hit me? Already happened."

That shut his father up good. Jan heaved his bag onto his shoulder and went out into the corridor, deliberately bumping into him on his way. It was his own fault for standing in the way.

"You don't have anywhere to go!" his father warned, though it sounded the slightest bit desperate.

Jan snorted as he slipped into his shoes and grabbed his jacket. "Anywhere will be better than this shithole."

Then he grabbed the door and slammed it shut behind him.

There was truly only one place Jan could go to. Or only one he wanted to go to. The docks, where he would buy some more MAGIC and wash the bitter taste of the altercation out of his mouth with beer.

He'd moved out, and all Jan could think was why it had taken him so long. His parents clearly detested his very existence, and he detested existing in their sphere. With him gone, they'd finally all be happy. He was free of their expectations, and they had their perfect little family with Anne.

"Back already!" Felix greeted him and clasped his hand.

Jan had only left the docks this morning in search of some cheap food. Now, the pang in his stomach reminded him that he'd never been able to grab something from the kitchen. Oh well, he'd grab a burger later. Now he wanted to do some MAGIC.

"Where's that old dealer?" He usually let Felix and Lutz buy any drugs, but occasionally he tagged along.

"It's a new guy," Felix told him. "Come, I'll bring you to him."

Felix knocked on the door of a shipping container just around the corner, which surprised Jan. He hadn't known the dealer was so close-by.

Felix banged against the metal. "Hey Mel!"

"Are we getting new stuff?" Suddenly, Lutz was there, his eyes shining with fervour. "I could use some."

"You just had some," Felix pointed out, then shut up when the door opened and an imposing man stepped into the frame.

There was something in the flash of those cold eyes that reminded Jan of someone, but he couldn't quite place him. The dealer held his gaze and, to Jan's annoyance, he was the first to look away.

"The price increased," the dealer said in a low drawl.

"Again?" Felix asked, outraged. "Are these things made of gold?"

The dealer glowered at him, not deigning him with an answer.

"Can't you make an exception?" Lutz asked, his eyes darting back and forth. Then he gave the dealer a toothy grin. "Please."

The dealer's hand shot out with enviable alacrity. His fingers dug into Lutz's chin and dragged him closer until he saw him straight in the eyes. Jan swallowed and studied his shoes, suddenly uncomfortable to watch.

"For you," the dealer hissed. And with a flick of his hand, he practically threw Lutz into the storage unit. "You two pay!"

Grumbling, Felix got his wallet out and paid for a new pack of pills. This time, he didn't dare protest.

Annoyed with himself, Jan cleared his throat. He'd fought demons, after all. He wouldn't be intimidated by this wannabe drug lord. "What are you doing with Lutz?"

"He'll work it off." And with that, the dealer closed his door.

"Do I want to know more about his supposed work?" Jan asked Felix as they strolled away from the storage unit. The thought of leaving Lutz behind to work at this creep's place bothered Jan. Lutz had been his friend. They'd gone to the docks together, even before Felix had joined them there. But that had been years ago, and Jan was worried about Lutz. He'd been down-spiralling for a while. Somehow, Jan doubted there would've been anything he could've done or said to prevent Lutz from going with the dealer. Not with the promise of free drugs.

Felix shook his head. "Better not ask. Lutz is beyond any help, if you ask me. You want one?"

Jan took the pill he offered and rolled it between his fingers. "I'll pay you back," he said, though he had no idea how exactly he'd get more money now that he didn't even have a home to live in. When it came to it, things weren't exactly looking good for him, either.

"Don't worry about it," Felix muttered. Then he bumped Jan's elbow. "Hey, isn't that your girl?"

Sure enough, Meg stood awkwardly among the others. Jan had to admire her courage for not just coming here but staying when she hadn't found him immediately. He supposed he shouldn't make her wait any longer than that and jogged over to her.

"Hey, babe." He moved in to kiss her, but Meg pulled back. "What's wrong?" Deep inside, Jan thought he already knew why she was here. She'd come to break up with him. It would be the perfect end to this day.

Meg hugged herself while trying her hardest to glare at him. "You owe me an apology."

"For what?"

"Your behaviour last night."

"I didn't force you to drink." In fact, Meg had surprised him by how readily she'd tried everything.

She rolled her eyes and sighed. "No, you didn't. I told Sam it was my choice."

"Ah, your lovely sister. And what did she have to say about that?" At that moment, it was hard to remind himself that Samantha was a friend of his. Or if not really a friend, then someone he'd spent quite some time with since school started. And though they were on opposites of the student spectrum, he had liked her well enough. Until she'd butted into his relationship.

Meg's lips twitched. "She told me you're a wretched boyfriend. She wants me to stay away from you."

And yet, Meg was here. "And?"

She threw her chin up. "Well, I think Sam just doesn't know how to have fun."

Jan's lips stretched into a grin. He put an arm around her and kissed her forehead. Then he hollered, "Does someone have a beer for my girl?"

Lucille

Shopping with Rachel should have come with a warning. There was nothing Lucille liked more. She prided herself on her sense of fashion and style, and what was better as date preparation than a girly afternoon picking out new clothes? For starters, the afternoon would've been infinitely better if Rachel were a girly girl. As it turned out, she was everything but.

"That's too colourful," she said to a bright yellow dress that would've suited her complexion perfectly.

"Don't worry," Lucille trilled, determined not to be beaten this easily. "We'll find something that will blow Fabian away. He won't have any choice but to kiss you."

Rachel sighed with a distinct lack of enthusiasm. "We're going to the cinema. He won't even see me."

Lucille clicked her tongue as she flicked through a rack of clothes. "But he'll see you when you two meet, and then he won't think about anything else during the movie but how amazing you're looking in *this* outfit."

She pulled a pretty combination of a cream blouse and pink-tinged miniskirt from the rack and held it up to Rachel. Yes, that worked perfectly. The blouse was cut in a way Rachel couldn't hide her cleavage, and the miniskirt would definitely fire up Fabian's imagination.

Rachel looked as if she'd eaten a batch of sauerkraut. "This isn't my style."

As if Lucille didn't know that. In her opinion, Rachel didn't have a style. "Boys like this."

"It's winter," Rachel pointed out.

Lucille had to concede the point. It was rather cold outside. But then something else caught her eye. She pushed the outfit into Rachel's unwilling arms and dashed over to the table on the opposite side. "Legwarmers." Triumphantly, she held up a pair the same cream as the blouse.

"I was thinking more about wearing a pullover," Rachel said as she dragged her feet over.

"How is Fabian supposed to fantasise about all the things he wants to do with you if you don't give him even a hint of what you're hiding under your clothes? You need to give him something."

"But it's cold!" Rachel protested. She shot a longing glance at the outside, as if she couldn't wait to get out of the store.

"That's perfect," Lucille claimed triumphantly. "If you're shivering, he'll have to give you his jacket."

Rachel stared at her in dismay. "But then he'll be cold!"

There was nothing Lucille could say to that. She'd been beaten, completely beaten by this girl who didn't have a sexy bone in her body. "Sure. Well, I'm sure Fabian doesn't mind a pullover."

It certainly wasn't what she was going to wear tonight.

Lucille had decided that Rachel and Fabian needed proper supervision, so she had invited Chris, a cute upperclassman, on a date. They would watch the same movie as Rachel and Fabian: a horror movie. While Rachel had fended off all her attempts at dressing her sexily, she had reluctantly agreed to Lucille's choice for the movie. A horror movie was perfect for a date. Boys their age hated romantic comedies, so the second-best choice was out. A horror movie meant plenty of opportunities to hold on to each other, to bury one's face in the shoulder of the strong man beside them, stroking his ego. And once the kissing started, you didn't even have to watch the horrors unfolding on-screen.

It all went rather splendidly. Within the first ten minutes of the movie, Chris had put his arm around her, and as soon as Lucille used a jump scare to cling close to him—showing Rachel three rows behind her how it was done—he'd drawn her closer and begun kissing her. He was a very good kisser. A little bit on the wet side, but passionate, not shy at all, just as Lucille liked it.

The minutes ticked by, and she couldn't have said what had happened in the movie—something about people vanishing in the fog and then turning up dead. For the longest time, Chris made her forget why they were here in the first place. But when Lucille finally came up for breath, cheeks flushed with heat, she threw a glance at Fabian and Rachel.

They hadn't moved at all. Neither had Fabian put his arm around Rachel's shoulder, nor had she moved closer.

Damn it! She was supposed to pretend to be frightened, but from the looks of it, Fabian was the one frightened out of his mind. He'd gone entirely rigid, his eyes not moving an inch, and Lucille was almost sure that if they turned the light on at that moment, he would be white as a sheet.

Of course, Fabian would be the one guy who'd be scared of horror movies. And Rachel... Rachel looked bored.

Lucille caught her eye and gave her head a distinct shake to the side, indicating that Rachel should cuddle up with him. Perhaps the whole thing could still be saved if Rachel gave him the comfort he needed.

But Rachel misunderstood her, and instead of distracting Fabian, she gave the worst performance of a frightened girl Lucille had ever had the displeasure to witness. Sure, it didn't require an acting class, but one look into Rachel's impassive face would've given everybody the indication she was having a stroke rather than shivering from fear.

Chris tugged on her shoulder, and Lucille melted into him with a sigh. Suddenly, her own romance felt a whole lot less exciting. She let Chris kiss her again, but it didn't hold the same magic as just minutes before, and she was quite glad for the interruption when her phone vibrated in her pocket.

Lucille stole a glance at it, much to Chris' annoyance. It was a message from Samantha.

Samantha: Meg hasn't come home. It's getting late, and she's not answering my calls.

Lucille was suddenly glad she was an only child. A little sister seemed to be entirely too much work. She wrote back: *I can't. I'm watching the ship sink. Fast.*

Samantha: Never mind then. I'll ask someone else.

Samantha: Save the ship.

With a sigh, Lucille leaned back into Chris' embrace, her eyes frequently checking on the couple behind her. *Save the ship.* If only she still had her powerful spell. But no, she'd learned that particular lesson. Fabian and Rachel would have to find their way to each other on their own, because Lucille didn't have the slightest idea how to help them.

Matt

It was a Saturday night, and Matt was busy. The kind of busy that didn't do well with interruptions. His own shirt was somewhere on the floor while the guy on the bed in front of him was still dressed. But not for long.

Positioned between his legs, Matt gave his date a sly smile. Ever so slowly, he leaned forward and kissed him gently. As the kiss intensified, his hands slipped under the shirt and explored the other man's body. Just as Matt was about to trail the line of his date's jaw with his tongue, his phone vibrated in his back pocket. Without a moment's hesitation, he interrupted his foreplay and sat down on the bed to pull out his phone, ignoring the outraged look he drew.

Matt didn't get texts often. He refused to give out his number to the countless people he dated, so whoever contacted him was someone who deserved his attention. Even if just for a few seconds.

Samantha: Do you have time? I could use some help. Please.

Or a few minutes. She didn't even have to use the please with him. The moment Samantha's name had popped up on his screen, Matt had decided that he had a lot of time. Instead of writing back, he called her. It only rang once before she picked up the call. "What's the matter?"

She was breathing hard and gasping as if she'd been crying. Matt's chest tightened in a manner that was entirely unfamiliar to him. It only got worse when he heard her teary voice. "My little sister is missing, and I'm afraid she's doing something really stupid. I know where she is. At least, I think I know, but... it's not a good place, and I—"

"Say no more. I'm on my way." Matt got up, once again ignoring his would-be-lover. He supposed he should come up with some excuse. A family emergency or something acceptable like that. But he didn't really care enough about the other boy to make him feel better with a lie. "Got to go," he said instead, grabbed his T-shirt, and made his way out of the room.

"Did I interrupt you?" Samantha asked, sounding slightly aghast. She wasn't stupid and had probably guessed Matt's Saturday night plans. For some weird reason, he felt bad about it. Like he'd been doing something he shouldn't have been doing.

"Nothing important," he said, but the glib answer had a bitter taste. Not because he liked the boy he'd made out with. Matt couldn't quite put his finger on why it bothered him so. It never had before.

He decided to forge ahead and leave those confusing thoughts behind. "Do you need me to pick you up?"

"No. I'll meet you in front of the school, okay?"

A peculiar meeting point. There was nothing dangerous about school—unless the bogeyman had made another appearance. "I'll be there as soon as possible." And he meant it.

Instead of taking a step out of the house, Matt tore through space itself. A second later, he was in front of the school, shaking off the cold, greasy sensation that always accompanied a space jump.

Naturally, Samantha wasn't there yet, but it took her less than ten minutes to arrive. When he saw her, eyes wide with worry, his chest tightened some more. He didn't like seeing her like that. So fragile. Vulnerable. He didn't remember ever seeing someone vulnerable. And actually caring about it.

"Hey," Matt said, unusually shy.

Even in her state of distress, Samantha gave him a quick smile. Then she hugged him. "Thanks for coming!"

Her body pressed against his, and Matt didn't quite know what to do. He had practice in holding a woman if she wanted him, but never a friend who needed comfort. It was like those hugs René sometimes gave him. Matt never endured them for long, but for some reason, he didn't want to let go of Samantha.

Unfortunately, she did. Again, she smiled at him, while her eyes remained worried. "I hope I didn't ruin your Saturday night plans."

She had done so rather spectacularly, but all Matt said was, "As if I wouldn't let everything fall the moment you called me." At least he was still capable of a smooth answer. "So, Meg is missing."

Samantha sighed heavily and started walking into the direction of the river. "We had a fight. I'm pretty sure she bought an Emblem of Power and refused to give it to me. But what we were really fighting about was Jan. He..." Another sigh, one Matt easily echoed. Jan tended to make one feel that way. "He's a bad influence on her. Last night, he got her drunk, or they both got drunk, and he tried to get with her. You know what I mean."

Of course, he did. His annoyance at Jan deepened. Just a few weeks ago, he'd given Matt this big speech about waiting until his hypothetical girlfriend was ready for sex, and now that he had one, he couldn't get there fast enough. It was the hypocrisy that angered Matt. And the fact that he'd got Samantha's little sister drunk.

"Then he ignored her all day, and when I called Anne earlier to ask whether Meg was with her, she told me that he'd moved out, which is just great." Slowly, Samantha was talking herself into a rant, her voice shaking as she did so. "So, now he's a shitty boyfriend, a drunk, and homeless. I don't know the details, but he's not the right guy for Meg. And if my sister had more than one functioning brain cell, she would understand that. Unfortunately, Meg is... sixteen."

"You think she ran away with him?" Matt barely knew Meg. Samantha rarely talked about her, and it didn't sound like they had a lot in common. Estranged siblings were the norm for Matt, but what he didn't understand was why Samantha cared so much.

She swayed her head in indecision. "That's what I'm afraid of. She's only sixteen and thinks she knows everything." The explanation was followed by a significant eye roll. "Little siblings, you know."

Matt couldn't help but chuckle. "You're aware that I'm the little brother in my family?"

"But you're different."

Her words were like a blow from left-field. They left Matt stunned and speechless. Of course, he was different. At least he liked to think he was a bit more reasonable. A bit less... demonic. But if he was true to himself, he was every bit as depraved as his demonic half-siblings. Maybe not as much as Caspar, but he was no angel, either. Especially compared to human standards. Samantha had no idea of all that, and yet, she saw something special in him. A little bit like Chay always had. Only when Matt managed to live up to Chay's ridiculous standards, it filled him with pride. Living up to Samantha's standards... it filled him with longing. It made him want to be different.

"Either way, Jan usually hangs around the docks with his junkie friends and... well, he... or rather his friends... they make me uneasy." Matt picked up on the fear in her voice.

Though he had no idea why anyone should be afraid of Jan or guys like him, he nodded. "Don't worry. I'll keep you safe." And if he could smash his fist into Jan's face, the better.

"Thank you," Samantha whispered, and this time, her smile reached her eyes.

Matt found himself smiling back. It wasn't his usual seductive smile that was like second nature to him. This one was out of control, as if he couldn't do anything else but mirror her smile. It was soft and gentle, and every bit as grateful as hers.

He cleared his throat to say something when they heard loud cajoling. They'd reached the docks, and it looked like there was a bit of a party going on. A beer bottle smashed against the wall of a container, making Samantha jump. Three fires were burning, emitting a thick, black, and pungent smoke. Teenagers and young adults were singing or throwing what looked like a ball of liquid fire between each other.

Matt took Samantha's hand to drag her with him, suddenly quite aware of why this area would make her uncomfortable. Everyone here was intoxicated and in a rough mood. Matt could easily see the guys turn on them just because they didn't like their looks.

"Let's find Meg."

He pulled Samantha along, past three guys who were caught in a scuffle, taking no prisoners. Blood glistened in the dirty snow beneath them. Samantha's breath caught in her throat, her hand in his, cold and clammy.

"Don't worry, I'll keep you safe," Matt said gently. If it came to it, he'd easily keep her safe. Thanks to his mother's genes, he was stronger than the average human and could easily handle a bunch of rowdy teenagers. He would protect Samantha. And her sister.

He spotted a familiar figure standing by a container behind one of the fires, a smaller person next to him. "Is that Meg?"

She certainly was the only girl present here on the docks. Meg had her hood drawn deep and was rolling an unlit cigarette in her hand.

Samantha pulled from his hand and started running. "Meg!"

The girl got a fright and quickly hid the cigarette behind her back. Jan turned around as well, a dark scowl on his face as he regarded the two of them. Naturally, his gaze shot immediately to Matt. "Is she your next conquest? Ran out of the good ones, did you?"

Anger rose in Matt's chest, but he beat it down and resorted to a snarl. "You're such an idiot." This wasn't about him and Jan but the Kollmer sisters. And as much as Jan annoyed him, Matt would do everything to keep the situation from spinning out of control.

"Meg, what are you doing out here? You ignored all my calls. And Anne's."

Meg raised her chin and glared at her sister. "I'm hanging out with friends. Not that it's any of your business."

"You call these your friends?" Samantha glanced at the guys still fighting and the one smoking next to Meg.

Jan threw down his cigarette and stomped it into the snow. Then he clenched his fists and closed the distance between them. "You've got a problem with my friends, Sam?"

The hostile tone threw Matt. Jan was annoying, but he wasn't... like this. So aggressive. Matt put a hand on Samantha's shoulder, quietly letting her know he was there for her if need be.

Samantha sighed. "No, I don't. You're all adults and know what you're doing." Matt doubted that by quite a bit, but he kept his mouth shut. "My sister is—"

"Young and naïve?" Meg crossed her arms and noticed the cigarette she'd been hiding. Something set in her eyes. "Just because I'm not a bore like you doesn't mean I can't make my own decisions." She leaned over to the guy at the wall and let him light up her cigarette.

Matt thought the guy looked a bit out of it, but he managed to light the cigarette just fine. Meg inhaled the smoke and came up coughing. Jan grinned, but he quickly stopped when he saw Samantha glaring at him.

"Don't be like that, Kollmer. Your sister just wants to have some fun."

Matt noticed how much Samantha was struggling to stay calm. Her shoulders were bunched, and the muscles around her mouth worked tirelessly as she kept the more furious responses inside. He admired her greatly for keeping her voice level when she finally spoke. "I don't think your friends are a good influence on her."

Jan took another step closer and scrunched his up his nose. "You mean my friends and *me*?" When Samantha shrugged, he launched into a full-blown tirade. "Yeah, that figures. I'm the big bad wolf who wants to swallow your innocent sister. She told me how you tried to break us up. I always knew you were a busybody. Always butting in where you don't belong. Thanks to you, my parents kicked me out of the house. But I guess that serves me right, right?"

In Matt's opinion, it absolutely served him right. Deeply sarcastic, he said. "Sure, that's Sam's fault."

Samantha put a hand on his side, clearly not appreciating his interference. "I'm sorry that you got into a fight with your parents because of this whole thing with Meg. But I had nothing to do with that. I didn't call them."

"No, but you told Meg what a terrible boyfriend I am."

Matt bristled at the repeated hostility in Jan's voice. But before he could step in, Samantha's patience reached the end of the line. Her entire body burst into action, as her hands flew into the air and she shouted, "You were terrible! You got my sister drunk and tried to have your way with her!"

Behind them, Matt noticed that Meg was following the conflict closely. She no longer leapt to Jan's defence and Matt thought that, secretly, she must have thought that her older sister was right.

Jan came even closer. He was almost nose to nose with Samantha now. "Meg and I are together. We drank together, and we made out together." Each word was flung at Samantha with a good amount of vitriol and spittle. "And none of that is any. Of your. Business!"

Samantha crossed her arms, though it was a less defiant and more protective gesture. "She's my little sister."

"So?" Jan didn't give her any grace. "I've also got a little sister, but you don't see me meddling with her life. So, one last time. Stop. Butting. In!" And suddenly, he raised his arms and gave Samantha a push.

It happened so fast that Matt couldn't stop her from stumbling backwards and falling into a snowdrift. The anger Matt had kept so well contained all this time bubbled up. He grabbed Jan's shoulder with his left hand and pulled back his right fist, ready to knock him out flat. But when his fist came crushing down, Jan caught it. And before Matt really registered what had just happened, Jan twisted his arm and threw him down on his back.

The blow knocked the air from Matt's lungs as he hit the frozen concrete. This wasn't right. Jan might be a martial arts specialist, but he shouldn't be strong. Not like this.

Matt jumped back to his feet and clenched his fists, faintly noticing that Samantha had stood up as well. Jan grinned at him. "Oh, man, you have no idea how long I've waited for this moment to kick your arrogant ass."

They were such pompous words from a stupid human boy, Matt had to laugh. "Not today." He threw himself at Jan, determined to show him what it meant to challenge a half-demon to a fight.

Behind him, Samantha was screaming. "Matt! Jan! Stop this immediate—"

Even if Matt had wanted to listen to her, he never had a chance. He had no idea how Jan did it, but suddenly, he was back on the floor, sliding several metres until his head hit a garbage can hard enough for the skin to split. It felt like the bone had split as well, but Matt knew that couldn't be true. Still, his eyes blurred from the sharp pain, and for a few seconds, he could only gasp for air.

The noise had lured in the other guys, and they formed a tight circle around Matt and Jan, as well as Samantha and Meg. They pumped their fists into the air and their cheers rose high as Matt got back to his feet and lunged at Jan once more.

It wasn't right. He was stronger than Jan. Usually, Matt held back around the others so he wouldn't give himself away, but even with his full strength, Jan merely toyed with him. He blocked each of Matt's attacks and got hold of him when he shouldn't have been fast enough to stand a chance. Jan's knee hit the soft bits of his stomach several times, and Matt simply folded. Like an utter weakling. Caspar would be delighted. There was a ringing in his ear, and someone screamed in panic.

Samantha was worried about him, but there shouldn't have been anything to worry about, Matt thought in a daze. He should be mopping the ground with Jan, not the other way around. Just then, blinding pain erupted in his face and the crunching noise of his bones breaking rang in his ears.

When Matt's vision cleared again, he found himself face-first in the snow, a heavy weight on top of him. The snow cooled his broken nose, but a new pain shot through his right arm, as it was cruelly twisted behind his back until it jumped from the socket with a sickening wet sound.

Tears stung in Matt's eyes, and he felt himself pulled back to the days when Caspar had messed him up. Nowadays, he and his brother were more evenly matched, but back then, he hadn't stood a chance. How many times had Matt been pinned under his older brother until Caspar had been satisfied with the number of bruises he'd planted or bones he'd broken? Too often, Matt had passed out before his brother would ease up.

Jan, however, let him go. He threw up his arms while he bathed in his friends' adoration.

Matt rolled onto his knees and cradled his arm. He wasn't too worried about it, but at the moment, it hurt terribly. A quick glance told him that Samantha had seen everything. Her face was wet with tears, and she pressed her little sister to her chest. Meg must've searched for solace in her arms when the fighting began.

Jan was still hyping up the crowd when the others parted and let through an older man with a terribly cold stare. For a quick moment, Matt thought that they'd drawn the attention of the police, but this man wasn't a cop. He took one hateful glance at Matt before turning towards Jan.

"Kill him."

Samantha

"No!"

Samantha had hoped that the newcomer would stop this terrible disaster. Now she couldn't even breathe. Something was wrong with Jan. He'd always been a troublemaker, but he hadn't been like this. He wasn't this brutal and cruel, this aggressive.

A pocket knife flipped into Jan's hand, and Samantha thought her heart would stop. What she'd witnessed tonight was worse than any monster hunt. No one could blame the monsters for being bloodthirsty. Jan, however... Matt didn't stand a chance. Not in his beaten down state.

"Who made you the boss of everything?" Jan asked, and Samantha's knees almost gave way with relief.

"I'm the one who supplies your MAGIC," the stranger said coolly.

Samantha stopped short. This man supplied Jan with magic?

"So?" Jan spat, his aggressiveness not sparing the stranger. "I'm not letting some lame-ass dealer tell me what to do!" His friends cheered at that. "So, piss off!" His words were followed by a blinding strike of lightning.

Blinded, Samantha felt the earth shake. The vibrations rang through her bones as if she'd stood on top of the detonation. When her vision finally cleared again, the dealer's cheek was bleeding from a cut. That was all. A magic explosion, and all that had happened to him was a minor cut. "I have what you want," he said in a low drawl that froze Samantha's blood.

It affected Jan as well, even if he tried to hide it. "I said piss off." Though he repeated his words, he sounded much less sure this time.

"I want to go home," Meg whispered.

Samantha held her tighter to her chest. With Jan's and everyone else's attention on the frightful dealer, there was an opportunity to get out of here. "Let's go then."

Her heart pounded in her chest as she took Meg's hand and snuck around the dealer and Jan. The stranger had grabbed Jan by the neck and was pulling his head backwards. "You want to taste my power and refuse to pay?" he hissed.

Samantha raced towards Matt, who'd got himself up to his feet. She took his left arm, the one that wasn't hanging useless from its socket, and implored him with a desperate stare to follow her. She expected Matt to protest and insist on taking revenge, but he surprised her by nodding.

As he limped away, Samantha tried to steady him. Behind her back, she could hear a sizzling sound and some grunts, then the smack of a fist. Meg whimpered in distress and threw a glance over her shoulder. Samantha looked as well and saw that the crowd of teenagers had turned against the dealer. They were probably going to kill him.

But then Jan broke free from the scuffle, a mysterious bag in his hand. He jumped onto a trash can and crowed, "Freebies for all!" Then he popped something from the bag into his mouth, and for a moment, his eyes shone green. Green like the rivers of magic in the forest.

The others flocked to Jan, who threw the contents of the bag into the crowd, and they all scrambled for them like children in a lolly rain.

The dealer just stood there. Samantha expected him to attack Jan again, but he only turned around and vanished. And suddenly, Samantha knew who it was.

"The demon," she whispered.

He'd left them alone for three weeks, but now he was back. And it looked as if he was going after Jan next. Unless he'd concocted a bigger scheme.

When Jan couldn't find the dealer, he shouted. "Where's that asshole Matt? I think I might kill him after all."

Samantha gasped. At the same moment, Matt's grip on her arm tightened, and he pulled her and her sister into an empty storage hall. The door slammed shut behind them and dunked them into darkness. Someone had bolted up the windows of the abandoned hall. Matt pressed Samantha to his chest as he leaned against the wall, and for a while, her ragged breath matched his racing heartbeat. She hoped with all her might that Jan wouldn't find them in here. With his magic infusion and heightened aggressiveness, he was sure to kill Matt first and then her for daring to interfere with his relationship.

How were they supposed to stop him, powered up as he was?

"Your arm!" Samantha suddenly realised that Matt was pressing her to his chest with his injured arm.

She pulled away from him and got out her phone to shine a light at him. The arm didn't look as bad as it had. And there was something else. Jan had broken Matt's nose. Just minutes ago, Matt's left eye had been swollen almost shut. Now there was only a slight discolouring, as if the injury had occurred weeks ago. And while she watched, the blue faded from his skin, leaving only the blood splatters behind. His nose set before her eyes.

"How is that possible?" Nico had been the one with healing powers, but even his wounds had taken several hours to heal, and he'd never been hurt as badly. Or rather, the one time he had, no healing power had saved him.

Matt looked pained, tortured even. His voice was a little raspy as he spoke. "I... I'll explain it later, okay? Right now, we have to make sure your sister is okay."

Samantha had all but forgotten about Meg. She was in here with them, but she stood near one of the bolted windows and peeked through the boards, her face frightfully pale.

"I don't understand what happened," she whispered when Samantha made her way over to her. "This isn't Jan. Is it?" Meg turned to her, her eyes big in the darkness.

Samantha bit her lip. She'd heard stories about Jan. What a troublemaker he was, and that he'd got into fights when he'd been younger. There had been years where she found him utterly unpleasant, but Fabian had vouched for him and always told her that he wasn't as bad as everyone said. And Samantha knew *personally* that Jan wasn't as bad. He'd been fun on the monster hunts, and while he was a bit rough around the edges, he hadn't been an asshole. "It's the drugs," she said.

Meg groaned. "Right. He takes drugs, so he's a bad person."

Her mood change gave Samantha serious whiplash. "No. Meg! Do you know anything about the pills he's taken recently?"

A little cowed, her sister didn't lash out immediately. "It's called MAGIC. Pretty stupid name, if you ask me. They all take it. They swear it makes them powerful."

"Did you take one?" Worry made Samantha's heart beat faster again.

"No!" Indignation made Meg screw up her face. "I would never!"

Samantha shrugged a little. "Well, before you hung around with Jan you also never drank or smoked—"

"Oh my god!" Meg screeched. "You are such a rule stickler. Everyone drinks and smokes at our age. Everyone but you! You never do anything wrong. Jan was right about you."

"Stop defending him!" Samantha spat back. "Didn't you see how he beat up Matt? He could've killed him."

Meg threw a glance at Matt. "It doesn't look like he actually hurt him."

She was right. Apart from the blood splatters on Matt's shirt—he'd wiped his face—there was almost no sign that he'd received a brutal beating. He gave Samantha an apologetic shrug, as if sorry he wasn't in dire need of the emergency services.

"And Matt started it," Meg cried.

"Only because he pushed your sister," Matt said rather grumpily.

Meg snorted at him and then glared at Samantha. "If she falls over so easily."

Samantha gasped. "You are insane! I've heard of teenagers going crazy, but I never thought I'd see it firsthand."

"Oh, because you were never a teenager. You were a responsible adult the moment you turned thirteen."

Something crashed against the wall of the storage hall, and all three of them froze. Samantha was starkly reminded that Jan was still on a bloodthirsty hunt for Matt. They all held their breath and strained their ears to listen for sounds at the door. Someone was walking around the hall, banging against the hall's shuttered windows.

The moment they knocked against the one next to them, Meg flew into Samantha's arm, swallowing her gasps and tears. Samantha held her, shaking as much as Meg was, while she looked into Matt's frightened eyes. Their gazes remained locked until the banging stopped and the person moved on.

"That was close," Matt whispered.

"How do we get out of here?" Meg cried.

Samantha swallowed heavily. They had to get Meg safely home. And then they had to save Jan before he ran into his doom. And fight that demon. "We need reinforcements."

Rachel

Blood splattered on the screen, and a collective gasp went through the room. Fabian didn't make a sound. Or move.

Rachel threw another glance at him. The last three times she'd tried to act scared, he hadn't even noticed. As it was, she could probably sit here naked, and he'd still be staring at the screen with wide eyes, his lips moving in silent screams.

Why had she listened to Lucille? She'd known Fabian for much longer than her. The reason she loved him was that he wasn't like the other guys. He was kind and sensitive. No one you had to play games with. And no one you'd take to a horror movie.

"Do you want to go?" she whispered. "This movie is too gory for me." She'd found it rather boring, to be truthful, but Fabian didn't need to feel any worse than he already did.

Fabian nodded almost undetectably, and she had to take his hand so he would actually move and leave the movie theatre. As soon as the darkness of the room faded and they were back in the light, Fabian deflated with a sigh of relief.

Rachel held onto his hand. It was the only touch they'd had all evening, and she felt like he needed it more than she did. In the light, he was frightfully pale. "You okay?"

He was conscious enough to shake his head, though his eyes still stared into an undefined distance. "Never force me into a horror flick again."

"Okay." She wanted to say more, but Fabian tore away from her hand all of a sudden and ran to the restroom. No imagination was needed to realise what was going on in there.

Rachel sighed and checked her phone. Nothing. No one had inquired how it was going, and the group chat was empty as well. It was in that moment that she was overcome with a sudden longing for her brother. He could've given her advice. He'd actually known Fabian.

It took Fabian eight minutes to return. His colour was a bit healthier, but there was still a haunted look in his eyes. "Sorry about that." He seemed utterly dismayed. "I really am. I didn't know you liked horror movies. Don't we have enough horrors in Greenvalley?"

"I don't."

He started. "But didn't you want to watch that one?"

"I find horror movies boring. This one started okay, but then it was just splatter. I never wanted to watch it."

"But if you didn't want to watch it, why did you choose it?"

Rachel couldn't blame him for his confusion. It made absolutely no sense, and she didn't know at what point she had believed Lucille when she'd said that it would. "It was Lucille's idea. All of it."

"All of it?"

She tugged at the thin top Lucille had managed to talk her into. "My clothes." They showed off Rachel's figure way too suggestively, and she had the permanent urge to cover her breasts.

"Oh."

"You don't like it."

More colour filled Fabian's face as he flushed. "Of course I do. You look stunning. Lucille's got taste, which makes sense since her stepmum is a fashion designer." He took a deep breath. "But why are you letting Lucille dress you and send you into horror movies?"

Rachel thought she had nothing to lose after already telling the truth so far. "The plan was that you'd put your arm around me if I acted scared, and we'd kiss instead of watching."

It took him a moment to really get what she was saying. "Oh."

An awkward pause stretched between them, and Rachel felt unable to meet his eyes.

Fabian fidgeted with his shirt. "So, do you want to—"

"What are you doing out here?" Suddenly, Lucille was there, glaring at both of them. "You're supposed to be inside and snogging. Why is this so hard for you?"

"Uhm…" Fabian hesitated, while Rachel cleared her throat.

They were both saved by a three-fold hum of their phones. It could only mean one thing.

"Sam needs our help."

\#

The most peculiar thing about the message was that it hadn't come via their normal group chat, but an entirely new one that excluded Jan. There wasn't much information. Samantha and Matt were stuck in a storage hall with Samantha's little sister, Meg. And the demon was around, a fact that seemed to make Fabian wish he was back at the cinema.

But all three of them had hurried down to the docks. Some sort of ruckus was going on at the waterside, and they quickly decided to steer clear of that. Instead, they made it to a shipping container that could pass for a storage hall.

"Sam?" Fabian asked as he opened the door and stuck his head into the darkness. A second later, he pulled it out again. "I feel like I'm sick again."

"The effects of the movie we watched," Rachel explained to Lucille with a hint of annoyance.

Lucille looked at her apologetically and stepped into the container. Rachel followed her and was suddenly quite nauseous as well. She had no idea why. There was no smell or anything like that. But one step forward made her nauseous, and one step back made everything right again.

"What is that?" Lucille pointed towards a softly glowing animal at the back wall of the container.

At least, Rachel hoped it was an animal. It shimmered in a soft violet hue and looked like a cross between an oversized vine louse and a small cat. As they tried to determine what it was, it glowed brighter and extended into a sickening bulb. A handful of round pills dropped from its bottom, and the creature deflated again.

"Did it just poop?" Fabian asked. He'd managed to come in but held a hand in front of his mouth.

"I think they're eggs," Rachel suggested.

Lucille was a little more curious. She took a few steps forward, only to press her hands to her ears. "This is so loud."

Fabian and Rachel exchanged a look. They didn't hear anything. With another glance at each other, they decided to step forward and grab Lucille, who'd sunk to her knees.

They'd barely reached her when the room turned painfully bright, and a loud ringing filled Rachel's ears. She doubled over and fell to the floor next to Lucille as intense nausea hit her. Everything in her body hurt, her senses flooded to the extreme.

At last, someone grabbed her and dragged her back to where her senses weren't constantly overloaded.

Fabian broke down and threw up spittle and gall. "What is this?" he asked, gasping for air.

But before any of them could answer, a stranger barrelled through them and sprinted to the weird creature. He never stopped once. More surprisingly, he seemed entirely unaffected by the magical wards. Still, he was in some kind of frenzy as he grabbed the eggs and stuffed them into his mouth.

"What do you think you're doing?" Lucille asked. She was back on her feet and furious about the treatment by the hand of this stranger. "You can't just come in here and—"

She'd walked deeper into the room and screamed again as the effects assaulted her senses. Panicked, Lucille tried to step back, but the stranger grabbed her arm and pressed her against the container wall.

"Globus igneus," Lucille whispered.

The fireball appeared, but the stranger only raised a hand and waved it away. "I can do magic, too."

"Lucille!" Fabian stayed back where he was unaffected by the strange force and pummelled the guy with water.

He'd merely got him wet when the stranger turned around and grabbed the water as if it were of substance instead. With a gleam in his eyes, he yanked it, and Fabian fell forward as if pulled by an invisible rope. Then the water turned into a snake that wrapped itself first around Fabian's arm and chest, and then his neck.

Rachel wanted to help him, but Fabian shouted at her, "Run! Get Sam and Matt!"

Her heart wanted her to leap towards him, but her mind knew he was right. They needed help, not another one caught up in this weird force field. She turned around and stopped short.

A tall figure filled the entrance. His menacing gaze hit Rachel, and her heart skipped a beat. "You again," he hissed, and then he changed into a form she was more familiar with. Instead of a run-down junkie, the demon that had killed Nico stood before her.

Rachel knew she was going to die. Or rather, she thought she was going to die. But the demon merely barrelled through her and pushed her aside. Rachel slammed into the container wall, preparing herself for more pain that never came. Instead, the demon reached for Fabian.

With a slash of his dark magic, he cut the water stream turned snake off and glared at the unfamiliar guy who'd attacked them and was still holding Lucille. Tears were streaming down her face from the assault on her ears and eyes.

"Stop wasting my magic on something this ridiculous," the demon snarled. Then he grabbed the boy and hauled him into the middle of the room.

Rachel took her chance and darted forward to tug Lucille back into the safe zone. Fabian had somehow managed to roll himself there, coughing and sputtering.

"Are you guys okay?" she asked when she heard a bone-sickening crunch.

Shocked, Rachel whirled around, only to see the young attacker sink to the floor, where he remained unmoving. The demon stood above him and stretched out a hand. Green tendrils rose from the dead boy's body and sunk into the demon's hand.

"There you are," the demon said in a welcoming voice, and for a single moment, he looked exalted.

But soon enough, his face turned sour, and he shot a bolt of energy into the dead body at his feet. The green tendrils had vanished, and no new ones rose. With glowing eyes, he turned to the group of them near the door. "You! Did you take one of my eggs?"

Fabian shook his head, while the other two were still too shocked to respond.

The demon snorted. "This can't be happening. I want my payment! Now!" His anger caused a shockwave of energy that sent the three of them crashing to the floor.

When Rachel opened her eyes again, head ringing, the demon was gone.

"We're alive," Fabian breathed.

"I believe he is preoccupied with something else," Lucille whispered.

Rachel nodded. "Let's get out of here before he comes back."

Lucille

They got lucky with the next storage unit, a decrepit house with bolted-shut windows. Lucille was just about to knock when the door was ripped open by Meg shouting, "I'm not leaving without Jan!"

Then she stared at the three in front of her. Behind her stood Matt and Samantha. Samantha had her arms crossed and was glowering at Meg, while Matt seemed completely overwhelmed. Old blood splatters clung to his clothes, and Lucille's heartbeat lurched.

She pushed Meg back inside and asked, "What happened to you?"

Fabian blocked the door, effectively keeping Meg in, who stomped her foot and then withdrew into another corner.

Samantha sighed. "We've been hiding from Jan and his junkie friends. They're all acting weird and aggressive."

"And the demon's here," Lucille added. The memory of his sudden appearance still echoed in her mind. She'd been almost blind and deaf inside the weird magical forcefield as it pounded her senses, and quite preoccupied with the junkie who'd attacked her, but she could still hear the bone-snapping sound and see the eager look in the demon's eyes as he sucked up his magic.

"The one with the hellhounds?" Matt asked.

"The very same. He can shape-shift. Isn't that awesome?" She sighed, trying to calm her fried nerves. "I'm not completely sure, but I think he sells drugs to these junkies."

"Eggs," Rachel corrected her.

Lucille winced at the reminder. "That's right. Those drugs are actually eggs of a weird animal, probably another hell creature. We were attacked by one of those junkies, and after he popped a pill, he negated our magic and turned it against us. I thought I would die, but then the demon appeared... and killed him." The sickening sound was in her ears again, bringing back the nausea.

Samantha shared a glance with Matt. "Jan was much more powerful than he should've been."

"For sure." Matt's eyebrows narrowed as he regarded Lucille. "So, are you saying that the demon saved your life?" He sounded very doubtful.

Lucille hadn't thought about it like that. "I guess so, but it wasn't exactly his priority."

"He wanted the magic that was stored in the junkie," Rachel mused. "At least, I believe that's what it was."

"It was definitely magic rising from the..." Lucille had to swallow. "The boy. It was a boy." She shuddered.

For a moment, the multi-sensual assault caught up with her, and a few tears ran down her cheeks. A boy had died tonight. He had tried to kill her, and... Lucille took a deep breath and focused on the demon again. "He was angry because it wasn't enough. I don't know what he'd expected, but it was more than what he got."

She wouldn't have expected Samantha and Matt to follow what she'd just told them, but it looked like their hasty recounting had filled the gaps of their own theories, because Samantha said thoughtfully to Matt, "So, the demon developed these new drugs, which are technically the eggs of some Hell creature, and which saturate the affected with magic until they are... ripe for the taking."

"Like a harvest," Matt said.

Samantha nodded, then her eyes widened. "We need to save Jan! He isn't possessed or anything. He's high! And once he's full of magic, that demon will kill him."

"I don't want to go anywhere near him tonight, but I guess you've got a point," Matt muttered.

Now it was Lucille's turn to find it hard to follow. "Wait! Is that why you've excluded Jan from the chat? He's taken these drugs? He takes drugs?"

Samantha shrugged. "That's what people say."

"It doesn't surprise me," Fabian said.

"That creature," Matt asked, while Lucille filed that new information about Jan away. "What did it look like?" After Rachel described it, he rubbed his chin thoughtfully. "I've heard of it. It's called a Viresci. They're animals that are nourished by magic. They lay these eggs to lure in a symbiont. Once the symbiont gets addicted, they come back for more until the symbiont is so full of magic that the Viresci can feast on them."

"How—?" Samantha asked, but Matt gave a small shake of his head, and she kept her mouth shut.

Lucille narrowed her eyes. There was an understanding between these two that was new. Deeper somehow.

It didn't matter right now. They had a demon to fight. "So, this demon breaks the cycle and takes the magic for himself? He's been after the spring of magic in the forest as well. Why does he need so much magic?"

"We've got more immediate problems. Outside are a bunch of magic-addicted youths who're ready to lynch anyone in their way," Samantha said.

Matt nodded. "If we kill the Viresci, the effect should lessen quickly."

"But it's impossible to reach it," Rachel protested.

Once more, Lucille recalled the noise, nausea, and bright light that had tormented them when they'd tried to approach the creature. And how that junkie had just walked in. "Unless you're high."

Samantha picked up the thread immediately. "Jan is high."

"Do you think he'll help us?" Matt asked doubtfully. "We're not exactly his favourite people today."

Samantha looked over her shoulder to where her little sister stood, arms crossed and pouting. "We're not, but Meg is."

Jan

Jan couldn't remember when he'd ever had this much fun. To be honest, some details were a bit blurry, but they didn't matter in the glory that was MAGIC. He'd never truly wanted magic, just knew it existed. Turned out, he had no idea what he'd been missing all the time.

The power. The strength. This pure feeling of being alive.

He was strong. He was powerful. He was invincible!

Magic coursed through his veins, both the drug and the real thing, and it was everything. Who cared if he'd moved out from home? He could easily build himself a home with magic. He could make a fire, grab some food, and make the cashier forget he hadn't paid for it, or make himself invisible altogether if he needed to.

Jan had quickly decided that this was the life. Running around with his friends and seeing how far magic would get him. He'd beaten Matt! Beaten that cocky grin right out of the wannabe demon hunter. All this time, Matt had acted superior to them all, and now Jan had shown him who was really boss.

"Over there!" Felix shouted. "I can see him over there."

Finally! Matt had reappeared. Jan knew he wouldn't flee the scene. That wasn't his style. And now they would get him. No more cocky smiles from him.

Jan and his friends hollered and gave chase when a splash of water hit Jan in the face and made him slip on the icy ground.

"Did you hurt yourself?" Suddenly, Meg was at his side, her blue eyes wide with concern. "Are you okay?" He'd thought she'd be long gone by now.

"Of course I'm okay." Jan stretched his neck, but he couldn't see the others anymore, just heard them jeering in the distance. He turned to his girlfriend, annoyance simmering under his skin. "I thought you left with your stupid sister."

Meg grimaced. "Jan, please. What is going on with you?"

"What's going on with me?" He got up to his feet, dragging Meg with him. "I'm feeling the best I ever have. Until you came along. We were going to catch Matt and mess him up for real this time." He almost tasted the blood on his lips.

Meg's eyes grew even wider. "Jan! Do you even hear yourself speaking?"

Jan rolled his eyes heavily. He had no time for this drama. "Meg, I—"

"I know that you're cool and tough and all of these things." Meg put her hands on his chest. "But living on the streets, addicted to drugs? That's not tough. That's... sad."

"I'm not an addict."

She very nearly stared him down. "Then why are you taking this MAGIC stuff?"

"Did you see what I can do with it?" He walked backwards and raised his hands. Electricity sprung back and forth between his fingers until it became one big ball, sparks flying.

Meg took a hasty step back, and he threw the ball of electricity into the lantern. Lightning struck and glass burst. The light turned off, leaving him and Meg in darkness. "Pretty cool, huh?"

"You're scaring me." She had slung her arms around herself and kept her distance this time.

Why was she acting so stupid? Why couldn't she see how much better he was now that he had magic? "I'm still Jan. Just a stronger, more powerful version."

"You mean more violent and aggressive?"

That was it. He had enough of her drama-queen behaviour. "Either you take me as I am or—"

"But this isn't *you!*" Meg shouted, her arms flailing at him as if she couldn't decide whether to keep embracing herself or pushing him hard. "It's this stupid MAGIC talking. And you know what? What you're digging into are eggs. Not pills. Eggs! You're getting high on disgusting little eggs from some magical psycho creature."

"You sure *you* aren't high?" Jan almost burst out laughing. That was the most ridiculous story he'd ever heard.

Meg's eyes were blazing. "You don't believe me? Check it out yourself." She pointed at one of the storage units. "That's where your dealer keeps it."

Jan didn't believe a single word of this magical creature, but that last info was useful. He needed more MAGIC, and where better to get it from than from the source itself? "Okay, I'll check. But you owe me a kiss if there's no magic psycho creature." He strode across the lot and ripped the door nearly from its hinges.

Meg was right. There was a little animal inside. And it looked outright weird with its glowing, near-translucent skin. He ventured closer and marvelled at the weird creature. "You're right, this is magical."

He turned around and found out that Meg hadn't come into the room alone. Instead, she'd been joined by her stupid sister. Just what he needed.

"Stay away, Sam, before I give you some of your own medicine." He stretched his hands out when the creature began to swell and light up. A moment later, it popped out a bunch of shiny white eggs. MAGIC. An endless supply of it. "Damn, that's rad!"

"You need to kill it," Samantha said.

Jan almost laughed in her face. "Kill it? This treasure trove? Never!"

Next to her sister, Meg stamped her foot. "You're such an idiot. Give this to me, and I'll do it." She ran towards him but folded halfway through.

While Samantha was running to help her sister, Jan grabbed the creature with one hand and stuffed his pockets full of eggs with the others. Now he only had to get rid of the Kollmer sisters, and his new life as a rich man would begin.

He turned around and nearly stumbled over the body on the floor. He recognised that body. Why was Lutz on the floor? And why wasn't he moving while his eyes stared into nothingness?

"Jan, please don't do this," Samantha begged.

He tore his eyes away from Lutz and glared at her. "You again."

"Yes, me again. I know you think I'm meddling, but Meg is important to me." Her little sister was huddled into her embrace, tears streaming down her face.

"She's important to me as well." She was his girlfriend, after all.

Samantha scoffed. "Oh, is she? How can she be important to you if you'd rather be high than around her?"

She was confusing him. Why would he have to decide between Meg and the MAGIC pills? Why couldn't he have both?

"If you truly love her, you'd give up on those drugs. You don't need to prove how cool and tough you are to anyone. Meg loves you as you are. She sees more in you—"

"Than you do?" His voice dripped with sarcasm. Let Samantha wriggle herself out of that one. She was just as haughty as Matt, always thinking she was better than everybody else. Just because she didn't go to parties or drink, and had never even taken a single puff from a cigarette.

But Samantha didn't protest. She only shrugged. "So, who's right then? Is there more? Or are you just an idiot who ruins his own life and doesn't care at all about those who love him?"

"Jan," Meg whispered, her eyes begging him to choose her.

He couldn't stand looking at them, and so he turned his gaze down to the ground again. Lutz still hadn't moved. "Why isn't he moving?"

"Was that a friend of yours?" Samantha asked, sounding awfully compassionate.

Jan refused to look at her. "His name's Lutz."

"I'm sorry."

Why was she sorry? Why was Lutz not moving? Why wasn't he moving, dammit!

"It's that demon, Jan." Samantha's voice was still so awfully calm. A stupid voice of reason in a sea of magic and fury. "He murdered Lutz. He's planning to kill all of you when... when you've taken enough of those eggs."

Lutz, who'd been so frantic lately. Who couldn't wait to get his next kick. Who'd gone with the dealer into this very container. To get more

MAGIC. For free, because at that point, he was more valuable to the demon high than strung-out.

He grabbed a handful of pills from his pockets and let them fall. The pills hit the floor, cracking as they did so. How had he never noticed they were actually eggs?

He looked down at the weird little creature. *Kill it,* Samantha had said. Well, if he couldn't kill Matt, he might as well kill this thing. "For Lutz," he whispered, slung his arm around it, and wrung that little beast's neck.

It was as if the fog had cleared. Green tendrils sifted from his clothes and sunk into the ground. He suddenly felt weak and tired, but unfortunately clearer.

"Lutz." He sunk to his knees next to his friend, finally realising why he wasn't moving. "Oh, man." It wasn't like they'd been the best of friends, but they'd been through some shit together, and he had always been able to complain about his parents to Lutz, because Lutz understood him. Lutz got it. Like no one else had.

But Lutz had been lost for a while. They'd both gone to the docks together, yet Jan was still here, while Lutz's addiction had cost him his life.

And Jan had almost shared his fate.

What was he doing here? Taking hard drugs? Running away from home? Beating up his friend? Wanting to kill him?

"Jan?" Samantha had stayed back, but Meg had come closer, her face full of worry.

Who's right? Is there more? Or are you just an idiot who ruins his own life and doesn't care at all for those who love him?

He wanted Samantha to be right, wanted to be more, but right now, Jan was afraid he was still the same old idiot as always. "I'm sorry," he whispered.

Meg fell around his neck with a cry. "It's you! You're you again." She kissed his cheeks while tears ran down her face. "I knew it. I knew you weren't as bad as Sammy said."

Jan glanced at the doorway, where Samantha still stood, arms crossed and with a weary look in her eyes. They both knew he was every bit as bad. But did he have to stay that way? He didn't need the drugs. Didn't need to make every chat with his parents a standoff. Maybe it was time to outgrow the docks and step away from the downward spiral.

The last thing Jan wanted was to end up like Lutz. He was sure his friend would agree.

Matt

"The demon came and killed a few of them," Matt explained to Samantha after they'd met up again and left the docks before the police arrived. "He was so furious. Screaming about how they had to pay him. And when the magic vanished and the survivors returned to normal, he told us that we owe him." He shuddered. "It's definitely a greed demon."

Matt thought greed demons were the worst. Not that any of the deadly sins were pleasant—well, except for the one—but dealing with greed never turned out well. He much preferred the clean anger of wrath or the easy-going nature of sloth demons. A greed demon never settled. They always wanted more, and they'd literally kill for it.

Next to him, Samantha only nodded. She was probably tired. It was late, and they'd spent the last few hours in a nightmare. Her eyes were fixed on Jan and Meg, who were walking a couple of paces ahead of them, a distance Samantha had chosen, not the happy couple.

"If it helps, I'll kill him if he breaks her heart," Matt said.

Samantha grimaced—probably the wrong thing to say after the night they'd had. "Oh, no she's not!"

Matt turned his eyes to the front again. They were near the Kollmer house, and the couple had stopped. Meg was handing something to Jan, no, tying it to his wrist. "Is that…"

"The Bond of Levante, yes," Samantha hissed. She let out an enormous sigh. "I can't believe she's giving it to *him*!"

He remembered what Chay had said, that the Emblems of Power found their way to their bearers. "Perhaps it was meant for him."

"If I'd bought it, it would've been mine," Samantha said, her eyes still fixed on the couple.

Gently, Matt took her hand. "But you didn't." As much as he commiserated with her, he trusted Chay. The seer would intervene if one of the emblems went to the wrong person.

"Then where's mine?" Samantha said, swallowing heavily.

Matt couldn't be sure, but he thought he saw tears glistening in her eyes. With Rachel and her dreamweb, and Jan receiving the bracelet, Samantha was the only one still missing hers. If they were truly meant to have all six. "It'll find its way to you," he said, nonetheless.

Someone else found their way to them, and Samantha hastily wiped her eyes before taking a step towards Jan. "I would've thought you'd want to stay."

"And get in trouble with you again?" Jan joked. He shook his head with a soft smile. "I'm sorry I dragged her down with me. It won't happen again. I promise. So, step one, I'm going back home and…" He made a face. "Apologising to my parents."

Samantha smiled at him. "You can do it."

From the corner of his eye, Jan glanced at Matt, then sighed. "Actually, step one is apologising to you two, and especially you, Matt. I don't know how I'm ever going to—"

"It's fine," Matt hurried to say. This whole thing was starting to become embarrassing. "You were possessed or whatever. That wasn't you." It still grated on him how easily Jan had beaten him. He hadn't received such a beating since he'd been half the size of his older brother. And from a mere human at that. A magic-fuelled human, but still.

Jan frowned. "You're sure?"

Matt nodded quickly. "Yeah, all good. Just stay away from drugs," he said in an exceedingly grumpier voice.

"Say no to drugs." Jan chuckled. "Yeah, I think the idea of eating mini eggs from some Hell creature cured me of that one." He glanced over his shoulder to where Meg had gone inside. "Well, thanks for setting me straight. I can't promise you'll never have to do it again, but I'll try."

Since Matt had no idea what to say to that, he let Samantha do the talking. Promises didn't mean anything to him. People either did what they were saying or they didn't. He'd learned not to rely on anyone but himself from a young age. Least of all on his family.

They said goodbye to Jan and watched him leave. Matt expected Samantha to head inside as well, but she surprised him when she said, "Do you want to go to the playground?"

"To the playground?" It was early morning, almost four o'clock by his watch, not exactly the time to play.

"It's better than standing on the street."

"Sure." What else was he supposed to say? Samantha didn't seem ready to leave him yet, and for some reason, the idea made him inexplicably happy.

He followed her to a small playground with some monkey bars, a slide, and a swing set. Samantha steered him to the swings, and they sat next to each other.

"Do you do this often?" Matt couldn't help asking. He was still learning about humans. Maybe that was something they did. During the day, the kids took to the playground, and at night, the adults—or teenagers—played.

But Samantha didn't play. She swayed slightly as she balanced on her tiptoes and regarded him with a seriousness that made him uneasy. "You were going to explain something to me."

Oh dear. With everything else that had happened, Matt had forgotten that she'd seen him heal from a broken nose and a torn shoulder muscle. The blood was still on his shirt.

"Why your injuries were gone so quickly?" she asked helpfully, still unnervingly calm. "And why you know a whole lot about monsters, especially creatures from Hell."

Damn, she was good. But of course she was. This was Samantha, the brightest mind in their school. And she had read up on magic for years. How did he think he could keep his secret from her? And more importantly, did he even want to keep his secret?

Suddenly, there was this urge inside him to tell her. He hated that he'd lied to her and was desperate to come clean. He wanted to tell her all about himself, his youth, his family. All of it. "It's complicated."

"Try me," she said with a wistful smile, and Matt almost spilled it all right there. "I mean, if you don't want to talk about it, that's fine." Samantha rolled her eyes with a little chuckle. "Don't want to be meddling again."

"I want to!" Matt surprised himself by his vehemence, but he did. He really wanted to tell her. He was simply... afraid. This was so wrong, so different from anything he knew. What was there to be afraid of? This was Samantha. She wouldn't jump up and run away. Or try to kill him. She was far too sensible for that.

He cleared his throat. "Well..."

Gravel crunched under light steps, and Samantha's head flew towards the newcomer who approached them. Matt turned more slowly, and immediately wished he hadn't. He usually liked Chay, but he couldn't have come at a more inopportune moment. Unfortunately, Chay knew exactly which moments to pick.

"Chay."

"You two know each other?" Samantha's head moved back and forth between them, and Matt realised that Chay's sudden appearance had scared her. So, hanging out in abandoned playgrounds at night was not a normal human thing.

Matt got up from his swing and acknowledged Chay with a nod. "He's an old friend of mine."

"I'm not that old," Chay muttered.

"Debatable," Matt said through pressed teeth. He didn't want Chay to out him to Samantha. As much as he dreaded it, he wanted to do this himself. It seemed important.

Chay smiled at Samantha. His smiles always gave him a deceivingly boyish look. Samantha wouldn't assume he was any older than twenty-five. "You must be Samantha." The bastard was well aware of her name. "I'm Chay. I believe you've read my book."

Matt gasped. So, he wanted to reveal *that* to her?

Meanwhile, Samantha was confused. "Which book?"

"She reads a lot," Matt said quite acidly. "You need to be a little more specific."

Chay had only a smile for him. "*The Circle of Magic.*" As Samantha's eyes widened, he grinned. "Let me introduce myself again. I'm Chay, also known as the Seer."

Samantha's gaze flew from Chay to Matt and back again. "How is this...?"

"Chay can see the future," Matt replied grumpily.

He still didn't know why Chay had chosen this exact moment to appear and tell her. Surely, he must've known that Matt was about to tell her something important. And then it hit him. Chay had known. And he had chosen this moment because it wasn't to be. It wasn't the time to tell Samantha the truth about himself. And somehow that made Matt sad.

"You can?" Now, she was utterly fascinated by Chay. "Does that mean—?"

"Don't ask." Chay raised his hands. "I'll explain everything—well, what I can—later. But right now, I need to steal Matt from you."

Samantha turned to Matt, and the betrayal in her eyes hit him unexpectedly. "Did you know all this time?"

It took him a moment to understand what she meant, but Chay was quicker. "No, I kept him in the dark until a few weeks ago. Don't blame Matt for my secrecy. I try my best not to get too involved in the course of the future. And it was important that you all met without fate dangling over your heads. But I'll get to that later. I promise."

"I'm sorry," Matt breathed. He wasn't quite sure what he was apologising for, only that it was important.

Samantha nodded, still looking rather dejected. She got up from the swing and pretended to check the time. "It's rather late, so I'll better head inside. I'll see you... guys... later."

Matt would much rather have stayed with her, talked a little bit more, alone in the darkness, but he raised his hand in a half-wave and let her go. He'd always fared best when he trusted Chay.

Still, it hurt him to see her walk away. It was an unfamiliar ache, as if something was missing in his chest, torn from it the wider the distance grew. Matt blinked and turned to Chay. "I was about to tell her everything."

"I know." The smile was gone, and only sadness remained in Chay's eyes.

"Then why didn't you let me?" Matt didn't want to keep this secret any longer. He owed Samantha the truth. He wanted her to learn the truth. As scary as that was, for some reason.

The sadness in Chay's eyes only grew deeper. "Because the moment she learns of it, she'll hate you."

Fabian

It had been a very long night, and when Fabian finally rose from his bed, it was past noon. And on such a glorious day. The sun was peeking through his blinds, a faint promise of warmth. But Fabian knew better. Sunshine only made a winter day colder.

Unwilling to leave the bed right now, he checked his messages and found out that Jan had made up with his parents and even sat down to talk to them.

Jan: They're not the greatest fans of my relationship with Meg, but they came to their senses when I pointed out that they were twelve years apart. Anyway, all good, I guess.

Lucille: Parents. My father probably wouldn't even notice if I moved out.

Rachel: Same.

When Fabian saw her name, his heart ached. Last night—before the real-life horror had begun—she'd dragged him into a horror movie just because she wanted him to make a move on her. And he hadn't even noticed, although Samantha had prepared him for it. Or perhaps he'd been a tad distracted by all the gore on the screen and later on the street.

What a mess that date had been. But Fabian refused to think of their relationship as a mess. Rachel was desperate for him to do something, while he'd been waiting for a sign. Well, he'd been hit over the head with a fence pole of signs, so he'd better give their relationship a real chance.

And so he began typing.

An hour later, Fabian waited for Rachel at the eastern entrance of the Christmas market in town. It had snowed earlier in the day, and a soft blanket of real snow covered the huts and the houses behind it. Now, this was his kind of magic. He couldn't have been in a better mood.

When Rachel arrived, she was much more sensibly clad in a thick coat and warm pants. Her signature braids popped out from under a colourful hat that Lucille wouldn't even have dared to touch, but which looked perfect on Rachel. She usually wore muted colours, but whenever she chose a splash of colour, it made her eyes shine.

"There you are," he greeted her and held out his gloved hand.

The thick wool made it harder to feel her fingers, but at least they were warm. Fabian preferred pragmatism over style any day.

"Did you have to wait for long? My mother wanted to talk for some reason." She rolled her eyes, but her cheeks were glowing slightly.

"Anything good?" Fabian asked as they slowly started walking down the street.

Rachel sighed. "I don't know. It's hard for me to believe that she cares. I mean, some part of me knows that. It's been written all over her dreams for years, but well, addiction and... I guess trauma is stronger. And I don't see how that's going to change. But..." She licked her lips as if she had to prepare herself for what would come next. "I told her that she needed therapy. Not in a mean way, but it felt appropriate, and she promised to look into it. So, we'll see."

It was highly unusual for Rachel to say so much, which told Fabian all he needed to know about how important this talk had been. He squeezed her hand a little tighter. "I hope she gets better."

"Yeah, me too."

Last night, he'd had a front seat to what addiction could do to people. To imagine Rachel had lived with that most of her life made Fabian see her in an entirely new light. She was quiet, yes, but underneath all that mousy exterior was a strength that far surpassed his own.

"Shall we go get some hot cocoa?" He much preferred the mulled wine, but he was suddenly unsure how Rachel would take it if he asked for wine, even if there wasn't much alcohol in it.

To his surprise, she saw right through him. "You always get mulled wine from Elvira and me, too. It's Sam who prefers cocoa."

Now that she said it, Fabian remembered it as well. "Two mulled wines then."

As they got in line, Rachel explained in a low voice, "I'm not the biggest fan of alcohol, and getting drunk is a no-go, but I don't mind it in something like mulled wine. Or a cocktail."

"Cocktails. Maybe that's what we should do for our next date," Fabian quipped.

Rachel wrapped her free arm around his and put her head against his shoulder. "I much prefer this one."

"Me too." Then they were at the front of the line, and Elvira's familiar face looked out at them. "I swear you get taller each year. No Samantha today?"

The problem in a city this small was that almost everybody knew each other. Elvira had run this hut as long as Fabian could remember, back when he'd definitely been on the hot cocoa list. "No. She already went without us. And we're on a date."

"Uhh." Elvira grinned, then put two mugs in front of them. "Well, then. Don't let me keep you two."

Fabian and Rachel managed to grab one of the round standing tables and warmed their hands against the mugs. This year's design was the city hall and a bunch of stars in white on blue. At home, his mother had a whole collection of mulled wine mugs from the Christmas market. You were supposed to return them, but the deposit was only six euros. Hefty for a deposit, but not expensive for pretty mug memorabilia.

They had to let go of each other to drink their wine. Rachel's cheeks were still glowing, but whether it was from the cold or the contents of her mug, Fabian didn't know. She looked over her shoulder at Elvira and whispered, "Why did you have to announce it?"

"Well, we are dating, aren't we?"

"Yes, but..." She stopped to stare longingly into his eyes.

Was that one of the signs Samantha had said he was missing all this time? "We can make it official, can't we?"

"Sure," was the slightly stretched answer. Then Rachel smiled. "Does that mean yesterday wasn't a total fail?"

"Oh, yesterday was a total fail. Never drag me into a horror movie and then top it off with a real-life horror show," Fabian joked, though the smile didn't come easy. They'd met the demon again. And that surely couldn't be a good thing.

But the sun was shining, and the snow was glistening. And Rachel's eyes shone in the warmest brown. He slid his arm around her, pressing her closer to him. "And that's why we're here today. To have a real date. Without Lucille and Samantha holding the ropes."

She smiled at that. "I should've known you'd hate Lucille's ideas. You're not like the guys she dates."

"No, because then I'd be dating her," he quipped. "And I don't want that. Because you're much more my type. And..." His gaze fell onto her lips. "I should've done this much earlier."

Fabian bent down and lightly kissed her lips. At first, Rachel seemed to hold her breath, but then she leaned into him. And while their lips and tongues discovered each other, their mulled wine grew cold.

Part 2
Mistletoes & Cookies

Samantha

December brought a spell of cold temperatures and more snow. It was one of the most magical times of the year when Greenvalley looked like a fairy-tale postcard. At school, they still had another round of exams to get through, but after that, it would be mostly fun and games until the holidays.

Samantha turned away from the winter wonderland outside of her room and went downstairs to grab something to eat and prepare her lunchbox. Meg was blocking the bathroom, and her father was already at work. But her mother was still in the kitchen when she walked in.

"Good morning, darling," her mother greeted her as she made herself a cup of coffee. "Glad I caught you before I left."

"Why? Was there something you wanted to talk about?" Samantha paused slicing her bread to check with her mother.

Her mother smiled, her hands wrapped around her coffee mug as she leaned against the counter. "You know that I've been asked to organise the Christmas Gala for the council."

"You mean you volunteered because you wanted to invite the agency people here for Christmas, so they can fall in love with Greenvalley?" Despite being over forty, her mother still dreamed of becoming an actress. She'd had small features in TV ads, but nothing to write home about. Instead, she ran the little town theatre and worked part-time for the council.

Her mother grinned. "You got me." Despite her smile, Samantha thought her mother wasn't truly serious about her acting career. Otherwise, she would've convinced her father to move to one of the big cities ages ago. If there was one thing you couldn't find in the Harz, it was a blooming film industry.

Samantha turned to the fridge to get out spread and cheese for her sandwich. "Is Dad still cranky about it?" The Christmas Gala took place on Christmas Eve. It was an annual event for those who were spending the holidays on their own. It also doubled as a fundraiser for those willing to open their pockets at Christmas, like the de Cerques.

"He's on board after I promised to invite your grandmother," her mother explained and took a deep breath. "What about you?"

When her mother had first told them about it a week ago, Samantha had been annoyed. She loved Christmas with her family. The cosiness of it, the cookies, and the roast dinner. The candles and the songs. But most of all, she loved spending this day just with her family. The Christmas Gala was a big function. There was nothing cosy about it. "I think if we don't do this every year, it's fine." She shrugged. "I like the general idea of it, to be honest." Not everybody had a family to celebrate with.

Surprised, her mother's smile widened. "I'm so glad to hear it. Well, I've got another proposition for you."

Samantha didn't like the tone of that. She put her sandwich together and asked, "Another proposition?"

"Yes, we're in dire need of a singer. There's always live music and—"

"Mum, no!" Samantha whirled around to face her. "I only sing in the choir. I don't do solos." That would mean standing out—and standing on stage alone.

Her mother protested instantly, "Well, you should! Your singing voice is beautiful." Upon Samantha's glare, she quickly changed strategy. "You wouldn't be alone—we've also arranged for a male singer. But I kind of already promised you'd take the job."

Why did her mother always do this to her? Most of the time, she left Samantha alone, but once in a while, she had the great idea of pushing her out into the world. To make sure she lived a little, as she often put it.

"I can't do this. There are people, and I..." Years of bullying had made it impossible for Samantha to even imagine taking the spotlight for herself. It shone on her often enough, usually in conjunction with a cruel joke. If Cheryl and her cronies learned about this engagement, they'd have a field day.

Her mother stepped forward and cradled Samantha's cheek with her hand. "You can do this." She snorted a little. "Believe me, most of the guests will be in good spirits—so to speak—and it's only Christmas songs. The main thing is to spread some cheer."

"Because I'm so good at that. I'm the born entertainer..."

"For whom? Nursery children?" Meg had come down to prepare her lunchbox.

Samantha took a deep breath. Her sister was the prime example of why she shouldn't say yes to her mother's wild scheme.

"Meg, please," her mother warned. "Sammy, you really don't need to worry so much. And it's one time only. And..." She sighed. "I'll pay you for it. We have a small budget."

"I want money!" Meg cried out. "What do I need to do? I have sooooo many presents to buy."

"Try self-made ones," Samantha hissed, unduly annoyed at her little sister. Of course, she could use some extra money, and truth be told she enjoyed singing. Even Christmas songs. "Fine, I'll do it. But only this time."

Her mother's face split into a wide smile. "Oh, Sammy, thank you so much. If you could come to the town hall at four thirty after school, we're going to have our first rehearsal."

Samantha immediately regretted saying yes. "I had plans..." Matt and she were going shopping for his birthday. They'd probably be able to finish before then if they left right after school, but still. "I'll try to be there."

"You're the best."

Samantha took her sandwich and grabbed an apple before leaving her mother to Meg, who was complaining that she wanted a holiday job too. Hopefully, it wouldn't be singing. No one deserved that on Christmas Eve.

Since their late-night chat had been interrupted by Matt's strange friend, Matt hadn't tried to talk to her again. Sure, they were still joking around at school, but whenever Samantha tried to get him alone, he managed to slip away. Until today.

After school, they crossed the river and walked into the city centre, currently occupied by the Christmas market. It was snowing a little, and a cold wind blew through the alleys.

"So, you've really never celebrated a birthday?" Samantha asked, hoping to work herself towards the things she really wanted to find out. What kind of strange sect did he belong to that didn't celebrate birthdays? He didn't particularly strike her as the religious kind, but one could never know. He was obviously keeping secrets from her and the rest of the group.

"Is it that weird?" Matt asked. He was studying his feet, as if avoiding her.

Samantha shrugged and decided to nudge him some more. "Well, not weirder than anything else about you." Sect or no sect, he had some powerful internal magic that helped him heal and shoot black energy from his hands. And Chay—whose book was worth several *decades* of work—was the same. She wasn't even sure if it was truly Matt's eighteenth birthday, except for the fact that his father couldn't have been that much younger when he'd had him.

Matt's shoulders bunched, and his face twitched. For a moment, Samantha worried that she'd pushed too far. It didn't actually matter to her what he was. She knew him for *who* he was, and that was quite enough.

"I'm sorry," he muttered. "It... No, I can't remember celebrating a birthday. Perhaps my dad did when I was still living with him, but my mum never cared."

"That's horrible," Samantha whispered. Or perhaps those secrets held too much pain for him to let her in. Quickly making up her mind, she took his hand. "You know what? We're going to make this the best birthday party ever. Practically eighteen birthdays at once."

Matt burst out laughing. It was a beautiful sound, and Samantha felt some of the tension flow out of him. "What's that going to look like?"

She instantly had a bunch of ideas. "Follow me to find out." She teased him with what she hoped was a mysterious smile, but it was slightly ruined by a grin, then dragged him forward to a stall that sold Christmas lights. "You're in luck. My mum's paying me extra money this year to do some stupid singing, so we've got a good budget for this."

Matt put his hand on hers when she went for a string of lights. "I'm paying. It's my birthday party, and you've already offered to organise it."

There was an intensity in his chocolatey eyes that made Samantha's heart beat just a little faster. Quickly, she turned back to the goods in front of them. "Very well. Then tell me your budget, and we'll operate from there. I was thinking of getting two or three of these fairy lights. Look, these are even green, like the spring in the forest."

"A magical birthday party? I like it."

Samantha blushed. Surely, he only said it to humour her. Leave it to Witchy Sam to come up with a magic theme. Oh well, she might as well embrace it. Matt had never laughed at her, after all, and he knew that magic was real. "Magic could save us from spending too much. We can ask Lucille to conjure up some never-melting giant snowflakes or icy flowers. Or Fabian could draw some with his feather, though that stuff vanishes within an hour."

"Yeah, I was planning to celebrate a little longer than that."

"Of course. We're going to start on the thirty-first and celebrate your birthday in style with some fireworks."

He raised an eyebrow. "Are we now?"

She held her breath. "Too bossy?" Fabian always claimed that she was too bossy, but that was only when she was with him. He was safe around to be herself, which she guessed was a bit bossy. But Matt... when had Matt become safe enough for her true personality to shine through? "I'm sorry, you probably want to celebrate New Year's Eve with your dad. The party doesn't actually have to be on your birthday, though it's a Saturday."

"I want the New Year's party," he said with a smile that turned her knees to butter. A usual effect he had on pretty much anybody, Samantha was sure. "And everything else you come up with."

Full creative control for the birthday party of the coolest guy in school. "Right... uhm, how many people are we expecting?" If this was one of those huge parties, she would restrain herself from a big magic statement.

"Just you guys," Matt said, his fingers running over the fake icicles of another string of fairy lights. "My father, I guess. And probably Chay."

"Probably?" Samantha was doing her very best not to burst from curiosity. Chay had promised to talk to her about the book, after all.

Matt shrugged. "You never know with him. He's a busy man. He doesn't usually stick around for such a long time."

"Why do you think he is?"

"You know as much as I do in that regard." He nodded towards the green lights and addressed the stall holder. "Can I have three of those, please?"

If there ever was a sure sign Matt didn't want to talk about a topic, it was this one. Samantha let him buy the fairy lights and thought about what else they needed for the party.

Once they'd started walking again, a pretty good idea had formed in her head. "So, normally, people have raclette or fondue for New Year's, but with eight people... well, it could work, but I was thinking a buffet would be nice instead. I've got a couple of recipe books I've been waiting to try out."

Matt stopped and turned around to her. "Isn't that an awful lot of work for you? Because I can't cook. So..."

She smiled at him. "I told you I was going to give you eighteen birthdays at once. Okay, maybe it won't be that extreme, but I like cooking."

For a moment, he looked terribly lost, as if worried about hidden costs or something like that.

"Friends do this for each other," she said firmly. Friendship like family seemed to be something he wasn't quite as used to as he should be.

"Sam." Matt took both of her hands in his and wet his lips. "I... thank you."

"Don't worry about it."

He looked down at their hands, as if unable to bear her kindness. His thumbs rubbed over her palms slightly. "Your hands are cold."

"It is winter," Samantha pointed out, but her voice tapered off a little, unsure of what to make of his weird mood.

Then Matt stepped closer until his toes almost touched hers, and he placed her hands flat against his stomach. Heat radiated from his abs, warming her fingertips. Samantha blushed heavily as she registered the motions of his breathing. She was awfully close to him, her skin only separated from his by a few layers of fabric. It was impossible for her to raise her eyes higher than his chest. She had no idea what would await her if she looked into his face. And she was too scared to find out.

Snow swirled around them as the wind picked up a little, and all Samantha could think of was the heat emanating from his body that warmed so much more than just her hands.

After their shopping trip, Samantha had to hurry to make it in time for the rehearsal. The town hall was nearby, but there had been minutes of awkward silence with her frozen in place.

Matt confused her. He was different than before. When she was alone with him, he wasn't flirty or cocky. Quite the opposite. There was this vulnerability in him, one she wasn't even sure he realised he was showing. And just now... Didn't he realise what it did to a girl when he let her touch him like that?

Samantha would've liked to be completely immune to his good looks and charms. His reputation alone was cause enough to run the other way. And it wasn't just a reputation. Every word was true, confirmed by Matt himself. But this vulnerability. It was as if he were two people at once. The terrible flirt and suave monster hunter everyone else got to see, and the boy who'd never had a birthday party in his life that only she seemed to catch a glimpse of.

The problem was Samantha had no idea if she wanted to be the one in the know. This was a crush, nothing but a crush on a guy who would break her heart into little pieces. It didn't matter that Matt was showing her this other side. He was still the one who left broken hearts left and right. And Samantha had no illusions that he'd change enough for her. She wasn't that stupid. She...

Her foot slipped out from under her, and she fell backwards. It was too late to do anything about it. She was falling and about to land on her backside.

"Oops." Someone caught her before she hit the ground and brought her back to her feet.

Breathing heavily, Samantha turned around to her saviour. He was a young man, maybe three to four years older than her, with brown hair peeking out from under a woollen hat, curling slightly. He was a bit taller than her, almost reaching Fabian's height, and had a backpack slung over his shoulder.

"Are you hurt?" He smiled gently, and a little dimple appeared on the left side of his mouth.

Samantha had forgotten how to speak and shook her head. The fall, she told herself. It must've knocked the breath out from her lungs. Only, he'd caught her quite gently.

"Were you also heading inside?" The stranger asked and pointed towards the doors of the town hall.

She found herself nodding, still unable to speak. He didn't seem to mind and stayed by her side, ready to catch her again, before opening the door.

The hall where the gala would take place was already halfway decorated. Her mother was talking to an older guy who always played piano at town events. Mr Meise. As they heard the door open, Samantha's mother turned around and waved them closer.

"Come here, you two." She got hold of the guy's hand and shook it. "Juliane Kollmer. We talked on the phone," she told him.

And Samantha's brain finally restarted and told her this must be her duet partner. "You sing?"

It was her mother who answered. "Daniel called me last week, responding to a flyer we posted at the university. He'll be your partner on stage." She smiled at Daniel. "This is my daughter Samantha, by the way."

"Nice to meet you, Samantha."

His smile was like butter, and her tongue felt big and unwieldy once again, but she managed a squeaky, "Likewise."

Her mother looked back and forth between the two of them and then grinned for some reason. "Well, I'm glad you're both here. Mr Meise has already built us a set list."

The pianist handed them a small booklet that had clearly been printed in the office upstairs and tucked together. "You probably know most of these songs from your childhood."

They both leafed through the booklet. Daniel kept looking at her, and his eyebrows managed to communicate exactly what he thought of the set list. "What's the audience going to be like? I mean... could we perhaps sing a few more modern songs?"

The booklet was kept extremely traditional, with most of the songs working well as carols or background music, but none were exactly suitable for dancing.

"Young man. It is *Christmas*, a holiday of contemplation and peace."

"Sure," Daniel said, not eager to get in a fight about it.

Samantha's mother stepped in. "No, no, I think Daniel is right. This is a big gala, and we don't want to put everybody to sleep. How about mixing old and new? Then we have some nice traditional Christmas songs that everybody can sing along and something to dance to in between."

"I don't know if I can learn many new songs," Mr Meise protested, but he was no match for her mother.

Or Daniel. "Then we'll find some karaoke tracks. The hall has a music system, doesn't it?" He smiled encouragingly. "We can do this. Right?" And for some reason, he looked straight at Samantha.

He was absolutely right. The supplied set list didn't excite Samantha at all, but she would've done whatever the adults thought was best. "Uhm, yeah, we can." It wasn't much more than a whisper.

She was startled when her mother clapped her hands with way too much enthusiasm. "Wonderful. Then I suggest you two sit down and build us a new set list, and we'll leave you to it." All three of them stared at her in surprise. "This way you get to know each other. That's important to harmonise on stage, right?" She reached into her pocket and held out the key to Samantha with a wink. "You can close up when you're done." Then she took Mr Meise's arm and steered him towards the exit. "Let's go."

Mr Meise was clearly confused, but he let himself be led out of the hall. When the door shut behind them, Daniel raised an eyebrow. "Am I seeing things, or did your mother just try to set us up?"

"I wouldn't put it past her." Samantha wished the floor would open up beneath her and swallow her whole.

Daniel laughed. "Alright." He put his booklet on the stage, then pushed himself up to sit on the edge. With a grin, he patted the floorboards next to him. "Come on up."

Samantha hesitated. She was still suffering from whiplash after her mother had left her alone with a stranger so suddenly. A stranger she was going to spend quite some time with to rehearse their songs. She got over herself and handed him her backpack before climbing up herself.

"What have you got in there? Stones?" Daniel joked.

"Books. I had an exam this morning."

"Are you still going to school?" he asked, then got out his phone to search up Christmas songs.

Samantha snorted. "Why? Do I look too old for that?"

Daniel grinned and shrugged. "I would never dare guess a woman's age."

"I'm seventeen and you?"

"Twenty."

"Do you study in Greenvalley?" Her mother had said he'd responded to a flyer at the university.

He pushed up his shoulders and laughed. "That's why I need the money."

The amusement sparkling in his eyes made it easier to talk to him. "And here I thought you did it out of the goodness of your heart. To bring joy to lonely people on a Christmas night."

"Do I look like a good guy?" He did, but Samantha couldn't tell him that. So she shook her head and almost managed a grin. "Well, thanks. And how did you get roped in?"

Samantha thought back to the morning. "My mother pretty much had everything already set up. But I'm getting a bonus."

"Yeah, me," Daniel said with a straight face.

Samantha blinked at him as the words slowly sank into her brain. Then she burst out laughing. "You must be very sure of yourself."

Daniel grinned, then looked down on his smartphone. "I'm usually not, but, uhm... Oh, listen to this one." He got out some earphones and handed an earbud to Samantha.

Samantha took hers and tentatively rolled it between her fingers. Something about Daniel set her senses buzzing. To listen to the song, she would have to get even closer to him. Before she could come to a decision, he slid a little towards her and put one earbud into his ear. Samantha decided to just get over herself and do it.

Initially, the feeling of his shoulder against hers made it impossible for her to take note of the song, but then the beat cut through the fog in her brain, and she found herself nodding along with the music. This was so much better than the dated set list.

"That's a good one," she said, initiating conversation for the first time this afternoon.

Daniel turned to her with his signature grin. "It is. It's my favourite Christmas hit. If you don't mind, I'd say it goes on the list."

"I don't mind," she said, unable to keep herself from answering his grin with a smile.

"Awesome. What's your favourite song?" He held out his phone to her.

Once again, Samantha was micro-focusing on their bodies: the warmth and pressure of his shoulder, the length of his thigh against hers, and the tingling feeling in her fingertips when they brushed his as she took his phone to type in her favourite song. "This one."

"Oh, good choice." Even his voice had a velvety quality to it that she couldn't wait to hear him sing with.

But they didn't sing that afternoon, only exchanged songs peppered with personal questions. And as time progressed, Samantha warmed completely to him, laughed and joked, and marvelled at how good it felt to be around him. When the sun had set, she knew he had no family in Greenvalley, had moved here from the Ruhrpott region in the west, and studied architecture, though his parents would've liked him to do a business degree instead to take over the company one day.

She was also pretty sure she had a major crush on him.

Lucille

Lucille knew she should've been at home studying for her history exam the next morning, but her head was feeling bloated from all the dates and contract details she'd crammed in. So, instead, she had invited Rachel to a shopping spree under the guise of making up for the disastrous date.

Not that anyone could call it truly disastrous. Fabian and Rachel might still be a rather low-key couple who weren't constantly all over each other, but they were most definitely a couple now. Lucille's bad dating advice *had* propelled them to take the necessary steps themselves. Not her strongest argument, but one that could be made.

There was also a second reason why Rachel was the perfect partner today: none of the others had to buy presents for parents they barely saw.

"Honestly, it's more the act of giving," Lucille said. "And I don't mean this in a wholesome way. It's 'get a few expensive stock pieces together to show each other how much we love each other', and afterwards, those pieces will gather dust for the rest of their life. Not that anything gathers dust at our place."

"Of course not," Rachel muttered.

They were an odd pair. Lucille chatted without pause, while Rachel kept to short answers. "What are you getting your mother?"

"Nothing. Or I'll wrap something up that's already there." She shrugged. "Three out of five Christmases, she forgets presents."

"Ugh." It was hard to imagine there could be a worse parent than her father, but Rachel's mother definitely took home that questionable award. "Very well, what are you getting Fabian? I always find it so hard to buy for boys."

Rachel glanced at her, as if she found that hard to imagine. "A sketch pad, some special pens."

Apparently, it wasn't hard to buy for Fabian at all. "Nothing romantic?"

"Please don't talk me into a romantic present."

Lucille giggled and raised her hands. "All right, all right, I won't. If art supplies are the way to Fabian's heart, I'll defer to your judgement. What is the way to your heart?" She still had to buy presents for most of her friends, and while Samantha would be more than happy with the Magic Circle collection that Lucille had had Caroline set aside, the others were harder to buy for.

Crystals for Jan perhaps, and Fabian apparently liked art supplies. But Matt? A year's supply of condoms? A jewelled scabbard for his sword? And Rachel was just as much an enigma.

"I like to read," Rachel said. "Fabian always gets me a book voucher. I also like to dream."

"Can you gift dreams?"

"Sure." Rachel shrugged her shoulders. "It's not easy to craft a whole dream, easier to change an existing one or travel on tangents, but theoretically, it would be possible. Not that the person receiving the dream would know the difference."

Lucille hadn't expected such an elaborate answer to her silly idea. *She* definitely couldn't gift a dream to Rachel. And she'd better not try to make the perfect date happen, like paying for a night in a hotel. But the dream powers sounded interesting. "You can actually make a dream? I thought you only had visions."

"Oh, dream wandering is much easier. Or rather controllable. The visions are sudden. They find me." Rachel's dark eyes shone as she finally talked about a topic with passion. "But the dream wandering is like second nature. It's like a sixth sense that tells me which paths I have to take in order to change what I see. And it's fun. Sometimes people have the weirdest dreams, and they're open to even weirder ones. And Nico said I haven't even touched the surface of the dreamworld's potential."

Lucille stopped short. "Nico said?" Nico was dead. Had he come back as a ghost?

Rachel's face darkened. "He's in my dreams. It's not really him, just... another dreamer. Apparently, I chose to see Nico." Her gaze fell to the cobbles beneath her. "It's rather silly to seek him out, I guess."

"No, no, I get it. You must miss him terribly." Even Lucille, who'd known him for only two short months missed him. He'd always managed to lighten the mood.

"I do." Rachel looked up, blinking heavily as she tried for a smile and came up short. Then her eyes focused on something further away. "Who's that with Sam?"

"Samantha is here?" Lucille whirled around. Ahead of them, she could see Samantha standing at one of those little round tables with a mug in her hand, laughing with an unfamiliar guy. "You have no idea who he is?" Surely, it must be someone they knew. The Head Boy, maybe? No, Adrian had more fashion sense. "Let's get closer."

"Are you mad?" Rachel hissed, but she followed Lucille anyway until they could duck behind the little fence of the Christmas play area, a few metres behind Samantha and her guy friend.

Samantha could easily see them if she turned, but her eyes were practically glued to the man in front of her. She was tucking her locks behind her ears, unaware of how the guy's eyes followed the gesture without fail. And she was smiling the whole time. Her cheeks would be hurting tomorrow. Just as his would.

"I need to know who he is," Lucille whispered.

"We could go and say hi," Rachel suggested.

"And ruin their date?"

Rachel only shrugged at that. She probably thought that ruining dates was Lucille's style now.

The longer Lucille kept watching Samantha and her new beau, the more she was convinced they were flirting the hell out of each other. She'd never seen Samantha so energised, her cheeks bright pink from the flush of excitement. So many giggles and exaggerated gestures. It was entirely unlike her, which told Lucille all she needed to know about her friend's feelings for this guy.

With a contented sigh, Lucille tugged on Rachel's jacket. "Let's leave those two lovebirds alone. We can find out who he is tomorrow."

\#

The History exam went well enough, all things considered. Lucille had mixed up a few dates, but her arguments had been detailed and well-drawn from the source material. She'd even finished early.

Most of the subject majors had their exams today, so it was no surprise to her that she met the others in the cafeteria. The only decoration in the hall was a Christmas tree and some paintings from younger classes on the wall. The cafeteria itself was advertising special holiday prices that seemed to be more expensive than usual.

Lucille shook her head at that and slid into a seat next to Jan. "How was Geography?"

She only got a snort from him. Meanwhile, Fabian was hitting his forehead against the table, while Rachel patted his back. "I had a total blackout in Physics. I'm sure everything is wrong."

"Don't be silly. You learned so much with Sam and Rachel. Your mind probably did some of it on autopilot," Lucille tried to cheer him up.

"That's a spell I'd like to have," Jan said.

Fabian stopped his head-bashing to throw her a devastated glance. "Don't you have a spell that will open up the earth and swallow me? For ever and ever?"

"It can't be that bad." Rachel intensified her comforting efforts.

Lucille was saved from her cheering-up obligations by Matt's arrival, though he seemed to be in just as bad a mood. He slammed his bag against the table and dropped into a chair.

"Did you also think those questions were way too hard?" Jan asked.

"What questions?" Matt barked.

Jan frowned at him. "Geography. The exam we just sat. I had no idea what I was supposed to write so many words about. I barely made it to five hundred."

"I noticed that when you handed it in after only forty minutes." In a two-hour exam, that was awfully early.

"Sorry if I'm bothering you, Your Highness." Jan crossed his arms now, adopting an equally bad temper.

Lucille tried her charm once more. "Was it that bad?" she asked with as much compassion as she could muster.

"Nah, it was fine. Nothing too difficult." Matt looked around the table. "Where's Sam?"

"Still writing," Fabian answered in misery. "She's probably going to hand in her PhD thesis at the same time. Oh, there she is."

With only five minutes to spare, Samantha arrived in the hall, a happy smile on her face. Lucille noticed how Matt's mood lightened as he watched her approach. When she reached the table, he pulled out the chair for her so she would have to sit next to him.

If the rest of the group was wallowing in failure, Samantha was positively buzzing. "That was quite tough, wasn't it? Certainly some tricky questions."

Rachel grimaced. "Not in the wound."

"Just shoot me now," Fabian muttered and resumed his head-bashing.

"Oh, dear. I assume it didn't go so well for you?" Fabian only sighed deeply, and Rachel rubbed his back again. "Sorry." Samantha turned to Matt. "Hey, I checked my recipe books last night, and I had a couple of ideas. Monster snacks." She got out her phone and showed Matt some pictures on it. "I was thinking sausage krakens, cheese stick mummies, boiled eggs with olive spiders. I even found this awesome veggie skeleton. Probably a bit big for eight people, but maybe if we only do the skull."

Lucille had no idea what was going on, but she was intrigued, because Matt had started to smile as soon as Samantha had moved closer to show him her pictures. "What is going on?"

"Oh, this is for Matt's birthday party in the holidays," Samantha said and showed them all the skeletons made from capsicum, cucumbers, and carrot sticks. "Invitations will come. I just haven't had time to design those yet. Or rather, find an appropriate template. Unless you want to draw up some witchy-themed invites." She gently poked Fabian, obviously trying to distract him with an offer of art expression.

"I'll do witches, but no monsters," he muttered, thankfully having stopped maltreating his head. "When's the party?"

"New Year's Eve." Matt nodded at the pictures. "Those look cool."

Samantha beamed at him. "Perfect. If you like, I can come by your house on the weekend and we'll try those. Then we won't have to stress on New Year's."

"Yes, please," Matt said in a voice that made Lucille uncomfortable, as if she was intruding on something intimate.

Which reminded her... "Sam, I'm dying to know this—Rachel can attest to it—who was the handsome guy we saw you with last night?"

If she hadn't been sure about Matt's interest before, it was written on his face at very moment. He sat frozen, the smile wiped from his face so completely it looked as if his soul had left his body.

Meanwhile, Samantha blushed heavily and laughed softly. She even started picking at her ponytail's tip. "You mean Daniel?"

"Is that his name?" Now that Lucille had started her interrogation, she was unable to stop.

"Who's Daniel?" Fabian asked, frowning.

Put on the spot, Samantha seemed a bit speechless for a moment. "Uhm... he's my singing partner. My mother roped me into singing for the Christmas Gala, and that's it. That's all there is."

Lucille had no idea who Samantha was trying to convince because she didn't fool anyone. "It looked a bit different when we saw you sharing a drink on the Christmas market. And I didn't hear you sing either."

"Uh..." Samantha turned even redder. "We just talked. Got to know each other." She took a deep breath, then continued a little calmer. "He told me about his family and why he's not going home this year, and I talked about my meddling mum and stuff. We really just talked."

Lucille grinned wildly. She definitely had to grill Samantha more about this mystery man. "I didn't even know—"

"Chay wants to meet you all," Matt rudely interrupted her. "He was thinking perhaps at a café on the weekend."

"Dude, who's Chay? Your boyfriend of the week?" Jan asked.

Matt glared at him with a ferocity that made Jan flinch. "He's a friend of mine who can see the future, which makes him the Seer, as in the author-of-the-*Circle-of-Magic*-book Seer."

"He can see the future?" Rachel asked, her voice full of awe.

"You're friends with the book's author?" Fabian stared at Matt with wide eyes.

Lucille was still dealing with the whiplash of Matt's sudden and absolute topic change. She was utterly torn between wanting to learn more about Samantha's new acquaintance and this shocking revelation.

"Weird, but okay," Jan said with a shrug.

Matt's eyes narrowed. "Why is that weird?"

"Well, isn't he old?"

"Depends on your definition of old."

"Well, how old is he, then?"

There was no answer from Matt. He just glowered at each of them in turn, as if daring them to protest.

Samantha put a hand on his arm and gave him a soft smile. "I would love to meet him again. There's a cute café in the city centre where we can book a table."

Matt stared at her hand as if it was a worm. Lucille watched with interest as he fought some inner battle with himself. He resented Samantha's touch, but he also yearned for it, she thought. In the end, Samantha's kindness won him over, and his shoulders slackened. His face softened, and he said gently, "That sounds good."

Lucille put her chin on her upright fist and watched him more closely. She'd known Matt for three months now. And for three months, he'd made no secret of the fact that he had no interest in a committed relationship and was only looking for the next intercourse. And yet, he looked at Samantha with adoring puppy eyes, and boy, had he been jealous when Lucille had mentioned Daniel. The others might be blind to it. He himself might be blind to it, but Lucille was convinced she'd just witnessed a Christmas miracle.

Matt Traidous, notorious high-school playboy and cool charmer, had caught feelings for the nerdy girl.

Rachel

Saturday morning, Rachel woke up excited. So excited, she didn't even care about the nightmare she'd had—something with a bunch of candles drowning in hot blood. Today, she would meet the Seer! Someone who had visions and dreams like her. Who knew what it was like to see a glimpse of the future.

She had so many questions to ask him she'd even made a list. And she would take the dreamweb to verify it was what she thought it was. Rachel was in such a good mood that she even wished her mother good morning.

"You've got another date today?" her mother asked.

Surprised, Rachel paused. "How do you know I have one?"

"Haven't you been dating Fabian for a month?"

Rachel was speechless. For years, she had been convinced her mother took no notice of her life at all. If she tried to talk about it, her mother had never shown interest. But now she knew about Fabian. And the dates. "Yes..." Rachel said carefully, unsure of how to proceed.

Her mother gave her a sad smile. "He's a good boy. I saw him comforting you at..." She took a shaky breath. "At the funeral. I'm glad you have someone like him."

A splintered life. Happy memories that cut deep because they no longer fit together. Rachel remembered the nightmare she'd found her mother in vividly. She'd been so lonely.

"He *is* a pretty good guy. The best I know. Fabian has such a big heart. He'd do anything for the people he loves. And I feel very blessed that I seem to be one of those people." Rachel had no idea why she suddenly felt the need to give her mother all these details, these open windows into her soul. It had never meant anything to her mother before.

But something had changed. Maybe it was the therapy. Or perhaps losing Nico had been the rock bottom she'd needed to experience to turn her life around. No one would blame Rachel if she'd closed the door between them and walked away. But after years of wishing her mother would change, could she really ignore it when she actually seemed to do so?

Pain flashed in her mother's eyes, and she quickly lowered her gaze to the heap of laundry she was taking care of, as if Rachel's words had hurt her. "First love is a wonderful thing. You should relish it."

Rachel frowned. That made it sound as if her relationship with Fabian was a doomed thing. Not meant to last for long. "I guess that's what I get for oversharing."

She took her keys from the bowl and walked away to get dressed.

If Rachel had needed any proof of Chay's visionary talents, she got it when she walked into the café an hour early to avoid her mother. Matt and an unfamiliar man were already sitting at the reserved table.

"I told you she'd be early," the stranger said to Matt, who looked a bit annoyed. "Hello, Rachel," he greeted her with a friendly smile and got up to shake her hand. "I'm Chay."

He was much younger than Rachel had expected. In his twenties, unless he was the youngest-looking forty-year-old on the planet. His hair was the colour of honey, and his eyes were pale blue. The shadow of a blond beard showed on his cheeks. He might gain a few years with a full beard, but even then, he was way too young to have written the book in Elda's library. Perhaps he'd taken over from another seer. It could be a title given from master to apprentice.

Rachel noticed that Matt was staring at their touching hands as if they had slapped each other. "You... never mind." He waved it off, crossed his arms, and stared out of the window.

Chay let go of her hand and sat down again. "Do you want something to drink? I'm paying today."

"Yes." It took Rachel a moment to realise she should probably tell him what she wanted to drink. But something about being alone with Chay and Matt made her nervous, and so she slipped out of her chair again. "I'll go and order at the counter."

As she waited to be served, she saw Matt hissing at Chay and pointing to his hand. Chay merely shrugged, leaving Rachel to wonder why Matt was making such a fuss about a normal handshake. She decided not to add that question to her list and ordered her coffee.

When she returned to the table, Chay was still smiling in a friendly way, while Matt had once again crossed his arms in a sour mood.

"You can ask me whatever you want. But I can't promise to answer all of it or in a way that makes it inherently clear," Chay told her. "I'm told I'm a bit of a closed book."

"You wrote a lot in the book about the Emblems of Power." The retort slipped from Rachel's mouth, and she gasped. She hadn't meant to offend him. Any answer would make her happy.

But Chay wasn't taking offence. "Most of it is history. There's one prophecy in its pages, and I'd say it's an important one, but I wasn't the one who spoke it. It's another piece of history, even though its events are yet to come. Many scholars over many years have discussed and analysed and interpreted parts of it. I merely wrote down what I believe to be relevant."

Suddenly Rachel wanted the book here so she could flick through its pages and find the prophecy to read for herself. In lieu of that option, she asked the source. "What does it say?"

"It's very long, and you should read it in its original words, but I don't see the need to make a secret out of it. Here's the most important bit for now." Chay straightened, and this time, Matt was listening as well. "When Twelve become Six, all will be reborn at the same time in the same place to fight the same battle until the Greedy One fails twice, or all will perish." He broke into a near-boyish smile. "Pretty grim, isn't it?"

One line and Rachel already had a dozen questions. Who were all? Those reborn? Everyone involved in the battle? Or simply everyone and everything? And the Greedy One. Could he be the demon they'd been facing off against in the last three months? Had he already failed once? Or had it been twice? Or was it someone entirely different who had nothing to do with them?

In the end, Rachel focused on a single word. "Reborn? Can people be reborn?" Her heart ached for a yes, and she quickly added, "How?"

Chay rubbed his chin. "I fear it's in the Buddhist sense of the word. Not that any religion gets it right, but there are approximations. Scholars have been trying to determine the length it takes for a soul to be reborn, and they all tend to agree that it's about half a millennium, and without any recollection of their prior selves."

Half a millennium. Rachel sank back into her seat. She'd be long dead before Nico would walk the earth again.

"It is the whole crux of the prophecy though," Chay said. "I'll say it now, because I fear it might scare the others, but you seem to be more receptive to the twists and turns of the universe."

Rachel held her breath as she waited for him to continue.

"The Twelve the prophecy speaks of are legendary heroes of a time no one even remembers. They were the original bearers of the Emblems of Power, which were either crafted by them or gifted by divine beings. Their souls then travelled through time, being reborn approximately every five hundred years. They've been kings and queens, servants and beggars, lucky, rich, poor, bad, and good. It's a blank slate each time, and so much depends on the environment they're born into." Chay took a deep breath, as if he remembered his own. It seemed to have shaped him into a well-adjusted young man. "The prophecy speaks of a time when they come together in more senses than one. They will all be born around the same time and in the same place. This time. This place."

Rachel felt the words falling like stones into her stomach.

Chay's tongue flicked over his lips, and his strange pale eyes bored into hers. "And all twelve will meld—it happens sometimes, just as other souls are torn into two. From two, one is born."

"When Twelve become Six," Rachel whispered. She couldn't even blink while she tried to digest what Chay had said.

"Here's your latte." Rachel jumped when the server set the cup in front of her. "Anything else I can bring you guys?"

Chay shook his head. "No, we're good for now. Still waiting for the others."

His answer gave Rachel time to steady herself and take a few deep breaths. Her eyes met Matt's, and she saw that he was equally disturbed by the revelations. "Fabian will freak out," she whispered.

"As I said, I don't think the others are quite ready for that information yet." Chay raised his black coffee and took a sip. "Knowing the future can be quite disconcerting. As can knowing one's future be portent."

"What's in that coffee?" Matt asked, reaching for the cup. "You never drop that much information. Especially not on your first meeting."

Chay held the cup out of his reach, and for a moment, the two seemed perfectly normal, just two old friends bickering. "I *do*. To the people it matters." He turned to Rachel with a smile. "And those who can deal with it responsibly. Like you."

"Like me?" How did he know so much about her? There couldn't possibly have been such a detailed vision of herself, could there? "Are you the dreamer?" The depth of knowledge Chay claimed was the one she usually touched on in dreams.

"No, but it's because *you* are that I know you're capable of handling the future. You know the most inner self of people. Their worries, their dreams, what they show the world, and what they keep from it. You might just be learning how to dream, but your power requires an enormous amount of responsibility. Because..."

"I can change them."

Chay smiled. "Yes, you can. And when you change someone's dreams, you change their heart."

Rachel's eyes widened. "My mother!" Once again, the nightmare with the broken memories flashed in front of her eyes. "I reached out to her. Pulled her from the sharp edges of her failures. And now... now she sees me." It was a thin bond, incredibly fragile, but Rachel had forged it when she'd led her mother back to the meadow, back to safety and companionship.

Suddenly, her own power frightened her. Dream wandering had been something she enjoyed. She'd loved digging deeper into people's dreams, to find out who they truly were at their core. How many had she changed that way? However small it might be, she'd evoked change. And now her wonderful, magical power felt a whole lot like brain surgery.

She thought of Fabian and how many times she'd visited his dreams. What if her love had affected him there? What if she'd changed him and he didn't actually love her, just thought he did because she kept showing up in his dreams?

"Take a breath," Chay said, and Rachel found herself blinking away tears. "The Emblem of Devotion wouldn't have found its way to you if you weren't the right person to handle it."

That answered at least one of her questions. Rachel took a deep breath, then drank her milk coffee in one long gulp. "I think I need another coffee."

"The others will be here any minute," Chay said.

Instantly, Matt groaned and complained, "Stop speaking in the future tense."

But it was true. Within the next ten minutes, the others appeared one by one. Chay greeted each of them as he had her, and while Matt's reaction to their handshakes lessened each time, it still seemed to befuddle him more than it should. Naturally, Fabian and Samantha arrived together.

Fabian shook Chay's hand first, then took his seat next to Rachel and gave her a quick kiss. Still shaken by Chay's revelations and her own musings, she turned her attention to Samantha and Chay.

It was the first time Rachel saw Chay hesitate before giving her his hand. And as soon as their fingers touched, he winced and let go again. If Rachel hadn't been watching him so intently, she would've missed it. His smile certainly didn't give anything away. "...really sorry that I had to take Matt from you last time."

"No worries," Samantha answered, slightly confused. "You probably had a lot to catch up on."

Matt had got to his feet and put his hand on her back in a weirdly possessive way. "Nothing important, really." He guided her towards the seat next to him and helped her into it.

With a conspiratorial twinkle in her eye, Lucille leaned over the table to Chay, who'd been watching Matt's actions with a frown. "You see it, too, don't you?"

Rachel very nearly groaned, reminded of how she had grilled Samantha on Wednesday in front of everybody. Lucille was way too obsessed with everybody else's love life. Perhaps because her own wasn't quite met with success.

As expected Chay's frown only deepened. "See what?" Lucille probably had to be a bit clearer with someone who saw the future regularly.

She gave it a quick wave. "Never mind." Then she regarded Chay with an appreciative glance. "You're not what I expected."

"Understatement of the year," Jan announced. "It didn't click right away, but Matt, didn't you say Chay was your private teacher? The one who taught you to read and write, and magic and swords?"

Matt was unexpectedly taken aback. When he noticed that Samantha stared at him in confusion, he turned to Chay. "It's complicated, right?" There was the slightest of tremors in his voice.

"Yeah. It's not like I taught you from birth," Chay said.

"And you're older than you look," Matt said likewise.

Rachel didn't say anything. It was obvious to her that they'd quickly played off each other, probably not even lying, but it wasn't exactly an answer. Still, Chay had trusted her with his knowledge, and she found it inappropriate to call their bluff and demand more information than he was willing to give her.

Chay turned back to Jan. "Anyway, yes, I have tried to teach Matt a thing or two."

"A thing or two? Dude, it sounded like a full-on program. Where does one sign up for it?" Jan's eyes were gleaming.

Chay laughed at that. "I fear you'll have to learn on the fly. There isn't enough time to give you that education."

Because they were the Six, born in the same place at the same time. And they had already faced off against a greedy demon more times than any of them liked. Rachel shuddered.

"Everything okay?" Fabian whispered.

She nodded at him and smiled. Secretly, she worried whether his concern was true or whether it was all because she'd accidentally changed his dreams.

"Well, I'm not really the education type, anyway," Jan said, leaning back and stretching out.

"Understatement of the year," Lucille muttered, and giggles erupted across the table. Even Jan's face twitched with amusement. "Matt says you can see into the future." Lucille's eyes were gleaming as she leaned forward. "What's in mine?"

Chay sank a little deeper into his chair. "I'm not a fortune teller."

Rachel felt immense sympathy for him. He must get asked to tell the future ten times a week. She found it already difficult to share her dream glimpses of the future. They seemed too intimate. Too hard to handle. And besides, it never changed anything. Everything she dreamed of happened exactly as it was shown.

"It's all right. I like surprises." Nevertheless, Lucille looked a bit disappointed. "So, why did you want to meet with us?"

"Well, Matt told me so much about you. I had to get to know you." Just minutes ago, Chay had sung a different tune. He'd been so open with Rachel yet kept up this act of an old friend with the others. Though she supposed he hadn't told a lie. He probably *did* want to meet the six people his prophecy revolved around. And see what they were worth. "You found the Emblems of Power, I heard."

"You gave me mine," Matt muttered.

Chay gave him a small nod. "You were always destined to have it."

"We didn't find all of them," Samantha chimed in. "Lucille has the amulet, Fabian has the feather, Rachel the dreamweb, and because of my idiot sister, Jan has the Bond of Levante."

"I do?" Jan asked at the same time as Lucille asked the same question. "He does?"

Samantha sighed heavily. "The bracelet Meg gave you is an Emblem of Power. We found it together, but she got her hands on it first. And now you've got it, and you can't even see the golden thread of magic woven into it."

Jan pushed up the sleeve of his jacket to reveal a tightly woven bracelet, similar to the friendship bracelets young girls gave each other in grade school. He scrutinised it intensely, but obviously couldn't see the magic Samantha spoke of. "This is a powerful artefact?"

"It is," Chay confirmed with a gentle voice.

"Huh." Jan stared at Samantha. "And Meg bought it. How much did she pay for it?"

"Obviously not what it's worth." Samantha searched out Chay's face. "My sister gave it to Jan, but I could've easily been the one who'd bought it."

Regret filled Chay's eyes. "But you didn't. It's not yours. Jan is the bearer of the Power of Love."

Jan coughed heavily. "Power of Love? Are you kidding me?"

Lucille grinned brightly at him. "Well, you only got it because of your girlfriend. Must be your one true love," she teased him.

"Please tell me, this is a joke." Jan's entire face had gone slack while Samantha seemed to fervently wish for the same.

Matt raised his eyebrow. "Not cool enough for you?" he asked with a mocking voice.

Jan glared at him. "What's yours? The Power of Sex?"

The two boys glared at each other until Chay cleared his throat. "In either case, Levante's bracelet is yours, and one day, you might tap into that power. But probably not before you mature a little."

"So, practically never," Lucille quipped.

Meanwhile, Matt leaned over to Samantha and whispered something in her ear that seemed to surprise her. A few more whispers, and she nodded. They both got up together and put on their winter jackets. "We've got something else to do."

"Se-e-hex," Jan mumbled into his cup.

"Matt." Chay was frowning, and Rachel thought he looked terribly worried.

Matt patted his shoulder with a big cheesy smile. "You'll be fine. Rachel will look after you."

"What?" Rachel looked up, startled, but Matt ignored her, pulling on Samantha's sleeve instead.

Samantha put some money for her drink onto the table and waved at the others. "We'll see you later."

"Have fun," Lucille called after them in an annoying sing-song voice. When the two of them had left, she grinned at the others. "Did you all notice how he looks at her?"

"Looks at her how?" Fabian cried out, while Chay seemed to be utterly stricken when he said, "Yes."

With Matt's history, Rachel wondered if Chay had been a little more to him than just his teacher and friend. He'd clearly been hurt by Matt's action, and not just because he'd been abandoned in a group of strangers by his friend.

"He looks at her as if he's in love." Lucille had definitely been watching too many romance movies.

"Nah." Jan shook his head. "Take it from the expert in love now. He's into Sam. I give you that. But he only wants to get into her pants. And good for her. Might loosen her up a little."

Next to Rachel, Fabian had paled. "That's not good for her. Samantha isn't looking for something like that."

Rachel pressed her lips together, trying her hardest not to read too much into it. But wasn't that it? Fabian was only taking a chance on her because Samantha had rejected him. That and her dream wandering.

She almost wanted to slap herself. Why didn't she trust Fabian a little more? He would never hurt her. She'd known going into this relationship how deeply he'd loved Samantha. It was only natural that he hadn't completely turned off those feelings yet. It was part of the reason she wanted him to be in love with her so much.

"It's more than sex!" Lucille and Jan were still fighting over Matt. "I happen to know what he's like if he wants sex. This is deeper."

"Didn't you say on Wednesday she had a date with her singing partner?" Fabian asked, sounding as if he was sick. Or maybe he was just having trouble following Lucille's amorous daydreams.

She nodded at him. "Daniel, yes. They were flirting up a storm when I saw them. Which means Sam gets to choose between two cute guys." Lucille turned back to Jan. "Now *that* is a good thing for her."

Chay sighed and looked out the window. Rachel felt sorry for him. He'd come here to meet the prophesied heroes—or whatever they were—and was stuck in a teenage quarrel. Then suddenly, he flinched and turned back to them. "Is there a problem with your gnome population?"

All four of them stared at him. "Gnome what?" Jan asked.

Chay pointed at the window. "Usually gnomes are much more careful and only come out at night."

They all looked in the direction he pointed. And sure enough, there was a tiny creature, the size of a winter boot, with a pointy bright-red hat and a long wiry beard hopping up and down in front of the window. At last, it grabbed a shiny decoration and took off.

"Did it just steal a Christmas bauble?" Fabian asked.

Jan jumped up and grabbed his jacket. "Let's go and get it."

Before he could sprint away, he ran into their classmate, Robert, who lit up with a bright smile. "Hey guys. What are you doing here?"

"We're leaving." Jan elbowed Robert to the side and ran out the door, Lucille and Chay on his trail.

Fabian was deliberately slow. "It's Christmas. Why can't they give us a break?"

"School, hmm?" Robert commiserated. "Good thing it's only one more week."

Fabian stared at him as if he was the one wearing a pointy red hat. To be fair, Rachel completely trusted Robert to pull off such a thing. He was dorky like that. Instead of answering, Fabian took her hand and the warmth she'd missed all meeting shot through her. "Let's go."

"You haven't even finished your coffee!" Robert called after them.

"It's yours!" Rachel answered, then realised they hadn't exactly paid for it yet. She let go of Fabian, got a note from her purse, and slammed it into a confused Robert's hand. "Enjoy."

Then she left in hot pursuit of the rampant gnome population.

Matt

Matt just had to leave the café. Too many things had been said that sent his mind swirling. More importantly, he had to get out of there with Samantha. He couldn't quite explain it, but he had this urge to spend time with her. Not with all the others, but with her alone. Especially after what he'd learned of on Wednesday.

"Chay didn't seem happy about you leaving him with the others." Samantha looked over her shoulder to where the café was located.

That wasn't why Chay's voice had carried this warning tone. He was scared that Matt was about to tell Samantha what he really was. That was the reason he'd pulled her out of the café. "He'll survive. He's a big boy."

Samantha rolled her eyes, smiling as she did so. "Yes, he is. Big enough to raise you. Or was he older than he looks?"

How was he going to stop her from finding out? She was too smart. When Jan had accused him of being every monster in the book, Matt had easily thrown him off course with ridicule. Jan's guesses were wild and lacked substance, but Samantha would find out. He'd be disappointed if she didn't.

And then she would hate him.

Because he was a monster from her books. Or at least half a monster. Her grandmother had seen right through him, probably alerted by some defence spell when he'd first visited her house. She'd lured him into the kitchen under the guise of needing his help, then poisoned him with tea until he was sure he'd choke. Only the fact that he was the bearer of the divine sword had saved him that day. And still, Elda had promised to kill him should he ever hurt Samantha or her friends. And Matt fully believed the witch was capable of that.

"Matt?" Samantha had paused, looking at him with worry in her green eyes. "Is everything okay?"

Her hand was slightly raised towards him, and he was unable to resist and took it. Holding her fingers tight in his, he took a deep breath. "Sam..." *The moment she learns of it, she'll hate you.* He couldn't bear that. Could bear that even less than the other thing. The other thing named Daniel. "What is it with you and your... Daniel?"

Samantha chuckled and pulled her hand from his grip. "Are you trying to distract me?" When Matt shrugged helplessly, she clicked her tongue. "To be honest, I have no idea. We're just going to sing together." Nevertheless, thinking of Daniel brought a blush to her cheeks that Matt wanted to rub off instantly.

"Lucille said you had a date."

"We just bought some gifts together after rehearsal, and he invited me for hot cocoa."

The blush intensified, and Matt grew nervous. He wasn't stupid. He'd been in Ashuan long enough to know what it looked like if someone had a crush. Matt was the recipient of far too many of them. Girls—and boys—still blushed when he passed them in the hall, and not a day went by without him finding a love note in his locker. They were amusing, but there was nothing amusing about Samantha's crush right now. Because this time, he wasn't the recipient.

"Do you like hot cocoa?" he asked, grabbing her hand again.

Samantha stared at their hands, then his face in confusion. "What?"

"Do you want to drink hot cocoa with me?" One thing Matt had no experience with was this whole dating business. He never had to put effort into finding a date for sex. However, inviting someone for a hot drink seemed easy enough. If Daniel could do it, he could too.

She was still confused. "I thought you wanted to buy some more supplies for the party?" That was the reason he'd given her in the café.

"It's not like they're running away." He gave her hand a slight tug. "I..."

Jan ran past them, in hot pursuit of something small. Then Lucille followed, and behind her, Fabian and Rachel.

"What is going on?" Samantha asked.

"Gnome problem!" Fabian called out before they passed by.

Samantha turned back to Matt. "A gnome problem. I guess your party supplies will have to wait."

"I guess so," Matt replied tensely and watched her run off to catch up with the others. He couldn't care less about the party supplies. Or gnomes. All he knew was that he'd almost had Samantha in his hands—quite literally as they stood in the falling snow—and now she was slipping away from him.

\#

Matt didn't feel like hunting gnomes, which were annoying at best, so he jumped home instead. It looked like Chay had had the same idea, as he awaited him in his room with Crumbs on his lap.

The puppy perked up as he saw Matt and bounded happily towards him. Matt bent down and ruffled his fur, sinking into the unconditional love of the little creature and feeling some of the weight lift. Trust the little dog to make him feel better just with the wag of his tail and his slobbery, wet kisses.

Once Crumbs got over the initial joy of seeing him after such a long two hours, Matt looked up at Chay. "I didn't tell her."

Chay nodded. "I know."

"I just don't get why. Samantha is smart and kind. She's not narrow-minded. I don't believe that she hears demon and jumps at my throat, and I'm only half-demon, anyway. Surely, that must count for something." Why was he rambling so much? He didn't do that normally.

"Why her, Matt?" Chay asked, his voice heavy with sorrow. "Of all the people in all the worlds, why her?"

Matt had no answer for him. He wasn't even sure he understood the question. "I thought that was the whole point. That we got together in this place. Didn't you tell Rachel it was prophesied?"

"You're not falling for any of the others," Chay said gently, as if he was trying to soften the blow.

"I'm not falling for anyone." Matt let go of Crumbs and straightened up, picking the fur from his leather jacket. "And why would I? I could have whoever I wanted."

"But not her." Chay got up from the bed, and Matt knew he wasn't going to let him get away with it.

If there was one thing Chay harped on and on about, it was that he shouldn't ignore his human half. The one that—according to Chay—longed for company and comfort on an emotional level, where his demon half only needed the physical touch. So far, Matt wasn't convinced that he truly had different needs from the demons he grew up with. He'd been perfectly fine in Hell. It was Ashuan that was demanding and made him feel all these confusing emotions he'd never encountered before, much less learned how to cope with.

"I'm sorry, Matt. I rarely want to change the future more than when I look at you."

Matt snorted. That was great. Perfect, really. "So, she *will* find out. And she *will* hate me. And there's nothing I can do about it."

"Oh, there's plenty you could do about it. The problem is you won't. I know you think it won't matter because you're not really in love. You don't believe in love. And I hope you're right. Because if that's true, it'll save you from a world of pain. So, forget her. Find someone else. Or no one at all. Or everyone." He put a hand on Matt's shoulder, taking great care not to touch his skin. "Take it from someone who *actually* knows. There's nothing in this universe that hurts as much as love."

Matt couldn't help but snort again. He and Chay were alike in some ways, yet so different. Whereas Matt had grown up in Hell, surrounded by demons, fully aware of all his potential, Chay had been raised human and hadn't taken a step into Hell until he'd already lived a full human life. He'd once told him he'd only found out his father was a demon when he'd been 118 years old, by which time he'd figured there was more that separated him from other humans than an unfortunate penchant for seeing the future at skin contact.

His experiences had shaped Chay. Demons lived hundreds and hundreds of years, yet they rarely evolved. They lived as they wanted, took what they could, and enjoyed life as it was. Chay, however, had used his long life to study a myriad of subjects, to forge diplomatic relationships, to bring people together, and to use his unique powers to save a handful of worlds from complete destruction. He was known across the worlds, his title invoking awe and envy alike.

Once, when Matt had been about eight years old, he'd asked Chay why he even bothered. He'd been miffed that his favourite person in the world had to leave yet again to solve some foreign conflict or save a species from extinction. And Chay's answer had been because *he cared*. No matter how much he tried not to care, and how much he removed himself from human societies, he never managed to turn off his human side and stop caring.

It'd sounded awful to eight-year-old Matt, and now that he had the tiniest taste of it—what with Nico dying on them, and Samantha confusing him—he knew for a fact how awful it was.

"So, you're scared that when Samantha finds out and hates me, it'll hurt me somehow?" When Chay nodded, Matt shrugged. "There's nothing to worry about. She'll come around eventually, and I'll be fine."

Chay's mouth thinned, but he didn't argue with him. Instead, he nodded. "That's good to hear. In that case, I would advise you to celebrate your birthday in Hell."

"With the others?" Matt doubted that would go down well with Fabian.

"Of course not. With your family."

Matt burst out laughing. "What? They never celebrate my birthday. No one does. As if anyone can keep track of their years."

"They will celebrate it with you this year."

"No, they won't." Uneasy, Matt shifted his feet. "My party is already set. Here." Samantha had organised so much already. She was coming tomorrow to practice her finger food. They'd bought decorations. "There's no way I'll miss my eighteenth birthday to play target practice for Caspar."

While his demonic family was much bigger than any of his friends could guess, most of his half-siblings had no relevance to his life. Matt hadn't even met most of them in the sixteen years he'd lived with his mother. There were really only three that mattered, and he could well do without two of them. His half-brothers Caspar and Balthasar. One brutal, the other manipulative. Only his half-sister, Menuha, was somewhat bearable. She happened to be Caspar's twin sister, but where he hated anything human—and thus, by extension, Matt—she loved humans and had always protected him from Caspar's worst. Still, Matt didn't relish having her at his birthday party, if that meant Caspar came as well.

Something in Chay's pale eyes broke. There was a deep sadness in him that scared Matt to the bone, afraid that the same sadness would look at him in the mirror one day. But as so often, Chay shut it away and nodded. "Very well. I guess your friends are meeting at Elda's soon. They could probably use your help."

Matt frowned. "Where are you going?"

"Trying something else." And with that, Chay simply vanished, leaving Matt alone with his dog.

Crumbs barked, startled at the sudden disappearance, and Matt lowered himself to once again cuddle the puppy and stroke his back until he calmed down. "Yeah, he often does that to me—has to save the world or something—leaving me with too much to think about and enigmatic words." He bumped his nose against Crumbs' wet snout. "You're lucky he's not interested in *your* future."

His phone vibrated with a text, and Matt took it out of his pocket to look at the message. As soon as he saw Samantha's name, his stomach made the weirdest little flip.

Samantha: Hey. I hope you're okay. We're going over to my grandmother's. The gnomes are completely out of control, and we could use all the help we can get. Only if you want to, of course.

Matt's chest tightened as he read the message again and again. Leave it to Samantha to respect his need for space, yet keep him in the loop. Would he miss that when she hated him? Or would it no longer matter, just as nothing had ever mattered before?

Somehow, Matt didn't need Chay to tell him that *this* one would matter. Because Samantha changed everything.

Hate or no hate, he could never stay away from her. Chay just had to be wrong. Just this once.

Fabian

Whoever said gnomes weren't a problem had never met one. They weren't the helpful creatures from stories. They were a menace.

While trying to catch the one they'd seen in the city centre, Fabian and Jan had quickly lost the others and landed in a dead-end. It should have been the end of the merry chase, but instead of one gnome, there had suddenly been three, and all of them were bombarding them with snowballs. By the time Fabian had found his footing again, they'd run off back the way they'd come.

"I'm too old for this," he muttered, rubbing his hurt backside. Under the assault of snowballs, he'd slipped and landed badly.

Jan chuckled and sank deeper into the comfy chair in Elda's living room. "Sure, grandpa." Not that he had fared any better. One of the snowballs had hit him right on the cheekbone, leaving behind a bruise.

Samantha's grandmother came in with a tray of Christmas cookies. "Well, I'm sorry to say, but the gnome population is out of bounds this year."

"We really do have a gnome population?" Fabian asked, still trying to wrap his head around it.

"Of course, Fabian. Where do you think all the gnome stories originate from? There are dozens of them in the forests." Elda batted Jan's hand away as he tried to grab a cookie. "These are not for you."

Jan blinked at her. "Who are they for?"

"Does that mean the gnomes aren't actually a problem?" Lucille asked, sitting on the sofa with Samantha and Matt.

"Oh, they are. Especially around Christmas time. Those gnomes are incredibly naughty and worse than any magpie." Elda sighed heavily. "It's all that sugar. The rest of the year, they can be quite helpful. They clean and fix things, but only until they get bored. However, around Christmas, they're a pest. They steal anything that glitters."

Jan's hand was creeping towards the cookies again. Elda noticed it and shooed him away. "Those are for the gnomes."

"I'm sorry, what?" Jan's mouth fell open. "They're a literal pest, so you're baking cookies for them?"

Elda laughed and shook her head. "These aren't normal cookies, my dear. We bake them every year with a shot of direction loss and put them out for the gnomes. This way, we can pick them up, bring them deep into the forest, and they won't find their way back until springtime."

"So, theoretically, these are *special* cookies." Jan eyed them even more intensely now.

"I thought you were off the drugs," Matt said, then shrugged. "Abandoning you in the forest until spring sounds good to me."

Jan glared at him, while Samantha jabbed Matt's side with her elbow. "You're mean."

And there it was, the look Lucille had described. Fabian watched as Matt grinned at Samantha before bumping her arm in retaliation. She laughed quietly, and he wrapped his hand around her arm, coming dangerously close to holding her hand.

How long had this been going on? Since when had Matt only had eyes for Samantha? Fabian remembered the day they'd buried Nico. Samantha had been unable to search for solace in the arms of her best friend, but she'd gone to Matt. Was that when it had all started? What was he giving her that Fabian couldn't?

It certainly wasn't sex, as Jan had suggested. It couldn't be. If so, Matt would've already moved on, and Fabian was almost sure that Samantha would've told him. Perhaps not the details, but the fact itself. She wouldn't keep that from him, would she?

The fact that he couldn't be a hundred percent sure of that grated on Fabian. He'd been fine with their break-up for a while now—heck, he was even in a new relationship with Rachel—but all this time, Samantha hadn't moved on. Despite her speech to him that she was looking for something more than what Fabian could give her, she hadn't found it. As much as he hated to admit it to himself, he had still held out hope. Only a little bit, but an undeniable bit.

He sighed and searched for Rachel, who was in the corner, leafing through the horrible book Matt's future-seeing friend had apparently written. Fabian liked her a lot. Their relationship was different, but he cared for her. Could one care for more than one person at a time? Or was he being unfair to his girlfriend because watching his ex-girlfriend move on still hurt?

Ever since the café this morning, Rachel had been avoiding him, even when they'd sat together. Had she noticed his doubts? Or was something else going on? Fabian wished he could just talk to her. Talking to Samantha was easy, whereas Rachel barely said a word more than was needed and seemed to live inside her head most of the time.

Just as she was right now. While the others were discussion gnome-catching techniques, Rachel had completely disconnected from the group, her focus entirely on Chay's book. Whatever she'd been looking for, she'd found it, intensely reading the words on the page.

Fabian got out of his chair and walked over to her. That was his girlfriend. And instead of worrying about whether his best friend was in love with this guy or that, he should be trying to figure out what was bothering her.

When Rachel noticed him coming, she quickly slammed the book shut. Fabian faltered, and for a moment, they simply stared at each other. He was the first to look away. "I... I'm sorry." Quickly, he returned to his chair and sat back down.

His pulse was racing, and he knew he was blushing from embarrassment. Thoughts ran wild in his head. Why had she closed the book? There was no doubt now that she wanted to keep her distance from him. If only Fabian knew what he'd done wrong. Why did girls have to be so complicated?

"Here!" Jan threw something at Fabian he didn't recognise fast enough before he was entangled in it.

A weighted net. Fabian pulled it from his face and shoulders and held it before him. He hadn't really been listening to the strategy session the others had started. "What are we supposed to do with these?"

"We're going to place some traps," Jan said. He had a net as well and handed the rest of them to the others.

Samantha had helped her grandmother put the cookies in little tins. "We're going to drop these cookies in the city centre, leading them to the traps. Once they're sitting there munching cookies, we'll catch them in the nets."

Fabian had never handled a net, but the plan was sound. "How hard can it be, huh?"

He knew he never should've asked that question. After three hours of scouring the city centre, Fabian had been kicked, scratched, and bitten. And all he had to show for it was an empty net.

Now he stood waiting in the shadows of a dead end. With only a single flickering lantern to light up the corner, it was starting to get creepy. Only *he* was the creep with the weighted net, hiding in the corner. He sighed. The cold seeped in through his clothes, and his fingers were stiff from holding onto the net.

A pile of cookies sat two metres away from him in what he hoped was an enticing position. From it led a trace of cookies—Samantha's idea to lead the gnomes to him, but he'd been standing in this corner for half an hour now, not a gnome in sight.

Then he heard them. Further down the street, three tiny gnomes were chattering in high-pitched voices impossible to understand. One of them always hopped ahead to pick up the cookie, and all three of them were as excited about the find as they were about the previous one. Adrenaline flushed through Fabian's veins, and he got ready to pounce.

The three gnomes took their sweet time discussing the second-to-last cookie on the road, which had turned out a bit smaller than the others, and apparently, judging by their gestures, wasn't perfectly round. Then one of the gnomes saw the pile of cookies, and Fabian could practically see its eyes growing bigger. With delighted squeals, the gnomes dashed to the pile and began to congratulate each other on the find, repeatedly shaking their tiny hands and nodding their heads.

As they began packing the cookies into their bags, Fabian crept forward. One and a half metres. One metre. Half a metre. His shadow loomed over the gnomes. One of them slowly turned its head to look at him. Fabian jumped forward and threw his net at the same moment as the gnomes flew into different directions.

The gnomes escaped, and the net landed on the remaining two cookies.

Fabian blinked away tears of frustration when he saw one of the gnomes returning, too greedy to let even those two cookies go. The gnome bent down to grab them through the holes in the net, and Fabian dashed forward to grab it. His fingers closed around its tiny body as his knees hit the ground, but before he could hold on tight, the gnome bit down on his finger.

With a cry, Fabian let go. At that moment, the other two gnomes jumped in, pulled up the net, and had it knotted within a few seconds. The weight of the knots pulled Fabian down. He fell onto his side, landing in the snow. The rope dug into his skin. It didn't hurt, but it was annoying, and hindered him from getting into a better position. While he squirmed in the net, the three gnomes ran off laughing with their spoils.

"Fabian!" Samantha came running. "What happened?"

He'd never been happier to see her. Samantha knelt down next to him and began working on the knots. "I suck at this," he muttered.

"Yeah, you do." The drawl belonged to Matt, who had a net with a total of five gnomes hanging over his shoulder. Among them were the three that had brought Fabian into this situation. With a grin, he set the net down and crossed his arms. "That's quite a feat, you know? Getting entangled in your own net."

"Don't worry, I'll have you free in a minute," Samantha whispered. "Gosh, these knots are tight."

A few minutes later, Fabian was able to sit up and free himself. Samantha brushed the snow out of his hair and regarded him with pity, while Fabian wanted to bury himself in the snow.

She pulled him up to his feet. "Come on, we'll bring the ones we have into the forest, and then we'll get some mulled wine to warm up."

Fabian's gaze fell onto the net Matt had carried. "Which ones do you mean?" The net was cut through, not a gnome inside.

Matt spun around, only now noticing the escape. "What the—?"

"Yeah, the gnome population is really something this year." Fabian grinned from ear to ear. At least, he wasn't the only one being completely outfoxed by the little beasts.

Samantha started giggling, and Fabian fell in with her, while Matt glowered at the both of them. "How is this funny?"

"It isn't," Samantha said, laughing. "Not really. But laughing is better than crying." She leaned into Fabian, unable to keep a straight face.

Matt rolled his eyes, stuffing the useless net into his backpack. "I'm not going to chase after them again."

"Why didn't we use sleeping cookies?" Fabian asked. The gnomes they'd lured in must be disoriented as heck, but that didn't stop them from being naughty and pulling all kinds of stunts.

"Sleeping spells don't work well with sugar," Samantha said with a serious face. "Otherwise, that would have been our go-to recipe."

"I didn't actually expect an answer to that."

"I know."

Fabian grinned. Maybe Samantha had moved on from their relationship, but she was still his best friend who knew him better than anyone. Lately, they hadn't spent a lot of time alone together, and he realised he'd missed that. This little conversation alone had cheered him up faster than he would've thought possible.

He gave her a quick sideways hug, then asked Matt. "What do we do now?"

"It's dark and late. I say we get that mulled wine now and give it another go tomorrow. And the day after that. And after that..." He sighed. "Can't we just let them steal their stuff?"

Fabian commiserated strongly. "I'm fine with no decorations this year."

"Well, I'm not," Samantha declared. "We'll get it under control, one gnome after the other."

"How many did you catch?" Fabian asked.

"None." She grinned sheepishly. "But surely, we can all catch one gnome tomorrow. And the day after that. And after that..." Matt poked out his tongue at her, and she laughed. "Let's call the other three and tell them to meet us at Elvira's. Unless *they've* caught any gnomes."

Later that night, after they'd spent a fun-filled evening drinking mulled wine and hot cocoa, Fabian walked Rachel home. Something about seeing her under the Christmas lights where they'd had their first kiss had reignited the fire inside of him. The mulled wine had warmed him up, and he felt bold enough to put his arm around her shoulders, when Rachel side-stepped him.

"Rachel, what's wrong?" Fabian asked. "What did I do?" It was always his fault somehow.

She sighed heavily. "Nothing. I'm sorry. It's just..." She stopped under a lantern and looked up at him. There was something unnerving in her big brown eyes, something steely. "You're still not over Sam, are you?"

Fabian stared at his shoes. There was no use in lying to her. He didn't really want to, either. "Not completely."

Rachel breathed in through her teeth. The hard look had vanished, and she'd reverted to the shy girl. "That's to be expected, I guess. You really loved her."

With a sigh, Fabian pushed his hands into his pockets and shuffled in the snow. "Sure, but what's the point if she doesn't love me back? She's falling for Matt or for that singer guy. Or someone else. Anybody else. And I'm fine with that." The moment he spoke the words, he was surprised to realise they were true. "I just want her to be happy, which I don't think she'll be with Matt if his previous relationships are anything to go by. And I don't know the other one. She hasn't told me anything about him. And that's what I'm struggling with most."

Rachel didn't say a word, letting him speak. And since he couldn't spill his heart out to Samantha, it poured all over Rachel. "We're still not quite where we were before we started dating. She's my best friend. But what good is it if she's not talking to me about what's going on in her life?"

"Maybe she can't."

Fabian frowned. "What do you mean?"

"Well, I assume Samantha knows that you're still not over her, so she can't go to you and talk about the boys she likes. Especially not after she hurt you so much. You didn't talk to her for over a month," she reminded him. Then she stretched her hand out and gave his arm a quick rub. "Don't worry, you'll rebuild your friendship. She'll never leave you behind."

Now she was building him up while he was complaining about his ex. "I'm sorry, Rachel."

Rachel huffed softly. "You're just being honest. And I appreciate that. It... it makes it more real."

"What does that mean, exactly?"

She sighed again. "Sometimes I'm worried that you're only with me because I accidentally affected your subconsciousness." Fabian stared at her dumbfounded, and she hurried to explain, "In your dreams. I... This is really embarrassing, but you were honest with me, so... I can visit other people's dreams, and I often end up in yours."

Now that she said it, Fabian realised she *had* appeared quite often in his dreams. He couldn't always remember them and never really read much into it, other than that he dreamed of a friend, and then his girlfriend. "You're spying on my dreams?"

Rachel gasped and took a stumbling step back. "I didn't do it on purpose. Initially, I mean. At first, I thought I was just dreaming of you. Because I do that quite frequently, have been since we were in the same class together. You know, after you helped me when my bag burst, while everyone else laughed."

Fabian couldn't help but grin. "Rachel, you're rambling." She barely said a word too many, but now random things were flowing out of her mouth.

"I am." She clapped her hands in front of her mouth, then found his gaze and giggled softly. Fabian laughed, and soon she was lowering her hands to laugh with him. "I'm sorry."

He took a step closer to take her hands. "No. *I'm* sorry."

"For what?"

"For never realising how much I meant to you. And for being unable to let Samantha go. You deserve so much more than that. I'm a terrible boyfriend."

Rachel shook her head, and the pressure of her fingers in his intensified. "But you're my boyfriend. That's all I ever wanted. If anything, it makes me love you even more. There aren't many boys our age who can say that they've ever been in love."

"I—"

"Don't. You don't have to say it. I was afraid that my dream presence had altered your feelings, but it hasn't. There is still that love for Samantha. And I might only be your second choice for now, but that's quite enough for me."

It wasn't enough for Fabian. He hated that she would accept as much for herself. But then he realised it was what she'd grown up with. Never being someone's first choice. Not even her parents'.

"You deserve better," he repeated, then kissed her on the forehead. "And I'll do my best to give that to you." He nodded emphatically. "From now on, you will have my full attention. I'll be happy for Samantha when she makes her choice, so she can stop thinking she can't tell me things. And it'll all work out. It might take me a little time to say I love you, but I *do* care for you. I always have." Surely, love could bloom in a place where he was wanted.

Rachel's eyes softened. "Oh, Fabian." Shyly, she wrapped her arms around his neck and pulled him down for a kiss.

Samantha

The gnome hunt had to be interrupted for school, and then for rehearsal. Samantha was running a little late after a school council meeting that had dragged on and on, until she told Adrian she had to leave. Now, the closer she got to the town hall, the faster her heart beat. She was going to see Daniel again! The gnome shenanigans had worked well in distracting her from that fact, but today she'd been a mess, willing the clock to move faster and for Adrian to stop talking.

"You're late." There he was, sitting on the stage, his head shaking in mock-disappointment. "Women, huh?" He kept one eye closed, squinting up at her, but the corner of his mouth was already twitching.

Samantha gasped unnaturally loud to keep herself from smiling. "How am I supposed to know if someone's finally on time?" She'd spent many dates waiting for Fabian because he'd forgotten the time or been running late.

"You'll better get used to it. I'm always on time," Daniel boasted and hopped down from the stage to grab his scoresheet.

It was only then Samantha noticed they were alone again. "Where's Mr Meise?"

"He's not on time."

Samantha burst out giggling, and Daniel grinned in response, as if he'd been waiting for that sound all day long. "Nah, he excused himself. Has to pick up his kids and will be along later, perhaps. And perhaps with kids." He grimaced slightly.

"Don't you like kids?"

Daniel hesitated. "That's a trick question, isn't it? Because I'll say it highly depends on the kids, and then you're gonna say you work part-time as a babysitter and can't wait to start your own family with at least five kids."

"Stop!" Samantha's cheeks hurt too much from laughing as he went on this weird little tangent. "I do not. I... I haven't actually planned that far."

"In that case, I *will* say I'm not sure if I will like Mr Meise's kids because he sounded very exhausted on the phone. Though I can't really complain that he's late, because..." He squinted at her again, hesitating. "Never mind. Shall we get started?"

Samantha was too curious about what else could bother him about the children, but she only found herself nodding. "Sure. How do you want to go about this?"

"Well, I thought I'd still need to find out whether you're actually good." Daniel bit his lip, as if he wasn't quite sure if he'd laid it on too thick.

"You know the drill." Samantha shrugged, feeling rather bold. "I only got the gig because I'm the organiser's daughter."

Daniel shook his head with a straight face. "Nepotism, shocking."

She couldn't quite keep up her mask and had to chuckle again. "I'll show you nepotism."

Once Samantha was on stage, though, her bravado fizzled out. Suddenly, she was overly aware of the fact that it was just her and Daniel. That he looked up at her, his lips open a bit in expectation. That she'd never sung in front of anybody, not without the security of inside the choir. And certainly never a private concert.

The increased blood flow was filling her ears with static, and her mind was skipping ahead. She would open her mouth, and he'd grimace. Or laugh. And whatever little thing had been blooming between them would shrivel and die as he realised he'd been paired with the loser. The girl everyone made fun of.

"Do you want some music?" Daniel asked softly, for once not joking. "Just tell me which song."

"I've never done this before," Samantha whispered.

His eyebrows rose. "Singing?"

"Solo. In front of anyone." Her throat had dried out, and no amount of licking her lips changed that.

"Do you want me to turn around?"

Samantha found herself nodding. She felt silly when Daniel turned. Her stomach twisted, but there was no backing out now. For a few more moments, she stared at the back of his head. He wasn't wearing a beanie today, and his hair curled into tiny tangles. She wanted to sink her fingers into it and find out how soft it was.

But first, she had to sing to him. The beginning was too quiet, but when she closed her eyes, the words flew from her mind, settling into the melody of 'Silent Night'. Though no music played, she could hear it fill her ears from memory, and her voice rose to meet the instruments in her mind. Everything else fell away. There was only her and the song. It didn't matter that she was alone on a stage. Or that she was practically serenading a guy she wanted to spend more time with.

When Samantha opened her eyes again, Daniel had turned back around. It seemed like he had been holding his breath, because he suddenly gasped. "Uhm. Let me put those classics back into the program."

"What?" Samantha's cheeks flushed with heat.

"You sing like an angel. I can't take that away from the poor families wanting to celebrate Christmas."

"Stop." Her voice was shaky. Did that mean he liked it? Or was he making fun of her?

Daniel lowered his head ruefully. "How am I supposed to top that?"

"You don't need to," Samantha said out of reflex. She licked her lips and added on the off-chance he'd meant it, "You only need to match it."

Daniel laughed. "Alright." He came closer and hopped onto the stage before she'd had a chance to climb down. "I'll try my best." As he looked through his phone for a track, he added, "We should sing a duet. You know, matching our voices for real."

The blood returned to her cheeks. A duet seemed so intimate. It wasn't just two people singing but two people singing to each other.

"But first." He pressed play on his phone. "Let me convince you I'm up for the job."

It would've been awkward to leave the stage now, so Samantha kept standing as Daniel launched into a more modern Christmas song with a rockier tune. He was good. Not just his singing voice, but the way he performed. Watching him was fun, and Samantha quickly found she couldn't keep still—or the grin from her face.

Emboldened by her reaction, Daniel cranked his performance up another level, leaning into the lines and playing with his voice to lay down some impressive runs. He even played some air guitar when the solo came through. When he dropped to his knees at the end of the song, Samantha was laughing and applauding with glee.

"That was amazing!" It was too energetic for the party, but she was well aware this version had been for her, not for anyone else.

Daniel stood up again, suddenly right in front of her and slightly out of breath. "So, am I good enough for you?"

"Are you...?" The words got stuck in her throat as she looked into his hazel eyes. They weren't completely uniform. The ring of his left eye was a little darker than his right. And his pupils grew as they focused in on her.

"The duet," he suggested helpfully. "Because I believe our voices match perfectly."

He leaned forward slightly. Samantha's heart almost jumped out of her chest in anticipation when suddenly, his gaze fell on something behind her shoulder. "Hey!"

Samantha whirled around, not sure what to expect. Then she saw it too. A gnome had got hold of a string of lights, ripped it from the wall, and was merrily sprinting towards the exit. "Bloody gnomes."

"What?" Daniel stopped short.

Samantha clapped a hand in front of her mouth, but it was too late. The words had already slipped from her lips. Embarrassed, she lowered her hand. "I... I just..." He'd laugh at her if she told him about gnomes stealing Christmas decorations. Or her efforts in catching them with magic cookies.

"Gnomes? That was a gnome? Like in the fairy tales?"

How was she going to stop this? She didn't want him to think she was a lunatic. Magic wasn't allowed to ruin this for her. "Uhm, yes."

Daniel was frowning. "Have you seen one before?"

"Maybe."

"Because I have."

He'd seen them before! In her surprise, Samantha asked, "Really? You know your way around magical creatures?"

"Magical—? There are magical creatures?" He stared at her as if she'd gone mad.

Samantha winced. She'd seen that look too often in her life. But the damage was already done. She might as well admit to it. "You'll probably think I'm crazy if I say yes."

"Why would I?"

His seemingly innocent question only hurt her more. Did she really have to spell this out for him? "Because I just claimed that magical creatures live in Greenvalley."

"You didn't claim anything," Daniel said. "I saw that gnome. What else could it be?"

Samantha blinked. Did he believe her? He didn't even try to argue? "You don't think I'm crazy?"

He shrugged and shook his head. "Honestly, your explanation makes sense, at least. When I first saw a gnome stealing from the big Christmas tree outside, I thought *I'd* gone crazy. It's a relief to know I haven't."

Relief was an understatement for the emotion that flooded Samantha. He believed her! He didn't think she was weird or a lunatic. The thing between them wasn't doomed before it had truly started. The emotions were so strong and sudden, Samantha blurted out, "Don't worry about the gnomes. My friends and I are onto them."

"You are?" Daniel looked at her in surprise.

Once again, Samantha wished she hadn't been quite so forthcoming. Claiming magical creatures were real was one thing, but admitting she regularly set out to fight them was a different story. Nevertheless, she'd come this far. He wouldn't stop asking, so he might as well hear the truth and then sprint the other way. "Not many people in Greenvalley know about this, so please don't tell anyone. But my friends and I, we take care of the town. The gnomes are pretty harmless compared to some of the other creatures we've met. But they're very cheeky. We're trying to catch them and take them back to the forest, but they've proven to be..."

"Slippery little bastards?" Daniel asked, his mouth twitching with amusement.

"Yes!" Samantha took a deep breath when the tension flowed from her body. He was taking the news pretty well, all things considered.

Daniel glanced at the door before grimacing. "Can I help somehow?"

"You want to help catch the gnomes?" She stared at him in confusion.

"It sounds to me like you could use an extra pair of hands."

"They're very naughty."

Daniel laughed. "Can't be worse than children."

"I'd rather babysit a dozen children than handle one gnome." When he grinned in return and didn't protest, Samantha nodded. "Okay. If you give me your number, I'll fill you in when we have another go at them."

"I thought you'd never ask."

Taken aback, Samantha felt the blood return to her cheeks. Had she really just asked for his number? Sure, for an entirely different reason, but nonetheless, she'd asked.

Daniel chuckled to himself, then stretched out his hand. "Give me your phone."

She took it from her pocket, unlocked it, and pulled up the contacts before handing it to him. Daniel was done in a minute, then called his phone to obtain her number as well. "All done."

As he handed it back to her, their fingers touched, sparks flying between them. Both of them held onto the phone, their eyes locked.

The door of the hall flew open and two young boys came running in. Behind them, Mr Meise, hidden by a bunch of shopping bags, followed. The children quickly took control of the hall, screaming and laughing, while their father apologised. "The streets were completely blocked, or we would've been here sooner. Did you get started already?"

Samantha quietly put her phone away, while Daniel turned towards the pianist and sat down on the stage again. "We did." He gave her a grin that made her knees go soft. "You need to hear Samantha sing. She'll blow you away just like she did me."

The smile those words put on her face never quite faltered throughout rehearsal.

Lucille

"So, you're singing with Samantha?" Lucille asked when she finally got to meet Daniel the next day. Samantha was delayed, and so she had the handsome student all to herself.

Samantha definitely knew how to pick them. Sure, he was no Matt, but there was something easy-going about him, a smile that made her warm to him right away. He would make a great boyfriend for her friend.

"It's my privilege. Have you heard her sing?" Daniel asked. When Lucille shook her head—once, because she truly hadn't, and second, because she wanted him to tell her more about it—he continued, "She's got the most amazing voice. So clear and strong. I bet when she sings 'Silent Night' at the gala, the whole room will be quiet."

Lucille very nearly swooned. Now, *this* was an emotionally available man. "Please tell me you're single."

"Are you flirting with me?" Daniel asked, laughing.

"No! But as Samantha's friend, I need to know what your intentions for her are." No one would ever accuse her of not being direct.

Daniel rubbed his cheek, taking a little time to think about it. "To answer your question, yes, I've been single for seven months. As for my intentions... well, it's quite obvious I'm head over heels for Samantha. I only took the job because I needed the money, but now I'm sad that the gala is so soon."

"Well, now that you know our secret, you can always join us on our monster hunts." It had been quite a surprise when Samantha had informed the group that Daniel would be joining them. "You'll find

Samantha is even more brilliant than you can imagine. She's super smart, and she can brew potions."

"Magic potions?"

Lucille nodded. "Yes. She's pretty awesome. I wouldn't know how we'd fare without her." They certainly wouldn't have even got out of school when the bogeyman had come for them.

For a moment, Lucille worried she had said a little too much in her attempt to hype up Samantha, but it only took him a few seconds to work through the information before he smiled. "I feel like my whole world has shifted."

"Yeah, Samantha can have that effect on people."

"Lucille!" Samantha, Fabian, and Rachel were coming up the road. "And Daniel. You're here already."

Fabian and Rachel stopped to take in Daniel, while Samantha joined them. Lucille loved nothing more than to watch Daniel's face light up at her sight. "I told you I'm always on time." It must've been some inside joke because Samantha giggled delightfully. "And besides, if I hadn't been here so early, Lucille couldn't have told me all those interesting things about you."

Samantha's eyes widened, and her gaze shifted to Lucille. "Can I speak to you for a moment?" She hooked her arm into Lucille's and drew her away from the others, leaving Daniel to make Fabian's and Rachel's acquaintance. "What did you tell him?" she asked once they were out of earshot.

"Only what an amazing witch you are."

"You told him about my magic?" Samantha's eyes grew even wider, and there was a slight panicky lilt in her voice. "Didn't Matt say we should be careful with how much we tell him?"

Matt had reacted anything but graciously to Samantha's announcement in their group chat. Lucille knew why. She put her hand on Samantha's arm and patted it. "Matt's just jealous."

"Why would he be jealous?" Samantha huffed, trying to sound amused about it.

"At the moment, Matt is into you. And before I saw you with Daniel, I was convinced you were also developing feelings for him."

Samantha shook her head with far more vehemence than necessary. "No! I mean he... we were just teasing each other."

"Something you seemed to enjoy."

Samantha blushed heavily. "Maybe I did, but he's not serious about it. In three weeks, it'll be someone else again." Lucille understood where all the hesitation came from regarding Matt's reputation, but there had been an undeniable spark. "You must think I'm horrible. Flirting with one guy, then falling in love with another."

"No, not at all. Matt isn't exactly what I'd call boyfriend material." Lucille was all too well reminded of how he'd rejected that notion with her. "Yes, he's fun, and his charm can be irresistible, but you're too sensible for that. You know what you want, and that Matt isn't capable of giving it to you." He may have been exhibiting some un-Matt-like behaviour when it came to Samantha, but Lucille couldn't believe he'd changed enough. "And did you just say you're falling in love with Daniel?"

Immediately, Samantha glanced over her shoulder at Daniel, who was chatting amicably with the other two. "I think so. He makes me laugh."

Lucille sighed contentedly. "Well, I didn't just tell him things. I also found out he's been single for a while. So, go get him, girl!"

"Lucille!" Samantha hissed and slapped her arm.

Laughing, Lucille turned her back to the others. "Come on, we've got some gnomes to find and date to get you with your crooner."

\#

An hour later, they met with Matt at the fountain. So far, they'd secured three gnomes, one of which Daniel had managed to hold on to, making him jump to the top of their group's success rating. But that paled in comparison to what they saw in the giant Christmas tree next to the fountain. More than half a dozen gnomes were swinging between the branches and stealing the lights.

Matt turned around as he heard them coming, pausing for only a second when he noticed Daniel, and quickly glossing over him to focus on Lucille of all people. "We've got a bit of a problem."

"Hey, Matt," Samantha said and tugged on Daniel's arm. "This is Daniel. He—"

"I figured. Hey." Still no eye contact.

Daniel was oblivious to the tension and offered his hand. "It's nice to meet you, Matt."

"Sure." Matt brusquely walked past Daniel and stood next to Lucille. "How do we get the gnomes out?"

Lucille exchanged a quick look with Samantha, who tried to assure Daniel it didn't mean anything, when they all knew it did. Just then, her phone rang. "Jan? Where are you?"

"I have no clue. Somewhere in Greenvalley?" the familiar voice sounded from the other end of the call.

"That doesn't exactly pin your location down."

"Well, I'm standing in front of a red-brick house with stars in the window."

Lucille took a deep breath. She was the one fairly new to town, not him. "You mean the city council building? That's, like, only two streets from us."

"Three," Fabian added helpfully.

"Three," Lucille repeated. "We're in front of the church."

Jan hesitated. "So, which way do I go?"

"You just walk down the street until you get to the church."

"Left or right? Which way is left, by the way?"

Lucille groaned, a terrible thought slipping into her mind. "You ate a cookie!"

"They were delicious," Jan muttered.

"Tell him to stay where he is. I'm going to get him," Fabian declared.

Lucille conveyed the message and ended the call, rolling her eyes. Her only hope was that the dosage was far too little to keep him disoriented until springtime. "One day, I'll kill him."

"Be my guest," Matt muttered. Then he looked up at the tree, where the gnome population had grown again. "By the time those two are back, that entire tree will be empty."

"Instead of cookies, we should lure them away with lights," Daniel mused. "They can't seem to resist something glowing and glittery."

Matt very nearly snarled, but before he could say something, Samantha picked up on the idea. "That's not a bad thought. Catching them all one by one isn't really working for us. Lucille, you must have some light or spark spells. What do you think about using that to lure them back into the forest?"

"Instead of catching them, we're performing the Pied Piper of Hamelin?"

"Exactly." Samantha exclaimed. "Then we only have to give them the cookies in the forest, take care that we're not losing Jan while we're at it, and voilà, Christmas is saved."

"You have the best ideas," Matt said, completely ignoring that it had been Daniel who'd come up with it originally.

Daniel wasn't stupid. He'd picked up on the unveiled animosity pretty quickly, and frowned. Not wanting a scene, Lucille stepped forward and raised her hand. "Let's try it. Scintilla!"

Sparks flew from her hand into the air. Some of the gnomes stopped to see what was happening.

"Can you move them?" Samantha asked.

Lucille tried it by waving her hand, but nothing happened. Instead, the sparks slowly sizzled out. "I've got an idea." Once more, Lucille conjured up the sparks, then walked a bit before repeating the spell. One or two gnomes climbed down the tree and tried to catch the sparks. As Lucille kept walking, all the gnomes came after her. They seemed delighted with the little flecks of light, always happy to find the next one.

As the others fell into step next to her, Samantha grinned at her. "It's working."

"Now I just need someone to tell me how to get to the forest before I lose my voice," Lucille sighed. "Scintilla."

"Follow me." Rachel took the lead.

As they walked through the pedestrian zone, more and more gnomes came out to follow them. Some people stopped to watch them. There was no way to keep such a big group of gnomes a secret, but then Daniel started singing, and Samantha fell in with him, and the people smiled, not realising what they saw wasn't a cavalcade of children with lanterns.

Lucille had never heard Samantha sing before, but now she knew what Daniel meant. Their voices harmonised perfectly, and if they sang that way during their performance, the people at the Christmas Gala would be in for a treat.

Next to Lucille, Matt dragged his feet, burning holes into Daniel's back with his stare, though he kept his mouth shut for now. Fabian soon joined them with Jan as they came past the city council building, and together, they led the gnomes out of the town and deep into the forest.

By the time they reached their destination, Lucille was certainly feeling the effects of whispering her spell constantly. "This is far enough, don't you think?"

Rachel nodded. "Time to give them their cookies." She opened her tin and began handing them out one by one.

"Goodbye," Lucille waved to the gnomes. "Be nice, will you?"

She shouldn't have said anything. A couple of gnomes tugged at her pants, talking to her in their high voices. And then, before she could even guess what they were planning to do, they swept her off her feet and carried her away from the others so fast, she could only scream for help.

The others called after her, but they were too slow to stop the gnomes.

On and on it went. Lucille tried to wriggle free, while her mind came up with a bunch of horror scenarios. They would throw her down a cliff or eat her. Or maybe take her down into their suburban caves and force her to work for them.

Neither of those visions came true. Instead, the gnomes burst through a line of pine trees and deposited her upright into a clearing.

It was a marvellous sight. The trees around her were decorated with stolen lights and baubles. Piles of cookies were set on a buffet table, and a bunch of gnomes were tuning their tiny instruments, getting ready for a concert. "You're having a party?"

The gnomes wildly nodded their heads, and laughter bubbled from Lucille's lips. "And we're invited?"

The others burst into the clearing, stopping in confusion once they became aware of their surroundings. "It's beautiful," Lucille could hear Samantha whisper.

A gnome tugged on Lucille's pants. When she crouched down, it waved its little hands about as if they were exploding in the air, all while chattering in that too-high voice. "You want me to do more sparks?"

The gnome nodded. "Very well. It's Christmas, after all." And with that, she stood up and repeated her spell until the entire clearing lit up with sparks.

The gnome orchestra began to play a happy jig, and Daniel asked Samantha for a dance. Together with the gnomes, they led a merry round. Fabian and Rachel were kissing under the falling snow that glistened in the many lights, while Jan was accepting the gnomes' offer of more cookies. Lucille rolled her eyes at him before her gaze landed on Matt. He alone had not been taken by the fairy-tale-like cheer. With his arms crossed, he frowned heavily at Daniel and Samantha enjoying themselves.

Lucille sighed and decided to soften the blow. Who knew Matt Traidous could fall for someone? The one he couldn't have? "Come, dance with me." She pulled him into the clearing despite his obvious disinterest.

"Leave it," he grumbled, but Lucille took him by his hands, forcing him into the dance.

Though his feet moved with her, Matt kept observing Samantha with the most forlorn gaze. Laughing with the gnomes and Daniel, Samantha never noticed his stare, which Lucille thought was a good thing. She deserved to be happy.

"Let her go, Matt," she whispered. "Don't ruin this for her."

"I'm not..." He sighed heavily and finally looked away from Samantha. "I just don't get it. She's only known him for what? A week? Two weeks?"

Lucille smiled sadly at him, his pain all too familiar to her. "She's in love, Matt. Are you?"

Matt stared at her, open-mouthed. Then he caught himself. "No. Of course not."

"That's what I thought," Lucille muttered, though she was convinced more than ever that he was now.

Samantha

It had never been easier to face a crowd than with Daniel at her side. The town hall was glistening in the candlelight. Long festive tables were decorated with pine branches and fake snow. Every last seat was taken by functionaries, and those who hadn't wanted to spend Christmas alone. Samantha's family was sitting to the left of the stage, right next to the dance floor, and her parents had taken full advantage of it, dancing and laughing, while Meg entertained her grandmother.

Daniel and Samantha had performed two sets of roughly fifty minutes, and the entire time, Samantha hadn't minded the over one hundred eyes on her or the fact that she couldn't hide in the choir. Daniel's confidence in himself and in her had given wings to her performance. Who cared what everybody else thought? She only needed to look into his hazel eyes to find the only opinion that mattered.

And Samantha looked into his eyes a lot. While they sang their duet, their eyes remained locked until the very last note. They were in their own world, where nothing but them and the harmony between their voices existed. Only when applause sounded from the audience was Samantha transported back into the room.

Daniel broke the eye contact first, but he took her hand to raise it high into the air. "Applause for my magical partner!"

Samantha laughed while the hall erupted once again. Of course, he had to bring magic into it. Daniel pulled her close and wrapped his arm around her side. Where his fingers touched her hips, her skin tingled. Suddenly, she became aware of the many eyes on them.

Fortunately, her mother came onto the stage and took the microphone. "That was wonderful. Thank you so much, you two." To the crowd, she said, "Give it up for our two exceptional singers for making this Christmas Eve such a delight." Then she bent over to Samantha and gave her a hug. "That was amazing. Go get some more food. They've got the chocolate fondue out."

"Can't miss that," Daniel quipped. His hand had slipped back into hers, and together, they walked off the stage while the hall was still applauding. "I've got something for you," Daniel whispered into her ear as they climbed down the stairs.

His hot breath along with his words put a blush onto Samantha's cheeks. But before they could go anywhere, her father and Meg stopped them. He clapped Daniel's shoulder and gave Samantha one of his signature bear hugs. "Fantastic job. That was almost like a little concert. I'm proud of you, Sammy."

She hugged him as well and whispered, "Thank you."

"Yeah, it wasn't bad for two amateur singers," Meg said.

Laughter burst from Samantha's lips. The cool front was ridiculous. Daniel leaned into her and whispered very audibly, "That's high praise in teenager terms. We should count ourselves lucky." He withdrew slightly. "I'll see you in the back."

Samantha clicked her tongue at Meg. "Really?"

Meg watched Daniel leave, then told her, "Don't let that one go."

"I'm not planning to." The concert had filled Samantha with adrenaline. She was buzzing from the exhilaration, and she would make absolutely sure that today was *not* the last day she'd spend with Daniel.

She followed him into the little room in the back, where they had stored their things, and searched her bag for the tin of cookies she'd made for him. As she turned around, he presented her with a poinsettia: the winter rose. Before she could really take in its beauty, he saw the cookie tin and laughed. "Are those gnome cookie leftovers?"

"No, this is a fresh batch. They're not for gnomes, but they do have a little bit of magic inside of them," Samantha admitted coyly. It had taken her a couple of tries to get it right. "These are Christmas cookies. They're filled with physical and emotional warmth, childhood memories, and the fragrance of Christmas."

"Wow." The word was a mere whisper in his breath.

Samantha lowered her eyes, unable to hold his gaze. Instead, she regarded the beautiful red blossom of the poinsettia. "How did you know I love flowers?"

"A wild guess. I don't know that much about you yet, so a flower was a relatively safe guess. And I'm giving this to you because I want to get to know you more. I want to know everything."

Samantha held her breath, unsure of how to respond to what was clearly a declaration of interest. Could it be true? Was Daniel as much in love with her as she was with him?

They exchanged their presents and put them down on the bench. Daniel took one of the cookies. His eyes widened after the first bite. "Oh my god, I'll never be able to enjoy another cookie again. These are amazing. I want a batch of those for every Christmas from now on."

Samantha laughed again. "Every Christmas, huh?" She would like that very much.

"Absolutely." He returned to her, but then frowned and looked up at the ceiling.

Samantha followed his gaze, only to see a gnome quickly climbing down and out of the room. Instead of stealing something, it hung the fullest, most perfect mistletoe above them.

Daniel chuckled and lowered his eyes again. "I guess, in this case..."

"There's really no choice," Samantha whispered.

She held her breath as he leaned forward agonisingly slow. Her eyes focused on his lips, yearning for them to touch her while fearing what it would mean. Her heart was nearly jumping out of her chest. And then, his lips brushed against her, light as a feather, and Samantha leaned into him to feel more of it. His kiss was electrifying, their mouths made for each other.

He let go for a moment, but only to put his hands on her cheeks and gaze into her eyes with pure delight. Then he lowered his mouth onto hers again, and this time, she opened her lips to welcome him.

The moment their tongues touched, Samantha forgot everything else. All the wonderful tastes of Christmas she'd put into the cookies were on his tongue. They filled her with heat and belonging that opened her heart wide. Samantha slipped her arms around his body to press herself closer to him. She never, ever wanted to let go.

His kiss was everything. Better than the flowers, better than the cookies, better than the music. She'd never had a better Christmas present.

Part 3

Birthdays & Demons

Jan

It was New Year's Eve. Normally, Jan would meet his friends at the docks and get wasted long before the clock struck twelve, but he hadn't gone there since the demon had ruined everything. Instead, he was going to Matt's birthday party. He hadn't quite decided whether it was a shame to have one's birthday on New Year's Day or simply perfection. Who else could boast having fireworks each year for their birthday?

For once in his life, Jan was the first to reach Matt's house. He could've gone upstairs but preferred to wait for the others. He and Matt were still on shaky terms, never having quite synced. While he didn't mind attending the party, he definitely didn't want to spend time alone with him and his teacher father.

He only had to wait a couple of minutes before the car arrived that dropped off Lu. She'd barely stepped out, dressed as if she was going to the biggest party of the year, when the others came around the corner. Lu was still waiting by the car for her chauffeur to present her with a huge bouquet for the birthday boy. Leave it to Lu to go completely overboard.

Though Jan supposed the same could be said for him. He'd been in charge of getting the fireworks, and he carried two large bags with him. "Hey guys," he greeted them. "Ready for an awkward party?"

Samantha had brought her new boyfriend, which was pretty unfair, since Meg hadn't got permission to join them at the party. But Daniel endeared himself to Jan immediately when he glanced up at the apartment building and grimaced. "Let's hope awkward is the worst word to describe today."

"Don't say that," Samantha whispered. "He won't bite you."

"It certainly looked that way when I last saw him."

Jan clapped his shoulder. "Don't worry. Matt is all looks, no substance."

"That's not true," Samantha protested. Then she leaned into Daniel. "You'll be fine." She kissed him until Fabian cleared his throat.

"It's cold. Can we go upstairs?" he asked.

"Yes, please. These flowers are getting heavy," Lu complained.

"You know, a smaller bouquet would've been perfectly fine," Jan teased her as they got inside the building and started walking up the stairs.

Lucille clicked her tongue in annoyance. "He's turning eighteen. That's a big one. And remember, he never had a proper birthday party."

Jan still thought it was weird, but perhaps demon-hunter people didn't celebrate such irrelevant things as birthdays.

"Here we go." Rachel pressed the doorbell of the Traidous unit.

They heard the buzzer behind the door and then an excited bark and steps. The door opened, and a fur ball shot out to prance around Samantha's legs. That was the last thing Jan took note of before his mind was blown.

Neither Matt nor his father had opened the door. Instead, the most beautiful woman he'd ever seen, on and off-screen, leaned seductively against the wall. Her hair was midnight black and fell over her shoulders in long, luscious locks. Her skin was a warm bronze tone, as if kissed by the sun, and she had the fullest set of lips and most mesmerising cat-like eyes. Jan's gaze dropped, unable to restrain himself from travelling her perfect body with his eyes. She wore something like a corset, which pushed her already full breasts even higher, and a very, very short skirt. Her legs went on for days.

"You must be Matt's friends. Come on in." Even her voice was pure sex, sultry, and sweet like forbidden honey.

A sharp jab in his side brought Jan back from the edge. Lu stepped in front of them and greeted the woman. "Hi, I'm Lucille de Cerque."

"What a beautiful name." The beauty turned away from them to lead them inside, while singing out into the apartment, "Matt, your friends are here." As she walked away, her hips swayed from side to side seductively.

"Pull yourself together," Samantha hissed.

Jan startled, but the warning hadn't been for him. Fabian's head was cocked sideways to have a better view as the woman vanished into the living room. He jerked back and flashed Rachel an apologetic glance. His girlfriend only rolled her eyes and entered the flat. Of all three males, Daniel had been able to control himself the most, but Jan would be damned if he wasn't also affected. Even Lucille muttered, "She's gorgeous."

They'd barely made it into the living room when Matt met them. If the woman was female perfection, Matt was her counterpart. In his black shirt, he looked annoyingly handsome. If only he would smile a bit more. But Matt's face was like the tension in the air before an electrical storm. "There you are. My parents are driving me crazy."

Jan cleared his throat, his eyes already fixed again on the beautiful woman behind Matt. "I shouldn't say this because I'm in a happy relationship, but man, your sister is hot."

"That's my mother, you idiot!"

Surprised, Jan stumbled backwards. That beautiful woman was his *mother?* She couldn't be older than thirty at most. As she sauntered over again to put her hands on Matt's shoulders, Jan took a good look at her. If she'd given birth to Matt eighteen years ago, and presumably older siblings before that, she must've had access to the best beauty surgeons in the world. That or magic. It had to be magic.

"You're a bit tense, darling," Matt's mother whispered, her lips uncomfortably close to her son's ear.

Matt snapped at her, "Could you please get dressed? We have guests."

"I am dressed." Her gaze found Jan's, and the wicked smile she gave him did something funny to his stomach. "Your friends like it."

"My friends are idiots," Matt snarled. He shook off his mother's hands, and she let him go, withdrawing herself from the situation.

Jan was sorry to see her go, but also glad since he didn't know how much more he could take. He had a girlfriend, after all, and this was Matt's mother, goddammit!

Matt took a deep breath. "You have to excuse her. She's a bit... unique." He grimaced. "Come in, take a seat. I'll be back in a bit." And with that, he vanished into the bathroom.

"I guess we all know now where he gets his good looks from," Jan whispered to Lu, who made a strangled sound.

The living room was decorated with fake icicles and fairy lights. A buffet with monster-shaped finger food had already been set, with a champagne bottle cooling for midnight. Matt's mother had taken a seat on a chair and crossed her legs, sliding her skirt up even higher.

His father seemed to be busy in the kitchen, but Chay was there to greet them.

"Do you want something to drink?" If Jan didn't know better, he would've said the seer was a bit tense.

"A beer," he said, thinking he needed a bit of alcohol to clear his head from the conflicting emotions.

"I'll take a water," Lu said politely.

It was Fabian's choice as well. "Water, lots of water."

Jan let Lu, Rachel, and Fabian take the couch while he sat on the armrest. With eight guests, the little flat was already quite full. And awkward as hell when Jan considered who'd been invited apart from them.

He only noticed Samantha had vanished for a little when she returned to take a seat on Daniel's lap. "He's all right?" Daniel asked, apparently privy to where she'd gone.

Samantha scrunched up her nose and sighed. "Not really. He's got a headache."

"Oh no," Lu exclaimed. "Can't we do something about it? He should be able to enjoy his party."

"We all should." Jan got up. "Come on guys. This isn't a coffee group. It's New Year's, so let's party."

\#

Jan knew why he'd never attended any of the others' birthday parties. If he threw a party, there would be loud music and a lot of booze. And then maybe some strip poker. With the others, it was family games, courtesy of Samantha.

They had split into two groups and were playing *Pictionary*. Jan had the bad luck of being grouped with the birthday boy *and* Samantha and Daniel, which made him feel a little like sitting between a rock and a hard place. And to make matters worse, the other group had Fabian.

While Jan tried to will the little hourglass to release its sand faster, Fabian drew a perfectly recognisable saw followed by a chain in under twenty seconds.

"Saw. Chain. Chainsaw!" Rachel shouted.

"That's it," Fabian declared, while Lu cheered and gave Rachel a high-five.

Jan slapped the table. "This isn't fair. Fabian should be banned from all drawing tasks."

"Isn't the entire game based on drawing?" Matt asked. They'd failed the last three tasks, while the other team had a flawless run so far.

"Whatever. It's your turn."

Lu turned the hourglass around and gave Matt a card. Instead of beginning to draw, he frowned, then leaned over to Lu to ask her what it was he was supposed to draw.

"You don't know Batman?" she asked with a chuckle.

"Lucille!" Fabian groaned and pulled a new card for Matt, while attempting to stop the hourglass and reverse what little had trickled through already.

Jan couldn't believe it. It had been such an easy card, a sure point. Even he could have drawn a stick figure and a bat. Or the signature mask. "How do you not know who Batman is?"

"Not everyone is into Marvel," Samantha defended him and immediately got what she deserved when Fabian shouted, "DC!"

Samantha raised her hands in apology, laughing. "I'm so sorry."

"Don't worry," Daniel said to Matt. "I'm not good with superheroes, either."

"Good for you," Matt hissed, his voice pure poison.

The mirth evaporated, and Samantha rubbed Daniel's hand, who kept his cool despite the animosity. Meanwhile, Matt got up. "I'm going to get a drink."

"But it's your turn!" Jan protested.

Matt ignored him. Halfway to the kitchen, he paused and turned towards the outside door. A second later, the bell rang. Jan got up, curious who else was invited to this party. "You're expecting anyone else?"

"Why do we have to do this in such a complicated way?" an unfamiliar male voice could be heard behind the door.

Matt paled at the sound of it. A female voice answered, "Because that's how you're supposed to do it. Trust me."

"Do you want to open the door, or..." Jan asked carefully, not sure whether Matt wasn't going to pass out on him instead.

His voice must've pulled Matt back from the brink because his face contorted, and he strode towards the door, almost ripping it out of its hinges. "What the hell are you doing here?"

Three people stood in the corridor: two young men and a woman, one more beautiful than the others. The woman and one of the guys had white-blond hair and lighter skin. The man's lips twitched cruelly as he regarded Matt, marring his pretty features, while the woman hugged Matt exuberantly. "It's so good to see you!" she chirped.

The third was taller than the others, with the same midnight-black hair and bronze skin as Matt's mother. His green eyes glinted with unveiled amusement as he patted Matt's shoulder. "We've got a running bet on you and are just checking in. You're not too bad so far, little brother."

"Oh, please, the last one didn't even count," the white-blond guy complained. He ran into Matt's shoulder on his way inside. The look he gave his little brother—for Jan assumed those were his fabled siblings—was pure contempt.

Matt turned around, looking like his birthday had been cancelled.

"Don't worry," his sister said. "I'll keep him in line. I promise. I just really wanted to get to know your friends and... well, this is an important day. My little brother doesn't come of age every day. It'll all be fine. Matt." She said it like an afterthought, as if she wasn't used to calling him by his name.

The taller brother had found Chay and grinned, "Of course, you'd be here. Didn't want to miss this one, did you?"

Chay's tension grew. "Wouldn't miss it for the world."

"I still remember your eighteenth birthday. Legendary!"

Jan regarded Chay with newfound respect. Not everybody got his parties called legendary. "You were a party animal?"

Chay winced. "We don't all remember it that well."

"Got it." Jan grinned wildly. Yep, that sounded legendary. Not like this sad excuse for a party, fraught with tension and bad tempers. Even Matt's father was mostly hiding in the kitchen. Now he stood leaning against the wall, scowling heavily.

Matt gnashed his teeth and finally got around to introductions. "Looks like my siblings are bored. Those are my half-brothers, Balthasar—" he pointed towards the black-haired guy "—and Caspar." His voice dripped of acid. "And my half-sister Menuha."

"Hi everyone," she smiled at them, all sunshine to her blond brother's storm clouds. "It's so great to meet all of you."

"What a nice surprise." Naturally, Lu got up, matching Menuha's smile with one of her own. "I'm Lucille."

As the two girls shook hands, Matt cursed under his breath. "Right. Those are Fabian, Rachel, Samantha," he pointed at Daniel, "Samantha's guy, and Jan. And now I really need a drink." And with that, he stormed past his father into the kitchen.

It turned out Daniel's fears were right. Jan would've preferred an awkward party to whatever this had just become.

Matt

His birthday was a nightmare. Sure, Chay had warned Matt that his family would like to celebrate with him, but he would've never guessed they'd actually make the trip to Ashuan. Not that it took them more than a second from Hell. And he was also quite sure they weren't truly here to celebrate his birthday. No. His mother's presence he could somehow wrap his head around. She loved him in her weird, demonic ways. Or at least, he'd always been a favourite of hers. Menuha with her human-fetish was more of a surprise than it should've been. But Caspar and Balthasar? The latter had spoken fewer than five words to him in his entire life, and the former... well, Caspar hated his guts. Where his twin sister loved humans to bits, he hated them. Which only meant that this party was going to end in a bloodbath.

Matt stood in the kitchen, contemplating what he wanted to drink, when his gaze fell onto the vodka bottle his father had left out. René usually didn't drink, but Melaney's presence in his apartment had changed that. Very well, the vodka would do.

"Isn't that a bit too much?" His father had entered behind him, closing the door to the kitchen.

"Let's not start parenting now, shall we, René?" Matt took a shot glass from the cupboard and poured himself a drink.

His father stiffened, a mask slipping onto his face as he detached himself from the situation. "So, we're back to René."

Matt never understood why it bothered his father so much to be called by his name. It was his name, after all, and it wasn't as if René walked around and called Matt "son" all the time. Matt only knew that it *did* bother his father. That he preferred to be called Dad, and that it was somehow important to him. "Sorry. I'm having a bad day." And with that, he downed the shot.

René crossed his arms, unhappiness oozing out of him, yet Matt never knew him to complain. He'd taken to Matt's sudden appearance admirably, but there was little doubt between them that Matt saw him as anything more than someone partial to helping him find his way around Ashuan. Someone who would explain all the confusing rules of social conduct and technology. There was so much Matt was missing that everyone else had soaked up with their mother's milk. Such as who that "bat man" was, or what all those movies, stories, and books were his friends frequently referred to. René couldn't patch up all the gaps, but he tried. And he never asked for more than what Matt would give him.

"Why are they here? Your siblings. I told you that I don't want them here." That was the only thing he'd been very clear about. No demons allowed. Half-demons, okay, but no purebred demons.

"I didn't invite them, okay?" Matt poured himself another shot. Just knowing that Caspar was on the other side of that wall made his blood boil. "It's not my fault they seem to make their own decisions." He gave René a derisive snort and drank again. "I see you're not complaining about Melaney being here."

René sighed, and his shoulders sunk a little. "I know she's important to you."

"Liar." Matt filled his glass up a third time. "Do you think I don't see how you look at her?" And why shouldn't he? Everyone looked at Melaney. If they didn't, she wasn't doing her job right, but for some reason, it bothered Matt to think his parents would get back together. They just didn't seem to fit. René was teaching young children, nurturing the new generation of humans. While Melaney was busy on her back, making the new generation of demons. And though Matt should've cared less about how the two of them celebrated their reunion, he didn't want them together. René deserved better. He deserved some human woman as wholesome as him. Someone who truly loved him. Not someone who would ruin him for the next eighteen years with one night of mind-blowing sex.

Matt set the glass to his lips, but before he was able to drink it, René snatched it from his hand. "Slow down, Matt. You're the host of the party. You should at least be coherent when they congratulate you later." While Matt glared at him and then the bottle for good measure, René sighed. "And regarding your mother. I'm trying not to be in the same room as her. Which is quite hard in a flat as small as this one." It explained why he was so busy in the kitchen tonight.

"I didn't invite her either," Matt admitted. Something was underfoot, and it unnerved him that he didn't know what it was. Add to that the horrible headaches he'd had all day. He was rarely plagued by disease. His healing powers took care of most, and if they didn't, it was usually a magical illness—or a curse Caspar had found for him.

Caspar... perhaps that was their origin. He'd cursed Matt with headaches, and now he and Balthasar were betting on how long it would take for Matt's head to explode. As ridiculous as it sounded, it was something he'd come to expect from his brothers. "I'm going to kill them."

"Not in my flat," René muttered, then drank the vodka shot himself. "You should probably head back out unless you want Chay to handle the whole situation."

Chay was the perfect person to handle anything. He was a talented and well-experienced diplomat who'd brokered treaties between mortal enemies. Surely, he could keep Matt's human friends safe from his demon family. But René was right. He'd invited his friends. And he would be damned if he'd let Caspar ruin the one birthday party in his life.

A high-pitched squeal rose from the living room, and Matt ran out so fast he might as well have jumped through space. Somehow, Caspar had got hold of Crumbs and was holding the little puppy by the tail. Matt barrelled into him from behind and snatched the dog from his claws. "Touch Crumbs one more time and I'll kill you."

Caspar's perpetual scowl deepened as he got up from the ground. "I want to see you try." He stepped closer. They were roughly the same height, and Matt could feel Caspar's breath on his cheeks. "Come on, bastard."

Never once looking away, Matt held out the puppy. "René, hold Crumbs for me, will you?" This was his party. He might not have invited Caspar, but he sure was going to kick him out. And then kick him some more for all the times he'd been tormented. Maybe he really *would* kill him. Caspar wouldn't be able to say he didn't have it coming.

But René never took Crumbs from him, and suddenly there was Samantha, squeezing in between the two as if she had no regards for her own life. "Matt, leave it. Crumbs is fine." The little dog was shaking but seemed unharmed. "Ignore him and come celebrate with us. We haven't finished the game."

All this time, Matt had only had eyes for Caspar, who regarded the back of Samantha's head with unveiled contempt. Matt knew only too well what he was contemplating. Could he get away with murdering the human who had, quite literally, stepped on his toes and denied him his reckoning?

"He doesn't want to play your stupid little game," Caspar hissed. "He wants to play my game."

That was not a tone to take with Samantha. To Matt's dismay, she whirled around and unknowingly faced-off with a demon who could snap her neck in one quick move. "Who do you think you are? You come here uninvited, you hurt an innocent creature, and provoke your little brother. At. His. Birthday Party!"

Matt had never quite seen this side of Samantha, and he was simply in awe. Until the very next second, when Caspar's face darkened, and the veins in his stocky neck pulsed. "Come with me." Matt grabbed Samantha with an iron grip and dragged her into his bedroom. With one last glance, he saw Menuha hurrying to Caspar's side. He shut the door and let Crumbs go.

"What was that about?" Samantha looked at him in confusion.

Matt bit his lip. He very nearly told her how he'd just saved her life. But saying that would mean explaining to her that Caspar was a demon, and that this made him, Matt, a half-demon. And then she would hate him. With his demon family crashing his birthday party and the debilitating headaches, he couldn't also cope with *that* today. No, he needed Samantha. Needed her now more than anything.

"I was just trying to diffuse the situation," he answered vaguely, then dropped himself on his bed and ran his hands over his face.

"By removing me from it," Samantha said in a slightly sarcastic tone. She came closer and sat on the edge of his bed, her knee so close to his Matt sensed her presence. "I'm sorry that your party is a bit of a bust."

Matt covered his eyes with his left arm so he wouldn't be tempted to see her. And sit up. And kiss her. He wanted to kiss her as much as he had wanted to kill Caspar. Wanted it so much his head felt like exploding. Or perhaps that was just the headache. "It's not your fault."

"Well, you definitely weren't joking about how much your brother hates you."

"I don't particularly like him either," Matt muttered. But his anger was slowly subsiding in her presence.

Samantha scoffed. "Yeah, I noticed that. You never said your family was coming. Do you know why he's here?"

"Probably because Menuha dragged him along. She sees the good in everyone. Even him." Matt wasn't particularly invested in talking about his siblings, but if it kept him from thinking too much about the fact that he was in his room alone with Samantha—on his bed even—he would keep going.

"Menuha seems nice."

A stabbing pain pressed right behind his ears. "I like her, too, but she's too attached to Caspar, and I can really do without him."

"And your other brother? Balthasar? He seems to be okay."

Balthasar, okay? Never. "Don't fall into his trap! He's a conniving, manipulative, backstabbing liar." Where Caspar was all brawn, Balthasar was the brain. Sure, he easily pulled off the calm, mature elder brother, but he hadn't survived almost a thousand years and climbed the career ladder without his fair share of crimes. Not that anything was a crime in Hell. Not even fratricide.

Matt heard Samantha taking a deep breath. She was probably at the end of her rope with him. "You're quite irritated today. We're all a bit worried."

"It's the headache," Matt muttered, clamping his teeth against the pain.

"Still? I thought you took an aspirin." It was what she'd advised him to do when she'd first checked on him in the bathroom. It hadn't even taken off the sting.

"They're getting worse. My head is *this* short of exploding." He really wasn't sure how much more he could take.

And then he felt her hand patting his thigh like he would sometimes pat Crumbs' head. Only this was Samantha, and she was touching him. A red flash of pain stabbed right through him, and he sat up, wrapping his arms around her from behind. Underneath the weight of his chin, her shoulders bunched up, and Matt heard a delicious little gasp. Samantha held her breath, and he saw the vein on her neck pulsing rapidly. His lips almost touching her skin, he said, "You're the only good thing at this party. I was afraid you'd let me down."

She'd let him down so many times in the last month. Just when he'd thought she was his, she'd turned around and fallen in love with Daniel. Silly, stupid Daniel. He wasn't terribly smart, nor strong. He didn't even look good.

"Why would you think that? I promised I'd plan this party for you. I spent all morning in the kitchen." She had taken her hand away, her entire body stiff as a board.

"The food is delicious." It truly was, but Matt could think of something even more delicious he would like a taste of right now. His breath painted a trace along her neck.

Samantha put both her hands on his arms, and he knew what she was planning to do. He wasn't quite sure if he would let her. He should, but not doing so eased the pain in his head. "Shall we go and eat some more, then?"

"I'd rather stay here with you." His lips were practically touching her skin.

She managed to wriggle herself out of his embrace and stood up. It'd probably cost everything in her repertoire not to slap him at this stage. "This is your birthday party. You can't hide in your room."

She should have slapped him. Instead, Matt grabbed her wrist and pulled her, so she landed on his lap, forced to lean into him. "What if I want to? It's my birthday, so shouldn't I get what I want?" Why was he talking like that? Samantha didn't want him. She'd chosen Daniel, and he should accept that and move on to the next.

"Matt!" Samantha looked at him sternly, her voice like iron, giving up all pretence. "Let me go."

"So you can run back to Daniel?" The words kept jumping out of his mouth, driven by this insane pain in his head and its echo deep inside his chest. "Why, Sam? Why did you choose him? And don't deny that there was something between us. That I was *only a friend,*" he hissed and snarled at her for good measure.

Samantha's mouth opened and shut. Her cheeks turned pink, but then anger flashed in her eyes. "Because you make out with someone new every day. How am I supposed to know that there's more behind your flirting than with any of your other thousand conquests?"

"Maybe because... because..." What was he supposed to tell her? She was absolutely right. Matt had never made a secret of what he was looking for, and more importantly, what he *wasn't* looking for. He prided himself on not forming those stupid little attachments humans were so obsessed with. They curbed and limited their desires for some lofty idea that rarely ever became real. Love. Love was a fabrication, one of humanity's many shackles, when most of them just wanted sex. *He* certainly just wanted sex. Until... until he got to know Samantha. "Because you're not like any of the other thousand." And with that, he finally let go of her.

Samantha stared at him. For at least five seconds, she simply stared at him. Then she slowly stood, her gaze still locked with his. "I..." She inched towards the door. "I'm going to get something for your headache." As if suddenly put into fast-forward mode, she was through the door and out of his room in seconds.

Matt fell back on his bed, pressing his fists against his temples as the pain robbed him of his sanity. She'd left. She'd simply left him. Fled really. And he knew she was absolutely right to do so. With this pain and rage building up behind it, he wasn't sure he was in full control of his feelings tonight. Bah, feelings. He shouldn't even *have* feelings. He'd never bothered with them in Hell.

And perhaps it wasn't feelings he needed to worry about tonight, but the actions that might emerge from them.

If the headache didn't kill him first.

Samantha

Samantha left Matt's room in a daze. Why was he saying this to her now? They'd spent weeks fooling around, and he'd never once indicated that he was interested in more than that, instead of just being his usual charming self. And now this.

Because you're not like any of the other thousand.

It had to be a turn of phrase. It had to be. He couldn't possibly mean it. Samantha knew enough about herself and how people perceived her to understand that she wasn't the kind of girl who could turn a player into a serious boyfriend. If she even so much as dreamed of that, Cheryl would quickly bring her back to reality. No, it must've been one of Matt's go-to lines. When he didn't get what he wanted, he told a girl—or anyone, really—that he had only ever wanted them.

And now he'd done it to her. Fully aware that she had a boyfriend whom she was very much in love with. Samantha hadn't been cruel. She'd been aware that Matt was interested in her, but how was she supposed to trust him? It wasn't as if she hadn't been affected at all. That day, with the snow, she'd almost been ready to throw all caution to the wind and let him break her heart, as she was sure he would. But then there had been Daniel. Who was also charming, who made her laugh, and who wasn't a serial dater. He was honest and good, and how could she not have been swept away by him?

But now Matt's words tormented her with those dreadful "what if?" questions that would eat her alive. She needed time to think and some fresh air. And so, Samantha found herself in the corridor putting on her shoes, when Daniel approached her.

"Hey, are you okay?" he asked, and her determination began to waver under his concern.

"Yes... uhm, no. Actually, it's Matt, he..." She couldn't tell her boyfriend what he'd said. Not now, anyway, when she hadn't had any time to sort out her feelings. "He's got a terrible headache, so I'm going to get him something." That was actually a good plan. Matt shouldn't have to suffer from a splitting headache on his birthday, and she would have some time for herself to contemplate what his words meant. It might very well be the cause of his strange behaviour. This aggressiveness he'd shown towards his family and even her.

Daniel frowned. "You want to look for a pharmacy now? It's the middle of the night. New Year's Eve night."

A valid point, but Samantha didn't go to pharmacies for something as simple as a headache. "I've got a brew at home that might be a bit more potent."

To her dismay, he bent down to pick up his own shoes. "I'll come with you."

Her heart went out to him. He was only here because they'd wanted to celebrate the New Year together. Her friends had welcomed him well enough, but Matt... Matt had made no secret out of his animosity. Thinking of Matt... "I need a few minutes to myself." She truly, desperately needed them.

Daniel paused, his face showing signs of torment. But he swallowed and nodded. "Very well. Just take care and be back soon."

"Thank you." Samantha leaned forward and kissed him gently on the lips. The tender touch eased something inside of her, and when she let go of him, she felt a bit more certain that things would be alright. She would figure this out, clear things up with Matt, and be happy with Daniel.

\#

The long walk in the crisp winter air had cleared Samantha's head. By the time she had retrieved the potion from her secret stash in her wardrobe, she had a plan. Matt had simply missed his chance. With all his history, she wasn't sure what it would've taken for her to take a chance on him, but he hadn't even tried. He must've simply thought that she would fall under his spell like everybody else. Well, Samantha wasn't like everybody else, in all the good and bad ways that the turn of phrase suggested. She'd been an outsider for most of her teenage years, used to being ostracised because she didn't like parties and make-up, and was instead interested in books and witchcraft. She'd prided herself on that, even if it only meant numbing the pain of not belonging.

All of that had changed this year. Her friendship with Lucille had disproved all the lies Cheryl had whispered into her ears for years, and which she'd subsequently told herself. And with their little group of friends practically doubling—each and every one believing that magic was real—she had a place in the world now. And it had made her bolder, more sure of herself, and less willing to please everyone if it hurt her. And pleasing Matt most definitely would hurt the good thing she had with Daniel.

Samantha wanted to remain friends, and she fully believed that once Matt got over her, he'd be back to sleeping with whoever crossed his way. He simply had to accept that he didn't always get what he wanted, and that a girl could prefer someone else over him.

She left home with a promise to Meg that she'd send Jan past the house after midnight, and was now on the way back. This time, she took her bike to cut down the time, but she'd barely made it ten minutes in when her phone rang. Daniel.

Wondering what Matt had done now, she started pushing her bike and took the call. "Hey."

"Hey. Are you still on the way?" He sounded tense.

"Do you miss me already?" She hoped he wouldn't ask her to leave the party with him.

"Painfully so," Daniel admitted.

Her heart soared a little. She was starting to miss him too, her alone time sufficiently filled. "I'll be about ten minutes unless I have to push. It's been snowing *again*."

He didn't reciprocate her playful tone. "Be careful, okay? I don't want to make you nervous, but the police have put out a warning."

Startled, Samantha stopped. "What? Why?"

Daniel sighed heavily. "There have been three murders."

Samantha's stomach grew cold.

"You know what? Just knock on someone's door and ask them if they can drive you or stay there." Daniel's voice grew more and more agitated. "Please."

"I'm almost there." What would be the chances she'd cross the murderer's path? That he would murder her? "Ten minutes." But her heart pounded in her chest.

"Be careful."

"I will."

Her hands were shaking when she got back on her bike. It was eerily quiet in the streets, not a soul outside. Samantha rode as fast as she dared on the slippery street, singing softly to keep her own fear in check.

She'd reached the big crossing five minutes from Matt's flat when she heard a loud snap. The sound startled her so much she tore the handlebar around. Samantha lost complete control of the bicycle as it slipped on an icy patch. She barely managed to jump off and stumble back, landing in a snowdrift on the sidewalk. The bicycle slid into the middle of the road and remained lying there.

Samantha took a deep breath to calm her racing heart when a winged shadow fell on her bicycle. Her eyes shot to the opposite corner, and what she saw there twisted her stomach so violently, she tasted the sourness of bile. An old woman was lying dead in her own blood. She looked back at the shadow. It was a young man with midnight-black hair, a pretty but cruel face, and a set of clawed, bat-like leather wings.

A demon.

His eyes locked on hers, and she almost forgot to breathe as he started walking towards her. He stepped onto her bicycle, the metal screeching under his weight.

Samantha got into motion quickly. She wouldn't just wait here, staring at him while he murdered her too. Instead, she jumped up and grabbed her phone. Only, her phone wasn't in her pocket. Panicked, she cast around until she found it lying two metres from her position. It must've fallen in the snow when she'd jumped off the bike.

She scrambled after it, when a shot of black energy hit the phone and destroyed it in front of her fingers. Screaming, Samantha jumped back. Her eyes fell on the demon who had almost reached her, a sadistic smile twisting his lips. Panicked, she retreated until she felt a wall in her back.

Before she could lunge to the side, the demon reached her, pressing so close she was unable to move even a centimetre.

Her heart thumped in her throat. Her entire body was shaking. She wet her lips again and again as her mind scrambled for a way out of this. The demon took her in with a slow, deliberate gaze. Then he hooked a finger under her chin and raised it.

"I shall make this quick, okay?" His silky rich voice reminded her of someone. But mostly, it scared her in the most instinctive way, as if something in her brain recognised this as a human predator.

He leaned in. Samantha felt like passing out as she struggled to breathe when the sound of sirens in the distance startled her.

The demon heard it too, his attention slipping for a moment. Samantha's self-preservation kicked in. She pushed him away from her, twisted her body out of the trap, and ran, never minding her bike.

Behind her, the demon laughed. "I'll get you sooner or later," he called, then there was a swoosh of wings as he took off.

Samantha sprinted harder than she'd ever thought possible. Her feet slipped and slid on the icy patches in the road, and she twisted her legs painfully to keep from falling. At the next corner, she changed directions, almost stumbling over a hydrant in her panic. She kept up the pace until she ran into someone. Screaming, she flailed and kicked, but it was all for nothing. The man gripped her wrists and drew her close until she was pressed against his body.

His voice was soft and gentle. "Sam, stop. It's me."

Through the fog in her eyes, her vision was blurred at first, but then his shape fell into place. "Matt!" With a terrified squeal, she wrapped her arms around his neck and burst into tears.

Matt was with her. She was no longer alone. She was safe now.

"You've got a mean right hook, you know?" he whispered as he hesitantly stroked her hair.

Samantha pulled back her head a little and found his cheek had darkened slightly. "There was..." Tears ran down her throat, choking the words. "There was a demon."

"A demon? Are you sure about that?"

"He killed someone, and... we need to call the police!"

Matt frowned slightly. "The police can't take care of a demon." When she wanted to protest, he took her hand. "Let's go home first. We can still call the police and discuss what to do about the demon once you're safe."

"O-okay." Now that the adrenaline had left her body, Samantha felt all the little stabs of pain and sheer exhaustion. "You're right." She noticed the bruise on his cheek was already receding. "You're healing."

"Or you didn't hit as hard as I thought." He winced. "I wish I was able to say the same about my headache."

It reminded her of why she was out here in the first place. "I've got something for you." She reached into her other pocket and found the potion bottle unharmed. "This should help."

Matt took it off her in surprise. "You really went and got this for me?"

"Nobody should have a headache on their birthday." Samantha bit her lip. It wasn't the full truth, and she remembered why she had needed fresh air originally. "Matt..."

He glanced at her, and must've guessed what she was thinking, because his shoulders dropped. "I know. You're with Daniel now, and he's a sweet guy or whatever. I... I just need a little time to get used to it."

It was more than Samantha had expected, which led to her own apology. "I'm really sorry. If I'd known how you really felt..."

Matt pulled away from her and pushed his hands into his pockets. "But you didn't. And you were right. Who knew how long the fascination would've lasted?"

"Fascination?" Samantha asked, slightly amused. "Aren't there much better candidates for you to be fascinated with?"

She almost wished she could bite off her own tongue when Matt looked at her, so clearly pained. "No. Not really." He cleared his throat and quickly took a sip from the potion before she had a chance to react. "That's not too bad."

He kept drinking little sips, clearly avoiding her. Samantha let him and stewed in her own thoughts, somehow returning to point zero. If there hadn't been a murderous demon on the prowl, she would've needed more fresh air.

Lucille

Lucille was trying her very best to keep the party going, but even her substantial entertainment skills were tested by the weird tension in the room. Everybody seemed on edge, as if they were all just waiting for what would happen next. And Samantha and Matt were still missing. Ever since the news about the murders broke—thanks to Daniel reading the news when he could've been playing Lucille's party games instead—they'd all been holding their breath. If anyone could bring Samantha home safely, it was Matt. Even though it had taken Lucille all her diplomatic prowess to convince Daniel of that.

Now she feared she had given him the impression that they all preferred Samantha with Matt, which was absolutely not true. Lucille loved Daniel for Samantha. Her friend looked so happy with him.

Currently, he was sitting alone on the sofa, watching Fabian, Rachel, Jan, and her entertain themselves by playing with Crumbs. Lucille was about to invite him into their group when she saw Matt's mother sit down next to him. One arm snaked around Daniel's shoulder, while her other traced the shape of his arm and his thigh.

Lucille squinted as she witnessed the strange behaviour. Daniel leaned slightly away from the woman, but he was sitting on the edge and had nowhere to go. Matt's mother didn't seem to know any shame. The dance her fingertips performed brought her closer and closer towards Daniel's lap, and her sultry whisper was such a low frequency, even Lucille felt aroused by it. "Where did your little girlfriend go?"

"Away," Daniel gasped. His eyes were now locked on the opposite wall with sheer willpower to avoid looking sideways.

"I saw that. Tell me," Matt's mother breathed into his neck, "is she good?"

Was Samantha good? What kind of question was that? She couldn't possibly mean what Lucille thought. Who would ask that about someone's girlfriend? Whose *mother* would ask that?

To say Matt's family had been a surprise to them was a gross understatement. Lucille should've guessed that his mother was gorgeous, what with Matt's own good looks, but she was breathtakingly so. And not just gorgeous. She carried an air around her that promised something dark and delicious. Something depraved. Something Matt's *mother* shouldn't promise.

And she certainly shouldn't promise it to Daniel, who had stiffened now. His eyes were bulging as embarrassment crept into his cheeks.

The man needed help, and Lucille would provide it. "Who wants to play *Spin the Bottle?*" Almost instantly, she rolled her eyes at herself. *Spin the Bottle* would certainly not diffuse the sexual tension in this room.

"I'm in," Daniel said immediately and plopped himself down next to her, before muttering under his breath, "Thank you."

To Lucille's surprise, Matt's siblings Balthasar and Menuha came down to play with them as well. His other brother, Caspar, looked utterly disgusted with the suggestion, and Chay kept checking his watch. Matt's mother showed a quick flash of anger before she stood abruptly and stalked off into the kitchen.

"How does this game work?" Balthasar asked, balancing the bottle on his fingertip. Like Matt, he was a beautiful man, though his colouring took more after their mother. Only his eyes were different. They were green with flecks of gold, Lucille noticed, staring for way too long into them.

She cleared her throat and took the bottle from him. "It's quite simple. You spin the bottle, and the person it points to has to fulfil a little dare."

As Lucille had spun it already without formulating the dare in her haste to avoid looking at Balthasar, it landed on Fabian without instructions. That suited Lucille just fine. After all, she had to make up for a particularly disastrous date. "Fabian, I want you to give your girlfriend a passionate kiss."

"Lucille!" Rachel protested, before looking flustered at Fabian.

"Interesting," Balthasar mused softly, driving the heat into Lucille's cheeks.

"Come on, you two," Jan urged. "You're not twelve anymore."

Fabian huffed in indignation. "But... Fine!" He grabbed Rachel's face with two hands and kissed her until she gasped for breath.

Jan cheered and pumped his fist into the air, while Lucille grinned. Rachel's cheeks were flushed. She turned back to the game when Fabian pulled her onto his lap and kissed her yet again with a passion Lucille would've never thought him capable of. Rachel kissed him back, and to everyone's surprise, her hands slid under his pullover.

Lucille's and Jan's eyes met, and they both laughed. "Hey, you two, you don't need to take it too far."

Startled, Fabian let go of Rachel, his face beet-red. "Sorry. I-I need a drink." And with that, he hastily got to his feet and ran into the bathroom. Lucille decided she didn't want to know why he had to grab a drink from there if they had a perfectly welcoming selection on the table.

In the meantime, Balthasar had moved closer, the heat of his body impossible to ignore. "Why did you stop them?"

"Uhm..." For a moment, Lucille's mind was completely empty. Why *had* she stopped them? She looked at the bottle and found her voice again. "Because of the game. Everyone else wants a turn as well, right?"

But Fabian wasn't there to spin the bottle. Instead, Balthasar took it, decidedly *didn't* spin it, and pointed it at Lucille instead. "Okay, kiss me then."

Lucille was about to point out that the game wasn't just about kisses—when truly it was—but there was something in Balthasar's eyes that captivated her. He carried that same dark, delicious promise as his mother, only he was young and available and... very handsome indeed. Surely, it wouldn't hurt if she gave him a quick peck on the lips.

She leaned forward to do just that, but when her lips brushed his, it wasn't enough. They were so incredibly soft yet demanding. She wanted more of it. His hand slipped into her neck, pulling her closer into him as he opened her lips with his tongue. Lucille could tell he was an experienced kisser. Heat filled her from head to toe, and she very nearly forgot to breathe. Her entire body melted under his touch.

When he let go of her, the room was spinning. Then he leaned into her and kissed her just below the ear, before his hot breath brushed her skin. "Let me know when you're done playing games."

He got up in one swift movement and sauntered back to the table where his brother welcomed him with a sneer. "That was disgusting."

Somehow, Lucille knew he wasn't referring to Balthasar coaxing that kiss out of her and every bit to his brother having kissed *her*. The realisation cut through the dizziness and helped her centre herself. It wasn't every day that a de Cerque wasn't good enough for anyone. If only the kiss hadn't been that amazing.

It was impossible to meet anybody's eyes for at least a minute.

"Whatever you do, do not go into the kitchen." Fabian sat down, his face as red as it had been when he'd left.

"Why not?" Jan grabbed the bottle to balance it on its neck.

Fabian closed his eyes and shuddered. "Let's just say Matt's parents are reconnecting."

The bottle toppled as Jan scrambled for it. His eyes shot to the *open* kitchen door and back again. "Right now? Ew!"

Now that Lucille knew what to listen for, she could hear it. And she knew exactly what Fabian had stumbled on.

"Why is it 'ew'?" The five of them had all but forgotten that Menuha was still sitting with them. Her question was asked with such innocence, it was almost impossible to believe she was related to her family.

"Well..." Daniel started but couldn't quite find the words.

They were saved by the door and the sound of Samantha and Matt taking off their shoes. Daniel got up and made it halfway through the room before Samantha fell into his arms and hid her face in his chest, her shoulders bunching suspiciously.

Daniel held her close and whispered, "Are you okay?" Then he scowled at Matt.

Matt only shrugged, cranking up his cockiness to the maximum. "Was a good idea that I went to get her."

"It's alright," Samantha answered, her voice shaking. "My cell phone is ruined and my bicycle's lying somewhere on the road, but I'm here. I'm fine."

"What happened?" Fabian asked.

They all got up, no longer able to keep up the pretence that today was anything but a normal day.

"I'll tell you later," Samantha whispered, which served only to put Lucille on high alert. "Tell you later" meant there was a monster on the loose. Something they had to keep secret from the other guests at the party.

But the other guests didn't think so. Caspar had finally left his seat at the table, a little smile playing on his lips. "Did you find your bloodthirsty killer?"

"Why? Is that one of yours?" Matt shot back immediately. When Caspar started smirking, he lost the shred of cool he'd been trying to maintain and clenched his fists. "What's so funny about it?"

"Everything, my dear brother. Everything."

Matt pushed forward until he stood nose to nose with Caspar. "I'm not your *dear* brother or anything."

"If only that were true," Caspar retorted. His face had darkened, the amusement gone in a flash. Any minute, the two of them would come to blows.

Lucille glanced at the clock. It was almost twelve. She would not have these two bash their heads in when they could all have a celebration. "Stop this, you two."

They both ignored her. Matt grabbed Caspar by the collar, effectively snarling.

His brother only sneered. "Finally! But don't go crying to Mummy when your headaches worsen."

To the left of her, Lucille could hear Chay mutter, "I wouldn't be surprised if Caspar ended up with a headache tonight."

Neither one of them should have a headache, Lucille decided. With one minute to midnight, she strode over to the champagne bottle and ripped it from the cooler. Matt pulled Caspar even closer, his usually warm-brown eyes almost black. Caspar bared his teeth.

Pop.

The cork flew from the bottle, hit the ceiling, and fell on the table. Bubbly champagne poured over Lucille's hands about ten seconds early.

It had worked, however. Everyone was staring at her. Even the two brothers had let go of each other. "Happy New Year!" Lucille said with three seconds to spare.

As the clock ticked over into the next day, she only hoped that she hadn't just cursed the brand-new year.

Matt

"Happy New Year!"

"Happy birthday!"

Matt had no idea what was happening. One minute ago, he'd been ready to show Caspar the door. The next, he'd been through more hugs than he could register. The first thing that became clear through the daze was Daniel and Samantha lost in a kiss. Seeing them made his head hurt worse, so he turned away and saw his father exiting the kitchen while tucking his shirt back into his pants.

"I don't even want to know," Matt muttered, mostly because he already knew perfectly well what the cause of René's dishevelled appearance was.

René had a silly little grin on his face and scoffed. Then he pulled Matt into a hug. "Happy birthday, big boy."

"Yeah, yeah, whatever," Caspar muttered. "Is it time for presents now?"

Matt certainly *didn't* want any of Caspar's presents, but Lucille didn't know that. "Yes! Just a second." She ran off to get whatever it was she'd been preparing.

Meanwhile, Caspar pushed an elegant little box into Matt's hands. "Enjoy."

Curiosity won out over better judgement, and Matt opened the box a tiny bit. The moment he saw something wriggling, he shut it again and handed it over to Chay. "Get rid of this, please." He was so angry at Caspar he hadn't even had time to freeze. "I hate you."

"I hate you, too, little brother."

"What was in there?" Matt heard Jan asking.

"Probably worms," Samantha whispered, and then she was in front of Matt, hesitating to embrace him. "You okay?"

It physically hurt him that she was no longer secure enough in their relationship to hug him on his birthday, and he realised that it was his fault. "I'm fine."

Samantha half-raised her arm, and Matt stepped into the promise of the hug to get over the awkwardness. "Happy birthday, Matt." Her voice was like a balm to his soul, but he made sure not to hold on too long to her. A human tradition at New Year's was to make resolutions for a better self. And he decided that he wanted to do better by her.

And Daniel. The student only gave him a handshake along with congratulations, but Matt didn't even try to squash his hand as he thanked him. He thought he was doing splendidly so far.

Then Lucille was back with a gigantic basket, though he had no idea how it had made it up the stairs without him noticing. Perhaps one of Lucille's employees had delivered it just now. He certainly wouldn't put it past her.

"This is from all of us," she declared. "Half of it is probably for Crumbs, but I mean he's too cute." She handed the basket to Matt and bent down to the little puppy that was way overdue his sleep and stroked his fur. "So happy birthday, Crumbs, even if it's not your birthday."

Matt had absolutely no objection. He was spoiling the dog himself. There was so much in the basket he couldn't grasp all of it. Toys and special food for Crumbs, delicacies and candles from the Magic Circle. Self-made potions by Samantha. "A box of condoms?"

"You go through an awful lot," Jan joked, identifying himself as the one behind that particular present.

"There are eighteen presents in total," Samantha pointed out, her eyes sparkling. "One for every birthday."

Why, oh why did she have to be so thoughtful? Matt's heart longed for her, and his New Year's resolution was starting to weaken. "Thank you all," he said, swiftly looking at everybody else.

His mother had come out of the kitchen, not a single hair out of place. Contrary to his father, Melaney was perfection. Matt didn't like the sultry look she gave him. "What happens now? We go outside, right?"

Count on Jan to come through for him. "Yeah, absolutely! Let's go!"

Matt had never seen fireworks before. René had already informed him of this custom, and he'd seen a few videos to prepare himself, but nothing came close to the reality. Half an hour earlier, when he'd picked up Samantha, the streets had been deserted. Now everybody was outside, and the sky was on fire. There was an orchestra of bangs, whistling, and shrill sirens. Fabian and Jan set off the rockets that made colourful flowers bloom in the sky.

It was cold, but it was beautiful, and for the first time this night, Matt felt something like peace settle over him.

"Pretty, aren't they?" Lucille asked him. She was leaning against his arm. Whether in search of warmth or as an offer of companionship, Matt didn't know. "You should see the fireworks in Sydney. Or New York City."

"Show-off," Samantha teased her from her position in Daniel's arms. She certainly didn't have to freeze.

Lucille laughed at her. "Perhaps I'll take you all next year."

A phone went off, not the first one since midnight. As Matt noted, most of their families had called in to offer their congratulations. It was a nice custom, he thought.

This time, it was Jan's turn, but he frowned at the phone. "Who is this?" He took the call and his face fell. "Robert?" Bewildered as he was, he put their classmate on speaker.

"...just wanted to wish you a Happy New Year. I hope you're not outside."

"What the hell do you want from me? And how did you get my number?" Jan very nearly shouted.

Robert seemed unfazed. "Didn't you see the news? The police are looking for a bloodthirsty killer. If you ask me, they'll never find him. It's probably something supernatural again."

"And you're telling me this why?" It would have been funny if there wasn't truly a killer on the loose.

"Because I'm worried about you. You often party hard and might not have heard about it. I'm also going to call some others," Robert added hastily, as if he was trying to mask the fact he hadn't planned to do so a second ago.

Jan groaned. "Good night, Robert. Stop annoying good people and go to sleep!" He broke off the call and shook his head. "He's such a weirdo. I'm telling you—he's obsessed with me."

"Did he call about the demon?" Samantha asked softly.

Not softly enough, because Fabian picked it up and immediately blanched. "Demon? Please don't say it's that asshole again. What does he want from us?"

"It wasn't *him*." Samantha sighed. "I met this demon on my way back, before I ran into Matt."

Daniel turned her around, his face full of worry. "Did he hurt you?"

"No. He planned to, but I managed to escape."

"So, this murderer is truly a demon on a rampage?" Lucille asked. When Samantha nodded, she shrugged. "Looks like we've got our first job this year."

Fabian protested instantly. "Are you mad? It's New Year!"

"But the police won't know what hit them," Rachel said, sliding her hand into his. "They can't handle a demon."

"And you can?" Caspar had kept to the back with Balthasar, Menuha, and Chay, but he was stepping closer now, drawn in like a moth to the flame.

"Better than you think," Matt heard Chay mumble.

Fabian groaned in dismay. "I don't want to fight a demon again. It was horrible. Disastrous. I don't want to die on New Year!"

"We have to do something." Lucille took charge, having no patience for Fabian's sensibilities. "Samantha, you've seen this demon. Can you tell us what he looked like?"

"Uhm, he had black hair, dark eyes, and the same bat-like wings as the other one. He was much younger though and…" She suddenly blushed. "I mean, ignoring the fact that I was scared for my life, he was quite attractive." Hastily, she added, "In a predatory way. Like a lion is very pretty and will still very much kill you."

"I can't believe you'd notice that," Daniel muttered.

Matt was inexplicably pleased to learn that apparently Samantha hadn't fallen under Daniel's spell completely yet. "Save those complexes for later. We need to hunt a demon."

Behind him, Caspar burst into laughter. Matt's fingers itched, but he didn't turn. His brother probably found it hilarious that they'd go demon hunting after partying with the four of them through the night.

"Ignore him," Lucille said, throwing a deliciously dark glare at Caspar. "What's the plan? Split?"

"You've never seen a horror movie, right?" Fabian muttered.

"More than you!" Lucille shot back. "And I actually *saw* them."

Matt had no idea what they were on about, but he was eager to get hunting. His whole body was longing for the fight. This was the perfect opportunity to let off some steam. No one would complain if he took out a demon. "We need to find him first, so yeah, let's split up." He caught Daniel's worried look and snorted. "No, I'm not taking your Samantha away. You can take the south."

"I'll go with them," Jan declared. "They'll need help." Considering that Samantha was unarmed and Daniel utterly useless, it was a good idea.

"Sure, just call us as soon as you see anything." Matt turned to Fabian and Rachel and lowered his voice. "I want you to stay here with my family. Keep an eye on Caspar." The description didn't fit him, but Matt wouldn't put it past him to go onto his own killing spree.

Both of them looked confused. "Why?"

"Just do it. Lucille, you're with me." He would've preferred Fabian, but despite his whining, he was the only one Matt trusted to keep Caspar in check. At least for a little bit.

Their plan made, Matt turned to leave when Chay stepped into his way. "Matt. Perhaps you should sit this one out. Go back inside, or home."

There was no mistaking what Chay meant with home. A tiny voice inside of Matt whispered that he should listen. That listening to Chay was a survival strategy. But the headache made it impossible. He needed to punch someone. And if it couldn't be his brother, it had to be this demon. "We'll be back soon."

With midnight gone, the sky had stopped exploding. In a small town like Greenvalley, the action didn't last long. Matt and Lucille were walking through the park, so far unlucky with their search. The longer they went without encountering the demon, the more agitated Matt grew. The headache was so painful now, it made his vision go red. It had happened a few times this evening, but so far had passed after a few minutes. Now it was growing worse by the second.

"Sam's potion didn't work?" Lucille asked, taking note of his discomfort.

"Not really." It had done absolutely nothing, but Matt hadn't wanted to tell her that.

Lucille rubbed his back, a touch he found utterly grating in his current state. "Maybe you should see a doctor about it."

"Tomorrow." He needed something else. If only he knew what.

"What is going on with you?" Lucille stopped, the worry visible on her face.

Matt very nearly ripped her head off for not letting it go. "Nothing. I... It's just that the party wasn't what I hoped for." It had been a nightmare from Daniel's attendance to his ruined friendship with Samantha to his hated family's presence.

"Oh, come on," Lucille joked. "We even got a monster for you. You like monster hunting, don't you?"

A monster. If only she knew *he* was a monster. "Not like this. Not..."

There. Someone else was crossing their path. Or not really crossing their path, but nearby. A lonely figure, out for a midnight walk. "Wait here."

The pain became unbearable as he stalked away from Lucille. Then his vision turned completely red, and Matt cried out.

When it cleared again, he was on his knees, his hands covered in blood. Underneath him lay the bloodied corpse of a middle-aged man. And Matt finally understood.

Black hair, dark eyes, very attractive. Demon wings.

The wings whose weight was heavy on his back, balancing him in a way he'd never quite felt in his human form. Samantha had seen *him*. Melchior. His demon form.

"Matt?"

Lucille! She'd come running after him, her eyes wide, her face devoid of colour. Her breath caught in her throat, and Matt could taste her fear on the tip of his tongue. The red encroached on his vision. The pain that had eased a little after the kill came back tenfold. And she was so close.

With his last shred of humanity to cling to, Matt hauled himself away from her.

Fabian

Fabian should have been elated to sit out on a demon hunt. But sitting upstairs with Matt's weird family was somehow worse. Akin to sitting in a lion's den. He and Rachel played cards, trying their hardest to ignore everyone else. It was impossible. Matt's father was pacing the flat, pretending to tidy, and Chay seemed to grow more morose by the minute. Matt's siblings were surprisingly quiet, not even bored, as if they were just waiting for the right moment to spring into action.

And Fabian did not want to know what Matt's mother was doing in his bedroom. He'd made the mistake once of walking into a room she was in, and he didn't care to repeat it. The image of his elementary school teacher's bare backside while her legs wrapped around him on the kitchen table was more than enough to give him nightmares. Not even hearing his parents getting it on had had this effect.

He shuddered, annoyingly aroused, while utterly disgusted at the same time. Rachel raised her eyebrows, but he shook his head. He couldn't possibly discuss this with her. They hadn't even gotten close yet.

His phone rang, cutting through the silence. One glance at the display told him it was Lucille, and he almost sighed with relief. "What's up? Did you get him?"

"No," she gasped and then sobbed terribly.

Fabian's blood ran cold. He quickly did the mental exercise of remembering who had gone with whom. "Did something happen to Matt?"

"Matt..." More sobs. "Fabian, he's..." Lucille gasped for air. "Oh god, I can't... Fabian, it's him. He..."

He still had no idea what she meant. Or rather, he hoped it wasn't what he thought. Matt couldn't be... They'd just been celebrating his birthday. "Where are—?"

"He's the demon."

For a moment, the world stood still, not a sound to be heard. Then the words dropped, one by one. *He's. The. Demon.* "Matt is a demon?"

"He's actually just a half-demon," Caspar's slow drawl snaked up on him. "His father is obviously human." The disgust in his voice was palpable as he regarded René, who'd gone rigid.

Fabian's mouth was suddenly dry. Every fibre of his being was on edge. He knew deep inside his core that his next move might be his last. "Uhm, Lucille? I'll call you back later."

"No, Fabian!" she screamed. "Don't—"

He pressed the call away and let his hand sink, unable to break eye contact with Matt's hateful *half*-brother.

"They're all demons, right?" Rachel breathed.

Unable to answer, Fabian swallowed. Everyone in the room seemed to have transformed. They still looked the same, but they no longer felt the same. Caspar's intense glare, an unspoken fury burning in his eyes. Balthasar's unsettling calm, as if nothing could faze him. Even Menuha's friendliness seemed to be nothing more than a sickly sweet trap.

"You don't need to be afraid," Chay muttered, the sadness weighing heavily on his shoulders. "None of you are going to die tonight."

"Says who?" Caspar snarled.

And before Fabian could so much as register that Chay might have seen the future, Caspar was in front of him, grabbed him by the neck, and smashed him into the wall. Pain exploded in the back of his head, but it was nothing compared to the one in his lungs as he fought for his next breath. Caspar's fingers dug into his neck as if he was going to rip Fabian's throat out.

"Fabian, here!"

He glanced to the side as Caspar's grip lessened slightly. Rachel had ripped the flowers from the vase and held the vessel towards him. Caspar was confused, but Fabian stared at the wonderful, inviting water that sloshed inside.

The stream of water hit Caspar in the chest and pushed him away from Fabian with such force he rammed into the table, nearly cracking his head. The immediate threat removed, Fabian sank to his knees and coughed. It still felt as if someone was squeezing his throat. Over at the table, he heard Balthasar laughing. Not cruelly, but like he was having a grand old time.

"Told you so," Chay muttered.

"I will kill you." Caspar was back on his feet, completely unharmed by Fabian's attack. If the fire in his eyes had been intense before, it was hot enough to burn down the house now.

A portentous click sounded, and the demon stood still. His gaze moved to the side, following René's steps as he put himself between Fabian and Rachel, and Caspar. Fabian knew what kind of weapon was in René's hand.

"Not in my house." The entire evening, René had been somewhat flustered, like a fish out of water. Now his voice was cold steel. Fabian had no doubt that René would pull the trigger on the gun.

"You never told us his father was a demon hunter," Balthasar commented drily.

Matt's mother must've emerged from the bedroom when the fighting had begun. "As far as I'm aware, he left his training unfinished." Her voice took a mocking turn. "For me."

"Well, I'm gonna kill him, too, then," Caspar snarled.

Fabian swallowed heavily. René was good, but the demon lady had just told them all he'd never finished his education. And when they'd fought against the other demon, he hadn't been able to defeat him either. Now they were up against four demons and whatever Chay was, and whomever he sided with.

"Don't." The gentle voice could only belong to Matt's sister. "We're guests here."

Did that mean anything to demons? Fabian wondered, but he was happy for her to take charge. And truly, Caspar must've had a soft spot for her, because he grunted and returned to his seat. Fabian knew he'd escaped with his life by the breadth of a hair.

Rachel sank into him, also shuddering with relief. "What do we do now?"

"We call Lucille back."

Jan

The demon hunt was a bust, but the night had turned out rather well, regardless. Jan had left Samantha and Daniel to enjoy some quiet time, while he made a little detour to visit his girlfriend. Meg had managed to sneak him into her room, and they'd welcomed the new year with cuddles and kisses. Now she was sleeping soundly while he lay fully dressed on her bed, feeling utterly content.

His phone vibrated. Jan carefully extracted his arm from under Meg and withdrew to the far end of the bed before taking Fabian's call. He kept his voice low. "Hey. Sorry, I got a little distracted."

"Is Matt with you?" Fabian asked, his voice also quite low.

"Nah, he's out with Lu. Don't you remember?"

"Not anymore." Fabian sighed. "Listen, we're all meeting at his flat. It's important, okay?"

Jan looked down at Meg's sleeping form. He had to leave anyway if he wanted to avoid detection by her parents. "Sure." Softly, he got up and crept towards the door. "I'll just pick up Sam and Daniel."

If he'd known what an effect his words would've had, he would've never admitted to splitting up. "You're not with Sam?" Fabian asked loudly.

"I am... I mean, theoretically." Her parents were fortunately asleep, and so he made it to the ground floor without a hitch. "I'm technically at her place. She's just still outside." He slipped out of the house and gently closed the door behind him. "And now I am too."

Fabian groaned. "Oh man, Jan. She can't defend herself against this monster! And Daniel's got nothing either."

"I love how protective you are of her, but Samantha is clever. She can do more than you think." In a fight between Fabian and Samantha, Jan would definitely bet on Meg's older sister.

"Not against this demon." Fabian's voice sounded extremely strained, as if he wanted to throw the phone at Jan. "Get here, pronto. And if possible, bring them with you."

Jan rolled his eyes, wondering what all the fuss was suddenly about. "Aye, aye."

Unfortunately, he had no means of contacting Samantha since her phone was broken, and the two weren't where Jan had left them. He searched for five minutes, calling their names, then gave up and returned to the worst birthday party known to humankind.

Jan had barely reached the Traidous flat when the door opened. Matt's father grabbed his arm and dragged him through the flat, past Matt's weirdo family, and into Matt's bedroom. To Jan's surprise, everyone else was here, even the dog.

Lu was on the bed, crying her eyes out, while Rachel awkwardly tried to comfort her. Fabian was pacing the bedroom, only stopping when the door closed behind René, who, for some reason, kept guard at the door, his demon-slaying weapon out for show. Matt's future-telling friend leaned against the wall, arms crossed.

"Where is Samantha?" Fabian asked in a tone as if he was accusing Jan of pushing his best friend in front of a car.

"Couldn't find her." Jan shrugged. He didn't see how he was responsible for someone as sensible as Samantha. "They seem to have wandered off. Don't you have Daniel's number?"

"Why would I have it?" Fabian hissed.

"Sit down." Despite his gentle demeanour, Chay carried a surprising authority in his voice.

Jan just didn't do well with authorities. He opened his mouth to protest, but Fabian tugged his arm, and disgruntled, Jan followed him to the bed, where Lu sniffled and tried to stop crying. She failed miserably.

"I know that you have a lot of questions," Chay started.

"I just want to know what's going on here!" Jan glared at him and then at his friends.

The glare was reciprocated by Fabian of all people. "Matt's the demon."

Lucille let out a squealing sob and broke apart once more in Rachel's embrace.

"Matt is *what*?" Jan must've misheard Fabian. Surely, Matt wasn't a demon, much less *the* demon.

"He's a half-demon," Chay explained. "Like me, since we're all sharing now."

Jan's back turned rigid. Did Matt's friend just casually confess to being a half-demon?

"Relax. I won't turn on you," Chay said, though he sounded exhausted as he did so. "I'm not so inclined."

"Why not?" whispered Rachel, as if there needed to be a reason. Jan was perfectly happy not to discuss why they weren't dead yet.

Chay waved the question away. "It doesn't matter. The important thing is that Matt is a half-demon. René is human, but his mother is a demon. In fact, Melaney is the Archdemon of Lust."

It must've been the overload of information, because Jan's brain only processed the last part. "That explains a lot."

Fabian jabbed his side hard.

"It does!" Jan protested. He'd always been baffled at how sex-crazy Matt was. Not that there was anything wrong with a healthy appetite during puberty, but Matt's success rate was extreme. Now that Jan knew his mother was *the* Archdemon of Lust—whatever that meant—it all made sense.

"In any case, his half-siblings are all demons. Not all of them are terribly powerful, but Balthasar and Caspar *are*." Jan's entire takeaway from Chay's explanation was that Matt had even more siblings. His mother must've kept very busy indeed. "The reason they're here has nothing to do with Matt's birthday. They couldn't care less about that, having had hundreds themselves. They're here because of his Blood Night."

"His Blood Night?" Lu had dried her tears, now listening closely.

Meanwhile, Rachel whispered, "I should've counted the candles."

"You had a dream?" Chay asked, mildly interested.

Rachel nodded. "Candles in a sea of blood. There were a lot, so I didn't count them, but I bet there were eighteen of them."

Creepy, Jan thought, but he knew better than to voice that aloud.

Chay breathed in, centring himself. For a half-demon, he had marvellous control. "The Blood Night refers to a point in time, though it's really a length in time, when a demon... comes of age. It usually isn't at eighteen, because eighteen-year-old demons have barely left the cradle, but half-demons mature like humans. It's still coincidence it happened today." He shook his head as if he remembered his own awakening. "During the Blood Night, the full potential of a demon awakens. Unfortunately, it is accompanied by an unquenchable thirst for blood, hence the name. Other demons regard a... *successful* night as a badge of honour, which is ridiculous, because if that were the case, Caspar over there would be scraping the bottom of the barrel. I am told his Blood Night was less than impressive."

He took a very deep breath. "In any case, it's horrible and terrifying, and half-demons experience it as well."

"Does that mean," Lu began carefully, "Matt isn't in control of himself?"

"Yes, that's right." The sadness in Chay's eyes deepened. "Which is why I want you to support him when he comes out of it. He'll need you when he wakes. My own Blood Night still haunts me to this day. When I woke from it, I wanted to die."

Jan took a shuddering breath at the reminder that the nice guy in front of them had killed at least one person in his horrifying Blood Night. And then he realised that Matt was already past the count of one. If, in fact, he really *was* the demon.

"So, Matt is being possessed by this demon," Fabian asked, "who forces him to kill other people?"

Next to him, Rachel shook her head, but it was Matt's father who answered, pain lacing his voice. "Matt is as much demon as he is human.

In fact, he's probably more demon, since he's spent most of his life in Hell."

"In Hell?" Fabian exclaimed in shock.

"It's where demons live," Chay explained. "Their world is officially called Hescaryn, but everyone around here calls it Hell."

Jan smacked his lips, trying to relieve some of the tension. "Sounds like a bad part of town to grow up in."

"It's quite literally Hell." Chay shook his head, relaxing ever so slightly. "Since Matt came to Greenvalley, he's developed his human side in leaps and bounds. And that's thanks to you. You're a good influence on him, and I would owe you if you continued the good work."

Fabian stared at him. "You want us to be friends with a demon?"

"Half-demon. That's an important distinction," Chay said sharply. "He has all the instincts of a demon, but he's got a human heart. The boy prowling the night right now isn't the one I've raised."

"What exactly are you to him?" Jan asked, still struggling to put all the information together. "You're not his father. A teacher? Another of his many siblings?"

"I'm his friend. And if you want to say so, his guardian. I took care of him when Melaney abandoned him for more interesting activities."

That was one way to put it. Jan couldn't help but feel sorry for Matt. He'd always known that something was different about him. Hell, he'd gotten awfully close with his random guesses. But imagining what it would be like growing up in a world that was all base instincts with no one to love or care for him, he found a new appreciation for Matt. He'd done well for someone with no human experience. Until tonight.

"He didn't want to hurt me," Lu whispered. "When he turned into his demon form... I was right there, but he looked at me... For a moment, I thought my time had come. There was so much blood... but he vanished. He didn't do it." She took a shuddering breath, and suddenly her shoulders were tighter, and her voice was stronger. "Chay is right. Our Matt is still in there. We need to stop him before he does any worse."

Jan thought they were already past that point if Matt had indeed killed several innocent people, but Chay looked as if he'd been invited to stay until Easter. "Thank you. Thanks for being his friends. I wish I'd had someone like that when I went through it."

"When did you go through it?" Fabian asked carefully, probably assessing how many years were needed to absolve someone from a murder—or several—in their youth.

"I wrote the book in Elda's library; it's been a while." Chay shrugged a little, then continued on. "Demons don't age like humans. They die only if killed. It's the same for half-demons."

Jan stared at him, then laughed. He didn't know what was so funny, but he couldn't help it. "That's a joke, right?" Chay's face was blank. "Are you saying we aren't truly celebrating Matt's eighteenth birthday?"

"Sure you are." René spoke up for the first time since he'd dragged Jan into the room. "I had a child young, but not *that* young."

"He's still young. You're still so young," Chay muttered, then breathed in. "I'm sorry, you'll have to carry this burden."

Fabian swallowed heavily. "Burden?"

"Matt," Chay answered after only a moment's hesitation. "He needs you. Now more than ever."

"What can we do?" asked Lu, suddenly eager to jump into action.

"First, we need to stop him," René said coolly. "I will not let him become some depraved monster."

Again, Jan held his tongue. Next to him, Fabian asked instead, "Stop Matt, okay. But what do we do with his just as dangerous family?" He nodded at the wall where a bunch of demons were idly sitting in the living room.

It was a good question, but Chay never got around to answer it, because in that moment, a terrible crash sounded from next door. Within seconds, they all pushed out of the door and into a brutal battle.

Matt's brother Caspar was rolling over the ground with an unfamiliar second demon. At first, Jan thought it was Balthasar since the demon had the same black hair, but the older brother was standing at the wall next to them, a wine glass in hand, and toasted Chay. "He's ambitious. I'll give him that."

"That's Matt?" Fabian whisper-hissed.

"Melchior," Chay corrected. "Matt is—"

"...the name I gave my son," René ended.

Caspar was bleeding from a head wound, but he barely seemed to notice. He held down Matt—or Melchior—with one hand, while black energy sizzled in his other. Before he could bring it down, Matt grasped his wrist and twisted it with a bone-crunching noise. The energy hit a picture on the wall and ripped it apart instead.

Menuha was trying to get in between the two, but she couldn't do so without getting hurt. His mother stood on the other side, her eyes glistening with delight while she watched her sons trying to kill each other.

"What are they doing?" Jan asked no one in particular.

Balthasar answered him. "Oh, just righting some old wrongs." He nodded to Chay with some appreciation. "Interesting choice to go after Caspar."

"He's half-demon," was Chay's confounding answer.

Jan had no idea what the two were talking about. Heck, he didn't even know whether it was safe to stand between a demon and a half-demon. Safer than between the other pair, though, he thought, as he ducked under a stray shot of energy.

Matt had got on top of Caspar and was punching him continuously. "That's for the firelake." The next punch broke Caspar's nose. "This is for the *riding lesson*." The bones crunched under his fist. "And this is for the hellworms."

"That sounds like a lot of wrongs," Fabian muttered.

"Shouldn't we do something?" Lu asked, before moving her lips as she went through her repertoire of spells.

Balthasar bowed to her. "Be my guest. I'd be interested to see what else you can do."

"Don't!" Melaney's glittering eyes found them. "I want to see who's the stronger one."

Meanwhile, Caspar had managed to grab Matt and throw him into the table, which broke in two under him. The flower vase crashed to the ground among a set of glasses, spraying shards and flowers everywhere. Caspar's nose righted itself with an equally sickening crunch, and his head wound had healed.

Matt jumped back to his feet and shot at Caspar, his energy ripping the couch apart.

"Matt!" René shouted, and Jan quickly braced himself for the inevitable attention he would draw.

But Matt ignored his father. He threw himself on Caspar, and just before the two hit the ground, they vanished.

"What just happened?" Lu asked.

"A jump through space. A sort of teleport all demons can do," Chay explained.

"I knew it!" Jan clenched his fist, then looked at the confused faces of the others. "Did you never think he always arrived awfully fast when you called him?"

Lu just rolled her eyes. "No."

But Rachel said, "Sometimes."

Meanwhile, Fabian whined, "Great. How are we going to stop him if he jumps away all the time? Is it too much to hope they moved their fight into Hell?"

Lu got out her phone. "If he still has his smartphone with him, we can track him. Assuming he didn't know enough about it to turn the feature off." She checked her phone and announced, "Nope, he didn't. He's at the park."

"I'll say one thing for you humans," Balthasar mused, surprisingly without any sarcasm. "You *are* inventive."

Jan and Fabian glanced at each other, deciding it would be best to keep their mouths shut.

\#

A little later, they had reached the small park near Matt's flat. Fabian and Jan had their phone lights on as they followed Lu's lead.

"He should be around here." She stopped and turned around.

"He or that thing on the ground?" Balthasar asked. For some reason, Matt's entire family had trekked out with them. They really had a perverse interest in getting first seats to the Blood Night.

Matt's phone was on the ground. While Fabian picked it up, Jan found a groove in the snow. "They came past here. Look, they broke through there." A row of bushes had been disturbed, broken branches everywhere.

Lu whispered her light spell, which made for a nice proper lantern, and they continued. Soon, they heard a moan. Then Fabian pointed to the blood in the snow and made a soft noise as if he was throwing up in his mouth.

Jan stepped forward and bent the branches to the side. His gaze fell on Caspar, lying in a pool of blood that had melted the snow. He was still moaning as he woke from unconsciousness. Groaning, he rolled onto his side.

Laughter rang through the night. Appalled, Jan watched Balthasar as he jumped to the other side of the thicket and nudged Caspar with the tip of his shoe. "It's really not your day, is it? Maybe next time you should bring your guard."

Caspar was grunting in pain, but he slowly got up on all fours.

"His guard?" Jan asked. He had no idea why a demon would need a guard on top of their own prowess.

"Caspar is the Commander of the Black Guard," Chay explained in a low voice. "Hell's army."

Fabian instantly stumbled backwards, almost falling into Menuha, who patted his shoulder in a calming manner. "He's got the day off." Somehow, that didn't reassure Fabian in the slightest.

Jan wasn't quite sure what to make of all of this. They'd only known the one demon so far, and he'd been everything a demon was supposed to be, brutal and ruthless. These others were different. He wasn't underestimating Caspar. He surely made a terrifying general, but he was also so... unfocused. Or rather singularly focused on making Matt's life miserable, when he should've been off leading his guard to victory, pilfering and looting, or something scary like that. And Balthasar and Menuha... if people hadn't told Jan they were demons too, he never would've guessed. Especially the sister, who was so kind, befuddled him. Who had ever heard of a demon adoring humans?

"We found Caspar, but where is Matt?" Lu asked.

Unfortunately, Caspar was back on his feet. He spat blood and grunted again. "Ran off. Probably searching for someone he could kill."

"He more likely thought you were dead. You looked dead," Balthasar said with a shrug.

The look Caspar threw him would've turned Jan's stomach, and the fact that the older brother completely brushed it off scared him even more. If he had to fight one of them, he'd choose Caspar any day. On the other hand, Caspar looked remarkably well for someone who'd been left for dead. He stretched his neck, and with every second, he stood straighter. And then he focused in on Jan and the others. "And now it's my time to enjoy a bloodbath."

Jan hastily took a step back—forget about fighting Caspar—as the demon raised a hand. Energy sizzled. And then it fizzled out.

Menuha had teleported to her brother and gently pressed down his arm. "Don't do this. I like them."

And Caspar—the terrifying general of Hell's army—became putty in her hands. He groaned, but it sounded more annoyed than angry. "Do you need to adopt every human?"

"Please, Casp."

"Fine." He spat again, not a drop of blood in his mouth. "I'm bored, anyway." And with that, he vanished into thin air.

"Let me guess," Jan muttered to Chay. "Those extreme self-healing skills are also part of the standard repertoire?" Chay nodded tiredly, and Jan sighed. It was another thing no one had believed him about. And the most annoying thing was, he hadn't fully believed himself either. Never again, he swore to himself, just as a terrified scream cut through the air.

Instantly, Jan ran towards the sound, Lu, Fabian, and Rachel on his heels. They returned to the main path and stopped short. The demon was in front of them, holding Robert by his throat and pushing him up against a lantern.

"Ma... Melchior!" Lu called.

Matt glanced at her, then squeezed harder. Robert was kicking hard, but his face was already turning blue.

"Hey!" Jan stepped closer, both arms ready to defend himself. "I know Robert's annoying, but that's no reason to kill him."

"Jan!" Lu exclaimed in horror.

But it helped. His words had some effect on Matt. Robert slid down the pole as Matt let him go. A moment later, Jan found himself backwards in a snow drift.

"You mean I should kill you instead?" Matt asked in a low drawl.

Jan wasn't a coward. Up until now, he had risen to every challenge and never backed down, but when he looked into Matt's dark eyes, he very nearly peed himself. There was no sign of his friend in there. Not an inkling of the Matt he knew. This was a monster, and it would rip him apart as painfully as it possibly could.

Matt's fist came crushing down when a thin shield lit up between them. Lu! The impact made the magic wobble. Matt raised his fist again and started bashing it. Unable to move, Jan could only watch him from behind his raised arms as the shield grew thinner and thinner with each impact. Soon those fists would smash into his head, his chest, his stomach. And he wouldn't heal as fast as Caspar. If Matt left him for dead, it would be because he was dead.

"Matt!" Lu cried. She was pulling on his wing in her desperation instead of using her magic to attack him. The wing snapped out and hit her in the side.

Jan didn't hesitate. He used Matt's momentary distraction to roll out from underneath him and get to his feet. But before he could fully stand up, Matt's knee hit him in the stomach.

There was no air in his lungs. Matt hadn't even hit his chest, but Jan couldn't breathe. He folded in two, landing face-first in the snow.

"You have no idea how long I've wanted to do this." The words were hissed into Jan's ears, dragging him back to when he had uttered them to Matt. What a fool he had been. Matt could've killed him any day, and yet Jan had kept provoking him. And now it was coming back to bite him.

With an iron grip, Matt hauled Jan back to his feet. Black energy crackled in his right hand as he drew his arm back.

"Fabian!" Lu screamed.

Just as Matt was about to let go, a branch gave in above them, and a shower of ice-cold snow-slush came down on Matt.

"Vinculum!" Lu's spell was a set of chains that wrapped around Matt until he couldn't move, his teeth chattering from the cold.

Jan stumbled backwards, only to crash to the ground as his useless legs gave way. Someone was whistling appreciatively. For what reason, Jan had no idea. He only knew the insane pain in his stomach.

Then Rachel and Fabian were at his side. "Jan, are you okay?" Rachel asked, while Fabian steadied him.

Meanwhile, Lu, in her wonderful lack of self-preservation when it came to her friends, approached Matt. "We don't want to hurt you. We're your friends. Chay told us everything, and we don't care. But you need to fight this. You need to stop!"

For a moment, it looked as if Matt was giving in. Then his eyes got this dangerous gleam, his muscles bulged, and the chains exploded. His wings unfolded, snapping in the air, and he was free.

They all held their breath. Matt looked at each of them for a long time as if to decide which one to kill first. Or maybe just how. A stupid taunt to ease the tension popped onto Jan's lips, but before he could seal his fate, Matt simply vanished.

Everyone sagged in relief. A strangled sob escaped Lu's throat. Rachel shuddered next to Jan, and Fabian cried, "How are we supposed to stop him? He's going to kill everyone."

"If he does, at least it'll be easy to find him," Jan muttered before biting his tongue. This wasn't the time for humour. But the notion was true. They would have to find him again. But what to do then, Jan had no clue.

Melchior

He was restless. His body longed for the kill, but it had been denied him too many times. Five people who were still alive. Their lives had been in his hands, and yet they still breathed. It almost drove him insane.

No, he was insane. Had been insane for some while now, apart from these few clear moments when he'd been absolutely sure he didn't want to kill *them.* But he needed to kill someone. Anyone would do.

Melchior regarded the dark windows from his perch on top of a house on the other street. There was no fun in killing sleeping people. It wouldn't quench the bloodthirst, only make it worse. He needed a worthy victim. Someone he really wanted to kill. Like Caspar. Only, he'd already beaten Caspar.

"I'll visit you during the semester break, okay? I promise." A familiar voice cut through the night, and Melchior's lips curled upwards.

Now *that* was someone he wanted to kill.

"Dad, please... yes, okay. Whatever." There he was with his stupid beanie, all alone, no Samantha in sight.

Melchior followed Daniel silently along the roof as he walked down the street, trying to end a call to his daddy. It filled Melchior with anticipation to see the man he despised unaware of what was about to happen. And Melchior knew this wasn't going to be a quick kill.

"Hello, Daniel." He landed on top of a wall, perched like a bird.

Daniel whirled around, his eyes searching the area wildly until they landed on the demon. Melchior sighed in ecstasy the moment the other's eyes widened with fear. "Who are you?"

"Can't you guess?" Melchior landed in the snow in front of Daniel, deliberately dragging the tip of his wings through the snow to spray Daniel. "Come on, Dannyboy. You know me."

"No, I..." Daniel swallowed heavily as recognition hit him. "Matt?"

"It'd be a shame if Samantha had picked a complete dud, right?" Melchior stepped closer. "But you've passed. Sadly, that's all that can be said about you. You barely pass."

Daniel must've found a sliver of courage because he stopped backing up, annoyance flashing in his eyes. "Listen, Matt. I didn't steal her from you or something."

"She belonged to me." Melchior had never been a scholar of greed, but this one he knew in the depth of his heart.

Daniel's face tightened in anger. "She doesn't belong to anyone! Man, you're so immature. If a girl doesn't respond to weeks of flirting, but kisses a guy she's only met a few times, it generally means she wasn't interested. She chose me."

Melchior had no interest in who chose whom. He only wanted one thing from this guy. "Hit me."

"What?" Daniel scoffed. "I'm not going to fight you for her. This isn't the winner gets the girl or something like that."

"I said," Melchior lunged forward, grabbed Daniel's wrist, and smashed his fist into his face. Blood spurted. "Hit me."

Daniel whimpered, holding his nose. "Are you crazy? You can't—"

Annoyed, Melchior grabbed his shoulders and buried his knee in his stomach. Sputtering, the older one stumbled forward. Melchior waited for him to catch himself—he'd only put a little force into the hit, after all. When Daniel straightened again, his eyes blazed.

"Finally."

He let Daniel have a go at him, but the attacks were a joke. Daniel had obviously never fought for his life, never even hit anyone. Melchior easily blocked his attacks, and when he had enough of the useless flailing, he ripped his feet out from under him and flipped him on his back, then kicked him for good measure.

Daniel coughed and sputtered. He was panting as he rolled himself up on all fours. "Do you really think..." He had to catch his breath. "Do you really think Samantha will love you for this?"

Melchior didn't care whether Samantha would love or hate him. He raised his hands, calling the black magic coursing through his blood. It came alive in his hand, just as bloodthirsty as he was.

The energy hit Daniel in the stomach and threw him several metres through the snow and the concrete underneath. When Daniel's body came to a standstill, his clothes and skin were torn. Blood flew from beneath his fingers as he held his stomach. He was still alive, but the anger had fled his eyes. Only fear ruled his features now.

Despite his injuries, Daniel scrambled onto his belly and tried to drag himself away. Melchior jumped in front of him, grinning wildly. "Don't run away. I'm not done with you."

"Please," Daniel begged. The pain had etched lines into his face. "Please don't do this."

But nothing would stop Melchior now. "Die, Daniel."

Rachel

Rachel wished she would wake from this nightmare. When she'd been asleep, she'd felt in control. The blood, the candles—those were just images. The blood in the snow, however, that was real.

She didn't even know why they kept trying. The future was written, the vision would come true. Matt's birthday was drowning in a pool of blood.

But they kept marching on through the darkness and the snow, with no real lead to go on.

Everyone was on edge—or everyone *human* was on edge. The demons looked more like they were out on a stroll. Balthasar seemed to enjoy himself, and Menuha was happily chatting with Jan and Lucille about demon culture.

Rachel only listened with one ear, filing all the information away. Balthasar was nearly a thousand years old. There were about two hundred siblings born to Melaney, but no one bothered to keep track. And most weren't interesting, anyway. Hell had laws, or rather several councils, one of which was led by Balthasar, who'd helped Melaney assume the role of archdemon many years ago.

Next to her, Fabian stewed in silence, his eyes stuck to the ground. After a little while, he quietly said, "We haven't heard from Samantha."

"Her phone broke," Rachel reminded him softly. Samantha was painfully missing from their group. Somehow, Rachel believed she would've been able to talk sense into Matt. She had this peculiar way of handling him, and Rachel thought that at least half of the good changes Chay had seen in his protégé were because of her.

"You mean *Matt* broke her phone?" Fabian's voice was so sharp, she barely recognised him.

Rachel sighed, trying to find some positive angle to this mess. "But see, she'll be fine. She already met him in his demon form, and he let her go. Because deep down he recognises her. And he would never hurt her. He cares too much about Sam."

"Rubbish." Suddenly, Melaney was at their side, anger flashing in her eyes. "My son doesn't care for anyone."

It seemed to be important to her, so Rachel didn't protest.

René, however, didn't show the same self-preservation skills. "Sure, he does. Matt has changed."

"You mean you ruined him?" Melaney asked sweetly. "He should've never come here."

Fabian and Rachel exchanged a quick look, and both decided to keep their mouths shut.

"He came here because he had needs that Hescaryn couldn't provide for him. He's half human, Melaney."

Matt's mother laughed. "There are no needs Hescaryn can't fill. Don't you humans always turn to us for your needs? Like you did?"

René's face darkened considerably. "I never needed you."

He might as well have spoken gibberish. Matt's mother smiled in a way that made Rachel's insides clench. Melaney bridged the distance between her and René, then slowly opened his jacket. It was like a car crash. Rachel couldn't look away, though she was screaming in her head that she didn't want to see this.

"It looked different a few hours ago," Melaney purred.

René didn't answer. His eyes never left her face, and it seemed like he was holding his breath. Rachel found she was holding hers as well, and Fabian gasped next to her.

She was proud of him that he managed to speak. "Could we perhaps..."

He stilled when Melaney's sultry gaze hit him. "Join in? Of course you can. The more the merrier."

Rachel squirmed. This was all wrong.

Fabian's head was bright-red, and he stumbled over his words. "No... uhm... I..."

But René seemed to have regained his senses. "That's typical." He stomped away. "We need to find Matt."

Melaney let him go without a second glance, her gaze still locked on Fabian. When she moved towards him, Rachel thought she was like a black panther, beautiful but dangerous. Fabian swallowed heavily, unable to break the gaze, and Rachel couldn't help but feel a little annoyed.

"Melaney!" René's sharp voice reeled her in. "Let the boy go! You don't need to ruin everything."

And, to Rachel's relief, she turned away from Fabian to join René again. "I ruin everything?" Melaney sounded amused. "Do tell. Did I not give you almost three amazing years?"

Rachel didn't even want to know in which way they had been amazing. She rubbed Fabian's arm and quietly asked him whether he was okay. The redness had left his face, but he was now so pale she feared he'd pass out on her.

He shook his head. "She's... something."

"You left!" René scoffed and threw his hands in the air. "With my son!"

Melaney seemed unfazed and shrugged. "I couldn't stay away from Hescaryn forever. I have duties to fulfil, needs to meet."

Slowly, Rachel began to understand. Melaney was the Archdemon of Lust. In other words, she was lust incarnate. With one glance, she could make anyone want her. And for a few years, she had toyed with Matt's father. And now very nearly with Fabian.

"You didn't have to take Matt," René shot back, his face ravaged by an old pain. "He belongs here. With his friends. With me. He's building a life."

Melaney snorted and rolled her eyes. "Please. It's just a phase. Caspar had one of those. Gone for thirty years. Once he came back, he was a different man. Perfect. And Melchior will come back to me as well. Maybe as soon as today."

"Not as long as I've got a say in it."

"How fortunate for me then that you don't." And with that, Melaney sauntered to the front to hook her arm into Balthasar's.

As soon as she'd left, Lucille and Jan fell back to them. "What was that about?" Lucille whispered.

Rachel sighed. Until now, she'd always believed that Matt had got the better deal with his parents' separation. He always seemed so nonchalant about it, balanced, really. Now she realised that he just hadn't cared enough because he'd been raised in Hell. But his father had cared. His father had mourned the son ripped from his arms with no regard for their relationship.

How different would Matt have turned out if he'd grown up here in Greenvalley? Would he still have fallen into his Blood Night? Would he have killed less? Disappointing his demon relatives?

Fabian didn't seem in the mood to fill Lucille and Jan in either. He shrugged and said, "I don't claim to understand demons anymore."

"Did you ever?" Jan asked.

But Lucille hugged Fabian's arm. "I know what you mean. It's all terribly confusing. I wish Matt would've just told us before all of this."

Fabian was about to answer when his phone rang. He got it out of his jacket and frowned. "It's an unknown number."

Sam.

Samantha

"Daniel?"

His vacant eyes stared into the darkness. Blood had frozen on his face. On his neck. On his chest... everywhere.

"Daniel, please..."

She'd only been away for ten minutes. He'd taken a call from his father, with whom he had a strained relationship, and she'd given him the space to do so and checked out a noise she had heard. And when she'd come back... When she'd come back...

Images flashed in front of Samantha's eyes. The demon's wings spread, his sword rising high into the air. And his voice. His voice whispering that deadly word.

Sobs tore from her throat, and she fell into the snow, still two metres away from Daniel. She couldn't bring herself to go closer, to look into his hazel eyes, which were now broken and empty. It couldn't be true. It just couldn't be true.

Samantha looked to the sky, as if the stars would help her find the courage. As much as she dreaded it, she had to be with him. Had to be there for him. Even if he would never be with her again.

It took her five more minutes to cross the distance, only to burst into fresh tears when she reached Daniel. She cradled his face and tried to stroke his hair, but wherever the blood had soaked in, it had become stiff and unyielding. "Oh, Daniel."

Samantha knew that she couldn't stay like this for the whole night. The demon might come back, and as tempting as it was to have a devil-may-care attitude about it, she was scared. Scared to see him again. Scared to face him after what he'd done.

"I'll get help," she promised Daniel, though he was far beyond any help.

She got up, her body aching like that of an eighty-year-old. Every step away from Daniel felt like a betrayal. As if she left him behind.

Something glistened in the snow. Daniel's cell phone. Her own was broken, and this one's screen had splintered, but it flashed alive as she touched it.

Locked.

Samantha didn't have the code to unlock it. For a moment, she contemplated calling emergency services, but the word *"fingerprint"* drew her gaze. She looked back at Daniel and shuddered. What she was about to attempt was madness. It was disgusting. It was also her only chance.

Quickly, she returned to Daniel, then stared at him once more. Fresh tears rolled over her cheeks. She gathered her courage and bent down to lightly put Daniel's finger against the touch screen. The phone unlocked, causing her stomach to churn.

She hastened away, begging the insides of her stomach to stay inside. Once she had managed to ascertain a modicum of control over her body, she typed in Fabian's number. The only one besides her grandmother's she knew by heart.

As she waited for him to pick up, she walked further and further away from Daniel.

"Hello?"

Samantha burst into tears at the familiar sound.

"Hello?" Fabian sounded confused.

She tried to speak, but only moans and sobs came from her mouth. "Fa..."

It only took one syllable for him to recognise her. "Sam! Finally! Where are you? Are you okay?" His questions only made her cry some more. "Sammy? What happened? Where are you?"

"Dan..." She couldn't say it, couldn't bring herself to utter the words. Instead, she cast around until her eyes landed on the sculpture of a boar. "South shore. At the boar."

"Stay there!" Fabian commanded. "Don't move, okay? We'll come and get you. We'll be there in a minute."

Samantha couldn't have moved even if she wanted to. The demon had materialised right in front of her, a smile on his face. The cell phone fell from her limp hands and landed in the snow.

Fabian's voice rang up to her. "Sam? What was that?" He was panicking. "Say something. Sam!"

The demon bent down and took the phone while Samantha stared at him. "She's with me."

"Ma—"

The phone was crushed in the demon's hand, Fabian's voice gone. Samantha's heart fluttered nervously, and she closed her eyes until she was only able to see a white sliver of snow.

"I told you—I'll get you," the demon said in his deep, seductive voice.

His finger touched her cheek, and she forgot how to breathe. He was so close to her, his heat seeping into her frozen body.

"Hush." The finger touched her lips. "You don't have to be scared of me."

Then his other hand landed on her neck, and he drew her even closer. Samantha took a shuddering breath as her chest was pressed against his. Her legs were crumbling beneath her, and she was about to pass out.

"Normally, I wouldn't interrupt, but I've been looking for you, bastard."

The demon pushed Samantha away, and she fell into a boneless lump, blinking. In front of her, a second demon had arrived. It was the one they'd met before. The one with the hellhounds. He regarded the younger one with contempt.

"Melchior, is it?" the older demon asked, then scoffed. "I have to admit that your escapades tonight are a tad annoying. The numbers are better than I would've expected, but with regards to your potential... boy, you're far too driven by sentimentalities."

"What do you want from me?" Melchior asked, stalking away from Samantha.

The older demon grimaced. "Actually? For you and your little friends to stay away from me. Your interference is annoying. *You* are annoying."

To Samantha's horror, Melchior was grinning. "Well, you've picked the wrong day to take it up with me."

"Don't overestimate your capabilities."

Melchior lunged at the other demon, ramming his head into his stomach. The older demon stumbled back two steps, then he grabbed Melchior by the neck, clearly planning to break it. The younger demon grabbed his opponent by the forearms, twisted in his grip, and somehow managed to roll backwards, kicking the other in the face as he did so. Then he drew his sword and jumped behind the other, ready to skewer him.

The older demon knew how to jump through space as well, landing so precisely behind Melchior that he was able to wrap his arm around Melchior's neck and cut off his airflow. Melchior gasped for air, but none managed to enter his throat. He let his sword go, twisted his arm, and shot black energy at the other demon. While the older demon managed to escape the brunt of the attack, the energy hit his face, leaving behind a bloody groove.

With the two demons fighting, Samantha forced her body up from the snow. Her legs didn't seem to be able to hold her, so she grabbed the boar statue to pull herself up. Unbothered by her, the demons kept on fighting. The younger one, Melchior, was more agile. He jumped through space continually, attacking the older from all angles with his black energy and sword. But the other demon blocked most of his attacks, and when he shot back, he usually hit.

Samantha clawed at the fence behind her, then dragged herself along, one step behind the other, never letting her eyes leave the deadly monsters in front of her.

Suddenly, the older demon's eyes locked on hers. A second later, he shot his energy right at her face. Samantha gasped, staring into the lethal magic that would rip her apart, when Melchior appeared right in front of her and took the hit. The black magic tore through his right shoulder and wing, tearing the leather to pieces.

"Told you. Too sentimental," the older demon growled. "You are nothing but a human bastard, after all."

This time, when he attacked Melchior, he held nothing back. Samantha jumped to the side as they crashed into the fence. Melchior fought back with all his might, but the older demon had the upper hand now, and he beat Melchior almost artfully. Piece by piece, he ripped the wings apart, which seemed to be the most sensitive part of demons. Then he placed his blows perfectly across Melchior's body.

Samantha couldn't watch anymore. She pressed the heels of her hands against her eyes and tried not to breathe in the thick smell of blood.

It took several minutes for the fight to die down. When she opened her eyes again, Melchior was on the ground, and his breathing had become stertorous from his own blood. He tried to jump away, but his body only flickered without movement.

The older demon raised his hand, black energy crackling around him, when he was suddenly hit by a bullet. A different kind of energy paralysed him, seconds before he was hit by another demon's magic.

People had arrived. In the very front, Mr Traidous and Matt's mother. He was holding his gun while Melaney had her hand raised. Then she vanished as well, only to appear next to the fighting pair, ready to scratch the older demon's eyes out.

He groaned and pushed her off him, but not in the aggressive way he'd just shown before. "I should've known you'd be here today." He glared at Matt's mother.

"Touch my son one more time and I swear to you, you won't be able to sit your butt in the Seven's Council for three weeks," she shrieked at him.

Her son. The truth Samantha had been trying so hard not to acknowledge came crashing down on her. It could no longer be ignored. *Her son.*

The other demon spat. "I thought he had his sentimentalities from his father." Then he looked past her shoulder. "Is that him? The human you liked so much you played wifey for him?"

As Samantha scrambled backwards on her knees, she watched Mr Traidous settle down at Melchior's side. Methodically, he grabbed the demon's wrist and cut a rune into his flesh. When the circle was complete, Melchior's torn wings receded, and his hair grew blond.

Samantha whimpered, pushing back even further, while the demons kept arguing. "My children are taboo for you. Do you understand, Malcolm?" Melaney asked.

The older demon, Malcolm, wiped the remaining blood from his face, his wounds healed. "Then tell your spawn to stay out of my business. Otherwise, dearest sister, I can guarantee for nothing." Barely finished, he vanished for real this time.

Melaney huffed indignantly before she hurried back to Matt's side, only to push René away. "What did you do?" she screeched.

"I ended his Blood Night," René hissed back.

"You idiot! He cannot heal if you block his demon side."

"Sam?" Fabian sank into the snow next to her, blocking her view of a dying Matt. "Sam, are you okay?"

Was she okay? She didn't even understand what okay meant anymore. Matt was a demon. No, half-demon. And he'd killed Daniel.

Suddenly, Samantha was clawing at Fabian's back, pressing herself against his chest so hard she couldn't breathe, only gasp.

"Sam, calm down. Please." His arms wrapped around her, one hand in her hair, the other on her back. "Breathe. Breathe."

Slowly, Samantha calmed enough to fill her lungs with air. Looking over Fabian's shoulder, she saw the others staring in shock at Matt as he lay in René's arms. His mother was running the show now. She called out for Caspar, and the white-blond brother simply appeared at her side.

"Where's Daniel?" Fabian asked softly.

Samantha pulled away from the scene, just as Melaney bullied Caspar into *healing* his brother. She stared at Fabian, unable to speak until he asked again, "Sammy, where's Daniel?"

"He..." Her eyes flickered to the crumpled body in the snow that nobody was paying attention to.

Fabian followed her gaze, and his face fell. "Oh, Sam."

"It was him," she heard herself whisper, and her head shot back to the scene.

Caspar was truly healing Matt, a golden shimmer spreading under his hands as he grunted in pain himself. And Matt opened his eyes, recovering to live another day.

While Daniel was dead.

"He's not in control of himself," Fabian said softly. "It's a demon thing. Once in their lifetime, they go through this murderous frenzy and—"

"He killed Daniel." Her voice was suddenly as sharp as ice. There was nothing uncontrolled about that. Not after everything Matt had said or done prior to his demon rampage.

Fabian shut up and nodded, his face hardening as well. "You're right."

Samantha turned her attention back to the others. They were all crowding around Matt, pampering him with attention. Lucille even fell around his neck to tearfully tell him she'd be there for him.

For *him.*

Samantha stood, her mind in a trance. Fabian rose to her side. He put his arm around her waist and steadied her, but he let her take the lead as she set one foot in front of the other.

"...I wanted to tell you. Someday," Matt admitted, sounding exhausted from all his murdering.

"Sure. That would've been nice," Jan quipped. "A little, 'yes, Jan, you're absolutely right, I'm not a human, I'm a demon' would've been enough."

"Half-demon," Lucille corrected him and smiled at Matt. "You're half human and we all know that you didn't want this to happen."

Matt sniffled. *He sniffled.* "Does that mean you still... you still want to be my friends? Why?"

"Well, it's too late now," Jan said with a shrug.

"What Jan is *actually* saying," Lucille stressed, "is that we're your friends. Tonight, you weren't yourself. And knowing it will never happen again, I don't see why we should abandon you now. Right, Rachel?"

Rachel shrugged, then took a deep breath. "Right."

Even Rachel had welcomed him back into the fold. Samantha was beginning to feel as if she'd caught the wrong train. Everything was wrong.

"You're... you're the best," Matt cried, completely overwhelmed.

Lucille smiled at him. "You can count on us."

The bloody snow crunched under Samantha's feet. They had reached the group, and Matt looked up at her.

"Well, you can't count on me," Fabian said coolly.

Samantha almost shuddered with relief. At least someone wasn't swayed by this humble act.

"But, Fabian, didn't you hear what Chay said?" Lucille protested. "This isn't his fault."

"Yes, it is!" Samantha choked out.

Matt's puppy eyes met hers. "Samantha?" his voice was a mere whisper.

"You. Are. A. Monster." She had to swallow, each of the words burning in her throat. "And I... I hate you."

He knew why. His eyes lowered in shame. *He knew why!*

And that sealed it all. "I wish you were dead."

She spun around and strode away, unable to be near him anymore.

"Sam!" Lucille called after her, sounding almost outraged. "What happened?" she asked someone else.

Fabian. "Why don't you ask your demon friend?"

He hurried after her and pulled her back into his arms. Samantha cried into his jacket. Her knees gave way again, and she crumpled into his embrace, wishing with all her heart that none of this were true.

That none of it had happened.

Chay

Chay never bothered to turn on the light as he sat in Matt's room, counting the minutes until Matt would arrive. He'd cleaned up most of the mess in the living room, but he couldn't repair the broken furniture, just as he couldn't repair their broken futures.

It was around four thirty when he heard the door click open. A sliver of light fell into the room from below, and he made out a soft voice—René talking to Matt. The voice was too low for Chay to understand the words, but they wouldn't matter. None of it mattered anymore.

After a little while, Matt dragged his feet into his room. He had somewhat cleaned up, probably washed down with snow, but the traces of the night still clung to him. He pushed the light switch, then froze.

For a minute, they stared at each other. Chay saw the hurt in his eyes, the pain, and the agony of having his heart broken for the first time. It had never been breakable before. Then bitterness as Matt finally spoke. "You knew."

Chay always knew. That was his curse. He'd first seen Samantha telling Matt how much she hated him after his Blood Night when he'd arrived in Greenvalley. Then, after shaking Samantha's hand in the café, he'd seen Daniel and the horrible tragedy that was destined to unfold as Matt's new and unprobed feelings clashed with the terrors of the Blood Night.

"You knew," Matt repeated, harsher this time. "Why didn't you stop me?"

"I tried," Chay said truthfully. "I even warned you." But it hadn't mattered. If Chay had learned anything in the over 250 years he'd dealt with his power, it was that seeing the future was not the same as changing the future. He'd tried being blunt. He'd tried being subtle. It never mattered. The future always found a way to settle back into its path.

Matt scoffed. "You call that a warning? You told me she would hate me when she found out." His face paled, then anger flashed. "But not like *this*. I was going to tell her. I could've *told* her."

And Chay had stopped him. "You still would've killed Daniel." It would've been worse because Samantha would've trusted him more. Their bond would've been even tighter. And the pain as it broke, much more intense.

"I wouldn't..." Matt began pacing. "I... What about the Blood Night? Couldn't you have warned me about *that*?"

"You knew about the Blood Night."

Matt clicked his tongue. "Sure, I did, but not that mine would happen tonight. On my birthday! I'm only eighteen!"

"You're a half-demon. I was about the same age," Chay said calmly.

Matt's face twisted. "Well, you never told me about *yours*."

That was true. Chay had never told anyone who was alive today. But many had known about it then. And their shadows still held his heart today. Even after all these years.

"Matt..."

"What? Any other important life changes I should know about?"

Chay nearly broke his mask and laughed. Where should he even start with one of the *Six*? "You will get through this." Matt only snorted. "But if you really want to take my advice, let Samantha go. Find someone else. Find—"

"This isn't about her!" Matt shouted. "So what if she hates me? She's got no real reason to do so."

And so it began. Samantha was a lovely girl—important to Chay even—but what she would put Matt through, and what he would put her through... If Chay could change one thing about the future, it would be that. It might very well ruin them all.

"You killed her boyfriend," Chay gently reminded him.

"During my Blood Night. No one can control themselves during it. It's not my fault I stumbled across her stupid boyfriend." Matt had crossed his arms, looking particularly petulant as he summoned all the coldness he'd cultivated in Hell to cover up his pain. "Samantha isn't stupid. She'll realise I never *meant* to kill him."

Chay kept his face just as guarded. "She's not stupid at all." She'd seen right through the intricacies of the chaos that ruled half-demons' minds. Knew that Daniel's death wouldn't have been a certainty if it was a full demon on a rampage.

Matt nodded to himself. "I need to take a shower. And sleep." It couldn't have been a clearer dismissal. But when Chay rose from the chair, the confused and frightened boy was back. "Will we talk in the morning?"

It would've been kind to say yes. And to mean it. But there were things Matt had to learn on his own if he was really going to learn them, and this was one of them. "I'm afraid I won't be here."

Matt's bottom lip pushed out, and he swallowed. "You're leaving me? After what happened tonight?"

"You've got some things to figure out. And I have other things that need my immediate attention." Chay gave him a nod. "You *will* get through this."

There always came a time when Chay had to disappoint one of his protégés. This was Matt's. Like all children, he had to learn that his parents weren't infallible. And that Chay served one thing above everything else: the future.

Before Chay left Greenvalley, he had one more stop to make. This one brought him to the little cottage in the woods—the home of Elda Kollmer.

She'd still been Elda Bergmann when he'd first met her and Cecille. The visions had brought Chay to the witches, but it had taken him decades to understand why. Sure, Cecille had the Emblem of Power known as the Nadellyan Tears, and at first, Chay had thought it was that which had called him here. But it had only been the beginning. And so, he'd deposited his life's work here—in Elda's library.

Now was the time to finish what he'd started.

The sun was still in her winter slumber when the door of the library creaked open and Elda came in, a Thorak in her hand. The vicious little blade was poisonous to demon blood, the traditional weapon of a demon hunter and her late husband's weapon.

"It's you," she whispered.

Chay put aside the quill and blotted the last page he'd amended. "It's me."

Elda let the Thorak sink, but she snorted derisively. "Do you realise that my granddaughter cried herself to sleep next door? That I had to tell her your protégé would walk free? That there was nothing the police would do?"

"They can try," Chay said softly, but Elda was right. With the ability to jump through space, human police were powerless against demons. It would only lead to more deaths.

She scoffed again. "What is your game, Seer?"

He'd been asked that question again and again in his life. The answer never satisfied the asker. "I'm sorry for what he's putting her through. I'm sorry for all of them."

"All of them?"

"The Six. It's not an easy burden to bear." The prophecy of their destiny burned in Chay's veins. He needed them—everyone needed them—but if he could spare them their destiny, he would.

Elda shook her head. The Prophecy of the Six was not common knowledge in Ashuan as it was in some other worlds, but the witch had learned of it—through Chay. "That's impossible," she whispered. "Not now."

"It's them. The emblems are coming together. Five are already in the hands of their bearers."

"Not Samantha." The whisper was barely audible.

Chay sighed. "Change. The Flowers from Freya's Garden. The Power of Change. It's hers." If only she was able to change her own future.

Elda took a shaky breath. "He killed her boyfriend."

She understood now what role Matt would play in the grand scheme of things, if not Matt would find himself cursed before the night was out. Even if she understood, he might still suffer that fate, unless Chay made his case. "During his Blood Night. I tried to stop him, to get him to spend the night in Hell, but the future is written. Matt never stood a chance."

"It doesn't excuse anything."

Chay nodded his head. A fixed future didn't mean there was no choice. That there were no errors in judgement. It was fixed because no matter how much anybody tried, they would always make the same choice, because they were the same people with the same errors in judgement. But Matt wouldn't see it that way. Not yet. Not soon.

"I know," he said, pushing his own failings deeper, "but that is *their* problem to figure out, not ours."

"I pray that you're wrong, Seer." Elda was still seething, and rightfully so.

Chay gave her a pitiful look. "Me too. Every day."

And with that, he left Greenvalley.

Part 4

Tears & Stone

Lucille

Snow covered the gravestones, glistening in the low-hanging winter sun. Even though it was the middle of the day, they were the only people out here, and they were decidedly fewer than before. Lucille sighed as she watched Jan kick some snow, the tender flakes resettling on the ground. Fabian and Rachel were walking down a parallel row behind the graves, holding hands, and talking quietly. And that was it. Only four when they should've been six. Make that seven, Lucille thought as the spot where Nico's grave was came into sight.

Since the terrible New Year's night three weeks ago, neither Samantha nor Matt had joined them on their monster hunts. They hadn't attended school either. Samantha was grieving for Daniel in the safety of her home, and Matt had simply vanished. He didn't respond to any texts, and her calls always went straight to his mailbox.

For all Lucille knew, he had returned to Hell, just as his mother had wished. His *demon* mother. She was still struggling coming to terms with everything that had happened on that ill-fated birthday party. Everything had been so simple before. Demons had been monsters that needed to be stopped, or at the very least, avoided. And while for some of them that still held true, it wasn't that clear-cut anymore.

Like Matt. He didn't have a demon side he had to fight and suppress. He was simply a half-demon, raised by demons, still adjusting to the human world.

Even the pure-blood demons she'd met seemed to be more than bloodthirsty monsters. Caspar had been aggressive and ruthless, just as Lucille would expect a demon to be, but then his mother had forced him to heal Matt. And though he'd detested every second of it, he'd brought Matt back from the edge under great pain to himself. His brother Balthasar had never once been interested in joining the fight or shown any kind of demonic behaviour. Unless someone could call that kiss he'd given her wicked.

And Menuha had patiently answered all their questions about Hell while they'd searched for Matt. She'd told them how demons were governed by the Council of Seven—the seven archdemons of the deadly sins—and several other political factions that didn't fit Lucille's image of how monsters organised themselves. It was like they had a life beyond the horror tales of humanity.

Menuha had even admitted that most demons didn't care at all about humans. Only a couple left Hell to walk on Earth, or Ashuan, as they called it, and only a few of those did so with the intention of hurting people. Obviously, the demon they'd encountered in Greenvalley—Malcolm—was one of those few, but even he, while ruthless in his methods, had never gone on a killing spree. Unless someone meddled with his mysterious plans.

The four of them reached Nico's grave together, as if they'd planned it. Rachel crouched down on one knee and put her naked hand on the stone plate on the ground. "I miss you," she whispered.

"Me too," Jan admitted to Lucille's surprise. He cast around nervously. "Are you sure you've seen our cemetery in your dream?"

Rachel rose again. "I recognise our cemetery pretty well now."

The harsh comment made bile rise in Lucille's throat. Even though Daniel wasn't buried here—his parents had him transported to his hometown—she couldn't help but be reminded of his recent death. "And you're sure it was a *true* dream?"

Rachel had called them this morning that she'd dreamed of a zombie-like monster infestation at the cemetery. "It felt real," she stressed.

"How you do you determine that?" Fabian asked, more out of curiosity than protest. "I'm just saying that I sometimes dream of zombies rising, but they're normal nightmares. You must have normal dreams, don't you?"

Rachel shrugged. "I don't know. If I do, I can't remember them."

"Hush. I see something," Jan whispered.

Lucille grimaced and followed Jan's line of sight. A mysterious fog was hanging low over the gravestones in the distance, unwieldy figures moving through them. At first, Lucille thought it was a funeral procession, but the shapes didn't move like humans, and their proportions were all wrong. Their arms were too long, and their bodies bent forward as if weighed down by their arms. They stopped and started digging through the snow and soon the earth.

Rachel's dream was real. There truly were some grave-digging monsters in the cemetery.

"Please don't let them eat brains," Fabian muttered.

Lucille poked him with her elbow, not in the mood for all the clichés of a zombie apocalypse. The creatures reached deep inside the earth, their backs almost completely bent. Suddenly, wood splintered, and the four friends startled. A little later, they could hear crystal-clear smacking sounds.

Fabian turned around and loudly brought up his breakfast. Lucille almost followed his example when she realised what these creatures could possibly be eating. The noise of Fabian's stomach revolting reached the creatures, and they paused.

"Great." Jan clicked his tongue in annoyance. "So much for being qui—"

"Careful!" The creatures were now moving towards them. Lucille drew in some cold winter air and got herself ready for the fight.

Jan raised his hands. "Don't worry. Zombies are incredibly slow."

The creature in front straightened, its muscles stretching before it jumped, landing right in front of them. Its long arms ploughed through the snow and sprayed them with it.

"Okay, not these ones," Jan conceded, shuddering as the snow slid under his collar.

This close, Lucille could see the creature in its full zombie glory: grey, patchy skin, hollow eyes, and a little round mouth with needle-like, yellow teeth. Tonight, she would dream of them as well. And not in a good way.

"Globus igneus!" she cried and hurled her green fire at it as it raised its arm to knock Jan off his feet. The magical fire enveloped the creature, burning vividly, but that hardly seemed to bother it. It kept walking towards them. Jan took position, readying himself for close combat. When two others joined the burning one, he launched a flurry of kicks. With no sizeable success.

The creatures barely shook under the impact, then one of them reached out its long arm and flipped Jan in the air, landing him face-first in the snow.

Lucille screamed, "Jan!"

"Get back!" Fabian jumped in front of her, legs spread and hands stretched in front of him. As the water erupted from his hands, Lucille hurried to Jan's side and helped him up. Together with Rachel, they backed up.

Jan was still sputtering from the hit and shook his head to get rid of the snowflakes in his hair. "How's he doing?"

Fabian's water pushed the creatures back and killed the green flames on their leader. But then the creatures spread out, and while Fabian managed to hold one at bay, the others closed in on him.

"Fabian!" Rachel cried, just as Lucille put her shield spell around him.

As he saw the two monsters coming closer, Fabian tried to retreat, but he slipped on an icy patch and fell hard on his back, nearly knocking his head on a gravestone. One of the monsters jumped on him, opening its needle-like-teeth-filled mouth. Fabian screamed in terror and tried to block it with his arm, but the creature grabbed his wrist and pushed it to the side, leaning down to bite him.

Before it could do so, the creature lost its head. Steel glinted in the winter sun as the sword rose again and felled the other two. While the creature collapsed on Fabian, Lucille's eyes travelled down the length of the sword and the body it belonged to. Matt stood there, his face bearing an unfamiliar haughtiness. He ran his hand through his blond hair and scoffed. Then he reached down to offer Fabian a hand. "That was close."

Lucille stared at Matt, struggling to comprehend that he'd truly returned. And just in time to save them.

Then the daze lifted, and she found herself running towards him. His brown eyes widened in confusion, but she was already in his arms, crying. "You're back!"

Fabian had refused the offer of help and got up on his own. His eyes focused on the snow beneath him as he patted his backside and mumbled, "Great."

"Looks like you didn't unlearn the whole decapitation act," Jan grumbled, considerably less delighted than Lucille.

Matt freed himself from Lucille's embrace. His face darkened, and for a moment, Lucille worried about him lashing out. But his nostrils only flared as he took a deep breath and let it go. Instead, he focused on her, the only truly friendly face around him. "Looks like you've got a little ghoul problem here."

"True," Rachel said, her voice unreadable.

Lucille looked from Rachel's blank face to Jan's hostile glare, and then Fabian's more than obvious unwillingness to meet Matt's eyes. He even scratched his arm as if there was nothing more interesting to focus on. She turned back to Matt, catching an unfamiliar caution in his eyes. Her first bout of excitement had cooled.

The weight of what he'd done the last time they'd seen him settled on all their shoulders. The New Year's murders had shaken the entire city, and the crime remained unsolved, the criminal walking free. Right here in front of them.

Annoyed with herself, Lucille shook her head. She'd promised Matt not to judge him by his actions during his Blood Night. That hadn't been him. A little too cheerfully, she said, "And you obviously know how to deal with them. We missed you." The cheer didn't last for long as the doubts crept back in. "You're staying, aren't you?"

Matt didn't meet her eyes. "That's the plan." He shrugged, his gaze searching for something else. Or rather, someone else. "If Sam's grandma doesn't try to kill me, that is." He took a short breath. "She isn't with you?"

It was obvious he wasn't asking about Elda.

Fabian's head snapped up. "How dare you?" He crossed his arms and regarded Matt with an icy stare. "She's off sick. She's still trying to cope with what you've done to her *and the man she loved*."

"I see." Matt bit his lip, but only for a second.

Lucille looked back and forth between the two of them. Usually, Fabian was the one to back down, but this time Matt wouldn't meet his eyes. She reminded herself that Matt probably didn't know enough about humans to understand that three weeks weren't nearly enough time for Samantha to process what had happened.

"It's not easy," Lucille said gently. "Samantha needs a little more time. Just like... you did." After all, that was why he must've been avoiding them for so long. Chay had told them how much he regretted his own Blood Night, even after all these years. After learning that he'd accidentally killed Daniel, Matt must've been devastated. Guilt was probably eating him alive as they stood here.

Guilt that only Samantha would be capable of absolving him from. "She'll come around eventually." Lucille wanted to swallow her words. It sounded so callous, as if Samantha was only off sulking after a perceived slight, when, in fact, she'd seen her boyfriend brutally murdered. That wasn't something you'd simply come around to.

She sighed. "You're back. That's the first step for us to get back to normal. We'll get through this together."

Fabian snorted and started to stomp away, snow crunching under his feet. Rachel sighed, then hurried to his side, taking the easy way out.

"There was nothing I could've done to avoid it," Matt suddenly rushed to say. "Every demon goes through it. We have no control over it."

Jan took a deep breath, uncharacteristically sombre. "Yeah, that doesn't really change the fact that six people died. Including Daniel."

Lucille saw Matt swallowing. He was struggling to keep his apparent cool. Why he wouldn't just let them see the inner turmoil he was clearly grappling with, she didn't understand.

"I'm well aware of that. But I can't be held responsible for it," he said instead.

Jan screwed up his face. "Tell that to your mum. Maybe she'll care." With a shake of his head, he followed the other two.

Matt took a few shaky breaths, and Lucille's heart went out to him. "I didn't plan to kill him," he whispered.

Contrary to the others, Lucille believed him. "I know." She slipped her hand into his and squeezed it. "I told you we'll get through this together. And we will." A sad smile came to her lips. "I'm glad you're back."

It did little to ease the tension in his shoulders. His face was remarkably calm. "I'm not sure I am."

Lucille decided to ignore his reservations and pulled on his hand. "Let's go home."

Fabian

Fabian had never been this mad at someone. Three weeks, Matt had hidden in Hell, only to act as if he'd merely been on holiday. During the last month, Fabian had been inclined to believe Matt was ravaged by guilt, but his behaviour didn't show the slightest bit of remorse. He sat at their table as if he ruled the world, greeting classmates who expressed surprise at his return.

Meanwhile, Fabian was doing all he could to keep his anger at bay. The water bottle in front of him shook slightly, but the water stayed inside. So far.

"Excuse my curiosity," Lucille said at last. "But what did you do for all these weeks?" She was the reason he was sitting with them. Fabian wondered how she was going to look Samantha in the eye and tell her she'd welcomed Matt back with open arms.

Matt shrugged. "Thinking. Just hanging around Hell. Stuff like that."

"And now you're hanging around here," Jan said with a good amount of snark. "Awesome."

The mood dropped five degrees. "Do you have a problem with that?"

Jan's eyes narrowed as he took up the challenge. "Am I allowed to say so without fearing for my life?"

Everyone around the table tensed. Fabian's eyes focused on the water bottle, ready to pop it if needed. But Matt only rolled his eyes. "Funny, very funny."

It wasn't funny at all, and the dismissive tone grated on Fabian's self-control.

Jan leaned back, balancing his chair, and asked, "Why are you doing this to yourself?"

"I find it incredibly hard to follow you." Matt's voice grew even more condescending.

"I mean school. You don't need it, and it must be so boring compared to what you're used to. Don't say you missed Zobel."

Matt grinned a little, and the tension flew away. "Not particularly. Believe it or not, I enjoy going to school. It teaches me interesting things. Like history."

"History is the best." Lucille nodded emphatically and smiled. It was her major, after all.

Jan, however, scoffed at him. "You're such a weirdo. If I was a demon or something like that, I'd go anywhere, but I certainly wouldn't attend school."

"Jan," Fabian hissed, and the water in his bottle rose. "Keep your voice down. We don't want anyone else to know what he is. It's bad enough as it is."

Matt's eyes narrowed as he regarded Fabian. Fabian should've felt intimidated knowing what Matt could do to him, but the anger wouldn't let him. It even infuriated him having to worry about how Matt would retaliate.

"Guys, please," Lucille said softly. "Let's not start this here."

"I'm sorry I can't sit and pretend—" Fabian stopped himself when two girls stopped at their table.

Cheryl and Ani smiled and waved at Matt. Cheryl's eyes widened in mock-surprise. "Matt! It's so good to see you. We thought you'd caught Samantha's illness."

Cracks ran through Fabian's self-control, and he drummed his fingers on the table, praying that Cheryl would move on quickly.

"Because it's a very *mysterious* illness that Samantha got." Cheryl nodded in her self-important way. "Probably got a pimple or two."

The water bottle exploded. Water sprayed and spread over the table. Lucille shrieked as she jumped up and raised her books out of harm's way. Rachel was less fortunate and lifted one corner of her ruined Maths folder, while Jan wiped water from his face and jacket.

The blood rushed into Fabian's head, turning his face bright-red, and he quickly put the near-empty bottle on the ground.

Meanwhile, Cheryl sneered at him. "God, Fabian, how do you even tie your shoes in the morning?"

The water on the table suddenly drew back, ready to bend under Fabian's emotions. Matt hastened to stand up and pulled Cheryl and Ani away from their group. "I actually just had an extended holiday. A family thing." And then he had the audacity to wink at Cheryl before lowering his eyes. "I was planning to stay longer, but let's say…" His eyes were now firmly stuck on her breasts. "There were a few arguments that convinced me otherwise."

Cheryl responded to Matt's attention in an instant, switching into full-on flirting gear, twirling one of her blonde locks, and glancing at Matt from under her extended eyelashes. At the same time, she managed to put her arm under her breasts in an almost natural way to push them up even further.

Fabian stared at them in disbelief when he suddenly felt Rachel's hand on his arm. "Just ignore her, Fabian. She's not worth it."

He wanted to argue that it wasn't Cheryl he was worried about, but Matt. His gaze, however, fell on the water bottle, which was already half-full again, and he sighed.

Matt continued with his newfound interest in Cheryl. "Perhaps you've got a few more arguments for me."

Cheryl giggled and playfully batted his arm. "Matt!" She lowered her voice and gave him a supposedly sultry look. "I might have a few. Or make that a lot." Another giggle. "Do you have my number?"

Matt shook his head but produced a pen from his pants and offered it to her as well as his hand. Cheryl took both and bent a little, offering him an even better view, while she scribbled her number onto the back of his hand. "There you go. I put my address on as well."

"I'm sure I'll make use of it," Matt replied. Then he watched them walk away, apparently taking great pleasure in Cheryl's swaying hips.

When he turned back to the table, Fabian couldn't hold it inside any longer. "Wow. Cheryl." He normally didn't care who Matt slept with, but Cheryl felt personal. She was Samantha's worst bully.

"I just saved your ass. Again," Matt stressed, his voice pure ice.

"It actually looked like you were more *into* her ass," Lucille said, then sighed.

Matt screwed up his face and grabbed his bag. "Think whatever you want."

He stalked off in the opposite way from Cheryl and her clique at least. His empty chair didn't stay empty for long, though, as Robert squeezed into it. "Woah, you should have seen the look the cafeteria owner gave you." When all four of them stared at him in confusion, he pointed at the remainders of the water. "Because of that little accident. Shook it too much, right?"

Fabian struggled to find the right words. "Yeeeeeah." It was still water, but the explanation would have to serve.

"Happens to me all the time."

"Robert," Jan started, "what do you want?"

Robert beamed at them and began rummaging through his backpack. "I've got something for you. When I saw it, I thought of you guys." He pulled out a newspaper and showed a page to them. There was a picture of an open grave and the headline, "*Grave-robber gang strikes again.*"

"You see grave robbers and think of us?" Jan asked and pointed at Lucille and Rachel, who managed to look exceedingly prim and proper for Robert's benefit.

"I thought you were interested in stuff like that." Robert's face fell. "Mysterious murder cases, and the like."

Lucille smiled in a calming way. "Usually, we try not to get in the way of these people. But thanks for the warning. Now I know not to cut through the cemetery on my way home."

"Oh, man," Jan complained, before laying on the sarcasm. "I was so looking forward to our cemetery date."

"I know, but maybe you can take your girlfriend instead," Lucille played along.

"She doesn't like mysterious murder cases," Jan deadpanned.

When Lucille broke character to laugh, Robert got up again. "Very funny. Thought this was something for you." He took the newspaper back and hurried away.

Immediately, Lucille's and Jan's merriment evaporated. "They've multiplied," Lucille whispered.

"I hate zombies," Fabian muttered, while Rachel corrected him, "Ghouls. They're ghouls."

Like most of these days, Fabian had found Samantha at her grandmother's home. Today she was working in the little witch room, preparing dried plants and other components for later use. Fabian left his school bag by the door and walked over to have a look. Samantha never acknowledged him. The way she handled the fragile flowers had something meditative, calm, and deliberate.

"Zobel asked for you again," he said softly, after watching for a while. "We're finishing with the presentations next week and he wants to know whether you're still planning to give one or whether you want to hand in something else." Fabian had picked up notes for most of her subjects. Sometimes she did all the homework and then some. Other days, she never touched them.

Samantha took a deep breath. "I don't know."

"You'll have to go back one day." It seemed even more important now that Matt had returned. It wasn't fair that he should have a normal life while Samantha still hid out here.

"Now you sound like my parents." She sighed and turned away from the herbs and flowers. "Maybe Monday."

Fabian smiled, relieved. "Monday sounds perfect."

"What's that?" Samantha took his arm and looked at the patch where the ghoul had scratched him. The skin was reddened and itchy, especially after Fabian had scratched it so much.

"Just a scratch and a stupid rash. I think I'm allergic to monsters."

Samantha chuckled inadvertently. It was so rare to see her smile these days, and Fabian was glad he could make her laugh a little. But the weight of what he had to tell her became heavier, and he sighed.

"What's wrong?" Samantha asked.

It hurt Fabian to speak the words out loud. "He's back."

Samantha's breathing quickened, and she flexed her fingers nervously. Fabian had known she would react badly to it. Matt's cowardly flight had made it a bit easier for her. It hadn't brought Daniel back, but at least Matt had been gone too.

She took a shaky breath before whispering, "And?"

"He asked about you," Fabian answered and shook his head. After everything Matt had done to her, it shouldn't have been a surprise to him that she wasn't exactly waiting for his return. Fabian wanted to believe that the reason he asked for Samantha was because he'd come to make amends, but school had shown him that if they were waiting for an apology, they'd better pack some snacks. "I try not to talk to him." Which was difficult if Lucille invited him to their table.

Samantha turned away hastily to attend to her plants, as if they couldn't be left alone for too long. "You can talk to him. You don't have to ignore him on my behalf."

Fabian snorted. "What about my behalf? Matt killed how many people?" Samantha's shoulders bunched, and he realised he couldn't continue that line of thought. If Fabian were truly honest, Matt killing someone he'd known and hurting Samantha was the worst part for him. He hadn't known the other victims, hadn't even recognised their names in the newspaper.

"I don't know how the others do it," Fabian confessed. "I see him, and I want to scream at him. Lucille is so supportive—well, not completely, but she's all *'We're gonna get through this together'*, and Jan's joking about it. Badly, but still." His voice got louder and louder. "The whole time he's against Matt, but now that it turns out he's some monstrous psycho killer, everything's chill." That wasn't quite the truth. Jan was giving Matt a hard time, but he wasn't exactly flipping him off either. "And Rachel—"

"Stop!" Samantha cried. Tears were running down her cheeks, and she let out a strangled sob.

Fabian lowered his eyes in shame. "I'm sorry." He had let his anger get away with him when Samantha needed assurance and comfort, not a mad rant. "I... What do you want to do now?"

Frantically, Samantha wiped her face to dry all these tears. "There's nothing I *can* do. I can't take out a demon, and neither can the police.

They don't even have a clue, and apart from what I've seen, I have no proof. Granny even said persecuting demons is useless. They just jump straight out of prison." She blinked more tears away. "That means Matt can do whatever he wants. He can walk the streets, go to school, and pretend he's human."

"He is half human," Fabian said softly. "Apparently, he had no idea the Blood Night was going to happen and no control over..." This was all so horrible. "No control over who became his victims."

Samantha stared at him in disbelief. "Do you really think that?"

Fabian shrugged. It was how Chay had explained it to them, and perhaps a part of him simply wanted to believe it. If Matt didn't have control over his actions, then he could be redeemed. Sure, a little remorse would go a long way, but at least he wouldn't actually be a psycho killer.

"He picked Daniel," Samantha said, completely sure of it. "We were on the other side of town. He had all of Greenvalley at his feet, but he went out of his way to track down Daniel. Why do you think that is?"

Fabian lowered his face in shame. The anger was gone, buried under a mountain of pain he couldn't even imagine. Samantha's eyes filled with tears again, and she whimpered softly.

He might not be able to make sense of it or know the right words, but he could take Samantha in his arms, and so he did, swaying her gently in his embrace until her shoulders relaxed again, and her tears were cried.

Fabian hadn't told Samantha about the ghoul problem. Since they couldn't meet at Elda's, he'd bribed his mum with a few extra shifts to allow them to meet in the back room of her shop. There he found Rachel and Lucille already scouring a few monster compendia, while Jan tried to balance his pocketknife on the table's corner. When Fabian entered, he startled and grabbed the blade, almost cutting off his finger as he did so.

"Phew, it's only you."

"Yeah, lucky you. Mum will have your head if you poke a hole in her table. And then mine for letting you in here," Fabian grumbled.

Jan put the knife away with a groan. "Sometimes you're really stuck-up."

"I just like staying alive." Fabian sighed and sat down next to Rachel.

"How was Sam?" Rachel asked quietly.

"Upset." He rested his chin on his hands, feeling tired all of a sudden. "I almost got her to go back, but... the curveball undid every progress she might have made."

Nobody commented on the curveball. Instead, Lucille pointed at her book. "We could use her help. I don't know how she does it. Like, I've read the books, and now I know exactly how many teeth a grown ghoul has and how you can tell their general health from their skin colour, but nothing that helps against them."

"Killing them helps." They all startled when Matt appeared in the room. He either didn't notice or ignored them, and simply sat down at the corner of the table. "Just saying."

"Dude." Jan exhaled loudly. "Give us a warning."

Matt shrugged. "Didn't have time to walk."

"Cheryl?" Fabian asked, trying his best not to sound too confronting.

"Nah. Someone else."

Lucille was smiling through her teeth as she said, "Well, I'm glad you were able to make it. And about killing the ghouls, what's your suggestion?"

"Ghouls have a leader, something like a ghoul queen," Matt explained graciously.

"Like a bee queen?" Fabian asked, trying to wrap his head around a potential hive of ghouls.

Matt shrugged, giving off the appearance of someone who didn't care either way. "If bee queens keep making new ones, while the rest of them get them food, yes."

Fabian took small satisfaction from the fact that Matt's grasp on Earth's biology was far inferior to his monster knowledge and gave him a curt nod.

Meanwhile, Jan shook his head in disbelief. "There are girl ghouls?"

"Not sure if you can truly assign them any kind of gender, but the ghoul queen keeps procreating as long as there's food." Matt became more and more relaxed as he talked. "So, we need to kill her first. The rest of them will die off by themselves after that."

"And how do we recognise the ghoul queen?" If someone could match Matt's cold, unaffected tone, it was Rachel.

Matt pursed his lips for a moment to think. "She's taller than the others. Her arms are longer. Small stuff like that."

Even Lucille seemed to struggle with keeping calm in the face of such callousness. "And how do you suppose we should kill the ghoul queen?"

"Ghouls are like vermin. You distract the group, and I'll take care of the queen."

All of a sudden, Jan hit the table. "Why don't you just go alone?"

Matt frowned. "What's your problem?"

"I don't have one. You seem to have it all under control," Jan shot back.

Fabian bit his lip at the mention of control. It was the key word at the moment. How much control did Matt truly have over his demonic instincts? He scratched his arm as he pondered the question.

"Guys please." Lucille looked from one to the other. "It's a good plan. Matt obviously has no difficulty killing the ghouls."

"Obviously," Fabian muttered.

Matt's eyes narrowed, and he jerked up his chin. "Do you have something to say, Fabian?"

Fabian stared back. He had a lot to say, but everyone else was looking at him. Lucille was pleading with him not to make a scene, Rachel looked worried, and Jan seemed unsure of what was happening. Fabian's gaze returned to Matt and the way he oozed arrogance at the table. Samantha's broken heart came to his mind, and his resolve strengthened. There was too much he couldn't afford *not* to say.

"Oh, come on! Do we really want to keep pretending that Matt was on an extended ski holiday and didn't murder half a dozen people?"

Matt's face darkened several shades and Fabian swallowed, but he refused to back down. Some fights were too important to run from.

"For your information," Matt began, dragging each word out. "I wasn't truly conscious during my Blood Night. I didn't even notice

I kept skipping out to kill. I didn't do it on purpose. No demon can control themselves during their Blood Night." When Fabian snorted, Matt's voice softened a little. "Of course, I'm not proud of it, but I can't change it. That doesn't mean I'm a murderer."

Fabian scoffed at what was a very poor excuse for taking responsibility. "Tell that to Samantha."

Matt's face twitched, but then his gaze hardened. "I'm sorry her stupid boyfriend got killed that night, but it's not my fault. She shouldn't have brought him on the hunt."

"What?" Fabian gasped. "Are you saying it was Daniel's fault he died?"

Rachel put a hand on his arm while Lucille desperately tried to smooth the feathers. "Boys, please. This isn't helping anyone. We're a team, aren't we?"

"It's nobody's fault!" Matt shot back at last, showing something other than his blasé mask at last. "Do you fault the lightning for striking?"

Jan chuckled derisively. "Are you comparing yourself to a force of nature now?"

Matt glared at him, then smoothed his facial features until the mask was back in place. "I was more referring to the fact that I wasn't exactly sane during those episodes." Then he added more for his own benefit. "Gosh, in Hescaryn they celebrate your Blood Night."

It was too much. Way too much.

Fabian jumped up so quickly the table shook. "Are we supposed to congratulate you for the blood on your hands?"

Matt opened his mouth, but a wave of water sloshed into his face and completely drenched him. Fabian looked down at his hands. He'd never even raised them as he usually did when he used his powers.

Wiping his face, Matt glared at him. "Really, Fabian? Shouldn't you know what it's like not being in control of your powers? It's only water for you, but it's the same thing. Only for me, it was a one-time-only thing. For you, it's constant."

Ashamed, Fabian sat back down. If Matt put it like that, the parallels between them were undeniable.

"But Fabian's never killed anyone," Lucille whispered.

"He got lucky then." Matt turned to her. "And may I remind you of a certain someone who sent her stepmother into the abyss, nearly burnt her own house down, and almost killed four *innocents* and us via smoke inhalation?"

Lucille paled under his scrutiny. At last, Matt broke eye contact and started to wring out his pullover.

"What about the ghouls?" Rachel asked.

Fabian wasn't ready to return to the topic of monsters. He watched Matt's attempt to get rid of the excess water and digested his arguments. For all their logic and sense, they still didn't sit right. And not just because neither he nor Lucille had killed anyone. Matt *was* right. They both had powers they weren't fully in control of and that were potentially very dangerous. But Fabian had known that from the beginning. It was why he'd struggled so much with accepting it. Lucille had been in tears after her curse had been lifted. And Matt... Matt just shrugged it off.

It was the lack of reaction that got him. This act of his, the whole "it happened, nothing I can do about it now" was what grated so much on Fabian. He nodded to himself as he slowly came to terms with the idea. If he'd drowned six people—even if they were complete strangers—he'd never have been able to forgive himself. He'd have been a mess. And he'd be doing everything in his power to make amends, to search for forgiveness.

"What are you going to say to Samantha?" One day, the two would meet again.

For once, Matt paused for a moment, looking as if he was at a loss of words. Then he shrugged. "What am I supposed to tell her?"

"You could start with an apology," Fabian suggested. It was the very least Matt could do.

"And will that apology bring Daniel back to life?" Matt asked, almost as if he genuinely wanted an answer. Finally, he lowered his head and mumbled, "Nothing I do or say will ever change what has happened. So, let's take care of the ghoul problem."

Fabian let him have his distraction. He realised that as long as Matt thought that way, they'd never get anywhere.

Samantha

Magic played around Samantha's fingers. Carefully, she coaxed a green string from it. Right now, she didn't focus on the weave pattern and only on the vibrancy in the thread. Green magic was life. The popping bud in springtime, the splash of colour in flowers, the sweetness of nectar, the mewling of a newborn kitten.

She loved the feel of it, how it filled her and made her more alive, more aware. And then came the weaving.

With the help of her fingers, Samantha looped the thread around itself to form the starting knot. All spells needed an anchor. Otherwise, the magic would simply unravel, eager to keep flowing in an endless cycle.

After several weeks of practising, the knots came easily to Samantha. But not today. The thread kept slipping from her fingers. She tried to call the image of what it should look like to her mind: a simple ring to protect the seeds in the ground. To help them sleep and charge until the spring sun woke them.

But instead of spring flowers, she saw snow. Blood-red snow.

The thread sprang from her fingers and rejoined the flow. Samantha groaned and rolled her shoulders to relax her neck. Spring, growth, life.

Winter, blood, death.

Another pattern came to her mind. It wasn't one her grandmother had taught her, but it came together easily. Tighter and tighter, she wound the threads. She tugged the threads with necessary hardness until the magic became unrelenting. Unstoppable.

"What are you doing?" Her grandma's gentle voice disturbed her concentration and brought her back to the here and now. "That's not a pattern that gives life."

Samantha looked at her creation. The tight little pattern would choke the life from whatever it ensnared. It was meant to bring death. She sighed and tugged at the knot. The magic unravelled and brushed her cheek harshly. Then it was gone.

"I'm sorry."

"I guess we can still call it a success." Her grandmother got to her feet with a groan then offered her hands to Samantha.

After an hour of sitting on the floor, Samantha's knees were almost as stiff as her grandmother's. "How is that a success? I couldn't even form a basic knot."

"But you did." Elda smiled mysteriously. "You did the knot for your own creation, which, by the way, despite its harmful nature was a very intricate web." She nudged Samantha's hand. "You've got talent, kid. Intuition. But maybe you should keep that web of death for the monster hunts."

Automatically, Samantha replied, "I don't go on monster hunts anymore." When her grandmother cocked her head, she added, "Not when the real monsters get away."

Elda sighed. "Oh, darling. Is that why you're so distracted?"

"He's back." Samantha wanted to stomp her feet or scream. Why did he have to come back? It was bad enough to know he was still out there, but now she would have to see him. When she went back to school, she'd see him. He'd be in three of her classes and around Lucille, if what Fabian said was true. She'd have to deal with him on a day-to-day basis. "It's not fair."

Tears stung in her eyes, and the urge to throw something grew stronger. She needed a distraction fast, and her eyes fell on the book Chay had written. That blasted book.

She'd been working her way through it when her curiosity won over her contempt. It mostly contained a historical or mythological account titled the *"The Legend of the Twelve"*, information about each of the twelve heroes, detailed descriptions of the Emblems of Power, and a near-endless appendix she hadn't finished looking at yet.

"Why does he get the Sword of the Gods?" Samantha asked, her eyes fixed on the book with its pages and pages on Matt's sword. "It says that only someone who knows both sides, light and dark, can wield it. I know he's a half-demon, but I don't think he knows a lot about being human." Her voice shook as tears tried to overtake her.

"He might grow into it," Elda said softly.

Samantha almost threw up. "Not you, too."

Her grandmother put her hand on Samantha's shoulder. "Darling. I don't care about the Emblems of Power, ancient prophecies, or whatever Chay saw in the future. I'm on your side."

"But you won't put a curse on him." Samantha pressed her lips together and turned away.

"No, I won't," Elda said, slightly amused. "And you don't really want me to do that, either."

Why did she have to be the good one? Samantha thought. Matt could go around, murder people, and she wasn't even allowed a sliver of vengeance. But her grandmother was right; that wasn't her. Even if she hated him for what he'd done, she couldn't retaliate. Not even if that meant Daniel would never find justice.

The moment she thought of Daniel, she couldn't hold back the tears. Almost a month had passed, and it still hurt so much. They had a *week*. She only had him for a week. He'd made her feel things she never had before. He'd made her laugh, and they'd had so many plans. The things she wanted to show him when the weather got better. The things they wanted to do together. And the things she wanted to learn about him. A week hadn't been nearly enough.

Samantha knew that they were all thinking she should get over him. She'd only known him for so little time, but that was what made it so impossible. Not that it would've been better with more, but that this way, she felt cheated out of her time with him. Cheated out of her first relationship after Fabian. The first one that hit all the storybook notes on how love should be.

There were more photos of Matt and her on her phone than of Daniel and her. Or at least, there had been until she'd deleted them in a rush. But she couldn't erase the memories or the fact that she knew Daniel's murderer better, had more memories of spending time with

Matt and enjoying it. It made her want to shed her skin and tear her hair out, just to get the lie of him out of her head.

"Kairos"—the original bearer of the Sword of Amain—"was a hero," she stressed. "He went out of his way to learn about the different sides of the war he'd found himself in, and all without murdering innocents," she added, annoyed when she realised that, technically, Matt had also gone out of his way to learn about his human heritage. And failed miserably. "He defeated Draken and saved the world. Matt wouldn't even care to save a kitten." Maybe that wasn't fair to him, but it all appeared so wrong.

How could he be the rightful bearer of the divine sword, the heir of a true hero who'd fought against the odds and succeeded for all that lived, when he was so deplorable? "It shouldn't belong to him."

"Darling, I don't think it's a matter of worthiness. The sword is his, just like the flowers will be yours," Elda said gently. "Matt carries Kairos' soul."

"His soul?"

Her grandmother walked over to the table and opened the book to the many lists of the appendix. "Chay has managed to trace the souls of the twelve heroes throughout the centuries. It takes about five hundred years for a soul to be reborn. So, every five hundred years, a new bearer of the emblems emerges. Or rather, two, since the emblems belonged to two heroes."

"Great, we should find the second bearer then and give them the sword. Surely, they're more worthy than a half-demon."

Her grandmother's face fell, and she had to take a deep breath. "Read this."

Against her will, Samantha was drawn to the book. She hadn't paid much attention to the lists, thinking they'd be references, but the lists were titled *"Known reincarnations of the Twelve"* and below it were names upon names. Some she could read, some were in languages she didn't even recognise, and others were written in characters she'd never seen. But she could clearly read the name at the bottom of the Kairos-list: *Matt Traidous/Melchior of the House of Lust.*

"Lovely."

But her grandmother pointed at another list. "Now look at Hanna's list."

Hanna was the fierce warrior princess of Amain who had snuck the sword out of her father's treasury after he'd openly sided with Draken, and given it to Kairos, the true bearer. Without her, he would never have got as far as he had. And, even in that final battle, she'd been holding off the enemy forces while Kairos and Draken duelled.

And the name at the end of her list was…

Matt Traidous/Melchior of the House of Lust.

"What? How is that possible?" It wasn't that the soul of a woman had come to life again in a man—souls didn't seem to know gender, judging by the list above—but… "How can two souls be in the heart of one?"

"It happens. Sometimes souls that belonged together find their way to each other. Sometimes a soul is split—those would be twins and triplets. Souls might be eternal, but they're not static."

Samantha had to take a seat. "I didn't even know that reincarnation existed. Does that mean everyone has a prior life?"

Her grandmother sat down opposite of her, a hand on the book. "In general, it takes about five hundred years for a soul to be cleansed of all living memories. Then it will be reborn. A different life, in a different place, at a different time." With a momentous sigh, she let go of the book. "All your names are in the book."

"What?" Samantha pulled the book to her and hastily scanned the pages. Her grandmother was right. Just like Matt, each of her friends' names was at the bottom of two of the legendary heroes. Her own name stared back at her from the lists of Gwydion and Dianthos. A chill ran down her spine. "What does this mean?"

"When Twelve become Six, all will be reborn at the same time in the same place to fight the same battle until the Greedy One fails twice, or all will perish," her grandmother said in a toneless whisper. "It's an ancient prophecy of the end of all worlds. And it looks as if it's finally coming to pass." She stared balefully at the book. "If Chay is right about it."

Samantha shut the book and threw it off the table. They both winced at the impact, but neither of them moved to pick it up.

At last, Samantha whispered, "Everything that's written in here has been written by him. Some are copied, but those last names are fresh." The ink hadn't paled like the other. "He's a half-demon like Matt. It could all be a lie." Though what Chay would gain from it, she couldn't imagine.

Her grandmother nodded slightly. "It could, but the emblems..."

"Aren't complete." Samantha shivered. Chay had told her grandmother that Dianthos' flowers would be hers, but if they were, they certainly didn't bloom in winter. All this time, she'd longed for them, but now she wished spring would never come.

"Sammy..."

If that prophecy was right, if they carried the souls of the ancient heroes, all born in the same time, here in Greenvalley, then that meant... "I'll never be rid of him!" Samantha cried. "No!" She got up, her chair scraping over the wooden floor. "I refuse to believe it! It's a lie. It has to be. There is no such thing as destiny or prophecies or a fixed future. We're not the Six. Matt and I will not have to work together."

"Child, please." Elda leaned forward to take her hand. "Calm down. I'm with you. I find it impossible to trust anything is set in stone. And that prophecy might never come to pass. Draken's soul needs to be reborn as well."

"And if he isn't," Samantha held onto the line of logic like a drowning woman, "we don't have to be together. Matt can do his thing, and I can do mine. We'll take care of the emblems, but not together. Never together." Tears were streaming down her face as she willed the words into reality. How cruel could life be for her to witness her boyfriend's brutal murder and then be tied to his murderer by an undeniable fate?

Samantha sank to her knees, burying her face in her grandmother's lap as the inevitability of it all came crashing down on her.

\#

As usual, her dreams were nightmares these days, but the last dream she remembered had been the worst of all. Not only had Matt declared that she belonged to him, but they'd killed Daniel together—because of fate. Seeing Daniel's blood on her hands, Samantha had woken and cried for the better half of an hour. In some ways, she felt responsible for Daniel's death. She'd brought him along. She'd left him alone. Matt had only killed him because of her. If she'd only met Daniel a month later, he'd still be alive.

The guilt tormented her. It threatened to rip her heart out and eat her alive, and no amount of rationality kept it at bay.

When she met her grandmother at breakfast, Samantha's eyes were swollen. The book had been restored to its place on the shelf, and she gave it a baleful glance. As if the future Chay had seen and the past he'd written down were somehow at fault for Matt's actions in the present.

Her grandmother came in with her usual tray of tea and a selection of bread and spreads. But when she set the tray down on the table, Samantha caught a glint of steel.

"What's that?" Between the plates lay a slightly curved dagger of black steel, runes etched into the hilt and blade.

"That is your grandfather's Thorak. I want you to have it," Elda said with a sombre face. "I don't want Matt to have control over your life, in any shape or form. This will keep you safe."

Samantha carefully took the dagger by the hilt and felt its weight. "Granny, Matt has a sword. I don't think a dagger will be much use." Never mind Matt's proficiency in sword *and* weaponless fighting.

"The Thorak is the traditional weapon of a demon hunter. Its magic-forged steel hurts demons in a way little else does. Even half-demons. They fear its touch. I expect you to use it responsibly."

"You know me," Samantha muttered, but her focus was caught by the runes inscribed into the weapon. A weapon against demons. And half-demons.

With the recent infestation of demons in Greenvalley, she'd surely make good use of it.

Jan

Since Jan was dating Meg, he had a front-row seat to the Kollmer drama. Though it had been almost a month since Daniel's death, he still had to answer a series of questions before being allowed to take Meg on a date.

"Where are you taking her?" her father asked when he came to pick Meg up. "Will there be people around?"

"Dad!" protested Meg. "It's a *date*."

Normally, that question would be of a suspicious nature, a dad making sure the boyfriend wasn't alone with his daughter. But Jan knew that wasn't the reason why Ben Kollmer questioned him. "We were planning to see a movie and have a coffee afterwards. Surrounded by people, all the time." God, he wished it would be about sex.

"How are you getting there?" Ben kept asking. "Do you have a car? Shall I drive you?"

"Dad!" Meg looked utterly horrified.

Her father wasn't having any of it. "Meg, the streets are not safe."

For a moment, Jan considered telling him that he knew Daniel's murderer and didn't think he was in the mood to kill anybody else, but even Jan was aware that this wouldn't settle any nerves. Instead, he pointed out, "It's the middle of the day. There'll be lots of people on the streets. But we can take the bus if it makes you feel better."

"It would." Ben nodded slightly. "And if you miss it, give me a call."

"Why don't we stay home?" Meg asked, exasperated. "Jan and I will be safe in my room!"

Ben glared at her. "Absolutely not. You can stay here and watch a movie in the living room, but that's it. Actually, that might be an idea."

Watching a movie with his girlfriend in her parents' living room while her parents hung around was easily the stuff of nightmares for Jan. What could he say?

Help came in the form of Meg's mother. She hugged her husband from behind and gently tugged at him. "Let them go, Ben. I'm sure they'll be fine."

Ben was about to protest, but he relented with an unhappy grimace. "Just take care. And Meg, I want a check-in every hour."

Meg looked as if she was considering scratching her father's eyes out. "I will not text during a movie!" The words were spoken with such venom, Jan took a careful step back.

"Of course not," Ben conceded in a tired voice. "Go on, then."

Meg whirled around, grabbed Jan's hand, and pulled him out of the house before her father could come up with another ridiculous security measure. "I swear he's going to skip work and pick me up from school any day now."

"What's wrong with me picking you up?" That was their current arrangement.

"I have to wait around for you to finish. Your days are usually one or two hours longer." Then she added, "In theory."

Jan grinned at her pointed reminder that he skipped the last few classes in her favour. "I've really been struggling with headaches lately. And a sore tummy."

Meg rolled her eyes and leaned into him as they walked down the street. "I really shouldn't encourage you."

"See it this way: because I have to pick you up each day, I'm not skipping any full days. I'm attending more classes than ever." He spread out his arms and laughed.

"I guess it's true what they say. Love can heal anything," Meg joked.

He wrapped his arms around her waist and whirled her in a circle until she squealed, then set her down and kissed her lightly. "Let's go for a walk."

"What about the movie?" Meg asked, suddenly apprehensive.

"I don't even know what's on," Jan admitted. "But sure, we can buy some tickets for one of the duds and make out in the back." It held a certain appeal.

But Meg only looked more worried. She looked over her shoulder, as if only now realising where they'd been going. "The bus stop is over that way."

"Meg." Jan took her hands and squeezed them in what he hoped was a reassuring way. "You have nothing to worry about. Greenvalley isn't the cesspool of criminal activity your father thinks it is."

She stared into his eyes a little too long, and Jan saw her face falling. Her chin dropped. "But it's a cesspool of monster activity."

Jan had never been quite sure how much Meg knew or suspected. She'd been around for the demon's attempt to fill up Greenvalley's less wholesome teenagers with magic. She'd seen the little creature from Hell, but she'd never commented on it. And she'd never shown any interest in butting in on what she called "Jan's special friend time". Even though her sister was part of it too.

But now she'd admitted it, it made things a bit easier. Jan pulled her closer and kissed her brow. "Then take it from me. The..." he paused. He had been about to say person, but even if Meg was aware of the monster activity, he wasn't quite sure how she would take hearing it'd been Matt. She'd probably freak out and tell someone else—his sister or her parents—and then things would get *really* complicated and out of control. A part of Jan wished that on Matt for acting so asinine since his return, but the bigger part felt some messed-up loyalty to the half-demon.

Matt had blown it big time, but he also hadn't been in control of himself. And Jan just had to put himself in Matt's shoes to know that involving human law enforcement in a demon case would make a right mess of everything. How could anyone judge Matt fairly without knowing all there was about demons? And having been judged unfairly far too many times himself, Jan had to stick with Matt this time. Not that he condoned any of the killing, it just hadn't really been Matt's fault, and Jan had pulled enough stupid moves while drunk or high—like burning down the mine's office while someone was inside—to know he couldn't judge anyone for it. In fact, if it came down to assigning responsibility, Jan had chosen to drink and take drugs, while Matt had been completely overwhelmed by his killer instincts.

"The what?" Meg asked impatiently, her voice a little stronger and insolent, just as he liked it.

"The creature," Jan said with new confidence. "The creature that killed Daniel is no longer a danger to anyone."

Meg looked left and right, then leaned in to whisper, "Did you kill it?"

Chased it away? No, that would make her worry it'd be back. Yes? A bit bold but… "Not alone, but yes." Everyone had been crystal clear that the Blood Night had been a one-time thing, so that person was most definitely dead.

Meg's eyes shone with admiration. Then her look hardened. "Good!"

Jan laughed. "My, my, aren't you the vengeful angel?" He ran his hands through her blond hair and admired her beauty. "My vengeful angel."

"I'll leave the actual vengeance to you, and…" After that pointed word, she slipped her hands around his body and pressed her hips against his. "If you knew what I've got in mind, you wouldn't call me an angel either."

Jan responded to it right away. "Uh-uh. I think we'd better take the bus after all. Wouldn't want to miss the ads," he joked.

Meg grinned wildly and kissed him, giving him a little taste of what to expect in the darkness of the cinema.

\#

Later that day, when the sun had set and he'd delivered Meg safely home to her father, Jan met up with the others at the cemetery. They'd geared up for the fight. Rachel was wearing her crossbow with a face that told Jan to keep a healthy distance from her bolts, Lu had her spells, Fabian his water, and Jan had picked a solid staff from Eric Kollmer's weaponry that was easy enough to handle and had a good reach. Martial arts only got him so far with a monster, especially one he'd rather not touch.

Fabian was rubbing his arm and looked around nervously. "I don't see any ghouls." The cemetery was covered in snowdrifts, its graves almost completely hidden under the blanket.

"I can probably do something about that," Matt said. And without further ado, he raised his hands and shot black energy out in front of him.

Jan winced as he saw the magic plough through the snow, scattering it everywhere. Now that his secret was out, Matt didn't seem to bother hiding his true nature anymore. Jan would be lying if he said it wasn't a tad unsettling.

From the snow, shapes rose all around them. Many more than they'd anticipated. The grey monsters lumbered around, treacherously slow while they adjusted to the new situation.

"Did we have to wake them?" Fabian whispered.

Matt shrugged. "Better you know where they are than stumble into them." He drew his sword. "All right, see you on the other side." And with that, he vanished.

"Matt!" Lu cried out.

They all looked at each other in horror. Sure, the plan had been for them to distract the big mass of ghouls while Matt took on the queen, but his sudden disappearance wasn't exactly reassuring.

"Let's stick to the plan," Rachel said and proceeded to nock a bolt into her crossbow. It shot out and hit one of the ghouls in the chest, felling it neatly.

The remaining ghouls had no problem following the plan. They came at them all at once. And fast.

Jan gripped the long staff tighter and welcomed the first ghoul with a flurry of blows. Its arms were almost as long as the staff in Jan's hand, practically rendering his reach useless. Soon, he was puffing with exertion. Every block seemed to hit him right in the shoulder and fester there.

"To kill a zombie," Jan huffed and ducked under the arm, "you need to hit it hard." He blocked the second arm, wincing at the pain. "In the solar plexus." Rotating his staff, he pounded it straight into the chest of the ghoul. That should do it!

The ghoul stared at him, then grunted with such a delay, Jan felt mocked.

"But these aren't zombies," Jan conceded. He jumped backwards to catch his breath, ignoring the creeping wheeze in his lungs. The ghoul came after him, not particularly interested in a short reprieve.

Next to Jan, Fabian had somehow managed to get hold of a deluge of snow, which he directed towards the mass of ghouls in front of them. It rolled through the creatures like an avalanche. The ghouls fell over each other and got stuck in the resulting mud, where they became prime targets for Rachel's impeccable crossbow skills.

Lu raised one hand and whispered, "Sageat negru distrugere!" The spell sounded particularly vicious, and sure enough, an arrow of crackling black magic formed in her hands and shot at the ghoul in front of Jan. Count on Lu to look out for him.

Abruptly, Fabian jumped in front of the deadly arrow and spread his arms, as if planning to protect the ghoul.

"Stop!" Lu cried, clenching her hand in panic until the white on her knuckles showed.

The arrow stopped a centimetre before Fabian's chest, still crackling viciously for a few seconds before dissolving. Fabian swallowed visibly, and Jan thought he saw sweat dripping down his forehead.

"What was that?" Lu asked, half relieved, half shocked. "What were you doing?"

Fabian had paled. "I have no idea."

The ghoul between them turned around slowly.

"Careful!" Jan shouted as the ghoul raised its arm.

Instead of hitting Fabian, though, he gently pushed him to the side and went after Lu. Her eyes widened in terror, and Jan started sprinting. He had to get in front of her, had to...

"Stranca..." Lu said in a shaky voice.

Jan hit her full on and pulled her to the ground just in time before the powerful arms of the ghoul swung over them.

"Ghula," Lu finished.

And the world grew still.

Matt

The ghoul queen reeked of decay. She was taller than the other ghouls by almost a head and bloated like a pig. A sickening number of shapes moved under the grey skin of her stomach, like multiple limbs churning and turning, fighting for space. A dark liquid was slowly dripping from her mouth, while clouds of flies surrounded her.

Matt tried shooting her first, but the tough, leathery skin blocked most of the impact. It wounded her, but not enough to slow her down. And she was a lot faster than she should have been with that belly. He tried to attack her from behind with a swift stroke, but she spun around so fast her arm hit him right in the head.

The impact drove him sideways into a tombstone. One of his ribs cracked, and Matt drew a sharp gasp. His head was reeling from the pain, but his mind stayed alert. He jumped away just as her arm crashed into the stone, turning it to dust.

Leaning on his sword about thirty metres away from her, he took one painful breath after another. Slowly, the bone in his body set, though the motion brought a sweat to his face and made him shudder.

The ghoul queen didn't seem to catch on that he hadn't gone far. She stood around, looking confused, then dug into the earth below the gravestone to eat some more.

Matt waited until she was halfway in the soil before he jumped forward, sword ready. The rib hadn't yet healed, but this was his chance. He shot at her from one side to get her attention, then appeared on her other side, and brought the sword down on her neck.

The blade hit stone and vibrated awfully in his hand. As it was, the impact was strong enough for him to sprain both wrists and throw his balance, so he landed hard on his knees.

Very hard.

Instead of snow and soil, Matt had fallen onto solid stone. Perplexed, he stared at the grey surface that was so similar to ghoul skin and yet rough enough to chafe through his kneecaps. Blood soaked the fabric of his torn pants, and Matt winced. He glanced up at the ghoul queen, expecting her to strike him down, but she didn't move a muscle.

Matt blinked, before carefully extending his hand to knock on her skin. Stone. The ghoul queen had turned to stone. Impenetrable, unmoving stone.

"Lucille!"

He got back to his feet, ignoring the pain in his knees and wrists that was already fading, and let go of the sword. Then he jumped back to where he'd left the others.

"What the hell?" he shouted at Lucille, who was standing amid ghoul statues. Half the ground around her had turned to stone. "I almost had her."

Lucille whirled around, her eyes wide in shock. Her lip quivered, and she was blinking too much. "I'm sorry, but... this works as well, doesn't it?"

"This works as well?" Matt could've ripped her head off if she wasn't his friend. "Half the cemetery is massive stone now. When will you finally use that brain in your pretty head and test new spells before you use them?"

There was such a sudden change in her face, Matt stopped short. Gone was the quivering mess. Lucille pushed her hands into her hips and gasped in indignation. Her eyes blazed with fire. "Are you out of your mind? Are you even aware of how you're treating us?"

"Treating you? What's that got to do with you throwing spells around without care?" he shot back, but his heart was suddenly beating too fast.

"Look. I get that you're a half demon who grew up in Hell, but that doesn't mean you have to act like an asshole all the time now." She changed her pose to cross her arms. "You weren't like that before."

"Perhaps that was an act," Fabian muttered.

Bloody Fabian and his stupid anger by proxy! Matt hadn't killed *his* boyfriend. He bet Fabian had been jealous of Daniel, too, but had been too much of a coward to admit it. It was okay for Samantha to hate Matt for what he'd accidentally done to her. She was well within her rights to do so. But Fabian wasn't! He hadn't been wronged, and it grated on Matt that he still treated him like a pariah.

"It wasn't," Matt snarled.

"Then why do you act as if we're all imbeciles who can't live up to your awesomeness?" Lucille asked. The blaze in her eyes had dimmed, but what he saw in them now was even more disconcerting.

Matt looked away. "Lucille." He didn't deal well with these human emotions. Half the time, he didn't even understand them. Anger was easy, but that vulnerability she'd suddenly showed was harder to understand. Why couldn't she just stay angry at him?

"I told you we'll get through this together," she said emphatically. "That I'm on your side, despite the Blood Night. I'm really trying here. Reason is telling me to run, to turn my back on you, but I don't want to do that. I want to believe in you. So, please, don't let that be a mistake!"

Matt stared at the stony ground. There was a tension in him that made him bristle at her words. He wanted to push back, to tell her that he didn't need her support, that he didn't need anybody's support because he'd done nothing wrong. It hadn't been his fault. If only everyone would apply their logic skills, they'd come to see that. No demon would hold him responsible for something that wasn't in his control.

But his friends were giving him a hard time. They wouldn't let him move past the Blood Night, wouldn't let him put it behind him and move forward. His father always looked so disappointed when they saw each other at home—which happened seldom enough, as Matt made sure to spend as little time there as possible.

Fabian was full of self-righteous anger, defending Samantha in her absence. Matt was well-aware that Fabian only tolerated his presence because of Lucille. And maybe Rachel, but Rachel was unreadable as always. Matt didn't know whether she hated him, liked him, or judged him, or whether he was completely irrelevant to her. And while irrelevance was exactly what he would expect from demons, it grated on him when it came from Rachel. His... friend.

Friends, Matt thought, were what made this so difficult. He could've stayed in Hescaryn, declared the human experiment a failure, something not worth any more of his time. But the longer he'd stayed in his mother's residence, the more restless he'd become. Suddenly, he'd no longer belonged there, the sins and pleasures no longer fulfilled him. It had been a frightening feeling. For if he didn't belong in Hell, and he couldn't be here, then where was he meant to be?

Thus, Matt had returned, but everything had changed. They all knew what he was now, and they judged him for it. And yet, they stood here with him. They let him sit with them at school, valued his monster experience, and offered reconciliation—sometime in the future. Matt began to realise that this was what friendship actually meant. True friends didn't turn their backs on you, but they sure as hell didn't let you get away with it when you messed up.

The tension inside of him gave way. Like a brittle layer of clay, it broke first into pieces, then into dust. There was a pain underneath, so different from his physical injuries, that made Matt gasp with its vehemence. He wasn't ready for it, didn't have the tools to deal with it, so he pushed it back down and grappled for something else. Something softer but not as deep.

He rubbed the back of his neck and cast around, taking in the various stone statues and firm ground. The spell had hit each ghoul and the ground beneath them for a radius of five metres. It wasn't, as Matt had said, half the cemetery, but there was no denying its power.

"That's quite an impressive spell," he said, then went for a lopsided grin. "Perhaps a little overkill."

"Oh, Matt!" And like a few days before, Lucille fell into his arms and cried. "I'm so glad you're back."

Matt answered the hug with one of his own. "Me too." And he really was. As hard as this was—and sometimes it felt outright impossible—it was right. It was where he belonged.

Behind her, Fabian looked tired, but he didn't protest or lash out with a snide comment. And he didn't stalk off like he had on the first night.

"Well, I'm glad that's sorted," Rachel said in a voice that didn't particularly sound like she was glad. "Can we discuss what to do with Jan now?"

"What do you mean?" Lucille stepped out of the embrace with a frown, while Matt looked around to find Jan.

Now that he thought about it, he hadn't heard a stupid comment for quite some time, and Jan always had a stupid comment about everything. He wasn't the kind of guy who kept quiet for long.

Well, he was now. Because, like the ghouls, Lucille's spell had turned him into a solid stone statue.

Lucille

Jan was a stone statue.

Jan was a *stone statue.*

She had turned Jan into a stone statue.

Lucille very nearly screamed.

"No, no, no!" In her mind, she replayed what had happened in the minutes before Matt had arrived and had a go at her.

The ghouls had attacked, and they'd been near unstoppable. Her arrow of destruction had almost hit Fabian, and then she'd tried that turn-to-stone spell on the ghouls, but a ghoul had been coming at her, and Jan had pulled her to the ground. When she'd opened her eyes again, the ghouls had been turned to stone. And before she'd had time to check on Jan, Matt had appeared.

Jan's statue was half-crouched as he'd never managed to get up from the ground, perpetually petrified in the moment he'd saved her. "This... how could this happen?"

"You tell us," Matt said, slipping straight back into his self-righteous attitude.

"The spell is for ghouls. So, unless Jan is really a ghoul, he shouldn't have been petrified!" Lucille stressed. She walked around the statue and knocked on several parts as if that would wake Jan. A terrible thought crossed her mind. "Please tell me I didn't kill him." Surely, a body could survive temporary petrification. He *had* to.

Matt raised an eyebrow, but thankfully kept quiet. Fabian and Rachel shared a worried glance. "How would we find out?" Fabian asked.

"By turning him back," Rachel said almost immediately. "Undo the spell and... we'll know."

Lucille swallowed. She could see it happen. Jan's body would take on colour, then crumple to the floor. Dead. She whimpered. Her heart was beating so fast it almost jumped out of her chest. Her breath came quick and sharp.

"Breathe." Fabian quickly strode to her side and took her hands. "Breathe with me." For a minute, they did exactly that, and slowly, Lucille calmed again. "Look. It's magic," he said, but his words came out shaky. "I'm sure he's fine. You just do the counterspell and he'll be back to normal in no time."

Her eyes filled with water as she looked back to Jan. "There is no counterspell."

Fabian's eyes widened, while behind him Matt groaned and walked a few steps. When he turned back around, he had problems with keeping his voice level. "Isn't that something witches learn? Like spells and counterspells? I'd have thought that would be Witches 101."

"Too bad there's no counter-sword strike," Fabian shot back before Lucille could even find her voice.

Matt's eyes darkened. "How is *this* different? If Lucille's killed Jan, then how will that be different from what I've done? I didn't mean to kill Daniel, either. Just like Lucille didn't mean to kill Jan."

"I didn't kill him!" Lucille screamed. It couldn't be true. It couldn't be so easy. Then again, she very nearly killed Fabian when he'd jumped in front of her spell.

Her knees gave way, and she crumpled to the ground, tears streaming down her face. "I never had Witches 101, because there is no one to teach me. I haven't learned spells and counterspells from my mother since the day I was born," she explained more for her own benefit. "All I have are a bunch of diaries and lists and lists of spells. I did a lot of research to find this petrification spell against ghouls. There is no simple way of reversing it. That's not how spells work." She swallowed. "I think."

"We'll figure it out," Fabian said, but his voice was shaking.

"Of course, you'd say that!" Matt complained. "Funny how it's pick and choose with you, what we can work out and what we don't!"

"That might have to do with the fact that Lucille is actually beside herself at the very thought of it, while you prance around like it's no big deal you killed six people in one night!" Fabian shouted.

Lucille covered her ears and cried harder. Jan couldn't be dead! She'd never be able to forgive herself.

"I'm not prancing around!" Matt shot back.

"Stop it!"

Everyone shut up the moment Rachel raised her voice. Lucille even stopped crying, her breath catching in her throat.

"Jan's not dead," Rachel declared when it was sufficiently quiet. "He's still dreaming. But we won't figure out how to return him to normal by tearing each other apart." She turned to Matt and shook her head. "Shouldn't you know better? Isn't this what Chay prepared you for?"

Matt looked as confused as Lucille felt. "He prepared me for a petrified cemetery?"

Rachel rolled her eyes. "Not that. I mean the prophecy."

"What prophecy?" Fabian asked, sounding unsure.

"The one that says the six of us belong together. And look at us now," Rachel said scathingly. "We're already down two members, and the rest of us are rushing to burn down the rest. Now, we can continue fighting or we can get our act together and figure out how to help Jan."

"Rachel's right," Matt said, considerably calmer than a few minutes ago. "We need to put our personal issues aside and concentrate on the real problem."

Next to Lucille, Fabian muttered, "Samantha's personal issue happens to be a real problem." But it was too quiet to carry to Matt.

Nonetheless, Lucille grabbed his hand firmly and pulled herself to her feet. "He's one of us." Fabian turned his face away, but he didn't pull away from her. She decided to count that as a win. Louder, Lucille said, "I could really use your help, guys. How about this? We all go to my place and scour the books together until we find something. You can sleep over."

She added the last part because it was necessary. They needed to spend time together as friends again. Fabian had to see that Matt was trying—and she wholeheartedly believed that he was—and Matt had to understand that they weren't going to turn their backs on him. And Lucille had to know that her group of friends would survive this, mysterious prophecy or not.

Slowly, the others nodded and agreed to the plan.

"I'll get my dreamweb from home and meet you there," Rachel said. "Perhaps the way to return Jan to himself is through his dreams."

"That sounds like a good plan," Lucille said, though she had no idea what that meant or how it would work. It didn't truly matter. Right now, the important thing was that they all had the same goal. "He'll be back in no time."

Matt shrugged, "Sure. As soon as we find the counterspell." And while it was a dig at her lack of such a spell, it was spoken with much less venom.

They all turned to Fabian, who looked tormented. Lucille understood his loyalty to Samantha. If there was anything she could do to ease her friend's pain, she would. Until then, she'd tried not to bother her, to ask nothing of her, and leave the door wide open until Samantha decided to step back into her life.

And while also supporting Matt in his struggle with humanity seemed counter-productive, they were both her friends. Lucille saw both their sides, and how irreconcilable they were at the moment. If she could get Fabian on her side, they might be able to bring the group back together. She squeezed his hand. "Please."

He visibly deflated. "Well, Jan needs us, so I guess."

It was a start.

A few hours later, Lucille was once more discouraged. As expected, there was no counterspell listed with the one she'd found. Apparently, no witch had thought about what to do if they wanted to return the ghouls to life. The book solved the mystery of how Jan got turned, though. It said that to cast the spell, one should make sure that they were in an open space, not touching anything.

Which meant Jan was currently a stone statue because he'd tried to save Lucille's life. It made her feel even worse than before.

"Do you think he'll hate me?" she asked the others.

Matt was lying on his back on her bed, flicking through one of the spell books, and gave her a long stare that made Lucille thankful he didn't put his opinion into words. She knew that it shouldn't matter right now.

Rachel was preoccupied with her dreamweb, while half-heartedly reading through one of the diaries. "I'm sure he'd hate it much more if he stayed a statue."

"How would we know?" Matt asked, and there was a hint of humour in his question that made Lucille feel a little better.

"I would. When I visit his dreams," Rachel answered, so sombre the humour died again.

Lucille shuddered at what Rachel would find in the dreamworld. "Can you let him know that I'm really sorry?"

"Sure."

"Hey, what about this spell?" Fabian leaned over to show her the book he was searching. He scratched his arm while Lucille took a look.

"A liquefying spell?" she asked doubtfully.

Fabian shrugged and reached over to grab one of the puff pastry pockets Martha had whipped up for them. "Different state of matter. He's solid rock now, so we need to... liquefy him."

"And then you'll use your powers to give the resulting puddle a Jan-shape?" Matt asked scathingly and sat up. He threw the book onto the pile and shook his head. "There's nothing in here."

"There should be a stone-to-human spell!" Lucille protested, annoyed at herself that she'd got them into this impossible situation.

Matt's lip curled up a bit. "You'd be the one to make that one up. Just turning a random piece of rock into a human."

Lucille knew he was only joking—it was what she had hoped for from this sleepover—but the remark cut. "I'm really trying here."

"As are we all." He grabbed a new book and returned to his position.

"I would like to sleep," Rachel announced.

Slightly taken aback, Lucille needed a moment to switch gears and remember why sleep was so important to Rachel. "Of course, I'll show you where your guest room is."

She had had two rooms prepared down the hall, one for the boys and one for Rachel. "The bathroom is over there. There should be fresh towels in the linen closet. Just leave it in the basket afterwards," she explained as she led Rachel to her room. "And this is it. I hope you like it."

"If it has a bed in it, I'm happy," Rachel said, not appreciative of the luxury in her guest room.

Lucille pouted a little, but then her thoughts returned to Jan. "You will let him know I didn't mean for this to happen, won't you?"

"If I can," Rachel admitted. "Anything else?"

"That prophecy you mentioned. Was it a dream?"

Rachel shook her head. "No, Chay told me about it. Apparently, the six of us belong together. You know, because of the Emblems of Power. We'll have to use them one day to defeat some dangerous enemy. Perhaps that demon that keeps bothering us."

Lucille wished she had the capacity to talk more about it, but with Jan's fate hanging over them, prophecies weren't especially high on her priority high. Apart from one thing. "I don't know how prophecies work, but if it's been prophesied that the six of us will face this enemy, it means we'll find a way to turn Jan back, right?"

Rachel looked at her as if she wanted to explain in detail how prophecies worked and how they didn't, but in the end, she snapped into a nod. "Yeah. It should."

It would have to be enough. "Sleep well," Lucille said, trying for a smile.

When she returned to the room, Matt had got up. "I'm going to sleep as well. The books will be here in the morning."

Lucille didn't bother to protest and pointed to his room. "Have a good night." Then she turned to Fabian. "What about you?"

"I'm not giving up that easily," Fabian said pointedly, making Lucille wonder if he just didn't want to be alone in the room with Matt while the other was still awake.

"I could get another room prepared for you," Lucille offered.

Fabian blew up his cheeks. "It'll be fine. It's not like we're going to tell each other bedtime stories." He shuddered. "Imagine what demon bedtime stories are like."

Lucille sat back down and pulled another diary on her lap. "We've never talked about it," she said.

"Talked about what? Demon bedtime stories?"

"That Matt is half demon. That we met four demons who didn't want to kill us," she stressed.

"Three. Caspar totally tried to kill me, and I think his mother wanted to seduce me." Fabian looked absolutely horrified.

Lucille shuddered in response. "She was... something, that's for sure. It must've been hard to grow up in Hell, don't you think?"

Fabian sighed. "Lucille, if you're trying to make me feel sorry for Matt, please stop."

"I'm just saying that demons aren't as straight-cut evil as we thought they would be," Lucille protested. She was totally trying to make him feel sorry for Matt. For her, just imagining what his day-to-day life had been made her heart ache.

"No! Absolutely not." Fabian shook his head vehemently. "You've heard Matt. They'd be celebrating his Blood Night in Hell. That's not something good people do. I don't care whether we were beneath Balthasar's notice or whether Menuha was awfully chatty. Neither of them blinked when they heard about Matt's murders."

Lucille tried to remember and realised that he was right. Neither Balthasar nor Menuha had seemed bothered by Matt's unfortunate rampage. "Maybe it's just a fact of life for them. We really don't know much about demons."

"Well, I know enough about them, that if this is a fact of life for them, I want nothing to do with them," Fabian declared and buried his nose in the next book.

Lucille tried to read as well, but she couldn't concentrate. Her thoughts wouldn't give her any peace, and the lack of a real lead did the rest. "But Matt's not a demon."

"He grew up as one."

"We don't know that." Lucille shut her book as passion overcame her. "We don't know anything about Matt. There must been a reason why after seventeen—or fifteen—years he decided to move here. What if he ran away from home? His mother was very eager for him to return. Remember?"

Fabian took a deep breath. "Lucille, if you're so interested in what's going on in his mind, ask *him*. Because I'm not. I don't care if you think I see the world in black and white or if I'm making it easy for myself. I have principles, and not killing other people is one of them, whether you're secretly a demon or not."

"So, if your mum killed someone in a car accident, you'd cut her off?" Lucille had to swallow. She should know better than putting mums into car accidents.

"If my mum tells me afterwards that it was no big deal, it wasn't her fault, and I should just get over it, then yes." He looked at the books before shutting the one he was reading. "Perhaps I should go to sleep after all. Let's hope tonight's not a special demon night."

Lucille clicked her tongue. "Don't be like that, Fabian." She couldn't lose the only person willing to stick out with her. They'd never spent much time alone, but she understood him a little better now. It wasn't so much that he was afraid of Matt, but that he stuck to his principles in a rather admiring fashion. Her own were seriously shaken by the whole situation.

Fabian sighed again. "How often have you visited Samantha?"

Lucille bit her lip. She'd reached out to Samantha the very next day, then again, a couple of days later. But she'd only gone around once to drop off some homework. "Once."

"I visit her almost every day," Fabian admitted. "She was shaking when I told her that Matt was back in town. I don't know if it's because she really loved Daniel or because it happened so soon after we lost Nico, but she's not getting over this. Not now, maybe not ever. While Matt... he should be just as devastated. I know I would be. And I get that a demon wouldn't care, but that's why I don't see myself befriending a demon any time soon."

"I'm sure that deep inside he is devastated. He just doesn't know how to cope with it. Hence the constant lashing out."

Fabian gave her a long, tired look. "Are you really sure, or do you just want that to be true?"

Lucille swallowed her answer and thought about it. The uncomfortable truth was that she *did* want to believe in Matt more than anything. The alternative was simply too horrible to behold. Lucille understood repressing your feelings. That was a concept that made sense. Not having emotions, however—that was beyond comprehension.

She never gave Fabian his answer, and they both worked through the books in silence until neither could keep their eyes open anymore.

Fabian

Fabian was bone-tired, but he couldn't sleep. His arm was itching too much, the skin underneath burning with heat. He'd tried cooling it under the tap, but the irritation didn't go away, and he'd soon scratched it open again.

"Do you have fleas on you, or what's the problem?" a voice rang from the other side of the guest room. Matt.

"Go back to sleep!" Fabian told him, while wrapping his arm in the blanket to keep himself from making it worse.

Matt snorted. "I would love to, but it's literally impossible with you scratching yourself bloody."

At the mention, Fabian kept rubbing the arm against the fabric. It didn't bring enough relief, so he unwrapped it again. "It's itching. So?"

"What is?"

"The spot where the ghoul scratched me three days ago." He sank his nails into his arm and briefly enjoyed the relief the painful stimulation brought him.

Suddenly, the light flickered on, and Matt came over. "You were scratched by a ghoul? Show me!"

Fabian stared at him. He didn't want to show his arm to Matt, but it was either that or keep scratching it. "Why?"

Matt grabbed his arm and turned it into the light. The spot Fabian had been scratching for three days looked grey instead of red. Thanks to his attention, it had got bigger. Matt leaned forward to sniff it, then screwed up his face. "That smells disgusting."

Embarrassed, Fabian pulled his arm away again. "I took a shower."

"Doesn't take away from the smell of decay," Matt said drily.

"Decay?" Fabian's stomach clenched as the word filtered into his brain.

Matt poked at his arm. "That there is dead." When Fabian gasped for air, Matt added, "Which doesn't mean you're dead. At least not yet."

"I'm going to die?" Fabian asked in a high voice. His breath came hard and fast, his mind reeling. The ghoul had infected him with its ghoulishness, and Fabian hadn't known for three days.

"I don't think you're going to die," Matt answered, but shrugged. "You're probably going to turn into a ghoul."

That didn't make Fabian feel any better. He started to hyperventilate.

"I'm sure there's a cure for it," Matt offered, but he didn't sound particularly convincing.

It wasn't like they'd had a lot of luck with magical healing in the past, Fabian thought, remembering Nico's horrifying death. The cure had taken the curse away, but it hadn't saved his life. "What about your brother?" Fabian almost choked on the words. He didn't want a demon to heal him, but he didn't want to die, either. "You know the horrible one..."

Matt scoffed. "Caspar? He'd rather rip his own arm off than heal some random human. And it doesn't work with those kinds of curses, anyway. He'd only infect himself that way. Not that I'd be sad about that."

"Could you at least try to act like you're interested in my survival?" Fabian snapped. A random human. If that was what he was to Matt, their friendship was well and truly dead.

Matt kept his mouth shut for a few seconds, looking the tiniest bit disgruntled. At last he took a deep breath and said, "First, you need to calm down. As I said, I'm sure there's a cure for it."

"There wasn't a cure for werewolf bites, either."

"There *wasn't*, but there is now," Matt reminded him, sounding slightly awed. "I would show this to Samantha *if* she would see me."

For a moment, Fabian stopped thinking about his imminent ghoulification. For all of Matt's bravado and devil-may-care attitude, he still seemed to worry about Samantha's opinion of him. It was the first time since his return that Fabian had seen a hint of something human in him. That he knew how wrong he was and just had no idea on how to deal with it. Like Lucille had said.

"You should seek her out and apologise if you really care for her." Fabian had no idea why he was offering him a piece of advice. Matt didn't deserve Samantha's forgiveness. And Samantha didn't deserve Matt calling on her and bothering her while she was still grieving for Daniel. Perhaps, he thought, having Matt ask for forgiveness would help Samantha. That must be why.

Matt ignored him like a pro. "You should hurry. The decay will spread to your entire body and you'll..." He paused, then decided to rip the Band-Aid off. "You'll develop an appetite for dead things and slip into ghoulish behaviour long before your body follows suit."

The moment he'd jumped in front of Lucille's magic arrow came to his mind. Had that been his mind subconsciously trying to defend another ghoul? Fabian shuddered, before focusing on Matt who still seemed terribly disinterested in his fate. "Thanks for the pep talk."

"I'm just saying it like it is. You need facts more than this emotional crap," Matt said with a sneer. "And no, that doesn't mean I want to see you dead."

Fabian wasn't too sure about that. "It wouldn't exactly cost you any sleep, either. Emotions really aren't your strength, are they?"

Matt jumped up and snarled. "You know what? Just keep doing your thing—all whining, no doing. Demon minds work differently than you human ones. We prefer the truth."

"Right. So, it was your human side that lied to us for months. Charming." Fabian didn't know why he was provoking someone as deadly and short-tempered as Matt, but he just couldn't keep quiet lately. Not while Matt kept acting so high and mighty.

"Oh, forget it!" Matt shouted. With a turn on his heel, he vanished, half-naked as he was.

"Matt!" Fabian groaned. This space jumping ability of demons seriously got on his nerves. But with Matt gone and the room still, Fabian's attention quickly returned to his itching arm.

After scratching viciously at it, he sniffed the spot and almost threw up in his mouth. It was bad. Really bad.

He was turning into a ghoul, or worse.

As if they didn't have enough problems at the moment.

Matt

Nothing was as telling of a low point in your life as standing on the streets of Greenvalley in the middle of a late-January night in your boxers. The packed snow under Matt's naked feet quickly lowered his body temperature, but it did little to cool off his temper. As he saw it, he had three options.

One: he could return to the Villa de Cerque and face Fabian again, admitting that storming off during their fight without getting dressed had been a bit premature. That option was certainly out of the picture. He would *not* lose face in front of Fabian.

Two: he could return to his own room, pick up some clothes, or continue the sleep that had been interrupted by Fabian's stupid scratching. And while his father was most likely asleep, returning home was like admitting defeat. Even if it was only to himself.

Three: he could return to Hell, the one place where he wouldn't be underdressed, and which didn't have snow or rain or even colder weather. He could leave Ashuan behind and forget the whole experiment. Nobody would come after him and nobody would ask questions on the other side. It was perfect. And entirely too depressing to entertain.

Matt started walking to keep his muscles warm. Fabian was so frustrating. He'd tried to explain himself to Fabian, but to no avail. Stuck in his narrow human views, Fabian wouldn't even listen to him. There he was, dying from a ghoul infection, and instead of looking for a solution, he wanted to be coddled and told it would be all right. As if words could heal any wounds.

So what if Matt wasn't the emotional type? He had other qualities. But it seemed like none of those mattered to humans without the appropriate show of feelings.

He bent down to pick up some snow and hurled it at the wall of a nearby house. The cold was like a hundred needles on his fingertips and made him think of Caspar—his usual source of torture. If he could only see Matt now. His brother would call it "twisting himself to fulfil human expectations", but if Matt had learned one thing these last days, it was that he was as far from fulfilling human expectations as Caspar would be if he gave it a go.

Whatever he did or said, it was all wrong, and Matt began to wonder how he'd managed to fit in for four months when he was making such a mess out of it now. Of course, four months ago, none of them had known about his identity.

Unbidden, Chay's words came to him. He'd warned him that Samantha would hate him the moment she found out what he'd kept secret from everyone. Somehow, he'd failed to mention that everyone else would be judging him as well.

Matt stopped to lean his forehead against a lantern, almost welcoming the sharp bite of the cold metal. Physical pain he could deal with. It was this human emotion thing that was so foreign to him.

Funnily enough, apart from the first few minutes after he'd woken from his Blood Night, he hadn't actually seen Samantha. Who knew if she truly hated him? People said all sorts of things in the heat of the moment, and there was only Fabian's anger as an indication of how she might be feeling. Surely, if she hated him so much, she would let him know.

Matt groaned and pushed himself off the lantern. It didn't matter what Samantha thought of him. He didn't need her approval, much less her forgiveness. What he needed right now was to get somewhere warm.

He looked around at the houses and street numbers, and suddenly an idea struck him. Option four promised a lot of heat. It was uncomplicated with none of the emotional baggage his friends came with—exactly the thing he needed.

A space jump brought Matt right in front of Cheryl's house. He took a minute to figure out which room she slept in, then knocked on her window and waited. It didn't take long for her sleepy head to look out from the window. Without her styling, her hair looked a bit flat, while her face was puffy from sleep.

"Matt?" She rubbed her eyes. "What are you doing here and... are you naked?"

"Almost," he admitted and gave her a lopsided grin. "Want to take care of the rest?"

Her cheeks blushed. Flustered, she shook her head, then nodded. "Oh... uh... wait. I'll come down and let you in."

Matt's patience—and cold resistance—was severely tested while he waited for Cheryl to open the door for him. When she finally did, there was a fresh coat of make-up on her face, and she'd changed into much sexier pyjamas.

She laughed. "I still can't believe it. This isn't a dream, is it?"

Since she wasn't inviting him in, Matt stepped forward until he was so close, he felt the heat emanating from her body, and he breathed on her forehead. "It'll be better than your dreams," he whispered, then lowered his lips to seal the deal with a kiss.

Cheryl gasped, then sunk into the kiss. She wrapped her arms around him and pulled him even closer. Suddenly, she shuddered. "You're ice-cold!"

Matt took the opportunity to sidestep her and sink his feet into the doormat. It was almost better than the kiss. Not that he let any of that show. Instead, he cocked an eyebrow and grinned at her. "Looks like I need someone to warm me up. What do you think about a hot shower?"

Her eyes glistened feverishly. She nodded a little too fast, then joined him and closed the door. "Come with me."

Cheryl took his hand and pulled him up the stairs behind her until they stumbled into a good-sized bathroom. She turned the hot water on and turned around, a question on her lips. "How did you end up almost naked on the streets? Did someone show you the door?"

Not interested in discussing his recent life choices with her, Matt stripped out of his boxers. Her eyes bulged and the red on her cheeks deepened. He grinned and stepped into the shower. "Do you want to join me now or not?"

\#

The hot water had burnt away the cold, and Cheryl had burnt away his thoughts. But only for the time being. Now she was sleeping in his arms, and Matt was still wide awake.

This was ridiculous. He'd never been unable to sleep before. Just as he'd never run through every situation in his mind again, analysing it from different points of view. Could he have been more compassionate with Fabian, knowing how easily the other boy freaked out? Matt should've known better.

Back when Nico had been bitten, the others had been offended by his pragmatism. Matt hadn't understood it then, and he didn't understand it now...

That wasn't entirely true. After the others had annoyed him with their emotion-clouded reactions, he'd gone to Samantha, thinking that she would understand him. She had, and then she'd gently explained to him why his pragmatism wasn't appreciated at a time like this. Pragmatism was cold, distant, and in a time of crisis, people preferred an emotional connection that would make them feel less alone.

Matt swallowed, his throat tightening at the thought of how wonderful Samantha had been when nothing else had made sense. And on a serious lack of sleep as well. She hadn't judged him but had patiently explained it to him, unaware of how little he truly knew. And then she'd made the impossible possible and blown him completely away.

Was all of that really gone?

When Matt closed his eyes, he saw her in front of him, her eyes bloodshot, face wet with tears, her hair in tangles. And her eyes... her beautiful green eyes had been cold— colder than the snow on his skin tonight—and yet so empty, as if a hole had opened underneath her, threatening to pull them both under.

I wish you were dead.

How many times had he heard that from Caspar or some other demon he'd pissed off with his existence? And how little had it mattered to him? He'd *laughed* in Caspar's face and revelled in the fact that he'd defied the odds and stayed alive.

But when Samantha had said it to him, it had felt as if she'd grabbed a knife and plunged it into his heart. He didn't understand why it hurt him so much. Why wasn't he able to laugh this off? And why was he lying next to Cheryl and thinking of a girl who hated him with every fibre of her being?

Option four was turning out to be just as bad as all the others. Would Fabian be asleep by now? Probably not if he was worried about turning into a ghoul. And besides, he didn't want to meet him again in the morning.

You should seek her out and apologise if you really care for her, Fabian had said.

Matt didn't know if he really cared for Samantha. It went against every one of his instincts. Why should he care about someone who wished him dead? And what was there to apologise for? Would "I'm sorry" really change things? Would she change her mind about him if he said those words? He wasn't sorry he'd killed Daniel. It had happened. It was a shame, but... if Matt was truly honest with himself, it wasn't even that. He'd been completely indifferent to the university student who'd stolen Samantha's heart in a flash. Had he deserved to die? Probably not, but it'd happened, and just because Matt had been the one to end his life didn't mean it was necessarily his fault. If he'd known about the Blood Night, Matt would've cancelled his birthday party. He wouldn't have risked his friends. No matter what Chay had said.

Stupid Chay. Not only had he kept this vital information from Matt, he'd also left him alone with this mess. Suddenly, his best friend had decided Matt needed to figure this out for himself. Well, Matt wasn't figuring it out. He'd tried, but he was even more confused than before. And now he was lying awake, thinking, instead of enjoying the post-sex bliss like he used to.

Annoyed, Matt untangled himself from Cheryl and chose the only option that made sense. Admit defeat and return home to René. With luck, his father was still asleep, and they'd never have to talk about it. And then maybe tomorrow, he could take Crumbs out for a walk and find out how much Samantha truly hated him, instead of losing sleep over it.

Rachel

Rachel walked along the sides of Jan's dream. There had never been sides in a dream before—the dreams of every person were as endless as the universe—but this one was closed off. It was all that was left of his once endless imagination.

It made her sad, standing on the outside of the stone walls. No dream should be limited, much less this severely. And no matter how many times she told herself that at least there still *was* a dream, she kept wanting to pound the walls and tear them wide open.

"I wouldn't do that," the familiar voice of Nico said. He appeared next to her and put a hand on the stone next to her. "Usually, when people encase their dreams, it's to protect their minds," he explained. "You're connected to this one?"

His question reminded Rachel that this wasn't truly Nico. Her brother would've known Jan and how the two of them were connected. Nevertheless, she nodded. "We're friends. A spell turned him to stone in the waking world."

"Ah. In that case, breaking down these walls—while possible—would do serious harm to his mind. Imagine being wide awake but unable to move even a finger."

Rachel shuddered as understanding dawned on her. If she broke down Jan's dream walls, he'd be caught in an endless dream when he should've been awake. "So, we'll have to bring him back first."

"It cannot be fixed here," Nico confirmed.

She let go of the wall and turned her attention to him. Jan's dream slipped from her awareness, and they returned to her meadow. "Who are you really?"

The corners of Nico's mouth twitched upwards. A familiar gesture that made her heart ache for him. "I'm the dreamer, nothing more and nothing less."

"But your name is not Nico?" she asked.

"It can be," Nico said thoughtfully. "Names and forms don't really matter in this world. They're like dreams. Temporary and fleeting. There's not a single soul alive who remembers me," he admitted. "No one dreams *of* me."

"But I dream of my brother."

"Yes," Nico said, once again smiling like her brother always had. "Who am I to deny you your dream?"

Rachel had no idea how she knew, but she suddenly understood that his appearance was up to her. For him to change, she would have to let go of her brother. It wasn't something she could see herself doing any time soon. "I miss him."

"I miss you too," Nico whispered.

And though her mind told her that this wasn't truly Nico, she fled into his arms and hugged him tight. Nico wrapped his arms around her and said, "It's nice not to be alone here."

She could've asked him questions. Like how he had become the dreamer or what his world looked like when he'd been awake. How did the dreamweb work and what did the prophecy mean for her? But Nico wouldn't have the answers to that, and so she never asked.

"I think that vision is for you," he said after a while, nodding towards a blooming flower.

Rachel separated herself from him unwillingly. "What is it now?" She reached for it but had to hold her breath as the memories of an awful stink enveloped her.

Once, a couple of years ago, she'd gone downstairs to where her mother kept her wine. It wasn't a wine cellar, or anything fancy like that. Just a cold, dark room that was empty most of the time. Rachel no longer remembered what she'd been doing there, but she remembered the terrible stink. Nico had been with her, and together they'd gone into the room and found the source of it. A rat had entered the house and died behind the rack. Her mother had never noticed, or never bothered to remove it, and so it had been lying there to rot.

The very same smell was coming off the vision.

"I don't think I want to see that," Rachel said. Usually, the visions overcame her, but this one was waiting for her to explore. Just as she was about to turn away, something splashed her face.

Rachel rubbed the liquid off her skin, expecting it to be foul, but it was nothing more than water. *Water!*

She was inside the vision in a flash and almost screamed when she fell into the churning ocean of Fabian's panic.

I can't drown in dreams. I can't drown in dreams, Rachel told herself again and again as she clawed for air. At last, she broke through the surface and gasped. There was an island not too far from her. In fact, it was coming closer fast, or maybe the waves pushed her towards it.

At first, she grasped for the dry spot, but the moment she got a whiff of the air, she felt sick. It was the rotten stench again. It was clinging to her skin, making her feel itchy and sticky. She wanted to wash it off in the sea, but the sea had already retreated, leaving her alone on the island, and so Rachel had no choice but to make her way across the land.

It was a cemetery just like Greenvalley's cemetery, only this one was much bigger and stretched everywhere around her. Rachel slowly turned to gather her bearings. When she'd completed her turn, she screamed.

In front of her, the ghoul queen had appeared. She was a bizarre beauty, though her skin was sunken and grey, and there was no hair on her patchy head. Still, she exuded a radiance that was reflected in her shimmering black eyes. Rachel was attracted and repulsed at the same time, and then she saw who was worshipping at her feet.

"Fabian!" Terror filled her as she saw Fabian kiss the feet of his queen, before looking up at her with pure admiration.

The queen raised him up, and as he stood, his arms lengthened, the freckles vanished from his face, replaced by listless grey, and his beautiful ginger hair fell out until he was as bald as his queen. Then his blue eyes, the only part still unmistakably him, turned to her, and he spoke. But no words came out of his mouth, only grunts. And when he opened his lips further, needle-like teeth filled his mouth.

Rachel fled the vision. She screamed and pulled walls around it, sank it into a deep pool, then buried the pool. "No, no, no!" Anger flooded her, as if that ever did any good. "This will not happen!" Once more, she screamed, teetering at the point of waking, and turned away.

In front of her, Nico sat on the old swing that had hung in their garden when they'd been younger. "What will you do about it?"

"About what?" Rachel tried, but she knew she sounded ridiculous. The vision was a warning. It would come true whether she was ready to cope with it or not. "I will—"

Someone woke her.

#

"Rachel..." Fabian's voice called her back to the waking world.

Rachel blinked. It was still dark outside, but Fabian was in her room. Was he trying to get in her bed? No, Fabian would never do that unless she invited him in. "What is it?"

"I've got something to tell you," Fabian whispered.

"Now?" Rachel already knew what he was going to tell her and she didn't want to hear it. She just couldn't lose him, too.

Fabian crawled onto her bed and pulled up his legs. "Do you remember when we first fought the ghouls?" Rachel didn't say anything, dreading each word. "Just before Matt appeared, one of them had me in their grasp and... it scratched me." His voice shook, and when he took a couple of quick breaths, he almost choked on them.

A proper girlfriend would go to him and hug him tight. She would coo and care for him and tell him that it would be all right. But it wasn't going to be all right. Rachel sat frozen in her bed. It was Nico all over again. He was bleeding out, and she stood there and did nothing.

"I showed the scratch to Matt, and he said... he said..." Fabian took another shaky breath. "He said that I will turn into a ghoul. Or die. Or both. And then he vanished."

Rachel was tempted to concentrate on the last bit, though she didn't really think it was terribly interesting why Matt had vanished in the middle of the night. Instead, she pulled herself together and grappled for some clever words to say. The only thing she came up with was "Or neither?" and even that didn't come out right.

"He was pretty confident, and..." Fabian gasped. "My arm *is* rotting. I also jumped in front of Lucille's spell because... I didn't mean to, it just seemed really important at the time."

"I..." Rachel winced at her lack of emotional response. Her boyfriend was scared for his life, rotting while still breathing, and all she could say was, "I don't know what to do."

"I don't know either," came the prompt reply. Fabian rocked back and forth on the bed, clearly losing his mind.

Rachel had to do better. "Fabian..."

"Matt said that there would be a cure," he blurted. "He doesn't actually know of one, but he thinks it exists."

Rachel latched on to it. "You should show this to Samantha. She helped... Nico." Not that it had changed anything, but she could do the same for Fabian. Make sure he would die human.

Damn it! She wanted to slap herself out of this stupor. Losing Fabian would be the worst thing to happen to her and to Samantha. Whether he died a human or a ghoul didn't matter. It would devastate Samantha, and it would destroy Rachel. That wasn't allowed to happen. She couldn't allow that.

"I don't want to bother Samantha," Fabian whispered. "She's not ready."

"I'm sure Sam would want to be bothered if you were dying." The sarcasm in her voice hurt Rachel, and it made Fabian wince. She didn't want to be this cold. Not to the boy she'd loved for so many years. He was important to her, so why couldn't she show that to him? Why couldn't she be there for him when he needed her most? Like he'd been there for her when she'd needed it?

Because it would destroy her if she let herself feel all of what she should be feeling.

Rachel shivered as she realised the implications. It was incredibly selfish of her, and yet, she didn't have more to give. Not after losing Nico. So, instead of hugging him and telling him sweet nothings, she said, "We'll go to Sam in the morning. She'll know what to do." And then she tried her best not to see the desperation in his eyes.

Samantha

"Sammy! You need to come quick!"

Samantha jumped out of bed and almost fell over her shoes. She grabbed the Thorak from her little nightstand, her heart hammering in her chest. Her grandmother rarely called for help like that, and in her mind, she saw Matt towering over her, his sword raised high.

She blinked rapidly to banish the vision until she found out what was really going on. But the grip around the dagger's hilt tightened as she ran out of her room and down the corridor.

To her great relief, there was no sight of Matt or any other demon. Instead, Lucille and Rachel were there, pushing Fabian into a chair in the living room, while her grandmother was already in the kitchen, tinkering with pots.

Samantha slipped the dagger on the shelf and hugged herself, keenly aware that she was standing there in nothing but her nightshirt. "This is an early morning surprise." It couldn't be that late. The sun was barely in the sky.

Fabian grunted and threw himself against the others, but Lucille and Rachel pushed him back down, and then Samantha saw it. His left arm looked as if it had been dipped into grey paint.

"It's progressing faster now," Lucille cried out.

"What is?" Samantha asked as she dashed over and sank to her knees next to the chair in order to look at his arm. It reeked horrendously. "What happened?" She bit her lip to keep herself from asking whether Matt had done this. Matt had a sword and some demon magic, nothing that could explain the visible decay on Fabian's arm.

"Ghouls," Rachel said, then tentatively stroked Fabian's forehead. "Do you want water?"

He grunted again, then forced himself to speak. "Only if it can keep me from dying."

Samantha's heart fluttered. Fabian was *dying*? Surely, he was just being his overdramatic self. "Ghouls?"

Now, Lucille turned to her, her eyes wide with shock. "We didn't tell you because we thought you still needed time, but there is a ghoul infestation in the cemetery. Well, there was." She was clearly rambling, but Samantha let her go on in hopes of grasping the important details. "Fabian was injured three days ago, but he didn't tell us. And yesterday, we returned to it. We were supposed to distract the ghouls, but my spell went wrong, and now the ghouls, the cemetery, and Jan are all petrified, and every counterspell I found only leads to me killing Jan, if he isn't already dead because I turned his brain into gravel." She gasped for air and continued right away, "And now Fabian is turning into a ghoul and is decaying while he still breathes and—"

"You petrified Jan?" There was simply too much information at once.

Lucille sobbed. "It was an accident. If he hadn't tried to save me, I wouldn't have touched him while I said the spell. And I have no idea what to do now!" she shouted.

"Calm down," Samantha said gently, and pulled her into an embrace. While Lucille sobbed on her shoulder, she patted her back and looked at Fabian, who stared at her, practically threatening her to tell *him* to calm down. She mouthed, "It's going to be okay" to him, and concentrated on Lucille for the moment.

Meanwhile, her grandmother came back, a draught in her hand. "Here, drink this," she told Fabian.

Fabian snarled, but Rachel had him in her hands and pushed him back down. Then she took the draught from Elda. "Drink this."

His protests melted away and when he took a sip, he looked his old whiny self. "I don't want to die."

"You won't," Elda told him. "I can make a salve for your arm, which will stop and reverse the transformation."

"You can?" Rachel asked, almost more surprised than Fabian.

Elda smiled at them. "Yes, the recipe is in one of those books." She pointed at the potion books in the corner. "But I need the skin of the ghoul queen for it. She's got a special secrete on it that is the main ingredient of the salve. And it has to be the queen of this particular pack, because that's... your pack, so to speak."

Fabian screwed up his face and sank into his chair. "But she's stone."

When her grandmother looked confused, Samantha said, "Lucille petrified the ghouls."

"And Jan," Lucille sobbed.

"And Jan. Do you know a counterspell for that?" Samantha asked. Even if her grandmother didn't use that kind of magic, she had studied it a lot. Samantha had as well, but she couldn't remember ever reading about how to undo a petrification spell.

Elda shook her head. "It's not that easy. The magic of words is powerful, but it is also limited. There might be a very complicated spell that will do exactly what you want it to, but there's a much easier way."

Lucille eased out of Samantha's embrace and dried her tears. "An easier way? There *is* a way? A potion?"

"Easier." Elda smiled at her. "When you voice your spells, you bind magic to your words—or rather you bind magic into spells with the power of your words. But there are different ways spells can be fabricated." Samantha realised where her grandmother was going with this before she said it. "Spells can be woven, for example, and just as easily, they can be unravelled. Sammy, why don't you go with Lucille and take a look at her spell?"

"Sam?" Lucille turned to her in wonder.

Put on the spot, Samantha had no idea if she was capable of it. "I've never done this before." She could barely string a spell together as it was.

"The unravelling is easier than the weaving. You just have to find the main thread and pull it. However, in this situation, I would advise tying off parts of the spell, so you don't have to deal with all the ghouls at once."

It sounded so easy when her grandmother said it. Just find the main thread. Tie off the spell parts. She remembered the magic slipping from her fingers as she tried to knot it a few days ago. "Okay..." she said feebly.

"You've found your magic?" Lucille asked.

"Yes, but it's really not that impressive. Practically, I can see the spells, but I haven't woven a proper spell yet." It was for that reason Samantha had kept it to herself while she trained with her grandmother. Compared to Lucille's quick-fire spells, and Fabian's control over water, her magic ability seemed rather feeble. Samantha wasn't a stranger to studying and applying herself, but she had wanted to do a little bit more than a soft glimmer of light before she told her friends.

"If you can undo my petrification spell, it'll be very impressive!" Lucille's face was rigid with need.

Samantha sighed, feeling the pressure of expectation. "I don't know if I can."

"Which is why this is the perfect opportunity to test what you've learned," her grandmother said, stabbing her in the back. "I'll prepare the salve and take care that Fabian doesn't rejoin his pack." She patted Fabian's arm, which prompted him to snarl at her.

"I'll join you," Rachel said quickly. "You might need extra help. I don't know what to do about the ghoul queen, but three are better than two."

Samantha had expected her to stay with Fabian, but she nodded, convinced there wouldn't even be a ghoul queen to fight. "Okay, let me get dressed, and then I can take a look at it."

"If this works, I owe you!" Lucille whispered.

Samantha only managed half a smile and fled from the room.

Daniel isn't here, Samantha told herself as she walked into the cemetery a mere three-quarters of an hour later. Her dad had driven her to Daniel's funeral. The cemetery he was buried in looked completely different from the little overgrown Greenvalley Cemetery, but having been to Nico's funeral just two months earlier, her mind was mixing the two now.

Lucille hadn't lied when she'd said she'd turned all the ghouls to stone. With fresh snow on them, they looked like the most eerie grave guardians of all time. It was a marvel the cemetery hadn't had complaints about its creepy art installations yet.

This early in the morning, there were no visitors, which suited Samantha just fine for her first serious attempt at magic. Or rather anti-magic.

"So, how does this work?" Lucille asked. "Weaving magic. It sounds marvellous, but I can't quite imagine it."

For Samantha, it was the most natural way of casting spells. She'd watched her grandmother weave magic since she'd been a little child, and she'd read books and books about it, though she'd only recently been able to see the magic for herself. "You know how magic flows through the world in rivers?"

Lucille nodded. "Yes, I saw that once when... when that demon cursed me—or rather I cursed myself."

Next to her, Rachel trudged through the snow with her crossbow, watching for stray ghouls.

"Well, when you cast a spell, you force the magic into a pattern. Weaving magic does the same, only you build up the pattern thread by thread," Samantha explained.

"How do you know which pattern does what?"

"You've got to learn them. Just as you need to study spells, I need to study patterns. At some stage, it might come to me intuitively, but I'm certainly not there yet. Actually, I don't think I'm at any stage," Samantha admitted.

Lucille shook her head. "You sell yourself short. You might not have any practical experience yet, but I bet your theory is on point. I'm sure you'll catch up in no time."

Samantha ran her finger over a ghoul statue they passed, trying to dip into the spell. "Thanks for the vote of confidence." It was a pattern so intricate it barely made sense to her. Like looking at a colourful fabric without seeing the weave behind it.

"I believe in you. I have to," Lucille half-joked and sighed. "So, is there a pattern to undo petrification?"

"There could be, but it would be very complicated." She let go of the ghoul, not daring to dig deeper into the magic just yet. "Which means it's well beyond my abilities. Fortunately, the petrification is already a spell, so all I need to do is understand the fabric of it and unravel it."

"Sounds doable to me," Rachel muttered.

Samantha blushed. "I guess. The difficulty will be to control the unravelling, so we get Jan back and leave the ghouls until we can deal with them. And the ghoul queen, of course."

They arrived at a spot with almost a dozen ghoul statues. In between them, a familiar shape crouched near the floor. Even if Lucille hadn't told her that Jan had tried to save her, she could see it now. His stony features made her uncomfortable, and she cleared her throat. "Wow."

"I know," Lucille said softly.

Once again, Samantha put her fingers on the stone, gingerly placing them on Jan's shoulder. The fabric of magic looked exactly as it had on the ghoul. As she looked deeper, she saw the individual threads making up the spell. "That is impressive work. What spell was this?"

"From the Romanian spell book you gave me for Christmas. I had another one, a destructive arrow, but that one almost killed Fabian," Lucille said bitterly. "Maybe I should give up on this whole magic business."

Samantha's heart went out to her. She knew exactly how Lucille felt after her part in Nico's death. "Don't."

"It wasn't your fault," Rachel said, sounding almost annoyed. "Fabian jumped in front of it because he was being forced into loyalty by his infection. If I jump in front of your car, it doesn't mean you can't drive. And same with Jan. You didn't put a spell on him without knowing how to reverse it. He jumped into it. It was an accident."

Both Samantha and Lucille were stunned. It felt as if they'd been scolded by a teacher, but Rachel just sighed. "We need to stop fighting over every little thing and blaming each other."

"You're right," Lucille said, then put an arm around her and whispered, "Thanks."

Rachel looked stiff and uncomfortable in the embrace, but then her eyes met Samantha's, and she softened. "And I don't mean what happened on New Year's."

"I know," Samantha said, slightly choked up. "Which one is the ghoul queen?" she asked, to distract herself from the inflowing memories.

"Oh, we'd have to ask Matt. She was his responsibility," Lucille said, then clapped her hands in front of her mouth. "I'm sorry."

The memories came crashing down on Samantha. Blood on his hands. Blood in the snow. Daniel's empty eyes. Melchior raising her chin while he had her trapped between his body and the wall. "I know that he's back," she muttered. She'd also known that he was back in the group, welcomed by Lucille.

"One day, you'll have to see him," Lucille said gently. "When you come back to school..." Her voice drifted off.

"I know," Samantha whispered. She was well aware that she couldn't hide at her grandmother's for the rest of her life.

Lucille looked more and more desperate. "It's not an easy thing. I get this, but..." Her back straightened. "If the last few weeks and our ghoul adventure have taught me anything, it's that we need the both of you."

Surely, Lucille hadn't meant it that way, but her words reminded Samantha of the prophecy that bound her and Matt together, no matter how much she hated him. "I know," she repeated, this time with tears in her eyes.

"You do," Rachel said softly, and in her eyes, Samantha saw that she was well aware of the strings fate had tied around them.

"I'm sorry." Lucille lowered her head.

Samantha took a deep, shaky breath. "Let's get Jan back first, okay?"

She closed her eyes and dove deeper into the magic. It was a bit like using the microscopes at school. One minute, there was this big complicated and compact spell, and the next, she saw individual threads intricately woven into each other. The magic of the spell was more red than the usual green she worked with, which reminded her of the colour theory she'd once read about in a book. If she remembered correctly, red magic was an aggressive type of magic that forced spells to take shape. Like Lucille's words.

It was surprisingly easy to see where she had to tie off the spell to keep her interference limited to Jan. Samantha started around his feet, plucking strings from the web and knotting them, until a separation had formed between Jan and the rest of the stone. Her fingers burned under the vibrant touch as if she was pulling on plastic threads rather than soft natural ones. Red magic was not something she wanted to weave with any time soon, but it helped her stay concentrated on the task, for if she didn't, it would cut deep into her fingers.

After what felt like an eternity, Samantha stood back and examined her work. It looked like she'd managed to split the spell into two. "Alright. Get ready."

With one deep breath, she pulled on the threads she knew would unravel the spell. It looked like rain washing the stone from Jan's features. First his head took on colour, then his shoulders and the rest of him. Samantha held her breath as the unravelling reached the line of knots around his feet. The spell around the ghouls had held, and she let out a breath.

Jan was starting to move, while the spell unravelled from his arms and along the battle staff he was holding. And then Samantha saw it.

"No, no, no!"

She jumped forward to grab the magic, but she was a split second too late. The tip of the staff touched the foot of a ghoul, and the magic burst through the loophole like a river through a hole in the dam. Samantha stretched out her hands to keep hold of the unravelling strands, but the magic cut her, and she pulled away in reflex, unable to stop it.

Thin lines of blood crisscrossed her hands as she watched Lucille's spell unravel along everything that physically touched each other. About three statues remained, but the rest of the ghouls were moving just as Jan did. And he was about one second away from being attacked by the ghoul whose foot he'd touched.

A bolt buried itself in the ghoul's forehead, and the creature crumpled to the ground. Jan stumbled as gravity reclaimed him, landing on his butt. He looked up to see Rachel with her crossbow. "Oh, hey there. Where's..." His casting glance found Lucille. "There you are."

There was no time to bring him up to speed as the ghouls closed in on them. Jan got to his feet and whirled his staff around to push two of them away. Rachel sank another crossbow bolt, and Samantha tried to weave something with the green magic she was more familiar with, but it wouldn't work. Instead, an arrow of black magic hit the ghoul in front of her and dissolved it from the inside out.

"That's a cool spell," she admitted. "Just—"

"Not on the queen. Got it." Lucille nodded and spoke the spell again.

"Uhm, I could use some help here," Jan called, still struggling with the two ghouls.

Rachel raised her crossbow. "Get down." As soon as he had followed her lead, she shot the left one.

Meanwhile, Lucille called loudly, "Sageat negru distrugere!" Her spell hit the right one, but this time it wasn't quite as effective. The ghoul fell to the ground, yet only half-dissolved. "What's happening?"

Samantha got a quick read on the magic and gasped. "You're destroying magic." Black magic was of the destructive kind. "What I mean is, there's not enough magic in the area to support your spell." Her own attempts at weaving were useless, not just because of her inexperience but due to the lack of green magic after two powerful attacks.

"When did you get here, by the way?" Jan asked, confused.

"They're getting back up!" Rachel shouted, and sure enough, the ghouls she shot were clambering up again. They didn't even bother to remove the bolts and kept coming at them.

Only Lucille's destroyed ones didn't return. Samantha looked around frantically when she noticed the near-invisible brown strings that tied all ghouls to something further away. "The ghoul queen!" They couldn't die because they owed their life to the queen.

"Wasn't Matt going to take care of her?" Jan asked.

"Times change. Try to keep up!" Lucille barked at him, before casting a shield spell to protect their flank.

Jan opened his mouth, but by then, the ghouls were too close, and he quickly returned his focus to pushing them off. Rachel shot another one, who got up half a minute later. Samantha continued trying to weave a spell, but there just wasn't enough magic for her to hold onto.

The ghouls pushed them closer and closer together. An escape was getting more and more implausible. "What should we do?" Lucille cried.

Rachel pushed her crossbow into Samantha's hand and began to mumble something. Samantha managed to shoot one of the ghouls, but two others closed the gap. Next to her, Jan was huffing and wheezing as he tried to keep the creatures at bay.

"Help us if you value your peace!" Rachel shouted.

Samantha wanted to say that they were all doing their best, but her breath caught in her throat as shimmering forms rose from the graves around them. The ghosts of the dead flowed through the ghouls, which swatted at them like pesky flies, inadvertently opening up a little corridor.

"Let's go," Rachel whispered and led them through the ghouls and ghosts.

"Creepy," Jan whispered once they'd put a little distance between them.

Samantha took over the lead and followed the brown threads of magic deeper into the cemetery. "I almost forgot you were good with ghosts."

"Well, they'll help, but since they're not truly in this world, we can't count on their efforts for long," Rachel explained.

"Then we'd better hurry."

They started running down the rows of graves, snow flying behind them. In front of Samantha, the brown strings started to run together. She knew it was another form of magic, but it was so revolting, she didn't dare touch it.

The ghoul queen was still a stone statue, but she wasn't alone. Steel glinted in the morning sun, and for a moment, Samantha saw the black hair and pair of demon wings from her memory. She stopped short, catching her breath. She felt as if all the life was seeping out of her, and the world had come to a standstill.

Matt turned around, squinting against the sunlight. "There you are."

Matt

By morning, Matt had made a decision. Samantha might be avoiding him, but he was done avoiding her. He was done trying to read between the lines of their friends' reactions. He needed *her* reaction. By now, Matt was convinced that Chay had been wrong. He should have told Samantha everything from the start—or, at least, once things had become a little more permanent. Once he'd explained it all to her, how demons lived and dealt with things, and what the Blood Night truly meant, she'd see that it wasn't his fault. Samantha was smart and empathetic. If anyone could truly understand where he was coming from, it would be her. Matt was sure of it.

So, while the morning sun was still low, he made his way over to her grandmother's place, the most likely spot Samantha would be at. He would've preferred to call first, but she seemed to have blocked his number. A surprisingly irresponsible move from her.

Matt appeared down the driveway of Elda's house when he heard the old lady scream. Quickly, he ran around the corner and stopped short. Elda was on her front step, holding her backside after what looked like a fall in wet conditions. Very wet conditions.

A flash of ginger dashed into the forest. Matt wasted no time and took up pursuit. With his demon powers, he easily cut off Fabian's flight and wrapped his arms around the taller boy, pinning his arms to his body. Fabian grunted and snarled while kicking up a storm, but Matt handled him, and dragged him back to the house.

He met Elda's eyes and, for a moment, he faltered. She'd got up, though she was still leaning to one side. Her eyes regarded him with great caution, but then she nodded inside and led the way.

Matt carried Fabian into the house and down some stairs into the cellar. There, he pushed him inside, and Elda closed the door, quickly activating a rune. A second later, Fabian ran into the door, but the rune lit up and kept him inside.

"Well..." Elda said, meeting Matt's eyes again.

He wasn't able to stand her glance for long and nodded at the door. "I assume he wanted to play with the ghouls?" Just as Matt had predicted, Fabian's infection was turning him into a ghoul, or at least someone who valued their life over that of his fellow humans.

"I should've killed you back then." So much for small talk.

Matt got ready to jump. Last time, she'd poisoned him with her tea, but he wouldn't fall for it so easily again. Still, he believed that Elda was a formidable witch who'd fought her share of demons in her lifetime. And he couldn't exactly kill her, even if she attacked him first. "Why haven't you?" He took a stab in the dark. If Elda really wanted to kill him, she probably would've done so already.

"Chay came and made a plea for your case," she said carefully.

That took Matt by surprise. Chay had left him so abruptly, he half-thought he'd been angry with Matt as well. It was nice to discover he was still on his side. "Did he really?"

"Eric always said that sometimes we need to tolerate the lesser evil to stave off the bigger one."

Matt sobered instantly. Chay might have made his plea, but the jury still found him guilty. "Right."

"I will tolerate your presence here in Greenvalley," Elda continued. "But set one foot wrong, and I'll have your wings."

Matt bristled. Most of the time, he didn't bother with his wings. Partly because he barely needed to fly if he was able to space-jump, and partly because they were rather sensitive. Ripping them from his back would be a torment even Caspar hadn't put him through. Yet.

"I'm not planning to," he told Elda sullenly, before looking up the stairs. "Is Samantha here?"

"And why would I tell you that?" Elda crossed her arms.

"Because if you don't, I'll go looking for her."

Elda sighed heavily. "No, she's not. She's at the cemetery, cleaning up your mess."

"It's not *my* mess!" Matt hissed back. "I didn't do anything. It was all Lucille and her careless spell casting."

"You, of all people, should be careful about accusing others of carelessness."

Matt held his tongue. Lucille *had* been careless. Nothing had taken control over *her.* But then he remembered what she'd said to him about having no one to teach her. And maybe he *had* overreacted. It wasn't like she could've anticipated Jan being in the way. He'd hate to have people going hard on him if someone jumped into his sword. Heck, he *was* hating it.

"Never mind," he said at last. "I'll find her."

"Matt..." Elda's voice lost a little of her edge.

He didn't stick around long enough to find out what else she had to say to him.

A few seconds later, Matt arrived at the cemetery right next to the petrified ghoul queen. She stood still, but Matt found the stone shimmering. Unsure whether it would hold, he drew his sword. Just then, he heard people running towards him and turned.

And there she was. Leading the pack, her cheeks reddened by cold and exertion, her black hair flying. Their eyes met, and Matt swallowed while Samantha came to a stop. His mind came up empty. All he could think to say was: "There you are."

Samantha didn't reply. Instead, her face convulsed, caught between anger and surprise. And before he could say any more, Jan stepped into his field of vision. "Since when do we have a ghoul statue in the cemetery?"

"That's a long story," Lucille said, sounding exasperated. "Matt."

He lowered his eyes and cleared his voice. "Thought you could use some help." Somehow, he'd always imagined his first meeting with Samantha alone, not with everyone else around.

"Well, it's nice of you to say hello after vanishing in the middle of the night," Lucille said testily.

Apparently, Matt had reached the end of her patience as well. He rubbed the back of his neck while struggling to form words. "I—"

Samantha pushed past Lucille and came straight at him. Matt's heart jumped into his chest, pounding so heavily he forgot how to breathe. But instead of attacking him, she knelt at his feet—or rather at the ghoul queen's feet. "Get ready."

"Ready for what?" Matt asked, his voice breathless.

She didn't say. Instead, her fingers were flying through invisible patterns.

"Samantha can undo my spell," Lucille explained. "Which means that this ghoul queen will come alive in a few seconds."

"I see." He put the tip of his sword on the ghoul queen's chest, remembering how fast she was. Below him, Samantha worked in silence, never once looking up at him. It took Matt almost a minute to work up the courage to ask her again. "You can undo spells?" That was great, wasn't it? She'd always wanted to do magic.

But Samantha kept her silence and closed her eyes for good measure.

"They're coming," Rachel warned.

The rest of the ghouls were drawing near. A few ghosts shimmered between them, but they soon dropped behind, one by one. Jan did a show of whirling his staff around. "Here we go again."

"Sam, hurry!" Lucille shouted.

Samantha's shoulders lowered, her fingers paused, and she sighed. Matt would've bet his mother's bed that she was having to start again because Lucille had interrupted her.

While he stayed vigilant, waiting for the moment the ghoul queen would come alive, Matt watched the others fight off the ghouls. Things were getting urgent quickly. His hand twitched when he saw a ghoul strike Lucille to the ground. Rachel shot another of her bolts, but the ghoul she'd hit barely slowed down. Jan whirled his staff around until one of the ghouls grabbed it and tore it from his hands.

Matt itched to join the fight, but he knew that he had one job and one alone. He couldn't afford to let his attention stray enough to be of any help to them. He had to trust in Samantha. If she believed she could do this, he had no doubt about it.

Just then, the skin of the ghoul queen shimmered. She opened her eyes—and Matt drove the sword into her chest.

Around him, he suddenly heard the laboured breathing of the others. The ghouls, however, didn't move. They stood dumbly for a few seconds before sinking to the ground. Matt drew his sword back and watched the ghoul queen crumble.

Samantha switched gears and got out a little bag and a pocket knife. With it, she scraped something off the skin of the ghoul queen.

Matt cleared his throat. "So..."

Done with her work, Samantha got up and said to the others, "That should be enough for the salve. Ghouls rot very quickly, so we can just leave them here."

"Cool." Jan got to his feet and pulled up Lucille. "Now, if only someone could explain to me why the sun has risen, that would be perfect."

Lucille laughed nervously and hooked her arm into his and patted him. "As I already said, it's a really long story. Do you remember how the ghouls were coming at us?"

Samantha started moving, and the rest of them followed her lead, slowly walking away without ever looking back. Matt stood dumbfounded. He'd been prepared to explain his case, to discuss it, and fend off the ridiculous arguments that he could've somehow anticipated his actions and prevented them. Samantha was supposed to be the reasonable one. Instead, she'd treated him as if he didn't exist past his ability to put a sword into monsters.

Matt had no idea what to do next, and so he watched them leave with the sinking feeling in his gut that this wasn't going to be an easy fix.

\#

Unsure of where else to go, Matt went home. He sat on his bed and stared blankly at his desk while replaying his meeting with Samantha in his mind. What had he expected? He wasn't quite sure, just that she would still be Samantha. And of course, she still was, but things were different. She no longer looked at him the same way. Heck, she'd barely looked at him at all. Her voice when she'd spoken to him had been so empty of everything that made her *her*. Samantha was still competent, clever, and a true lifesaver, but everything else had changed. As if he stood on the outside of her little world, unable to get in.

The front door closed, and Matt heard the patter of Crumbs' little feet as he ran to his bowl, and his father's heavier footsteps. A key fell into a bowl. A bunch of letters landed on the table. Then water running in the kitchen.

The sounds made Matt feel even more lonely. As if his father's life, too, was his own little world. One that didn't need Matt in it to keep turning.

Annoyed, Matt shook himself from his stupor. Of course, his father didn't *need* him. He'd been living on his own for fifteen years and done just fine. And if *he* wanted to talk to his father, he could just do it. He got up and opened the door of his room.

"You're home," René said, carrying a glass of water into the living room and sitting down to open his letters.

"Why wouldn't I be?" Matt asked, as if there weren't a million reasons for him to be somewhere else.

René raised an eyebrow. "Well, you weren't last night."

"I was at Lucille's. With the others." And then he hadn't been. He'd left there in the middle of the night to go to Cheryl's house of all places. Now, several hours later, he couldn't believe he'd done that. And it hadn't even made anything better, or more bearable. "I'm an adult—and half demon. I can do whatever I want."

His father's eyebrows rose even higher. "Sure. You do you." He shook his head and started opening his letters.

Matt clenched his fists, still hearing the words. *You do you.* As if doing him was something bad. As if it didn't matter to his father. He was standing on the outside again, and this time, he couldn't bear it. "Shouldn't you be on my side? You're my father, aren't you?" He hated how whiny his voice suddenly sounded. Why would he need René's approval? He'd lived his whole life without it.

René looked up again, his face a little softer now. "I didn't know that meant anything to you."

Desperation crept up Matt's throat and made him gasp. "I-I..." What was he supposed to say to that? What did it even mean?

His father sat up straighter. "Look, Matt, I'm going to be honest with you." Matt felt as if he was going to be sick. "I don't know how to deal with you. What I mean to you or what you need... and want from me. I thought that we were getting to know each other and building something, but the moment you encountered a problem you couldn't solve, you ran away. Back to Hell. I would've been there for you."

"I ran from my problems, not you," Matt whispered in desperation. He almost wanted to swallow them. They sounded so weak, so needy. "I'm... Lucille says I'm being a jerk to everyone. Fabian is angry with me and mistrusts every word I say, and Samantha... Samantha won't even look at me. She's been missing school. For three weeks." He knew because he kept looking for her in every class they shared.

"Well, this isn't exactly easy for her," René said carefully.

Matt rolled his eyes. "I know that! But after three weeks, I thought she'd be a little bit over it."

His father frowned. "Matt, she was in love with Daniel. That's not something you get over quickly."

"Well, demons do!" Matt was growing impatient. He'd killed demons in Hell. None of their relatives had given him grief, or if they had, he'd killed them too, and everyone was fine with it.

"Demons aren't usually in love, are they now?" his father asked, sounding almost amused.

Matt glared at him. "Of course not! This whole love thing doesn't even make sense. How can you fall in love with someone you only met two or three weeks ago? Apparently, that's enough time."

"It happens." René shrugged with a sheepish smile. "I fell in love with your mother on the spot. Feelings don't need to make sense, Matt. Some of them grow slowly over time, some burst into existence, taking over everything else." He cocked his head. "What about your feelings?"

"My feelings?" Matt sputtered. He hadn't really thought about his feelings. "I don't have any. I mean, not those 'taking-over-everything' kind of feelings, or anything deep, like love." He shrugged, though his face muscles twitched terribly. "As you said, demons don't fall in love." He knew for a fact that his mother had never loved René. She might have been attracted to him and oddly fond of him, but if he died tomorrow, she wouldn't even spare another thought for him.

René nodded sagely to himself, as he took some time to formulate his answer. "That's true, I suppose. But you are part human, not just demon."

Matt was starting to hate that fact. While Caspar had given him grief about it all his life, most demons had never cared. His blood hadn't made him different from them. He was just as strong, just as fast, and just as skilled. Until he'd come here. "I don't really feel human. This whole emotional crap, the back and forth and twisted morals, the utter rejection of reason—that's not me." His father didn't say anything. "Truly."

"You came back for her," René said at last, as if he was making a point.

"What?" Matt scoffed. Come back for Samantha? "No! I came back because my life is here. I want to continue going to school and hanging out with my friends. I want to hunt monsters and get to know you better," he admitted. "There's not that much in Hescaryn for me, apart from evading Caspar's attacks or stumbling over one of Melaney's lovers at every corner." It had never bothered him before, but life seemed so slow in Hell, so static and inconsequential.

Naturally, his father tensed at the mention of Melaney's lovers. "You said you hoped she'd be over it by now."

"But just because of everything else. I mean everybody." Matt almost stumbled over his words. "I thought it would be for the best, so they have time to get used to the fact I'm not really human."

"Matt, you ran away," René called him out sharply.

Stubbornly, Matt crossed his arms. "Why would I do that?"

His father scoffed at first, then sighed. "Because you were scared."

"I was not!"

"You were scared, because the wholesome little life you'd built yourself had come falling apart, and because Samantha told you she wanted to see you dead."

Matt took a shaky breath, as if those words had etched themselves into his skin. "I'm not afraid of her." Samantha might want to see him dead, but she didn't have the guts to do it. She wasn't demon enough for it.

"Oh, Matt, you're not scared of that," René said, the amusement back in his voice.

This was starting to get frustrating. Matt bet it was some other emotional crap he didn't understand that he was unable to grasp. Why couldn't humans speak their mind clearly? "What am I afraid of, then?"

"That, my son, you'll have to find out for yourself."

Samantha

With the death of the ghoul queen, Fabian's aggressive behaviour had completely subsided. An hour later, Samantha and her grandmother had produced the salve that would reverse the necrosis on his arm and return him to normal.

Fabian sat in the armchair, trying his best not to look at his arm, while Rachel held his hand. "It's going to be fine now," she said. "You are *not* going to be a ghoul." There was something apologetic in her voice, but Samantha chose not to comment on it.

She gently put the salve onto the affected skin and watched it sink into the grey. A few minutes later, the flesh was healing and returning to the pale, freckled skin she was familiar with. It just looked a bit dry. "Best to use some moisturiser for a couple of days, and then your arm should be good as new."

"I thought I was going to die for sure." He looked at Rachel and kissed her, relieved. It was only a short kiss, as Rachel seemed unprepared for it, and Fabian turned back to Samantha. "So, you can do real magic now?"

Surprisingly, he sounded happy for her. Samantha wasn't sure if the ability to undo spells was terribly useful, but she was going to run with it until she could weave proper spells. "Apparently."

"Apparently?" Jan said behind her. "Because of you, I don't have to spend the rest of my life as a statue."

Lucille sat next to him on the couch. "But you were a really pretty statue."

Jan grinned. "Look at that, Lucille de Cerque is buttering up my ass."

Annoyed, she clicked her tongue. "It was an accident."

"I know," Jan answered and laughed. "I'm just winding you up, Lu. But please tell me once more how incredibly good-looking I am."

Lucille slapped his shoulder, laughing along. "I will say that if you were a statue, I would put you into our winter garden. Happy?"

"Extremely."

Samantha watched the exchange with amusement and giggled. When she turned back to Fabian and Rachel, they were both looking at her. "What?"

Fabian smiled warmly. "That's the first time I've heard you laugh this year."

The reality overwhelmed her all too quickly. She hadn't laughed for almost a month because she'd been crying so much. "Yeah."

"Does that mean you'll come back to school?" Rachel asked softly.

Samantha thought about it. Matt was back at school, too, but after meeting him today, she felt surprisingly confident that she could handle him. "Yes, I'll be back on Monday."

"Yes!" Fabian punched his fist into the air, while Lucille flew onto Samantha's back and wrapped her arms around her. "We've missed you so much!"

"Sure did. Who else am I going to copy our Politics and German homework from?" Jan asked.

"Hey, I've got first dibs on those," Fabian protested.

"And I'll get them after you. Everyone's happy," Jan declared.

Samantha clicked her tongue loudly. "Well, I'm glad to hear *that's* why you missed me!"

"Boys," Lucille said, and they both started laughing.

With Rachel smiling happily, and Fabian grinning at her as if she'd given him the best birthday gift ever, Samantha thought things might be all right again for the first time in a month. At least a little bit. She leaned into Lucille's embrace and grinned along with them.

Her new plan made, Samantha moved back home full time. Her heavy backpack on, she walked down her street when a voice called out to her. "Sam."

It was *him*. Her breath quickened, and she slid her hand into her coat pocket. By the time Matt reached her and touched her shoulder, the Thorak was in her hand, and she whirled around.

Instantly, Matt backed away, both hands in the air, his eyes fixed on the dagger. "Woah! What are you doing with that?"

"Don't come closer, Melchior!" Samantha was proud that her voice was almost steady.

Matt's gaze snapped up to meet her eyes. He snarled. "I'm still Matt." When she shook her head, he scoffed. "Fine. Call me whatever you want. As long as we're good."

"As long as we're good?" Samantha repeated, bewildered. "There is nothing good between us." How could he even think there would be? He'd *killed* her boyfriend!

He glanced back at the Thorak and licked his lips. "Well, not if you continue swinging that thing around. What is that?"

Samantha smiled with satisfaction. He might not recognise what it was, but he sensed the Thorak's power. Felt its threat. Smugly, she explained, "That is a Thorak, a weapon forged in magic to kill demons."

"So, you really want me dead?" Matt asked, screwing up his face. "It was an accident! I couldn't control my actions."

She barked a laugh at his ridiculousness. "An accident? You didn't fall onto Daniel with your sword," she said sharply. How stupid did he think she was?

Matt clicked his tongue and rolled his eyes. "I mean the Blood Night. You can't think clearly when you're in a murderous frenzy. I didn't even know I'd killed Daniel until you told me." Samantha didn't believe a word he said. "I didn't even care about that guy."

"But *I* did!" Samantha screamed at him. "And you're still a murderer. *His* murderer, whether you're a demon, human, or whatever."

He was getting angry now as well. "How often do I have to tell you guys that it wasn't MY FAULT!?"

Not his fault? The fury made her whole body shake. "Until you choke on your words!"

Matt gasped, speechless for a moment. "Huh." Irritated, he took a step back. "Wow." Then his face hardened again. "Just so you know. I'm staying in Greenvalley, and I'll keep fighting monsters with the others. You know, real monsters. And I don't care if you're good with this or not."

"Great."

"Fine."

They both stared at each other, fuming. Matt was the first to break away. He snorted and vanished right there on the street. Samantha took a deep breath, but the wrath still had her body in its grip. She was shaking. Her heart was pounding, and it took her a few minutes until she had her breathing back under control and was able to continue the walk home.

Inside, she hurried up the stairs to her room and locked her door. Then she ripped the zip of her backpack open and pulled out the book Chay had written. Samantha was very particular when it came to books. She treated them well, always put a towel around them if she transported them in her bag, and if it was borrowed, she made sure not to get a speck of dirt on any page.

Not with this book.

She located the page of Kairos' reincarnations. Not caring that her own name was on the back of it under Gwydion, she tore the page from the book and crumpled it up into a ball. Then she threw it at her wall with all her might. It still wasn't enough.

Samantha stepped towards it and pulled on the magic. This time, it came willingly. Her fingers wove from memory or intuition, and moments later, the ball of paper blackened, as if a fire had consumed it. When nothing was left of it but a thin layer of ash, Samantha sank to her knees and cried her heart out.

Part 5

Dreams & Nightmares

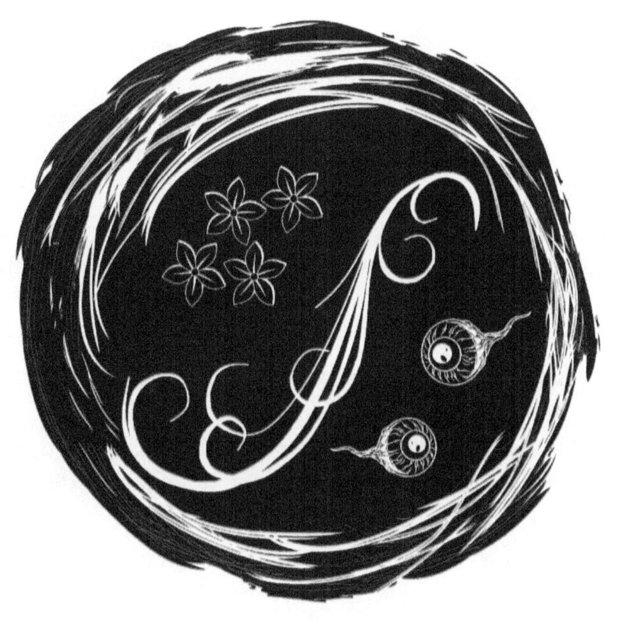

Rachel

"Are you going in?"

Rachel looked up from the flower she'd been walking around for ages. Not far from her, Nico watched with amusement. "Just saying..." He grinned.

Rachel sighed, focusing back on Fabian's dream instead. "I'm not sure." For some reason, things had got so complicated. She and Fabian were a couple. They'd been together for two months. All her dreams had come true, so why was she so reluctant to spend time with him?

It couldn't be the ghoul vision. Fabian had survived that. He was still living and breathing and laughing. It hadn't had anything to do with the attention he'd paid Samantha. They loved each other like brother and sister, and if someone understood how that felt, it was Rachel. Fabian was committed to her now. She'd seen it in her dreams and in real life. And still, something bothered her.

"How do you know if you love someone?" Rachel asked, stepping away from the flower. She'd never doubted her feelings before. Not until they'd been reciprocated.

Nico raised an eyebrow. "Are you asking me that?"

He'd been together with Svenja, which meant he had a little more experience in the department than her. But then Rachel remembered that this wasn't truly Nico, and whatever love story the dreamer might carry inside had happened a long time ago in a place completely foreign to her modern world. And if she asked him, she'd have to accept that he wasn't really Nico.

"No. I think I'm just confused. You know when you want something so badly for such a long time that once you get it it's—"

"Not as good as the dream of it?" Nico asked and strolled over to her. "I told you that you spend too much time chasing dreams and not enough living your life."

"But I like it here." Rachel crossed her arms. "I can dream as much as I want, and it's perfect. And if something bad occurs, it's only a nightmare."

Nico cocked his head and shrugged slightly. "Nightmares can be very powerful." He nodded his chin towards the flower. "He's having one right now."

"He…" Rachel whirled around. Fabian's dream flower was beginning to wilt. In her heart, she knew that dreams and nightmares were both parts of the dreamworld. People needed the occasional nightmare to work through the stuff they couldn't face awake. Fabian was probably dreaming of his ghoulishness.

"Do you care for him?" Nico asked quietly.

Rachel bristled. "Of course I do. He's my boyfriend."

"Then maybe you should give him a hand."

In front of her, the flower was growing darker and darker. This wasn't just a little nightmare, but a full-blown one. Perhaps he needed to experience it, but Rachel couldn't bear to watch him suffer. In the real world, she would've woken him. Here, she stepped inside.

And found herself at his home. The Bendtfeld house was a charming little cottage with two floors and a big garden, where they held chickens and grew vegetables. In this nightmare, the home was a mansion, dark and menacing, no door to the outside in sight.

It didn't take Rachel long to find Fabian. He was wearing an ill-fitted suit and carried a flat basket in the crook of his arm. When he saw her, relief washed over the dream. "Hi, Rachel."

"Hi." Rachel was yet unsure what to make of this nightmare. It was a bit creepy, but there was nothing ghoulish about Fabian.

Instead, Fabian searched the room, checking the dozens of drawers on a humongous dresser. "You haven't seen the eggs, have you?"

"What eggs?"

"The eggs from our chickens. Mum said I need to collect the eggs before I go. I don't really have time for this because I'm meeting Lucille's dad to clean up my company," Fabian explained in the earnestness of dreams.

Rachel couldn't help but giggle. "You've got a company?" She would love to discover what dreamy ambitions he had late at night. But that would've meant ignoring the growing desperation of his search. "Why don't you just go? Surely, the eggs can wait until after your appointment." And if she followed him, she might find out what he was trying to achieve.

But Fabian dug his fingernails into the tapestry and started ripping it off. "Have you met my mum? I'd rather be unemployed for the rest of my life than tell her I didn't collect the eggs. Work hard, party later. You know how it is."

Rachel had no idea what he meant, but Fabian cried out in joy when he found an egg under the tapestry. "I could help you," she said, feeling rather helpless.

"Excellent! Hold this." He handed her the basket, which was suddenly full of eggs and heavy, and started to dismantle the lamp in the corridor.

Just then, heavy footsteps fell onto the wooden planks. "Fabian!"

Caroline Bendtfeld was the sweetest person Rachel knew. She was her dream mum; calm, caring, always willing to listen. Hearing her screech Fabian's name was wildly out of character, and Rachel couldn't fathom why Fabian would dream of her like that. It got even worse when she entered the room, hair blazing with fire, her face twisted with fury. Five chickens accompanied her—or whatever counted as chickens in Hell, because these fiery creatures with black beaks, razor-sharp wings, and fire coming out of their nostrils were not Fabian's normal chickens.

Fabian was sweating profoundly, eyes wide in terror as he saw the flames lick the house. Within seconds, the house was burning.

"Water, Fabian! You need to fight the flames." This was a *nightmare*. Fabian's dreams were always full of water. Now the only liquid in his dream was the sweat on his forehead.

"I'd rather run. I stole the eggs, you know. She's not the forgiving type."

"Of course she is," Rachel exclaimed, but Fabian was already running from his mother.

Rachel took off after him, not wanting to be left alone in a burning house. Especially now that the roof was coming down, raining eggs instead of shingles and plaster. Behind her, she heard the flutter of chickens' wings. They overtook her in a flurry and threw themselves at Fabian, who crashed to the ground. Their sharp beaks attacked him in a fury, quickly drawing blood.

"Fabian!" Rachel got hold of one of the chickens and hurled it away from him. "Wake up!"

"Water," he croaked, suddenly looking as if he'd spent days in the desert.

Rachel shook him while the burning chickens continued to attack him. "Wake up! This is just a dream. This isn't real." When that didn't help, she changed it to, "You need to use your water."

"He doesn't want his power." Caroline was suddenly in front of them, smiling cruelly. "I'm doing him a favour."

Blue tendrils rose from Fabian's body and swirled towards Caroline, who held up a black egg. Something was different about her. As if she was too small for her body. But before Rachel could figure it out, Fabian's breath was rattling below her. "Water," he croaked once more.

As much as Rachel tried, she was entirely unable to summon water in this nightmare of feathers, fire, and blood.

Not surprisingly, Fabian looked like hell when they met at school on Monday. While waiting for Mr Zobel, his eyelids kept drooping, and he groaned in an effort to keep himself awake. Rachel watched him with concern, unsure of whether she should bring up the nightmare or not.

Her gaze fell on his water bottle. It had been ages since she'd felt this powerless in a dream. She should've been able to summon some water. Whether it helped his dream or not was a different matter, but it should've come to her.

Next to them, Lucille stood with Samantha, cheerfully chatting about something she'd seen on social media. It was nice to have Samantha back at school, even if just to prevent Lucille from talking to Rachel about topics she had no interest in.

She turned to Fabian, gently nudging his shoulder. "Didn't you sleep well?"

"Had a terrible nightmare," he muttered. "Something with flaming chickens and a deadly egg hunt. Ridiculous, now I think about it."

Nightmares had a tendency to be like that once you woke up, but even in the light of day, the memories of Fabian's water-drained dream made Rachel shudder. "You can sleep in fourth period. Your art teacher is off sick."

"I'd much rather sleep in Physics. Too bad Herbert is never sick."

The sudden lack of chatter made Rachel pay attention. At first, she thought Mr Zobel was approaching, but the other students weren't bothered, only Samantha and Lucille. And then she saw it too.

Matt had arrived, and for some reason, he had Cheryl clinging to his arm. "Good morning," he said, his voice slightly on edge.

"What do you want from us?" Samantha asked, irritated.

Immediately, Cheryl showed her claws. "Are you asking *me*? I'm allowed to bring my boyfriend to class, am I not?"

Lucille clenched her jaw in an effort to avoid saying something about Cheryl's claim. Samantha didn't even react. She half-turned away and muttered, "I meant him."

"Am I not allowed to come to school anymore?" Matt spat. "I wasn't aware you had a restraining order against me."

Rachel exchanged a glance with Fabian. Matt had been acting erratic ever since he'd returned from Hell, but up until now, she'd thought he was at least interested in patching things up with Samantha. Full-on attacking her didn't seem like a sound strategy. Fabian only shrugged, too tired to fully engage with the drama.

"Oh dear!" Cheryl said in her affected tone. "Did Matty blow you off?"

Lucille couldn't hold it in any longer. "Matty?" she spluttered, then quickly covered her mouth.

Cheryl sneered at her before batting her eyelashes at him. "You really need to get better friends."

"Yes, Matt," Samantha said, in rare agreement with Cheryl, "why don't you get some better friends who'll look past your frequent transgressions? I mean that could've happened to anyone."

And Samantha was fighting right back. *That* had never happened at school.

"Maybe I should get friends who won't keep harping on about the same old mistakes," Matt said, completely ignoring Cheryl's attentions.

"Mistakes?" Samantha asked and laughed joylessly. "That was a mistake for you?"

Cheryl didn't like to be left out of a verbal takedown and went for Samantha. "Not everyone can be Little Miss Perfect."

"Hey!" Fabian pushed himself off the wall. "You have no idea what you're talking about, so shut up!"

Rachel threw a quick glance at Fabian's water bottle. Surprisingly, the water remained completely still.

"Why don't you shut up?" Cheryl asked, giving him a dirty look.

"Just go away!" Usually, Fabian was a little more apprehensive when dealing with Cheryl, but today he seemed too tired to care. "Why did you even bring her?" he asked Matt.

Rachel kept an eye on his water bottle, but there was nothing. In the meantime, Mr Zobel had arrived and opened the classroom.

"She followed me," Matt said, sounding confused.

With a sharp laugh, Cheryl slapped him on the shoulder. "Aww, guys and their need to keep their cool in front of their friends." She leaned against him, still faking merriment. "I'll leave you alone with your loser friends. If they get too much, you know where to find me." Then she kissed him solely for all their benefit.

"Bullies recognise bullies," Samantha muttered and followed Mr Zobel inside.

Fabian picked up his backpack and water bottle and did the same. "Looks like it."

Cheryl seemed slightly disappointed that her performance had an interested audience of zero. She kissed Matt again, who looked as if he was merely enduring the physical contact, and walked off with swaying hips, despite the fact that he never once spared her a second glance.

"Do I want to know how that happened?" Lucille asked, amused.

"Not really," Matt muttered.

They all entered the classroom, and Rachel rushed to Samantha's side, but quickly turned in her seat to face Fabian, while the rest of the students still settled in. "Why was there no water?" she asked, pointing at his water bottle. Last week, it had flooded their entire cafeteria table when Cheryl had spread her poison.

"No clue," Fabian whispered. He glanced around, then concentrated on his water bottle.

Rachel began to worry when, after half a minute, nothing had happened. Fabian just sighed. "I'm probably just really tired."

"Okay. Try to keep awake." She turned back around to face their teacher.

While Mr Zobel started reviewing the material from the last semester, Rachel started to dissect Fabian's dream. The chickens made no sense. And neither had the egg hunt nor Fabian's business plan. It made no sense like most dreams, but like most dreams, there were kernels of truth hidden within. Important things.

And one important thing was that Fabian almost always dreamed of water. And last night, he'd dreamed of fire. And the water hadn't come to him. And now there was no movement in the water while he was awake. As if something—*his mother*—had stolen his magic overnight.

Unable to accept that meaning, Rachel sat there while her stomach clenched, completely droning out Mr Zobel's valuable review. Dreams couldn't have such an effect on reality.

Or could they?

Samantha

Samantha was back at the town hall, wearing the dress she'd worn on stage with Daniel, but more sensible shoes. Instead of lonely people and town functionaries, the hall was filled with people from her school, and it fell to her to organise everything—as usual. In her hands was a heavy folder with neat instructions.

"The streamers have to be higher," Samantha said, after consulting the incredibly detailed plan for the hall. Everyone else was here to amuse themselves and have a great party while she was working in the background, making sure everything was running smoothly.

She walked forward to fix a crumb on the buffet table, when she stepped into something. Irritated, Samantha lowered her eyes. A thin trickle of red had marred the wooden floor. Her stomach turned. She was looking at blood. Her eyes followed the trail with her breath hitching in her throat. Soft snow was falling.

And then she saw him. Leather wings spread behind him, Melchior pulled the sword out of the classmate he'd felled, and Samantha felt her knees grow soft.

"No," she whispered.

A cruel smile twisted Melchior's lips, and he walked over to the next person, Robert, as if he was out on a stroll. As he sunk his sword into Robert's chest, panic erupted in the room. People were running for the doors, but Samantha's feet were glued to the floor.

Melchior jumped through the room to cut off the fleeing and plunged his sword into Jan's back. Samantha covered her mouth. Their friend had never stood a chance.

"Matt." Now Lucille was approaching him. "I know you're still in there. You don't need—"

He killed her just as ruthlessly as he'd killed Jan. From there, it became a true bloodbath. Nobody escaped, and the blood ran so high Samantha's feet were sinking into it.

"Stop it," she whisper-cried. "Please stop it." It had to be a dream. It couldn't possibly be real. But no matter how much she wished to wake from the nightmare, she was stuck in it.

"Sam!" Her sister was running to her. "Sam, please help me."

Samantha opened her arms and enclosed Meg into them, but Melchior appeared right in front of her and tore her sister from her arms.

"No!" Samantha screeched, tears streaming down her face. "Matt, don't. This isn't you. Please!"

"Hey, leave the little one out of it." Fabian's voice was shaking as he approached Melchior. He raised his arm in a calming gesture.

Melchior didn't even fully turn. He shot black energy at Fabian and broke Meg's neck all in one swift movement. Samantha lost it. She screamed and screamed until she lost her voice. There was no one alive but her, the monster Matt had become... and Rachel.

"Rachel?" she asked.

Her friend was standing on the sidelines, not a spot of blood on her, even though the entire floor was swimming in it. Her eyes were wide with shock, but otherwise she seemed unaffected by the mindless massacre. As if she didn't really belong here.

"There you are," Melchior drawled, and Samantha's attention snapped back to him. He was right in front of her, and he reached for her. His hand settled on her neck almost gently, but then he pulled her to him until she stumbled against his chest.

"Don't do it." Rachel's voice rang clear as a bell.

Melchior extended his arm. Samantha could only watch as he shot Rachel, too. Surprised, her friend stumbled and fell. As she lay dying, Melchior changed back into Matt and looked deep into Samantha's eyes. Snow fell between them, but that wasn't the reason Samantha was shivering so forcefully she would've fallen to the ground if he weren't holding her.

"Now you're mine," he said softly.

Samantha pushed feebly against his chest. "Matt..."

He pressed his lips onto hers, and Samantha could feel her will to live leave her body. His kiss was hot, and it burned itself through her as if he'd sunk his sword into her as well.

In another time, in another place, when the snow fell from the sky and no blood had coloured it red yet, she might have welcomed his kiss. Right here, right now, all she could do was scream in her head. *Please let me wake up! Please let me wake...*

The nightmare still clung to Samantha as she sat in Mr Zobel's German class. The whiteboard was covered with a character diagram of *Nathan the Wise*, their current reading assignment. Samantha had read the play about religious tolerance during her time away from school, but today, her mind was completely blank. Even the names on the board told her absolutely nothing.

Next to her, Fabian was dozing, and Samantha had half of a mind to follow his example. But sleeping meant risking more nightmares, and after that absolute shocker last night, she never wanted to go to sleep again. She still felt as if her shoes were soaked in blood, and a dull pain in her chest made her shift in her chair constantly, unable to take part in the lesson as usual.

Mr Zobel pointed to someone behind her and said, "Matt?"

Samantha closed her eyes, a soft moan escaping her lips. His voice was the last one she wanted to hear right now.

"Just to be clear," he began. "One interpretation of the book is that there isn't just the one truth. Sometimes two views are perfectly valid. And they both have to be tolerated."

Samantha couldn't help but snort. If that wasn't the most far-fetched interpretation of the ring parable ever uttered, she would have to hand in her top marks.

"Samantha," Mr Zobel called her out. "Do you want to comment on that?"

And get into a fight with Matt in front of all her peers when she told him that murdering people was not a view to be tolerated, no matter what he believed in? "Sorry, I wasn't paying attention."

Mr Zobel sighed. "I see. It looks to me like the focus of this class is generally fading fast. I guess it's good we're almost at the end of the term." He took position in front of Fabian and loudly said his name.

Fabian's head jerked up. "What? What's happening?"

People snickered behind him, and Mr Zobel regarded him sternly. "I might have already written your reports for this term, but that does not mean you can all ease up. We will continue with Nathan in the second term." He returned to his desk and addressed all of them. "After the winter holidays, I want you to hand in your own version of the ring parable." Jan wasn't the only one who groaned at the announcement. Samantha's only thought was that she really didn't want to read Matt's version of it.

"Be creative but keep the message. Perhaps someone could repeat it?" Before Mr Zobel could pick anyone, the bell rang. "Oh, well. I'll see you Friday." His gaze returned to Fabian. "Try to be awake for that one."

"Sorry," Fabian murmured.

The students packed up their belongings and started to leave the room. Samantha felt too tired to even do that. Her arms were just too heavy.

Rachel came over and decided to help her, which surprised Samantha until she leaned in. "You didn't sleep particularly well, did you?"

"I still have nightmares," Samantha confessed. "Tonight was really bad."

Fabian put his arm around Rachel, though he looked like he was more interested in taking advantage of her shoulder to rest his head on. "I had to fight our chickens for the second night in a row."

"Chicken fights?" Samantha asked and giggled. "Tell me more."

The three of them left the room and joined Jan and Lucille. Matt was trying to escape, but his precious new girlfriend found him and showered him with kisses.

"I consider myself a very tolerant person," Lucille said, "but if Cheryl joins us on our monster hunts, I'm giving up magic for good."

Samantha was torn between amusement and the bitter taste in her mouth as she remembered Matt's feeble justification in class. "Well, I'll try to be more tolerant of misunderstood killers."

"What? How do you mean?" asked Fabian, who had slept through Matt's argument.

"Matt tried to use the ring parable to propose his own version of the truth," Rachel summarised helpfully.

Jan groaned. "I have no idea what Zobel wants us to do with our own version. I don't write plays."

"Or essays. Or homework," Lucille said sweetly.

Samantha couldn't help but yawn. "Lucille, can I have your notes for today? I'm afraid I only wrote down rubbish." If she'd written anything coherent at all.

"Of course. I'll send them to you later." Then she launched into a tirade. "Jan, it's really not that hard. The whole point is that there isn't one true religion, and that they're all valid and have to tolerate each other. We can do our own stories with similar arguments. But that doesn't mean *every* situation can be shoehorned into that." Lucille cast a pointed glance at Matt, who was being dragged down the corridor by Cheryl.

As they followed them much more slowly, Adrian stopped them. "Hey, Sam, I was looking for you. Did you have time to finish up the lists for the student exchange?"

Next to her, Lucille clapped her hands in excitement. She was one of the students taking part in the French school exchange next term. "Oh, can we pick our students?"

Adrian shook his head. "Nice try, but no."

"I'm sorry," Samantha said. "I wanted to finish them this morning, but I completely overslept."

"Really?" Adrian sounded surprised. "*You* overslept?"

"Yes, I barely made it to school in time."

Jan clapped his chest and announced solemnly, "Ladies and gents, Samantha's version of oversleeping."

Annoyed, Samantha pushed him, but Adrian grinned. "Oh well, it's not that big a deal. I just had a couple of ideas I wanted to talk through with you. Plus, I have feedback for the proposed programme. Do you have some time now?"

Samantha would've much rather gone back to bed, but she nodded. "I'll meet you in the cafeteria in ten minutes?"

"Awesome." Adrian waved to the others and hurried along.

"He's a nice guy," Lucille said, leaning into Samantha.

Samantha could only stare at her. "I hope you meant for yourself," she said sharply.

They both knew she hadn't, but Lucille nodded and smiled quickly. "Yeah, perhaps." Then she sighed. "Honestly, I don't think there's anyone in this school for me."

"Poor Lu," Jan said, despite grinning wildly. "It must be so hard being single."

Lucille clicked her tongue loud enough for everyone to hear. "Oh, please. Meg's only taking pity on you. Right, Samantha?"

"Pretty much," she answered readily, only too glad to take this chance to joke around. Better than thinking about what she'd lost—and couldn't just replace. Then she yawned again. "Oh, gosh. I'd better go talk to Adrian before I fall asleep walking."

"Wait!" Rachel called out.

Surprised, Samantha turned around. Fabian was snoring on Rachel's shoulder, which made her struggle for balance. "What is it?" Samantha half-expected her to say she needed help with getting Fabian into a bed.

"Your nightmare," Rachel said. "I was there."

A chill ran down Samantha's back, and suddenly, she was wide awake. In her mind, she saw Rachel's body as it sunk into the blood. "You all were," she whispered, remembering how each of them had died.

"Yes, but I was really there. And I've seen Fabian's chickens," Rachel explained, and woke Fabian with the last word. He looked around wildly until she patted and calmed him. "No chickens at school." Rachel faced the rest of them again. "I believe both nightmares are connected, and we need to talk about it. And other things." She took a deep breath, as if all that talking was already becoming too much for her. "We haven't had a proper group meeting in over a month."

Of course, they hadn't, Samantha thought. Her eyes strained against the tears forming behind them. "A proper group meeting?" she asked in a meek voice.

"Yes, all six of us, tonight, at my place," Rachel announced with sudden certainty.

Jan and Lucille exchanged a glance before nodding. "Sounds like a great idea to me," Lucille said and gifted Rachel with an encouraging smile that made Samantha's stomach turn.

"Yeah, let's order some pizza and talk," Jan suggested.

At the end of the corridor, Matt and Cheryl were fooling around, and shared a long kiss. Samantha found herself lamenting the fact that Matt hadn't joined the Elite Clique at the beginning of the year. He fitted in so much better with them, and that way she would've never had to deal with him, apart from some mean comments. But then she remembered the prophecy and how she would never truly be rid of him. No matter which group he belonged to.

"Sure, if Matt can tear himself away from his girlfriend for an hour."

Fabian

Fabian was too tired for the kind of talk Rachel had planned. Despite already downing two energy drinks, he kept drifting away while the others discussed the Emblems of Power. Somewhere in the back of his mind, Fabian was freaking out about what it all could possibly mean, but he was simply too tired to care.

"The Emblems of Power are definitely finding their way to us," Samantha said, yawning. "Apparently, the flowers belong to me, but... well, I don't see anyone bringing me flowers soon."

"If I bring you flowers, Meg will get the wrong idea," Jan joked.

Lucille boxed his shoulder. "Don't listen to him. Yes, four of the emblems found their way to us via a gift, but Fabian's simply appeared. Wrong delivery. You'll get yours soon."

"Yes, yes, I'm sure it'll come to me." Samantha smiled vaguely. Fabian knew that smile well. It was one of those "nothing here to see, move on" kind of smiles.

"The book says that apart from guarding my dreams, the dreamweb can absorb magic and throw it back," Rachel explained. "Kind of like a shield and amplifier in one. But the details were very vague, so I'd like to find out how it works before I have to use it in a fight."

"Do you want me to throw a fireball at it?" Lucille offered. Next to her, Matt massaged the bridge of his nose.

Rachel gave her a long glance. "No. I'd rather not risk burning it down." She nudged Fabian. "Hey, can you help?"

"What?" He shook his head, unable to remember what they were even talking about.

"Rachel wants you to throw some water at her dreamweb," Samantha explained.

"Isn't there a bathroom around the corner?" Fabian asked, still trying to understand why Rachel would want to make her magic artefact wet.

Samantha laughed. "With your magic, Fabi!"

Fabian shook his head to clear it before sitting up straighter to call his magic. Rachel was holding out her dreamweb expectantly. He tried to summon the water, but not a drop came from his hands. "I'm too tired," he complained.

Disappointed, Rachel lowered the dreamweb. "You had problems with your water yesterday."

"I wouldn't call them problems." Not embarrassing himself in front of Cheryl by spraying her with water was supposed to be a good thing. "I think I'm getting sick. Just in time for the break."

Jan patted his back. "Happens to me all the time." He nodded sagely at the great universal injustice.

"Let me have a look at this." Samantha frowned. "So, normally, when I see the magic around you, there's a blue shimmer to it." She squinted her eyes and the vertical fold on her forehead creased deeper. "There's nothing."

Fabian found himself swallowing. "You mean my magic is gone?"

Samantha shook her head. "No, I can see absolutely nothing. No magic anywhere. It's like before..." She blinked rapidly, close to tears, and her voice was almost inaudible. "No magic."

"You mean your magic is gone as well?" Fabian asked, blinking.

"Perhaps—" Rachel began, sitting up straight.

But Matt talked right over her. "Perhaps it just wasn't meant to be."

Lucille clicked her tongue at him and frowned. "I'm sure what Matt *actually* wanted to say is that you're still new at this. You need more practice, that's all."

"If I wanted to say that, I would have," Matt said sharply. "I can talk for myself."

"Is that so?" Lucille asked with mock surprise. "I was under the impression Cheryl did that for you now."

Confused, Matt frowned. "What does Cheryl have to do with this now?"

"That's what we're all asking ourselves," Samantha muttered.

Lucille picked up the thread. "Well, it is a bit weird to see you in a relationship all of a sudden. And with Cheryl of all people."

"We're *not* in a relationship!"

Now Jan chimed in as well. "Ay, man, she walks you to every class and picks you up as soon as the bell rings."

"I have no idea why she does that." Matt sounded confused. "It freaks me out. We just had sex, nothing more."

"Perhaps it has to do with the fact that most humans have sex with people they connect with on an emotional basis." Samantha gasped in a fake manner that would've made Cheryl proud. "Oh, shoot, I forgot. You're not human."

Matt glowered at her. "When would I have had the time to emotionally connect with Cheryl? She gave me her number, and I called."

Samantha nodded sagely. "It must have been the sexual frenzy. You forgot everything around you and having sex with Cheryl was only... an accident."

"Is that supposed to be a reference to Daniel?"

Samantha shrugged. "Why? Does it sound familiar to you? It sounds to me as if it's not really an accident if it happens all the time. More like a learned behaviour, or something like that. I mean, poor demon that you are, you never stood a chance. All these murderous instincts are just too hard to resist."

"Hey, guys," Lucille interjected carefully. "Rachel had an—"

"You don't want to understand it, right?" Matt's face had darkened with anger.

Samantha wasn't far behind him. "You're the one who doesn't want to understand. Sex and death might be a daily occurrence in Hell, but in this world, there are consequences."

"I'm going to get snacks," Rachel announced and slipped out of the room.

While Fabian sat there, staring dumbly, Jan took the chance to escape as well. "I'll help you carry them."

"Oh, and of course *you're* the one that dictates those consequences," Matt fought back before the two had even left the room.

"Of course not!" Samantha shook her head, unable to speak for a moment. "No, I... You should've faced consequences for your actions. There should've been an arrest and a trial at least, but because you're a demon, you walked off scot-free."

"So, no consequences in this world for me too," Matt replied smugly.

Samantha was so furious she groaned. "Why do you have to be so damn callous about it? You killed someone!"

"Six people, actually," Fabian said dumbly, as if that was somehow important to their argument.

"Guys," Lucille tried again, but both Samantha and Matt ignored her.

"Not on purpose!" Matt shouted.

Samantha grabbed her pencil case and threw it at Matt's face. It was so unexpected he never had a chance to evade it. In all the years Fabian had known Samantha, she'd never once resorted to physical violence. Now, tears were streaming down her face, and she seemed simply too angry to talk.

Matt rubbed his cheekbone, his eyes glaring at her. "Now *that* was on purpose."

"You're comparing a pencil case with a sword?" Samantha choked out.

"No, I'm comparing someone who hasn't got their emotions in check to what happened in an uncontrollable thirst for blood." Matt's words were biting.

"Well, you know—" Samantha had to interrupt herself. "I'd rather have too many emotions than none at all."

Now it was Matt who seemed speechless. In the ensuing silence, Lucille looked up hopefully. "Perhaps now that you—"

"No matter how you twist and turn it," Samantha started, her voice slowly gaining power again, "Daniel's blood is on your hands. You're the one to blame. Not some mystical demon state, not fate, only you. And if you had anything resembling a backbone, you'd admit it."

"Life must be incredibly easy when you have someone to blame," Matt said in a low voice. He got up slowly and lobbed the pencil case back to Samantha. "You want me to admit it?"

Fabian was certain that no one, not even Samantha, wanted Matt to do that when he was asking that way.

"Fine. I killed Daniel. He died at my hands. Happy?" When Samantha just hiccupped, fresh tears on her face, he snorted softly. "That's what I thought." And with that, he vanished.

Samantha covered her face and sobbed. Lucille let out a deep breath, then shuffled closer to put her arms around Samantha and stroke her back, but even she had nothing to say.

And Fabian's mind was blank. His heart ached for Samantha, but his mind refused to string any sentences together that would've made her feel better. Fabian doubted it would have been much better even if he wasn't so goddamned tired.

Samantha was still crying when Jan and Rachel returned with not just snacks but the pizzas they'd ordered earlier. Rachel took one look at the room and sighed. "I really hoped we could have a proper meeting."

At that, Samantha cried out loud and fled from the room as Matt had before her. Everyone was so paralysed none of them followed her.

Lucille closed her eyes and sighed. "Perhaps this won't work."

There were still two whole pizzas left when Lucille and Jan called it a very early night and left as well. Rachel tidied her room, her lips pursed in a scowl. Fabian recognised that look. She'd been desperate to discuss something with all of them, but the fight between Matt and Samantha, and the subsequent mood drop hadn't allowed for it.

With a spur of energy, Fabian got up from the floor and sat on her bed. "Rachel..." She looked at him, and he held out his hands to beckon her closer.

Still, she only came reluctantly. "What?"

He pulled her closer until she stood between his legs. "What did you want to say?"

Her eyes widened slightly before her lips curved into a smile. "I thought you'd slept through the whole afternoon."

"I may not have looked like it, but I was awake." He put his arms around her and buried his face against her stomach before smiling up at her. "So, why did you get us all together?"

"I hoped that if we got Matt and Sam into a room together while figuring out a monster attack, we could start building back some trust," Rachel explained. "They worked well together in the cemetery."

Fabian winced at her suggestion. "Rachel, I wouldn't get involved. Sam's right, you know? Let her have her time."

"What if the more time we give Samantha—and I know it's early—the higher the chances we lose Matt as well? He's already hanging out with Cheryl."

"That's his problem. All we can do is hope that she's part of his self-punishing plan." Fabian couldn't think of someone he'd want less for a girlfriend.

Rachel screwed up her face. "It might be." Then she waved it off and put both her hands on Fabian's shoulders. "Let's forget about Matt and Samantha for a moment."

Could it mean what he hoped? Fabian was a bit confused since she'd been the one who brought the topic up and orchestrated the whole afternoon. But if Rachel wanted to skip the talking and focus more on their relationship, he would keep himself awake enough for it.

"There's a monster attack," Rachel said and squashed all his hopes.

Fabian's shoulders slumped under the lack of enthusiasm. He was too tired for monsters. "There is?"

"I believe so, but I'm not sure." Rachel freed herself from his embrace and strode towards her dreamweb. "I've been having dreams."

"You and me both."

Rachel grimaced. "Yes, that's because I've been visiting your dream. I know about the flaming chickens and your mum."

"You do?" As cool as Rachel's powers were, there was something deeply unsettling about having her in his dreams. Especially one as embarrassing as this. "Uhm, okay."

"You don't like me visiting you," Rachel surmised mercilessly, her voice cutting through his subtlety like steel. "I shall refrain from it, then."

Fabian tried to take her hands again. "Don't be like that. You know me. These magic things all freak me out. What did you learn?" He had no idea what the dream could possibly mean. He loved his mum, and while strict, she wasn't the vengeful banshee of his dreams. And the chickens had never frightened him before. He used to cuddle them!

"Not much, until I visited Samantha's dream, and believe me, she's got it worse."

"No contest here." Fabian could only imagine the nightmares she must be having.

"I did learn that she has some very conflicting feelings about Matt, but that's beside the point." Rachel sat down next to him, suddenly in her element. "Do you remember the fire in your dream? You were begging for water, but your mum had taken it away. Only, I'm not quite sure that she truly was your mum."

"Woah, slow down," Fabian begged, trying to follow her. "What do you mean, she's not my mum?"

Rachel turned her eyes to the ceiling and considered her next words carefully. "Walking in dreams requires a touch of surrealism. Actually, more than a touch. Anything is possible, but there are still rules. Like, I can't put something completely new into your dream that you've never encountered before. So, if some... stranger"—she had a peculiar inward look on her face—"appeared, you wouldn't really be able to make sense of him. Instead, your subconscious would try to press it into a shape it knows."

She shook off whatever weird thoughts she was having and smiled vaguely at him. "See, when I appear in your dreams, it's not a big deal. You're just dreaming of your friend Rachel."

"Girlfriend."

"Yes, sorry." Flustered, she turned back to him. "Now, what you and I saw in your dream looked like your mum, because that's someone you're familiar with. She is someone who, on occasion, checks your behaviour, or at least has some control over you. But Dream-Caro didn't behave like your real mum, so that got me thinking it might be another dreamwalker who picked a shape from your subconscious to get close to you."

Dread settled in Fabian's stomach. "Another dreamwalker?"

Rachel nodded. "I didn't realise it right away, but then in Samantha's dream, we had Matt. And he was acting... well, I guess he was acting much more like himself than your mum did, but that's because Samantha's subconscious made it really easy for whoever has been visiting her to create that nightmare." She folded her hands in her lap and took a deep breath. "The reason I got suspicious is that he took something from her. It was all a bit blurry, because I was dying in her dream, but before I woke, I saw a soft green cloud leaving her body. Just as I saw your water magic flowing to your mum."

Fabian's tired mind was spinning with all the information. The fact that Rachel calmly talked about dying in someone else's dream made him shiver. "So, what are you saying?"

"Today confirmed it. Someone stole your magic," Rachel said with much aplomb. "And Samantha's too."

Fabian waited with bated breath for her to continue. When she didn't, he shook his head to wake up his spirits. "I'm sorry. My mind's too fried to understand this. Someone is visiting our dreams to steal our magic?"

"Exactly. And I'm pretty sure who's next on their hit list."

Again, Fabian stared at her stupendously. "Who?"

Rachel groaned surprisingly loud. "Me, Lucille, Jan, and Matt. They're targeting our group! That's why I wanted to get us all together." She threw her arms up and leaned backwards until she fell onto her bed.

Fabian watched her run her hands over her face. Pity welled up in him, and then something else. He carefully lowered himself on his side, planning to put an arm around her.

"What are you doing?" Rachel asked and shirked away.

Sheepishly, Fabian went for a smile. "Well, I thought you could use some cuddling, and maybe... more?" Gosh, why had that come out as a question?

Rachel blinked once, then twice. "I... I have to sleep. I mean, I need to dream." She sat up again. "If my theory is right, the other dreamwalker will target one of the others—or me. So, I need to try to catch them."

He might be a little dense sometimes, but Fabian knew when he was being rejected. Sighing heavily, he sat up again as well. "Rachel? Are we good?"

"Of course we're good," she answered a little too quickly. But then her face fell. "I need to figure some stuff out. Can you wait until I do?"

When Samantha had figured some stuff out, it had led to their breakup. "Can't we talk about it?" Not that talking about it had changed anything once Samantha had set her mind to it.

"I promise we will, just not now." Then she quickly added, "You're overtired, and I want to figure out this dreamwalking. I..." Rachel's voice faded out, and she bit her lip. "I can't do this now."

Fabian sighed. Part of him wanted to push and demand the conversation, but the other knew that pushing would only put her under pressure. And she was right about one thing: he was too tired to deal with the potential fallout today. He heaved himself up to his feet. "I'd better leave you to it."

Rachel watched him as he picked up his stuff and what Samantha had left behind in her hurry. "Well, I'm off. Sleep tight, or dream well or..." He couldn't think of what else to say as the brain fog continued to spread.

As Fabian turned towards the door, she called out to him. He turned back around to find her right in front of him. Rachel threw her arms around him and kissed him. Before he could kiss her back, she'd already let go again. "Good night."

Unable to decipher these mixed signals, Fabian left.

#

That night, Fabian dreamt of flaming chickens again. Only this time, he was stuck in the burning house and could feel himself desiccating. He woke up way too early with a parched throat that took ages to ease. The worst part was that he was still tired, but just the thought of going back to bed made him whiny. So, instead, he walked down into the kitchen and turned on the coffee machine.

It hadn't even finished running through the filter when his mother came down, wrapped in a robe, eyes squinting. "Fabian? What are you doing?"

"Making coffee?"

"It's not even four," she complained before blinking rapidly to open her eyes a little wider. "What's wrong?"

Fabian sighed and sank into the kitchen chair. "Everything."

His mother looked confused at first, but then she took a deep breath and sat down next to him. "Come on, tell me everything."

"Well, there's obviously the whole Samantha and Matt thing."

"Oh dear." His mum was one of the few adults who knew what had really happened.

Encouraged by his mother's sympathy, Fabian sat up straighter and complained, "I thought them ignoring each other was hard, but now they're fighting until one of them cries or runs away." To be fair, it was always Samantha who cried, and Matt who ran away.

Gradually more herself, his mother nodded emphatically. "This must be so hard for Sammy. I wish I could do more to help her."

"Same. And I don't know if it has anything to do with the whole drama, but Rachel is pulling away from me. Or she might not be, and I'm only now noticing how slowly our relationship is developing, but... I feel like she doesn't actually want to be around me. At least not alone." It was the first time Fabian had allowed himself to think those thoughts through to the end.

His only other relationship had been with Samantha, and though they'd been a lot younger when they'd first started dating, things had definitely heated up more quickly. He'd liked the constant cuddling and pecks and kisses. With Rachel, physical contact was almost solely initiated by him. After everyone telling him how much she loved him, it was a bit disappointing how little she was showing that love. And he couldn't help but think he'd got it all wrong, and now they were both trapped. Too nice to call it off.

"Did you talk to her about it?" his mother asked.

Fabian rolled his eyes. He should've expected that question. "Well, no, because when I asked her whether she wanted to talk about it, Rachel said she needed time to figure it out for herself first."

With a commiserating grimace, his mother reached out to him and rubbed his thumb. "Then give her the time she needs. Don't push. I'm sure it will all work out." She sighed a little. "You guys have been through some very traumatic experiences this past year. I honestly don't know how you do it. When Samantha's grandfather was killed, Ben, Juli, Jo, and I were all just fifteen or sixteen, and it changed all our relationships completely. It took us months to repair, and Ben nearly burned all bridges. I guess because it was his dad. He always felt kind of responsible for his death, so he was going through a lot."

Fabian thought he'd heard all the stories about the Fantastic Four, as he liked to call them ironically. His father and Ben used to tell stories of their childhood and youth all the time to him and Samantha. But apparently, they'd left out this period. Now that he thought of it, he noticed how magic had never played a role in their stories. Which was a bit odd, considering both of Ben's parents were heavily involved in monster hunting.

"Does Dad know about you being a witch and me being..." Fabian was unable to finish the sentence. Was he even still an elemental mage if he couldn't call his water?

His mother's eyes widened. "No! Not a thing. And neither does Juli, though to be fair, she only really became a part of our group after Ben's father died." She shook her head. "Magic had always been a thing between me and Ben, though he hated it." She snorted. "Which isn't quite the truth. He always told himself he hated it. He felt as if the magic had rejected him because he wasn't showing any talent for it, and his father refused to train him when he was nothing but a dumb teenager. Ben rejected the magic in turn, especially after his father's death. So, don't talk to him about magic. He'll throw a fit," his mother said with a little eye roll.

Fabian wasn't planning on doing so, but he thought it might be something Samantha would like to know. "Talking about magic." He started sliding in his chair. "Up until now, the water always came to me when I was a bit emotional. Sometimes more, sometimes less. Don't mistake me, it is incredibly annoying and sometimes outright embarrassing, but I was getting used to it." He interrupted himself to yawn. "The last few days, nothing's happened."

"Well, I would hope that not absolutely every day in your teenage day is packed with drama," his mother joked.

"But it *was!*" Fabian cried out, only to realise afterwards what he'd just claimed. "I mean, there have been moments that used to summon my water before. Even Rachel noticed its lack. And the problem is that I can't call it either when I want to." His ability in that regard was still a bit sketchy, and he *had* been really tired when he'd tried, but somehow, Fabian knew deep inside of him that the water was truly gone.

His mother regarded him with pity. "Perhaps you just don't have enough focus. You look like you've spent some long nights playing video games," she said, a little sharper.

Fabian shook his head. "I haven't. I'm just sleeping really badly lately." He rubbed his chest, which was starting to feel as if he'd bruised it. "I keep having the same nightmare. Our chickens are attacking the house and burning it down. It's ridiculous, but it keeps waking me up." He yawned again. "I think I might be getting sick." A horrible thought came to him. "What if I get that fever again?"

Concerned, his mother leaned forward to put her hand on his forehead. "Feels cool to me. I'd say you need more sleep. Go upstairs. Tell the chickens that we'll be moving into their coop if they burn the house down."

Fabian had to chuckle at the idea. "I'll try." The nightmare felt rather ridiculous when he was awake.

He pushed himself up and eyed the prepared coffee longingly. But the call to sleep was louder, and so he went upstairs to face the chickens once more.

Lucille

Whenever Lucille dreamed of her grandmother, she met her in Elda's cottage rather than the villa her family inhabited. The cottage seemed a better fit for the witchy side of her family, and she'd always imagined her grandmother and her great-grandmother living in a humble home, rather than the luxury Lucille had grown up with.

She had never known her great-grandmother or seen a picture of her. Lucille imagined her looking like the grandmother she'd loved but turning her nose up like Linda. The witches might have lived in a humble home, but her great-grandmother was not a humble woman. She was the Greenvalley Witch.

"You're doing it wrong," the Witch told Lucille as she did nothing but look at the beautiful necklace that was her Emblem of Power.

"Can you teach me?" Lucille asked, eager to learn what she couldn't learn from anyone else.

The witch snatched the emblem from her hands. "It doesn't belong to you."

"Yes, it does." Instantly, the necklace was back on Lucille's neck. Her beloved grandmother had kept it for her, and she felt connected to it in more ways than one.

"This is wrong," the witch repeated and snapped her fingers.

Suddenly, they were in a car, driving at such high speeds, the world outside ceased to exist. The speed made Lucille dizzy, and her dream darkened until there was only the car. "Please stop," she begged from the booster seat in the back.

The Witch turned around and became her grandmother. "Give me my necklace, darling."

In the dream, Lucille was seven years old when she saw her loving grandmother's face. She would've given the world to her.

"Don't," a new voice said sharply. Next to her, strapped into a similar booster seat, sat Rachel. "Don't hand over your magic."

"Lyssie, baby, don't cry."

"I'm not..." Lucille was indeed crying, because the woman now seated in the driver's seat was her mum. Her beautiful, gentle mother, who always smiled at her. "Mum?" Her voice was a childish squeal, which was no surprise since she'd been only two when she'd last been in a car with her mum.

Her mother's face brightened. "Yes, my darling. Would you give me that necklace, please? It's far too big for you."

"Mum! Watch out!" Lucille shouted as the darkness around them lifted and an insane amount of traffic appeared. Fear gripped her heart until her chest hurt.

"Just give me the necklace," her mother repeated, refusing to watch the road in front of her.

A truck was coming straight at them. "Mum!" Lucille screeched.

"We need to get out of here," Rachel mumbled, but she couldn't free herself from the restraint, and when she tried to open the door, it was locked.

"Safety locks," Lucille whispered.

The headlights of the truck blinded her. Wheels were screeching. Her mum smiled at her, then widened her eyes. Lucille wailed, stuck in her seat, though her adult conscience was telling her to stop, to step out, and most importantly, not to watch.

Then the truck hit them.

Lucille woke to a heaviness in her chest. She could barely breathe, and her heart felt as if it was squeezed beneath her ribs. Gasping, she tried to shake off the nightmare, only to realise that the weight on her chest belonged to a small, ugly hag. Her face was riddled with valleys and craters, her eyes dark pools of nothingness. Spindle-thin fingers reached out for Lucille's temples. They poked her skin like twigs; annoying but not hurtful. The strange woman might have been little, but her weight was immense.

Lucille struggled to gather enough air. At last, a scream tore from her throat. She freed one arm from her blanket and pointed her hand at the creature. "Globus igneus!"

Nothing happened. No green fire burst from her fingers. No heat warmed her.

The woman wouldn't budge. She laughed without making a sound and leaned closer. Her weight robbed Lucille of the last of her breath, and panic set in.

Suddenly, the door opened, and the creature turned into black smoke, dissipating quickly. Light flickered on and blinded Lucille as she took a rattling breath.

"What happened?" Her father stood in the door, still dressed, with his headset still on. "Are you okay?"

A hand on her chest, Lucille clambered up in her bed and drew several deep breaths. "I... There was someone in my room."

Now, Albert appeared as well, though contrary to her father, he was in a chequered morning robe. "Is there anything amiss?"

"I want you to alert security and search the room. My daughter saw someone," her father said, taking instant control of the situation. Lucille stared at the blanket, slightly embarrassed. Surprisingly, her father sat down on her bed and brushed her tangled, wet hair from her forehead. "Are you okay?"

Lucille was so astonished by his attention she wrapped her arms around him and pressed herself against his body. "Daddy." Her mind was still catching up, caught between the horrors of her nightmares and the one she woke up to.

"Looks like you had a bad dream," her father said softly.

That much was true. She almost never dreamed of her mother, but it was always the accident when she did. Slowly, the wheels of her mind started turning, and she realised that what had been in her room was a type of monster. Nothing that Albert or her father could catch, no matter how diligently they searched the house. "I'm sure that was it. There's nobody here, Albert."

Her father kissed her forehead. "We're still going to search the house. Do you want me to stay while you go back to sleep?"

Lucille regarded his headset and day-clothes. He was still working at this time of night. Or working already. Her scream had probably pulled him out of some important phone conference. But he *had* come. When it had really mattered, he'd come for her. And now she had to be a big girl. "No, I'll be all right," she said and disentangled herself from him.

"You're sure?"

"Yes. You need to go to sleep."

Her father gave her a wry smile. "Later." He and Albert left her room and turned off the light again.

Once the door was closed, Lucille pulled up her blanket, watching each shadow in her room as if it was going to jump out at her. At last, she opened her hand and whispered, "Erit lux."

The room stayed dark, and Lucille whimpered. Something had stolen her magic while she'd slept.

The next day, Lucille rushed out of her history class to meet up with the others. Jan was already there, reserving their table for them. Or, if she knew him at all, he'd only just bothered to come to school. By the time Lucille had sat down, Rachel, Fabian, and Samantha were coming over from Physics, all of them looking as if they were in desperate need of a good night's sleep.

Lucille impatiently waited for them to sit down before she blurted out, "I need to tell you something."

For once, Rachel matched her excitement. "Yes, we need to talk about your nightmare."

"You know about it?" Lucille leaned back, feeling slightly overwhelmed.

"First, it was Fabian, then Sam, and last night, the dreamwalker came for you." Rachel gave Fabian a pointed look, and he shrank in his seat.

Unsure of what to make of their interaction, Lucille clarified, "I was actually going to say there was a monster."

"A real nightmare monster?" Jan joked. When nobody returned his grin, he rolled his eyes. "Come on, hit us with the details."

Lucille clicked her tongue, then tried to find the right way to tell them about the nightly apparition. "When I woke up, somebody was sitting on me." Her chest was still hurting from it.

Jan snorted, unable to contain his amusement. "That's TMI, Lu."

Lucille boxed him hard. "It was humanoid, but quite small, and very heavy. It honestly seemed like an elephant was sitting on my chest." In fact, her chest was still a bit heavy today. Each breath was accompanied by a hollow pain.

Across from her, Fabian was rubbing his own chest. "Are you saying my chest is hurting because for the last three days, a little guy's been sitting on it?"

"I believe it was a little woman, though she turned to smoke when my father came in. It was some sort of hag: small, old, wizen." Lucille shuddered as she remembered. "And I believe she stole my magic."

"Mine too!" Fabian exclaimed, before checking with Samantha, who was much less enthused and only nodded vaguely.

Lucille wondered what had caught her attention and followed her line of sight. Predictably, it ended on Matt, who stood in the atrium, surrounded by the Elite Clique. Alan and Cian looked a bit annoyed, but the girls were all over Matt, and Cheryl was hanging onto his arm, kissing him frequently. From behind, Lucille couldn't make out what Matt thought of it, but he was clearly not running away from them to join his friends here in the hall.

Rachel's voice brought her back. "I think she's the dreamwalker that's been invading your dreams. She pulls you into terrible nightmares, then steals your magic. And she's definitely after the six of us."

"Five," Samantha muttered, but only Lucille heard her.

Just then, Jan burst out laughing. All four of them turned to glare at him. "What? It just sounds so weird. Little women sitting on your chests all night. That would give me nightmares, too."

"I actually find it quite unsettling that someone can enter my room at night," Lucille said sharply.

"And your dreams," Rachel added pointedly.

That didn't make Lucille feel much better. "Right. So, what do we do?" If this was a monster, she wanted to hunt it down and demand her magic back. The necklace was still there, but it was strangely cold against her skin. Everything was wrong without magic.

"I need to go to class," Samantha murmured, grabbed her bag, and practically ran off.

Lucille turned around to see Matt coming towards them. Samantha rushed past him, and he turned to glance at her before continuing. By the time he sat down at their table, he was scowling.

"And here's the expert," Jan announced. "Matt, you know your way around beds. Have you ever met a tiny old lady whose fetish is sitting on people's chest?"

A collective groan went around the table while Matt looked confused. "Is he high?" he asked the rest of them.

"No, just being Jan." Lucille massaged the bridge of her nose. "Something is entering our dreams, turning them into nightmares, and stealing our magic. It has already come for me, Fabian, and Samantha."

"And I believe the three of us are next," Rachel added.

Jan scoffed. "Not me. I don't have any magic."

"You're still one of us," Rachel stressed, then sighed. "This is serious."

"So, what's the plan?" Matt looked around the table.

"It's a nightmare monster…" Fabian said slowly. "Never going to sleep again would be an option."

Lucille rolled her eyes. "Don't you want your magic back?"

"I actually do." Fabian looked as surprised about that as the rest of them. "But I don't know how to fight something while I'm asleep."

Rachel set her jaw. "But I do. Or at least, I'm starting to figure it out."

Matt

Matt was supposed to meet the others at the Magic Circle so they could search the books for their nightmare monster. Instead, he was pulled along by Cheryl, who had got it into her head to track down the student council. Belatedly, he realised *who* was on the student council.

The group of five was sitting in the back of the student hall with a bunch of folders and papers between them. Matt's eyes fell straight on the black curls cascading down Samantha's back and swallowed. She'd given him the cut at school today, and he braced himself for whatever silly retaliation she'd come up with now.

"Hey guys," Cheryl said sweetly. It was a tone Matt was starting to hate, her fake chirpy voice grating on his nerves. But when Samantha looked over her shoulder and stiffened the moment she saw him, he felt the sudden need to keep pretending to be Cheryl's quasi-supportive boyfriend. "I heard that you're doing matching for the student exchange."

Adrian pointed at Samantha who was biting her tongue. "We're about to do that, yes," he said somewhat strained.

"Oh, perfect!" Cheryl clapped her hands. "Do you have pictures?" When nobody answered her, she simply snatched the folder from Samantha. "Give me that."

Matt stared at his feet. He didn't want to defend Samantha, and yet, seeing Cheryl treat her like that made him angry.

"I just want to make sure I'm not getting some weird-ass chick." Cheryl showed one of the pictures to him. "Have a look at this himbo." The boy with glasses looked perfectly fine to Matt.

"Cheryl, we're not making the pairing based on looks but on shared interests," Adrian said sharply, while the rest of the student council seemed completely overwhelmed by Cheryl's rudeness.

She smiled sweetly at Adrian. "Oh, but I would like to be paired with someone who shares my interest in looking good. Right, Matty?"

Matt bristled at the public use of the stupid nickname she insisted on calling him. "I don't care. Boy, girl, whoever's left over."

"Too bad the school doesn't do background checks," Samantha muttered.

When Cheryl came down on her, Samantha turned into this mousy, pale reflection of herself, but when Matt so much as opened his mouth, she was all poison and fire. He didn't know whether he should be flattered or annoyed. "Whatever."

"This one here is cute," Cheryl said, and showed him the picture of yet another French dude. Despite what else might be said about Cheryl, she did have taste. The guy named Dion was a good-looking African-French guy with a charming smile and beautiful eyes. "You should pick him."

"Nobody is picking anyone," Adrian protested. "We're doing the pairings."

Cheryl scoffed at him. "Don't be silly, Adrian! There's nothing wrong with making a choice. You want us all to get along, right?" She pushed a lock of hair behind her ear. "I want Amelie," she said, giving the folder back to Samantha. "Be a dear and make a note."

"Sure," Samantha said and wrote down Lucille's name on Amelie's page.

"Are you trying to mess with me?" Cheryl asked, all her sweetness draining from her.

"Hey, Matt," said one of the other girls on the council, Laura. He knew her from his Biology class. "Can't you take your girlfriend away and keep her busy? We're trying to work here."

"She's not my girlfriend," Matt said pointedly. Whatever Cheryl thought, he didn't do the whole boyfriend-girlfriend thing. And he sure as hell wouldn't change that for her.

Cheryl laughed nervously. "Matty..."

"Stop calling me that!" This was all getting too much. The stupid nicknames, the clinging, the constant showing him off to anyone who cared and everyone who didn't. And now here in front of Samantha. He was sick of it. "We had sex, Cheryl, nothing more, and it wasn't even particularly great sex." Cheryl gasped, and Laura snickered. "So, please, just lay off. If I wanted a relationship with anyone, I'd go for someone less needy."

He expected Cheryl to launch herself at him, but it was Samantha who glared at him. "Are you serious? You can't talk to Cheryl like that."

"Why do you care?" he asked, irritated. Samantha *hated* Cheryl. She shouldn't care a bit for how he spoke to Cheryl.

"You have absolutely no decency, do you?"

Finally, Cheryl got her wits together. The first thing she did was lash out at Samantha. "Keep your ugly nose out of my business!" Then she turned around to Matt, a million things happening at once on her face. For a moment, he was afraid she was going to kiss him again, but then she slapped him across the face. "The rumours about the sex with you are so over-the-top."

"If you say so." He couldn't care less for any rumours or disappointing Cheryl.

His lack of outrage, however, brought a shimmer to her eyes, and for once, Matt thought he saw something real in her face. "You disgust me," she exclaimed and stormed off.

Matt shook his head, feeling an immense wave of relief wash over him now that he was no longer attached to Cheryl. But then he caught Samantha glaring at him, the accusation plain in her eyes. He didn't get it. Was what he'd done really so terrible that she would side with her lifelong nemesis over him? Matt imagined siding with Caspar against anyone, and couldn't comprehend it in the slightest.

"Weren't you against us hanging out just yesterday?" he asked more confused than angry.

"I couldn't care less about who you want to hang out with. But just because I don't like Cheryl, I won't condone anyone treating her like trash. You've never been like this," she blurted out. Surprised with herself, her voice softened for a moment. "At least you weren't before."

The moment was over before he could latch on it. "But hey, the feelings of other people don't really matter to you, I guess."

Matt stared at her. A million explanations ran through his head. He automatically wanted to protest, but then he asked himself if she hadn't got it perfectly right. He *was* half demon, after all. He didn't know a single demon who'd give a second thought about someone else's feelings. That was what he identified with. And yet, she'd said he hadn't been like this before. And while his mind ran through all possible retorts, he kept coming back to that little titbit. It was like a piece that didn't fit. As if he didn't truly know himself anymore.

Unable to respond, Matt shook his head, and slowly backed away.

In his dreams, Matt returned to the dark corridors of the Dûr Lôrac, a dark system of caves full of monsters. There was no sky in Hell, just bigger caves, some large enough to hold entire cities, but Matt was far away from those. No sensible demon went into the Dûr Lôrac without need. Why flirt with greater danger if there was enough danger to go around in the cities?

Yet, at night, those black tunnels were all Matt got to see. Sometimes, he would walk for hours without meeting a single soul. At others—

Energy shot past him, narrowly missing his face. Matt whirled around and dropped down in a crouch, ready to defend himself. The demon he saw lit up against some foreign light was all too familiar to him. "Caspar."

"Weakling," Caspar replied likewise. His eyes gleamed with cruel intent, and he threw another bolt of deadly energy at Matt.

Matt managed to jump out of the way just in time. He stumbled around to see the energy tear through the walls of the tunnel and into what looked like a human living room, where it hit and instantly killed the couple watching TV. Blood splattered, and for a moment, Matt felt the weight of his sword in his hand. He swallowed heavily.

"Oh, did you like them?" Caspar was behind him, trickling his poison into his ear. "You've gone soft, haven't you? Human bastard."

The final words cut through Matt's skin like a whip. "Leave me alone!" He walked away, once more returning to the darkness of the Dûr Lôrac.

It took him quite some time to realise there was someone else with him. It was the lack of danger that had him fooled for so long. "Rachel?"

"Hey." She smiled vaguely at him, then asked, "What are we looking for?"

"Myself."

Matt walked through a gap in the tunnel and found himself back in Greenvalley, in a nightmare of blood and snow. Daniel's empty eyes stared up at him, full of wordless accusation. Someone sobbed nearby, crying their heart out. Samantha.

"No," Matt stumbled backwards. "It was an accident!"

"Was it?" Rachel asked, but she didn't matter.

When Matt turned away, he found himself face to face with his father. Only René had given up on him. His face was closed off, and he pointed his gun at Matt's chest. "I thought you were different. That you somehow wouldn't turn out like her."

Matt stumbled back, his feet sliding on the icy surface. "I'm still learning," he blurted out. "Give me time. I just need time."

"Time? So you can continue murdering innocent people?" René raised the gun, and a click sounded loudly in Matt's ears. "No, Matt. The bad apple needs to be squashed."

"Dad!"

The bullet was fired and hit Matt squarely in the chest. Pain seized him and threw him backwards, straight through the ground into his mother's bedroom. He coughed up blood as he grappled for air. The blood soaked the bed sheets under him. He tried to get up, but the pain forced him down again and again.

At last, he lay still, wondering if this was it now.

Then his mother leaned over him, wearing nothing but a sheer robe and high heels. She stroked his hair, and Matt turned into her hand, eager for her comfort. Melaney bore her nails into the skin of his head, drawing more blood. "I never should've let you go."

"I'm back," Matt said, desperate for her approval.

But his mother got up and sneered at him in her best Caspar impression. "He ruined you. Where did my perfect Melchior go?"

Still eager to please, Matt transformed. The demon powers healed his chest, and he rose from the bed, black wings spreading behind him. He knew how important it was to show no weakness in Hell. Weakness got you killed. "I'm here," he said, his voice almost as confident as it had to be.

Melaney snorted dismissively. "You're not my Melchior." Suddenly, she was behind him. "My Melchior is strong." And with that, she tore her long fingernails through the thin leather of his wings. A new searing type of pain erupted in his back, and he leaned forward, gasping for air. "He knows what he wants." The nails dug deeper until his wings hung in tatters. Matt whimpered in pain. "And he takes what he wants." She'd barely finished speaking when she ripped the wings from his back.

Hot blood streamed down his back as he fell forward, screaming. Matt tried to rise again, clawing for the strength so valued by his mother, but his body wouldn't comply. It was weak. It was human.

"I should have left you to Caspar," his mother said and kicked her pointy heel right in the wound of where his wings had once been attached to his back.

The world was alight with pain as Matt fell deeper and deeper, backwards into time, until he was no more than four years old and at Caspar's mercy. He landed in a worm-filled hole. Above him, Caspar stood, sneering down at him. "See. You're just as weak as your human daddy."

Matt felt the panic tighten his throat. He was only four, and the worms crawling over his skin left behind burning traces. Blood and pus welled from his arms, his legs, and his face. One of the creatures slid over his eye, and Matt screamed as he was blinded. He shot energy at the worms, but only succeeded in making the hole bigger, more worms falling into the pit.

Next to him, Rachel tried to wipe the worms from his body, but they turned to dust in her hands, only to reappear on Matt's skin. "This isn't working," she said, annoyed. "Come with me!"

The authority in her voice left Matt no choice. He followed her out of the pit and back into the Dûr Lôrac. As the darkness welcomed them back, his mind and body returned to his eighteen-year-old self. Around them, vaguely familiar faces appeared on the walls. And then the voices came.

"I thought you loved me!" Cheryl screeched.

Fabian scrambled away from him. "Don't touch me!"

Matt changed directions and almost ran into Balthasar, who regarded him coolly. "In the end, it all comes down to what's more important to you. Power or those puny humans you call friends. You can't have both."

"I know what you are now!" Jan exclaimed behind him, then accused him, "You're a demon!"

"Human bastard," Caspar corrected.

Matt let go of Rachel's hand to cover his ears. It didn't help. The comments kept coming. The demons found him lacking, weak, too emotional. The humans were disgusted, frightened, or angry. And then there was Chay. The only other half-demon he knew.

"Why did you ruin it?" Chay sighed, utterly disappointed with him. "I didn't give you the Sword of the Gods, so you could tear apart everything I've worked for. You don't deserve its power."

"I know that!" Matt shouted back at him. How could he not? The sword was heavy in his hand ever since he'd killed Daniel in the snow.

He stumbled backwards into a storage container and right into Samantha's arms. Instantly, there was peace. Samantha took care of his wounds, her face creased with beautiful worry. Here was someone who cared for him, until the wounds healed by themselves, and she recognised him for what he was.

"I wanted to tell you," he cried. "Please believe me."

Her eyes filled with tears. "You killed him."

"I didn't care for Daniel," he admitted. "I only ever wanted to be with you."

Samantha turned her face away from him. "You don't even know what you want." When she faced him again, something metallic glinted between them. Her Thorak.

Matt scrambled away and swallowed at its sight. "Explain it to me! Sam, please. I don't know what to think anymore. It all hurts."

Pity filled her face, and he started to hope. She put her hand on his face and whispered, "Not enough."

His eyes widened. "Please... I need you."

"It's too late." And without further hesitation, she plunged the dagger into his chest.

Matt gasped, unable to speak, while black smoke rose from his chest. Samantha twisted the dagger, still lovingly cradling his cheek. She was killing him.

"Erit lux!" Rachel said, and a sudden light brightened the dream.

Through his squinting eyes, Matt saw Samantha's face unravelling. In its place was a wizen, old woman. She snarled, her twig-like fingers tightening on his temple.

"To me!" Rachel ordered, and both black smoke and Matt followed her call.

The creature rose to her hackles and shot at Rachel. Rachel grabbed Matt's hand and pulled them through a door into a bright meadow with open skies, endless galaxies in a myriad of colours swirling above them. Matt fell on his back, staring up into the colourful galaxies, unable to move now that he was somehow safe again. "Where should I go?" he heard himself asking.

Rachel knelt over him and gently poured the black smoke back into his chest. It made Matt feel a little more complete, but also full of disgust for what he was. "If only I knew, Matt, things would be so much easier."

"Life in Hell is easier than this." It would be easier if he was one or the other, but not both. Never both.

She sighed, her hands resting on his unharmed body. "But you belong here."

"Do I?"

Rachel

After four nights of fighting the dreamwalker, Rachel felt as exhausted as her friends. At the same time, she was positively buzzing. She'd won! When the creature had gone for Matt and pulled his magic out of him, she'd stopped it. Matt was still in possession of all his powers.

Not that he looked like it as he sat on the far end of the classroom, eyes turned to the table, lost in his own thoughts. Last night, Rachel had been privy to the inner turmoil he kept so well in check these days. It seemed to her that the shared experience had caused a crack in his shield. Rachel could only hope that it meant that the rift between him and Samantha would eventually heal, but she doubted one single nightmare was enough to push him in the right direction.

She sighed and turned her attention back to the front, where Mr Zobel was handing out their report cards for the first semester. Fabian had been called to pick up his and returned with a slightly demented grin that Rachel attributed to his lack of sleep. "Herbert gave me nine points!"

Samantha clapped excitedly. "I told you that he couldn't get past the quality of your work. You nailed that first exam."

"What did you get?" Fabian asked, still delirious with joy.

"Thirteen."

That made Fabian roll his eyes. "Every other teacher would've given you the full fifteen. You understand everything."

"Rachel Hadden," Mr Zobel called. Rachel walked up to receive her report card. "Looks good, especially considering everything you went through last year." Mr Zobel's smile was kind, but she could've done without the reminder that her brother's report card had never been written.

She only nodded at the teacher and checked her grades. Fabian had been right about Mr Herbert's bias. Rachel had received twelve points from him, and there was no way that she was only one point below Samantha. Or three above Fabian. Not that she was going to complain, even if she would've preferred being marked without a hidden agenda.

The rest of her report card was a good mix. Music was her worst subject with seven points, and Rachel found she could live with that. Especially when she'd earned fourteen points in her Maths major.

"Twelve?" Fabian asked, singularly zoning in on her Physics grade. "Damn, he must like you."

"Or Rachel's just really good," Samantha said in the slightly condescending voice she only ever used with Fabian when he said something insensitive.

Fabian leaned on Rachel. "Of course she is. I only date smart girls, you know?" His hand twitched as if he planned to put his arm around her but thought better of it at the last second.

Meanwhile, Jan got his report card with a much sterner message. "Two below five. If you don't put in the work next semester, you might have to repeat the year."

"Yeah, yeah." Jan grabbed his report card and stuffed it into his bag, unseen.

Mr Zobel handed out the rest of the report cards and wished them a great break.

"What break?" Jan grumbled. "It's already packed with homework."

Robert immediately latched onto that comment. "Did you also get loads of homework? I'm going to do it all on the last weekend. We're going skiing tomorrow."

Jan grimaced. "That's nice, I guess." He got up and left the room quickly.

Rachel felt a bit sorry for Robert. While he might be mistaken, thinking he and Jan were friends, he was only overly friendly. "Have a great trip, Robert," Rachel told him as she went past.

The group met in the corridor, where Lucille was examining Matt's report card in detail. "I'm impressed. Chay prepared you well for school here." She turned the report card around for the rest of them to see. "Almost all double-digit marks. And fifteen in PE."

Jan snorted. "I got fourteen in PE, too. That's why you pick it as a major. Easy top marks, little homework."

"Yeah, but he also has thirteen points in Geography," Lu defended Matt. "What did you get?"

"Something." Jan shrugged dismissively.

Matt took his report card back and put it neatly into a folder. "Those grades don't matter. What matters is that we find the creature that's been tormenting us at night. Thanks for last night, Rachel."

"You remember me?" Rachel asked, excited. It happened very rarely, and never in a way that someone realised she'd actually been there, instead of just dreaming of her.

"You saved my life, or something like it."

Rachel blushed, but in her mind, she saw all the violence of his dream. Shot by his father, torn to pieces by his mother, tortured by Caspar... stabbed by Samantha. "Well, I didn't..." She hadn't been able to stop any of it. "I think I saved your magic, not your life."

Matt frowned a little. "That's pretty much the same." He glanced around before lowering his voice. "Demons are creatures of magic. Take it away and... poof, I guess."

"Interesting," Samantha muttered, earning herself an instant glare.

"Either way. We need to find out what it is that's targeting us and how to stop it. Magic Circle?"

Lucille nodded eagerly. "Yes! I want my magic back."

"Such weirdos!" an unmistakable voice announced. Cheryl flicked her hair at them as she walked past with her posse.

They all groaned and got moving with the mass of students pouring out the gates.

A little later, they'd buried themselves in the books in the back room of the Magic Circle. Samantha and Matt were both going through the pile of monster compendia, sitting as far away as possible from each other. Lucille stole glances at both of them but didn't say anything. Instead, she was trying her best to stay awake.

Rachel had found a thin book on dream interpretation. She figured if she was seeing her friends' dreams, she should at least get better at understanding them.

"Were the worms a metaphor for what Caspar truly did to you?" she asked, reading about the symbolism of worms. "Apparently, they stand for fake friends who are out to get you, which I guess could mean family as well. They're a symbol for dishonesty, rejection, betrayal, pretty much any negative emotion."

"Sounds fitting to me," Samantha murmured.

Matt glared at her, then turned to Rachel, suppressing a shudder. "The worms are a memory. Remember the hellworms?"

As understanding dawned on Rachel, her eyes widened. "Your brother truly dumped you into a pit of hellworms when you were just a little kid?" And she thought *she* had bad memories of her childhood.

Matt shifted uncomfortably in his chair. "Something like it," he murmured.

Rachel noticed that Samantha was watching him above the rim of her book, for once not a snippy comment on her tongue. Meanwhile, Lucille was cooing in pity. "No wonder you're afraid of them."

"I'm fine," Matt said a little too fast, and Rachel started to regret bringing it up.

Fortunately for him, Fabian chose that moment to return from the store front. "My mum says if succubus isn't a fit, we should check out drudes."

"Drudes are extremely territorial. They don't move to a new location all of a sudden," Matt said.

"Then why did she look exactly like this?" Lucille said, opening a page up in her book. On it was the old woman Rachel had seen in Matt's dream. "It's a drude."

Matt shook his head. "That makes no sense. Why would she suddenly be in Greenvalley?"

"Maybe she moved," Jan suggested.

Samantha giggled, but when she saw Matt's annoyed facial expression, she turned serious. "What if your uncle is behind it? It wouldn't be the first time."

"My uncle?" The rest of them were just as confused as Matt.

"He called your mother his dear sister," Samantha said, slightly frustrated at his slowness. "Remember? After he beat your ass and she came down on him like a fury for touching her precious son? The demon who's after the magic in our town is your uncle. I thought you knew that and just chose to keep it a secret like everything else." She shrugged uncomfortably.

Matt was still staring at her, but Lucille caught on. "Yes, I remember him saying that. I forgot all about it in the aftermath. The demon's your uncle?"

"Lucille." Matt took a deep breath and shook himself out of the stupor. "Demons have like a million relatives. They don't really care... oh." His face fell. "No, no, this is not good."

"I'd argue anything to do with demons isn't good," Fabian muttered.

"No. I have loads of siblings and probably nieces and nephews and whatever, but my mother only has one brother. They might even be full siblings. And he's... shit!" He banged his hand on the table. "He's an archdemon like her. The Archdemon of Greed. I'd never met him before. In Hescaryn, I mean."

While the rest of them were processing the news, Samantha was already putting things together. "And we know that he wants Greenvalley's magic. When we blocked him, he tried using this stupid drug Jan took to get a hold on the magic. And now... I guess we know why the drude is going after us and our magic. Looks like he hates his nephew as much as I do."

"Well, maybe you've got much more demon in you than you thought," Matt shot back, then massaged his temples. "You really think Malcolm is keeping a drude as a pet?"

"I have no idea. Demons keep a lot of pets most people would keep far, far away from." Samantha's vicious comeback lacked heat when she had to yawn.

"Wait a minute!" Jan exclaimed. "The hellhounds! They liked you because you're part demon!" He clicked his fingers. "And you all told me I was crazy. Thanks guys!"

Matt groaned. "Oh please, you *were* crazy. And you were miles off. You'd think I was sitting on people's chest at night if I hadn't told you the truth by now."

"Well, I don't know your fetishes..." Jan thankfully left the rest of his comment unsaid.

Lucille pounded her book on the table to make sure Jan wouldn't start again. "So, on the topic of drudes. It says here the drude, also known as the nighthag, is related to the incubi and succubi demon group. They sit on the chest of the sleeping and eat from their nightmares." She shuddered. "It's assumed she is actually creating the nightmares herself. Once the drude has claimed her victim, she keeps eating, no longer necessary for her to revisit the victim at night. The victim will show continuous symptoms of exhaustion and weakness. Instead of recovering while they sleep, the nights only lead to a state of further exhaustion. It usually ends in a near complete shutdown of all bodily functions a few days later."

"I'll never go back to sleep," Fabian said, his face pale as a bed sheet. Reminded of sleep, he yawned and rubbed his eyes. "Nightmares are one thing; I do not want my body to shut down."

"Well, I suppose it'll shut down whether you sleep or don't sleep," Lucille mused, while looking quite unsettled herself.

Samantha stifled a yawn of her own before she faced Matt. "Didn't you say that the drudes are extremely territorial? If their victims die every few days, they need to move, don't they?"

"As far as I know, they're not killing them," Matt explained. "I've heard the victims are in a comatose state, caught in an eternal nightmare. The drude usually keeps around a dozen of them and only rarely exchanges them for new victims."

"Yeah," Fabian whimpered.

Lucille's eyes moved across the page in a fury. At last, she found something. "It says here that there are protective runes which can be drawn around the drude, and potentially help kill her." She frowned.

"But for the latter we need a drude knife? I didn't see her carrying a knife."

"A drude knife is simply a sharp dagger coated in chalk. We can easily make one," Matt said.

Jan's arm shot up. "I'll do that! I love occult weapons, and that doesn't sound too hard."

"Okay, sure," Samantha said, after recovering from his sudden enthusiasm. "If we ask Caroline nicely, you can get started right away."

"Great idea," Jan said, and shot up to dash into the store.

Samantha took a look at the runes and sighed. "I wish I had my magic. Then I could attempt to weave them into a protective circle."

"Chalk marks should suffice," Lucille explained, pointing at the text. "They don't seem too hard to draw."

Fabian got out his phone and took a few pictures. "Look, I can go around and put them everywhere. It's not like I'm going to sleep until we get the drude."

"Who do you think she's going for next?" Rachel asked, the tension making her body rigid. "Jan or me?"

"Definitely you," Matt said.

"Jan is just as likely," Samantha said, which caused Matt to groan.

"You don't need to disagree with me just because!" Matt clicked his tongue. "Jan doesn't have any magic, so what is the drude going to feed on? What does Malcolm stand to gain from going after him?"

Behind him, Jan was returning with some chalk and two small daggers. "Vengeance? But yeah, I guess Matt is right. I don't have any magic."

"I don't believe that," Rachel said. "You're wearing an Emblem of Power, aren't you? Chay said it's definitely yours."

Jan checked the wristband. "This thing? The Power of Love? I don't really know what to do with it." He nodded at Samantha. "Even your clever little book only said that it gives me the power to surpass my own expectations, which is like magic mumbo-jumbo to me—or 'love-conquers-all' bullshit. I don't really see either happening, to be honest."

"Perhaps your expectations are too high," Matt quipped.

"No. Rachel is right." Samantha rubbed her eyes. "I believe there *is* some magic in you. You're the reincarnation of Herne and Vesta."

"I'm what?" Jan asked, perplexed.

Samantha took a deep breath. "Herne was called the Hunter of Levante, and Vesta was his wife. They were both major players in the War of Worlds." She paused, noticing how much she was jumping between topics. "There was a war, and at the end of it, the world broke into pieces... Gosh! What I'm saying is that there were once twelve heroes who were the original owners of the Emblems of Power." She rubbed her eyes. "I'm so tired."

Jan frowned. "Okay, but can you repeat that reincarnation thing? I'm not really firm on Buddhism."

It seemed to take Samantha quite some effort to get her thoughts straight. "The six of us are reincarnations of these twelve heroes. That's why the Emblems of Power are finding their way to us. We're all in the book Chay wrote. All six of us. So, even if Jan might not show any magic skill now, he likely will at one point. Just as I did."

Jan looked rather pleased with himself. "Sounds good to me."

"But not to me," Fabian protested. "Why are we in the book?" He looked from Samantha to Matt. "What does it mean?"

Matt exchanged a glance with Rachel. It seemed like an eternity since they'd sat at the café with Chay and he'd told them about the prophecy. Chay had told Rachel that the others weren't quite ready for the truth, but that had been before everything. "There's a prophecy," Matt muttered.

"When Twelve become Six, all will be reborn at the same time in the same place to fight the same battle until the Greedy One fails twice, or all will perish," Rachel recited. "That's the first line."

Samantha stared at her in surprise. "How do you know?"

Rachel assumed mentioning Chay would further widen the chasm between her and Matt. "I just do," she said simply, then noticed another thing. "The Greedy One! The demon we've been fighting again and again—he's the Archdemon of Greed. He's the one we have to face or die."

"But Granny said it's the prophecy for the end of the world." Samantha looked dismayed.

"Stop!" Fabian shouted, then rubbed his face. "Just stop. Please." When everyone quieted down, he took a shuddering breath. "Uhm... the drude. Right now, we need to take care of that one, right?" He closed his eyes. "Sorry. I know I should care more, and I do. But I'm too tired to freak out about more than one thing."

Samantha reached out to him and squeezed his hand. "You're right. We can figure out what to do with Matt's uncle afterwards. The drude is more important."

"Well, I've got two drude knives ready to go," Jan announced and held up the chalk-coated daggers. "So, what's next?"

"We split," Matt said. "I'll protect Rachel tonight. The rest of you have a sleepover at Jan's."

Rachel wasn't surprised he'd picked her after last night. She was more curious as to why he didn't want anyone else there with them.

Fabian noticed that, too. He leaned over to ask quietly, "Are you all right with him?"

"I will be. You go to Jan and put your art skills to good use," she told him.

He nodded earnestly. "After I put the runes up in your room."

Jan

Jan's room was way too small to have an actual sleepover with four people. Fortunately, Lu, Samantha, and Fabian were going to do their best to not fall asleep. They sat on his bedroom floor and talked in hushed voices, while Jan tried to sleep next to them. The problem was, their conversation was far too interesting to slip away from.

"So, there is a prophecy, which says that twelve heroes would be reborn into six new heroes? And that's us?" Lu asked.

"Well, I'm certainly not a hero," Fabian declared. "And the thought of being reborn is kind of creepy. Is that even possible?" Jan couldn't comprehend how being reborn as a hero—or two heroes at that—was anything other than cool.

Leave it to Samantha to have all the answers. "According to Granny, yes. And you can't remember a thing because the soul gets cleaned. It's more like... resource recovery?"

"Soul recycling," Fabian said with a sleep-deprived giggle. "Cool."

Lu laughed out loud. "Thanks, now I feel dirty."

"That's because you're the reincarnation of Mikaia, the Goddess of Earth." Fabian paused a moment. "Wait, if she's a goddess, why is her soul in Lucille?"

"Perhaps immortals don't have souls," Samantha mused. "Or even divine beings die."

Fabian huffed. "How boring."

Jan could hear the rustling of pages, then Lu spoke again. "At least we know why you've got so much water in you. The God of Weather and the God of Rain."

"Why are there always two?" Fabian asked.

"Why can't you be quiet?" Jan sat up in his bed. "Seriously, how am I supposed to fall asleep if you won't shut up?"

All three looked up at him. Lu picked up an energy drink. "The problem is *we* will fall asleep if we shut up."

"That makes me feel so much better about the whole thing." Jan fell back into his bed and sighed. The three of them were supposed to protect him against the drude. He could only hope the monster went after Rachel. Matt might be a psycho, but at least he was still able to think straight.

For a minute or so, there was blissful silence, and Jan closed his eyes. Then he heard a bump, and the girls burst into giggles.

"Enough is enough!" Jan pushed his blanket off and got out of bed.

Fabian seemed to be the instigator of the latest disruption, as he straightened himself from Samantha's lap with a loopy grin. At Jan's sight, he grew serious in an instant. "Where are you going?"

"Sorry, we'll be quiet," Samantha promised.

Jan didn't believe they could, and it wasn't just them. Falling asleep with the impending visitation of some nightmare hag hanging over him was near impossible. He needed help. And he found it in his family's medicine cabinet. With a blister packet of sleeping pills, he returned to the room.

"Don't do that, Jan!" Lu regarded him with concern.

"It's only sleeping pills." He popped a few into his mouth and washed them down with water.

"You should at least read—" Samantha warned.

Jan gave her the thumbs up and plopped down on his bed. Lu got up and turned off the light to aid him in his mission to fall asleep. When they continued their conversation, Jan actually liked the soft murmur.

"I would really like to have a spell at the ready," Lu complained. "It's weird to face a monster without magic."

"It's like before for me," Samantha admitted as Jan felt himself drift away. "Fabian?" There was no reply. "Fabian!" Her loud voice pulled Jan back to the surface.

It seemed to have worked for Fabian as well because he yawned loudly and mumbled, "Sorry, it's the darkness."

Lu replied with something, but Jan could no longer grasp her words. Slowly, he sank into sleep...

...and plunged straight into a nightmare. All the colours were fake and incredibly bright. Jan turned around sluggishly, fighting for his balance. It was as if he was completely high *and* drunk on top of it.

Then a softly-glowing, vine louse-like animal hopped past him. "That's the one that killed Lutz!" The violet, translucent skin brought back all the bad memories.

Jan jumped after the hellish creature, almost running into Rachel in his fervour to get hold of it. Rachel called after him, but he wouldn't stop. Instead, he followed the creature through an endless maze of shipping containers. Finally, Jan cornered it in a dead-end.

"Got you."

"No, I got *you*."

Jan whirled around and found himself face-to-face with the demon. Malcolm, or whatever his name was. As Jan watched, the demon grew, dark wings spreading behind him. Taller and taller, he rose, until Jan was nothing but a vine louse to him.

"Scum." The demon raised his foot.

Jan couldn't move. He'd be squashed under this demon's foot, like the human vermin he was. Just then, Rachel picked him up and saved him from his fate. Jan found himself next to her, in his normal size. The demon had vanished, but now his father stood there, as usual a disapproving frown on his face.

He shook his head before shouting at Jan, "Did you even look at your report card?"

Report card? What did his grades have to do with a demon out to kill him? "Yes. No... maybe..."

"Are you that keen to ruin your life? Well, this is how you're going to end, boy!" His father pointed at something behind Jan.

There in a corner, Lutz crouched. With shaking hands, he pulled out a package of MAGIC. His lips were bloody, and his eyes moved around constantly. Still, he popped a few of the pills. Instead of calming, though, Lutz screamed and convulsed on the floor.

"Lutz!" Jan ran to him, when he suddenly stumbled into a river of blood. Seconds later, he was drowning in it.

Rachel caught him in time and pulled him back on dry land. "We need to find the drude, Jan!"

But Jan suddenly found himself in his kitchen, traces of blood everywhere. "What happened here?" his mother exclaimed in despair.

Jan dashed to the sink to wash the mess away when he saw Lutz's face in the blood. He caught his breath and stumbled backwards.

"Are you high?" his mum asked.

"No... no." He was clean, had been for months.

Rachel grabbed his arm. "Jan, we really need to find the drude."

"I wish you were a little more like Anne." His mother shook her head, close to tears.

And sure enough, there was his perfect little sister. "Do you want me to tutor you?"

The walls were covered with equations, science facts, and complicated questions that stretched line over line. Rachel started wiping them away, but Anne was quicker writing them. Jan knew he had to solve them, but his head was bursting just from looking at them.

Rachel suddenly turned away from the wall and grabbed Jan's hand. "Let's get out of here."

"I can't," Jan said, his voice turning to a plea. "If I don't understand all of this, I'm going to end up like Lutz."

"No, you won't. Malcolm killed Lutz."

"And Nico." His late friend's face looked back at them from the bloody surfaces, reminding him how they'd both angered the demon, yet only one of them had paid the price.

Jan sank to the floor. "He'll kill me too."

Rachel

Rachel had never had a boy sleep over at her place, not even Fabian. Her mother wouldn't mind that she had Matt over, but there was something uncomfortable about going to sleep—and in her case, dreaming—with someone else in the room.

Not that Matt showed any interest in her. He sat in her desk chair, balancing the drude knife on his finger, while mostly staring into space. When he noticed her watching him, he straightened slightly. "You can go to sleep. I'll keep you safe."

"I know," Rachel answered, but she didn't lie down.

After a few moments of silence, Matt spoke again. "How much did you see of my dream?"

So, that was what was bothering him. "A lot." She didn't think she'd missed any vital information.

"I can barely remember it," Matt claimed, then paused. "Apart from the worms and everyone being against me."

It had been a lot more than simple rejection. The people in his dream hadn't just been against him. They'd wanted him dead. "Something like that, yes."

"What about you? Can you remember it all?" He put the knife aside before he took all the chalk off with his balancing act.

"Yes, Matt," Rachel said a little more softly. It was clear to her that he remembered it just as well, even if he pretended otherwise.

Matt sighed and leaned back in the chair. "Do you think she'll ever forgive me?"

She should've known that this was the only part of his dream he truly cared about. "I have no idea, Matt. I've never seen Sam like this." Samantha was kind and eager to avoid conflicts after navigating the bullies at school for most of her life. This new version of her was ravaged by grief and hate. She constantly provoked Matt, desperate to inflict as much pain with her words as he had with his deeds. There was no holding back, no trying to please.

"I hurt her." Matt's voice was surprisingly soft, and Rachel realised that he was showing her a vulnerability he usually kept even from himself. He took a deep breath and fought for some confidence. "What about you?"

"Me?" If Rachel was completely honest with herself, the New Year's killings hadn't impacted her as much as they had her friends. Of course, they were horrible, and what Samantha was going through was impossible to bear, but it didn't affect her personally. Or rather, she found it too easy to understand both sides. She understood Samantha's pain because she had lost her brother in a similar fashion, and she hated his murderer just as much. But, contrary to Malcolm, Matt hadn't killed Daniel for fun. She got where he came from, understood why he hadn't been in control of himself, and saw behind the arrogant front he'd put on. Even before last night's dream, she'd known that he was lost.

How could she hate him if she understood him so well?

"Would you be able to forgive me if I killed Fabian?" Matt clarified.

Talk about a difficult question. Her gut reaction was a resounding "No!", but Rachel never went with her gut reactions. She thought things through before she answered, and thus when she opened her mouth, she said, "Considering the circumstances... eventually."

Matt swallowed and returned to staring into nothing. Silence stretched between them. Rachel should've taken the opportunity to lie down and sleep, but Matt wasn't finished. He just didn't know how to put his feelings into words. So, Rachel asked a question of her own to nudge him along. "Why did you kill Daniel?"

He instantly shrugged his shoulders. "It was the bloodthirst."

Rachel raised her eyebrows. "Hmm."

"You don't believe me?" Matt asked and laughed mirthlessly. "See, that's what I don't get. I killed more people that night. I might be misinterpreting everything again, but nobody seems to care about them. Like... I feel like if I hadn't killed Daniel, you'd all be on my side. Samantha too." He looked almost desperate for approval.

"No!" Rachel said sharply. "It's not okay. They're just as bad, and they've got people who care about them, too." He was right, though. She had mostly forgotten about his other victims. She licked her lip before dropping the important point. "But none of them have featured in your dream."

Matt shifted in his chair and picked up the drude knife again. "What do you mean?"

So, he really wanted her to spell it out for him. "What I mean is that it seems very important to you what Samantha thinks of you. What about the other loved ones?"

"I don't know them," Matt answered immediately. "And they don't guilt-trip me every single day." He scoffed and shook his head. "And Samantha's not important to me."

Rachel gave him a pointed stare. "Remember, I was in your dream."

Matt deflated again. "Fine," he whispered.

"You like her, don't you?" Rachel asked, all the time wondering how that had happened. He'd never seemed the type who'd fall in love with a girl like Samantha. Or anyone.

"Does it matter? She hates me." He groaned, letting go of the knife again. "Listen, I don't really care that much about her. Yes, I liked her when she was nice and all. But that's it. The thing is demons don't really have emotions like this. Strong hate, love... that's not our thing." He shrugged. "I don't have feelings like that, so it doesn't really matter whether she hates me or not. It's just annoying."

Rachel almost laughed in his face. His entire dream had been drenched in emotions. The feeling of betrayal, of being lost, of not knowing where he belonged. "Maybe you're right. Demons don't have emotions, but you're only half demon." Matt swallowed heavily, blinking more often than usual. "I know I'm just some little human girl who's standing on the sidelines, letting life pass her by, but I see you. I see your pain. And hiding it, bottling it up, refusing to acknowledge it, it only makes it worse. I know that much."

He didn't reply. His chin dropped to his chest, and she could hear his jaw working tirelessly as he fought for control over his undeniable emotions.

Rachel decided that it was best to leave him alone to it. "I'll sleep now."

She lay down and welcomed the sleep that would bring her to the dreamworld.

Jan's nightmare changed so rapidly Rachel could hardly keep up with him. Whenever she concentrated on something, another thing popped up. It was shrill, loud, and chaotic. And he wasn't reacting to her presence at all.

Caught in his home's kitchen, the walls continued to be filled with equations and questions too hard for Jan to solve. Anne danced circles around him, and every time she corrected one of his false answers, the blood on the floor rose.

It was no use. Rachel had to fight the drude directly. "Okay, let's do this. Really sorry, Anne." She jumped onto Anne's back and knocked her into the dishwasher.

Anne whirled around with a screech. Her fingers reached for Rachel's face, suddenly growing into twigs. Rachel let go of her to avoid getting her eyes scratched out. But the drude was suddenly behind her, grabbing her shoulders with those thin yet strong fingers. Then she bit Rachel.

"Jan!" Rachel screamed as the memory of pain flooded her dreams.

"Got to solve these," Jan murmured without ever looking at her. He had trouble trying to determine the inflection point of a curve sketched currently on the wall.

Even dragged down by the drude, Rachel could solve it. "It's a third! The inflection point is at a third! You need to—"

The rest of her answer was drowned out when the drude dunked her into the blood. The sticky liquid ran down her throat, eager to fill her lungs.

No!

She was not going to drown in blood in her own dream. Rachel found herself back up, a meter away from the drude. The old, wizened hag snarled at her. "Give me your nightmares, little dreamer." Her voice was like gravel over sandpaper.

"No. And you can't have Jan's either!"

The drude hissed and flew at her. Rachel turned around and grabbed the chalk from Jan's hand. "Role change. You fight the drude; I do your homework."

It was working! Jan was a much better fighter, and he kept the drude in check, while Rachel flew through the equations on the wall. Then she had a better idea.

Instead of solving any more questions, she used the chalk to draw the runes from the book around the kitchen. As dreams worked, she was done the minute she put her mind to it.

Behind her, the drude screamed in agony and rage. Rachel turned to face her, only to notice Jan sinking into the blood.

"Jan!" Rachel dived after him, but the blood was endless and so dark she couldn't see her friend.

The blood was everywhere. It stuck to her clothes and her skin, was in her mouth and her lungs. Rachel spasmed, trying to catch a breath, but there was only blood. So much blood.

Nico's blood.

Samantha

"There's something in the shadows." Samantha pointed to the far end of Jan's bed.

Fabian pointed the flashlight of his cell phone at Jan, and sure enough, there sat the hunched-over figure of the drude, right on Jan's chest. "Shit!"

"Get drawing!" Samantha shouted at him and grabbed the drude knife.

Meanwhile, Lucille had run up to the drude and tried to shove her off Jan, whose breathing was getting more laboured by the minute. The creature didn't budge even a centimetre. "Sam, get over here!"

Samantha quickly checked with Fabian that the pre-drawn circle was now completed, then ran towards the drude, ready to plunge the knife into her back.

The drude turned around and hissed. Black smoke erupted from her mouth, quickly filling the room. When it cleared again, Samantha found herself in the snow, Daniel's corpse at her feet.

She screamed.

"Sam!"

Samantha raised her knife in a feeble attempt to defend herself against Daniel's murderer. Matt was approaching slowly, his bloodied sword still in his hand.

"Stay away from me!" Samantha shouted, her hand shaking in fear.

Matt kept coming, his face deceivingly gentle. His soft brown eyes were full of worry, but Samantha knew it was a lie. The blood on his sword gave him away. "Sam, put that knife down. Please."

Instead, she lunged at him. Matt grabbed her arms and used her momentum to push her away from him.

Samantha stumbled over the line of chalk runes, and suddenly her mind cleared. Matt wasn't here, and neither was Daniel. Instead, Fabian looked at her wide-eyed, a thin trail of blood on his arm. "Fabian?"

He quickly stepped out of the circle and sighed with relief. "Great, you're back. Come on, we need to kill the drude before she drags us all into our nightmares."

Samantha's mind overtook itself. Nightmares. The drude. Matt and Daniel. Blood. "Oh god..." Her knees felt weak, but she forced herself to take a step into the circle. Instantly, she saw Daniel again.

Screaming, she stumbled back into Fabian's arms and crumpled into his embrace. Sobbing, Samantha dragged him to the ground with her. "I can't. There's blood. So much blood... and snow." The snow made all of it worse.

"It's just a nightmare," Fabian urged her. "It's not true."

"But it is!" Samantha broke into tears again. "It's all true!" Matt *had* killed Daniel. Matt *was* a monster. And Daniel would never make her laugh again.

Fabian didn't answer. Helplessly, he glanced around the room until his gaze fell on Lucille. "Lucille!"

Samantha blinked through her tears, searching for her friend. Lucille was lying motionless on the ground, as if the drude was sitting on her too.

"Lucille!" Fabian let Samantha go and dashed into the circle. He got halfway in when he raised his arms, as if shielding himself from invisible flames. Nevertheless, he pushed his arms forward and formed a delta with his fingers. Nothing happened. His magic was gone, and Fabian sank to his knees whimpering.

There was no other choice. Samantha had to go in and face her nightmare to save her friends.

She took a shuddering breath, then pushed herself up and over the line.

Cold bit her fingers as she stepped into the snow. There was Daniel, his blood frozen around him, while he stared into the emptiness that was death. "Matt?" Samantha asked, her voice shaking.

She saw him a little further ahead as he pulled his sword out of Lucille's dead body. "No," Samantha whimpered and covered her mouth with one hand. "Please don't."

"Sam!" Fabian was at her side, blood running across his face from a pecking wound above his forehead. "What do you see?"

"Him," she breathed.

"Matt?"

No, this wasn't Matt. He couldn't be Matt. Matt had been kind and funny. Not a monster. "Melchior."

Fabian didn't answer. He dashed forward to throw himself over Lucille's corpse, protecting her from an invisible foe, never noticing how Matt regarded him. A cruel smile played on his lips.

"No, please don't take Fabian from me," Samantha pleaded, tears streaming over her face. "Please don't!"

"Sam, I'm fine!" Fabian shouted. "This isn't him! Melchior... Melchior is over there, with Jan."

Samantha followed the length of his arm until her gaze fell on Jan. Melchior was indeed on top of him, his hands wrapped around Jan's throat, choking him. She grabbed her knife tighter, carefully putting one foot in front of the other in the snow.

"I did it for you," Melchior said, his eyes gleaming with bloodlust. "I killed them all for you."

"Ass!" She pulled back her arm and plunged the dagger into his back.

Someone shrieked. Samantha pulled up her hands to cover her ears as Melchior turned into the drude, then Matt, then the drude again, and finally into black smoke.

There was no snow, no blood, no corpses. Samantha sank to her knees and buried her face in Jan's linens as the despair rolled over her. It shook her shoulders and burned her lungs as she gasped for breath. It was as if she'd lost Daniel all over again, and with him, Matt. She'd really liked him. Liked the little relationship that had been developing between them, but it was all gone, drowning in grief and hate, and bone-shattering despair.

"She's only sleeping," Fabian whispered behind her. "Lucille's only sleeping." He sounded as if he was going to fall asleep as well.

Samantha raised her head just high enough to check on Jan. His chest was rising and falling. He, too, was sleeping, not a drude in sight. The heavy weight on her chest that had resided there for the last few days was gone, but the weight on her shoulders was as bad as it had ever been.

Daniel was dead. And Matt was dead to her. And it all felt as if she'd never be happy again.

The exhaustion got her before she could slide back to the ground. Between aching sobs and spiralling thoughts, Samantha fell asleep on Jan's bed.

Matt

Matt was sitting in Rachel's room as she slept. To pass the time, he had pulled out a scrapbook. He probably shouldn't have been looking at her personal stuff, but his eyes caught the first picture of Samantha, and he couldn't tear his hands away.

Demons didn't keep scrapbooks. The first photo taken of Matt had been with Lucille's camera. One of those friend selfies human teenagers couldn't get enough of. There were countless photos of him on Lucille's phone, and a few on his own as well. But he'd never seen something like this.

The scrapbook didn't just hold recent pictures. It was so much more. A history of friendship between Rachel, Nico, Fabian, and Samantha. He saw them as eight-year-olds in an old class photo, and then a few years later when they got into the habit of taking photos of each other.

Matt barely registered the others, though Fabian's ginger hair was hard to miss. His eyes were always drawn to Samantha's black curls. She looked so happy, laughing in most of the pictures, and fooling around with Fabian. There was a picture of her kissing him when she was about fifteen years old, and Matt couldn't help but wince.

Seeing Samantha happy and in love with someone else made his chest ache in an unfamiliar fashion he was slowly getting used to these days. He thought about Rachel's words, how he was refusing to acknowledge the pain. What good would it do? Whether he was in pain or not, it didn't change the past, nor did it have any effect on the future.

He closed the scrapbook. Samantha was lost to him. She'd never been his, and it would be best to move on. And yet, Matt couldn't.

He didn't want to. Didn't want to leave his life here behind, the friends he'd made, the family he'd found. To stay around Samantha was going to be torture, but it was better than being alone in Hell.

His eyes shot to Rachel's bed as she started to thrash in her sleep. Matt grabbed the drude knife and approached her, but there was nothing on Rachel's chest.

He considered waking her, when he saw three silver drops falling from the dreamweb. They touched her skin and sank into her dreams, and immediately Rachel calmed. Matt withdrew again and let the dreamweb do its work. It obviously had power over the nightmares.

He waited for about half an hour longer, watching Rachel closely. Then he got a text from Fabian.

Fabian: Mission accomplished. The drude is dead.

Matt snorted softly. So, Samantha had been right, and the drude had gone for Jan. Good on them for taking the hag out. He texted back, asking for details, but never got a reply. Figuring that Fabian still hated him, he gave up on it.

With one last look at Rachel's peaceful sleep, he vanished from her room.

\#

He should've just gone to bed, but instead, Matt found himself knocking on his father's bedroom door. René opened it in confusion and rubbed his tired face. "Matt? Is everything okay?"

"No," Matt answered, despite his original intentions of apologising for how he had treated René since his return. "Nothing is."

That seemed to jolt René awake. He nodded thoughtfully and stepped out into the corridor, closing the door behind him. "Talk to me."

Matt had no idea where to start. How much Samantha hated him? How his friends no longer trusted him? Or how he had no idea what to do? "I made a big mess out of it, didn't I?"

"Do you want the rational answer or the fatherly?" René asked.

"Can I... can I have the fatherly?" Matt thought he already knew the rational answer.

René smiled, then jerked his head to the right. "Come on." He walked into the kitchen and turned on the light. "I'll make us some hot milk."

For a few minutes, he busied himself with boiling milk for two cups. "Honey?"

Matt wasn't quite sure what the milk business was all about, so he just shrugged.

A spoonful of honey went into each of their cups. René stirred them, then brought them to the living room where they sat down. "You probably don't remember this, but I used to make you hot milk when you were upset. Your mum would leave for days, and you missed her so much. As did I." He sipped on his own cup. "So, even though you should've already been in bed, I made you some milk and then I would talk to you or read you a story. And you'd fall asleep in my arms."

Something shifted inside of Matt, like a dusty old jigsaw tile found behind a cupboard. He had no recollection of the first two years of his life spent here in Ashuan. Until he'd met Chay, no one had taken care of him in Hell. If he'd been upset, he just had to get over it. Crying made you weak, and weakness got you killed. He couldn't help but wonder how different his life would've been if he'd grown up with his father. If there had been someone in his life who made him hot milk with honey and talked to him about his feelings, would he still have suffered through the Blood Night? Would he still have killed Daniel? Or would Daniel have been completely out of the picture because Matt would've been with Samantha?

"I..." Matt tried to sort through the mess in his brain. The nightmare he'd had, and the things Rachel had said to him. "I feel like I don't belong here," he admitted, though he kept the part to himself that felt like he didn't belong *anywhere*. "With my demon sensibilities, I feel like I'm constantly stepping on everybody's toes. They don't understand me. And now... I'm not sure I understand myself anymore."

That thought was new. For most of his life, Matt had been confident in who he was. He was a son of Melaney: strong, smart, sexy. Caspar had had it out for him since he'd been too small to defend himself, and he was still alive. He even believed that he could take Caspar in a fight to the death, whether he was Hescaryn's general or not. And look at him now. He was all the things Caspar said humans were, riddled by irrational feelings and weak, yearning for something power couldn't give him.

"I never really thought about what it meant to be half demon," Matt admitted. "I was no different from the other demon kids, apart from the fact that I matured much faster." A demon's childhood took between eighty and a hundred and twenty years. He'd grown up five times as fast. "I was as strong as them, as fast as them, as sturdy... If Caspar hadn't constantly called me a human bastard, I wouldn't even have known that I was different to everybody else. The only other half demon I ever met was Chay, and he always hung out in human worlds if he wasn't teaching me. Don't get me wrong, he's my hero. He runs around and saves worlds, but I never thought I was like him. Like, deep down inside, I identified as a demon. And I believe Chay is more on the human side."

"Because he grew up here, right?" René asked.

Matt nodded. "Yeah, I guess. Anyway, I came to Greenvalley out of curiosity. Chay urged me to do it to get in touch with my human side, but I wasn't really interested in that. I just wanted to find out what humans were like. And at first, that was fun and really interesting. The school, those little family units everybody lives in, how nobody tries to kill each other on a daily basis." His voice took a dive. "How people are there for each other."

His father reached over the table to grab his hand. "Matt, I *am* here for you."

"I don't even understand what that means!" Matt protested while pushing down the sudden fullness inside his chest that tightened his throat and strained his eyes.

René smiled gently. "It means you can always come to me. If you want to talk things through, or rant, or cry. I'm your father, Matt. I know that we've been robbed of our time together. You don't know how many nights I've lain awake in bed, wondering where you were. I had plans for us. The places I wanted to show you, the things I wanted to teach you... Melaney took that not only from me, but from you as well." He took his hand away. "And yes, you're eighteen now, which means you're technically an adult and don't need me anymore, but if you do, I'll be there for you. I might still be able to teach you some things, even if it's just what it means to be human."

Matt bit his lip. His knee-jerk reaction would've been to reject that help. He *was* independent, knew how to stand on his own two feet, and while he got that René had missed his son for the last fifteen years, Matt hadn't truly missed his father. But things had changed and with this confusing human world to navigate, he needed someone in his corner. Because the only other alternative would be to leave it all behind, and somehow Matt knew that a door had opened inside of him that could no longer be closed, even if he did return to Hell.

"I could use some help with putting up the wardrobe in my room."

René's eyes widened. "You haven't done that yet?"

His clothes had been lying on the floor for months now. Sheepishly, he shrugged. "I didn't know how."

"Oh, Matt." His father sighed and laughed softly to himself. "I should've asked... Yes! Do you want to do that now?"

Did he want to build a wardrobe in the middle of the night? "Yes, I think I'd like that." Matt paused for a moment, chewing on the word he needed to get off his chest. "Dad."

René's warm smile instantly healed a small part of the rift inside of Matt.

Rachel

Exhausted, Rachel sat down in the meadow. All around her, the traces of Nico's death were evaporating, pulled into the dreamweb in her hand. "Wouldn't it be fun if that worked in the real world as well?" Rachel said bitterly to the one Nico who remained. The one who wasn't him.

"The dreamworld belongs to the real world. Any healing you do here has an effect there." He got up to his feet, petals swirling around him. "Come, I'll show you."

Rachel followed his lead, wondering what he meant by that. The first dream they visited was Jan's. The blood was gone, but the questions were still on the wall, with Jan pondering them. "I didn't know school was important to you," she whispered.

"It's not." Jan never looked around. "Except my father says it is, and I..."

"You're just not the schooling type," Nico said, then took a sponge from the sink and began to wipe it all down. "A parent's expectations can be harrowing. You can try to meet them, but you'll always fall short. Or you figure out what you do best and pursue that, fathers be damned." There was a rebellious streak in him that reminded Rachel painfully of her brother. "Give him his magic back."

Confusion washed over Rachel, but then she remembered the dreamweb's function. She had soaked up all the magic the drude had possessed, and now she had to let it free again. Rachel stroked one of the long feathers and caught a golden drop. It didn't melt in her hand, nor did it run through her fingers.

She offered the drop to Jan. "What's your magic, Jan?"

"I don't know." Jan glanced at the drop. "Is that like this MAGIC stuff? If so, I don't want it."

Rachel chuckled. "That's good to hear." She leaned forward and wiped the drop on Jan's forehead. A soft golden shimmer surrounded him before vanishing.

When she stepped back, the room had changed. It was an unknown place to her, a run-down hall in bitter need of renovation, but it bore Jan's signature all over it.

"I think you need to fix this place up," Rachel mused. It was obviously a metaphor for the run-down state of Jan's actual life.

Nico handed Jan a toolbox and stood back with Rachel. "See? Dreams reflect reality, and reality can take inspiration from dreams."

They returned to the meadow and ventured into Lucille's dream next. The little girl sat on the curb, watching the car wreck in front of her. Rachel's heart went out to her. She'd never asked how Lucille's mum had died and seeing this memory-laced dream of hers made her feel like she knew Lucille more intimately than she should now.

But Lucille wasn't tormented by her mother's death today. Because she'd had her grandmother.

Rachel stroked her dreamweb, this time coming up with a bunch of red drops that looked like tears. "The Nadellyan Tears." It was the proper name of her necklace.

She let them fly towards the little girl. As soon as the tears reached Lucille, she looked up.

From the shadows came an old woman, Cecille de Cerque. "Lucy? Lucy!" She ran towards her granddaughter and closed her in an embrace, endless love pouring out of her.

Rachel watched the two holding each other, and knew that little Lucille would be fine. Until she lost her champion, as well.

With a sigh, Rachel turned around and walked into Samantha's dream. She found Samantha kneeling on the stage, eyes covered as she sobbed and sobbed.

"And sometimes, we need a little dream to escape," Nico said softly, pulling the green drops of Samantha's magic from the dreamweb.

The droplets floated through the room until there were enough of them to sink into each body on the ground. Slowly, the blood washed away, and Samantha's friends and family rose again. Christmas music rang through the room, and people swayed in dance. On the stage, Samantha stood in surprise, wearing a pretty green dress and a red ribbon in her hair. Her eyes flitted around until they landed on the stairs.

There, Daniel walked up, a big cheesy smile on his lips. He approached Samantha and gently brushed a lock of hair out of her face. "Shall we?" Rachel heard him ask.

Samantha beamed up at him and nodded. A mistletoe bloomed above them, its berries white as snow. Daniel bowed in front of Samantha, then took her hand to lead her in a slow dance. Samantha smiled all the way, happier than she'd been in weeks.

"Let's leave those two alone. They deserve a little more time together," Nico whispered.

Rachel left the town hall through the door and stepped into the blazing madness that was Fabian's nightmare. "Right, water."

She stroked the dreamweb one last time to bring out Fabian's magic. The blue drops splashed into the dream, instantly extinguishing the flames.

"My, he's rather powerful, isn't he?" Nico commented.

Water flowed through the house, washing all remnants of the flames away. A bunch of chickens squawked as they floated by, now back to their normal appearance. Outside, Caroline and Fabian worked together to put them back into their enclosure. It always made Rachel's heart ache a little to see mother and son genuinely enjoying each other's company.

"So, have you made your decision?" Nico asked.

"About what?"

"About him. And you."

Rachel sighed. There hadn't exactly been a lot of time to think about where to go next with their relationship. "I really like him. I'm just not sure whether I love him."

"Is that because he might die?" Nico asked softly and drew her back into the meadow. They settled into the flowers, each crossing their legs, just as they used to sit at home and discuss their mother. "I told you this when we first met. Living is hard. It's full of loss. The loss of innocence. The loss of a loved one. But it's full of love, too." He took her hands. "There is love for you out there, Rachel. And no dream, no matter how beautiful, will come close."

She thought back to Samantha's dream. She'd seemed happy with Daniel, but Daniel was dead, and all she could give Samantha were memories of their love.

"You deserve someone who loves you, Rachel," Nico whispered, and the old pain flashed over his face.

How many years had they longed for love? Nico would never find true happiness, but hers was still within her reach. If only she had the courage to grab hold of it.

Lucille

They'd all agreed to take the weekend off to recover from last week's ordeal. Lucille slept through most of Saturday and ordered herself a spa day for Sunday. By the time Monday came around, she felt well recovered and was ready to talk shop.

It was a beautiful winter's day. The freshly fallen snow glistened in the sun as it blanketed the houses and barren trees. The Reese was half frozen and crackled softly as sheets of thin ice bumped into each other.

The six of them chose to enjoy the weather and take a walk instead of hiding inside. Rachel and Fabian were holding hands, while Matt and Samantha kept as much distance between them as possible without breaking up the group. Lucille was grateful that they weren't fighting right now but concentrated on the things that truly mattered.

"So, the Prophecy of the Six," Lucille started. "That refers to us?"

Matt nodded. "Yeah, that's what Chay said. Apparently, it begins when all twelve heroes of old are reborn in the same place, same time." He shrugged. "Well, we've all been born around the same time here in Greenvalley, so I guess it's safe to say the time of the prophecy is now."

"And with now, you mean between next week and the ripe old age of eighty?" Fabian asked hopefully. "I mean, the exact timing is a bit vague. I guess not in the grand scheme of soul recycling, but that final battle could've happened when we were all toddlers, and it didn't. So, who's saying it's going to happen now, instead of in... sixty years? I'd be happy to save the world at eighty."

"Except there's a seventh person," Samantha said with a heavy sigh. "The prophecy is about facing the same enemy. Draken... or as the prophecy calls him the *Greedy One.*"

She gave them a pointed look that went far beyond Jan. "Meaning?"

Lucille poked her elbow into his side. "Matt's uncle Malcolm, he's the Archdemon of Greed. He could be the Greedy One. Right?"

Samantha nodded. "Yes, there was no reincarnation list for him in the book."

"Can we please stop calling him my uncle?" Matt asked. "I only met the guy here, and he doesn't seem very inclined to let me live for family's sake."

"Fair call." Lucille smiled. "I think it just takes off a little bit of the edge when we call him Uncle Malcolm, rather than... the Greedy One." She shivered, and not from the cold. "Samantha's theory makes sense to me. He seems to fit the prophecy to a T."

"What are the chances he's not interested in the end of the world right now?" Fabian asked.

Next to him, Rachel chuckled. "Not that high, but that's not saying we're going to fail. We just need to get all six emblems together, and we should have a fighting chance."

"Right." Samantha bit her lip and grimaced. "If only I knew how to look for the flowers."

"Have you tried flower shops?" Matt asked.

She glared at him. "Yes, I'm sure the bond between me and Freya's flowers is so strong, I'll be able to pick them out from thousands of other flowers."

Matt pulled a face but kept his thoughts to himself, for which Lucille was grateful.

"Well, I'm with Rachel on this one," she declared. "Guys, we've kicked Malcolm's butt again and again. We've survived his hellhounds, his psycho-drugs, and now his drude."

"I wouldn't call surviving a few attacks kicking butt," Matt said, wincing. "He *is* the Archdemon of Greed. He has powers far beyond any one of us. And yeah, if we can get all emblems together and figure out how to combine them, we might stand a chance, but those are a lot of ifs."

"So, you're a coward?" Jan asked. "The big and dangerous Matt Traidous is afraid of his uncle?"

He was obviously joking, but Matt groaned. "I'll show you how afraid I am!"

Jan laughed and bent down to gather some snow. "Yeah? Bring it on!" He pulled back his arm to throw the snowball.

Lucille had to bend her neck backwards to save her nose from getting hit by the missile. Meanwhile, Matt used his teleporting skills to jump out of the way, and the snowball hit Fabian in the face. Matt reappeared behind Jan and dumped a shower of snow down his collar, while Fabian bent down to gather some snow for himself.

"That's cheating!" Jan called out, indignant. Fabian's snowball hit him on the shoulder. "Just you wait."

Within seconds, the boys had gotten into a full snowball fight. Lucille shrieked and jumped out of the way to try to hide behind a tree, but Rachel saw her and threw a snowball of her own.

"Globus igneus!" Lucille shouted and melted the snowball with her green ball of fire just in time.

Rachel looked outraged but highly amused. Meanwhile, Samantha was already in the thick of the fight with the boys, after Fabian had lathered her face with a handful of snow. She kept from targeting Matt, and he didn't bother with her, but they both seemed to enjoy themselves independently.

Lucille's cheeks glowed in the cold as she grinned and threw all propriety into the wind to join the snowball fight.

None of them showed any mercy until their fingers were aching from the cold and their faces hurt from all the shrieking and laughing on the beautiful winter day.

Malcolm

Deep down in the Residence of Greed, Malcolm stood in front of the exquisite model he'd had made of Greenvalley and the surrounding forests. It wasn't the only item of value in his residence. The entire room was filled with priceless artifacts, some of them magical. Under a glass dome, silver magic flowed like the Moebius strip in endless circles. In a big copper pot, a plant grew at breathtaking speeds and bloomed. Every time the blossoms opened, black seeds fell onto its leaves, destroying the plant within seconds, only to then sprout again anew.

Multiple coins from at least a dozen different worlds were piled up against the walls, jewels glistening between them. Even the furniture was invaluable, some of it from the rarest woods known to demons. Malcolm even had a wall piece from the Red Tower of Magic, one of several legendary towers spread across all worlds, believed to be the source of all kinds of magic.

But all of that wasn't enough. He wanted more.

For years, Malcolm had researched the rivers of magic: how they flowed across the worlds, connecting them through the abstract space between them. They were the source of all that was living, and they were immensely powerful. He'd found several node points where the rivers flowed into their world, but none as powerful as the one feeding Greenvalley.

He had to have it, but the witches in the area had blocked him from accessing the source. He'd tried to break the web that hid the magic from him, but had failed so far. Still, the rivers kept running through town, and so he'd looked into harvesting it through proxies.

The drugged-up kids from the docks had been a waste of time, but the drude had proved more successful.

Until the little bastards had killed her and stolen *his* magic.

Malcolm had their houses marked on the model in front of him. From the huge villa in the Southeast to the tiny flat in the north. He knew where the annoying human friends of Melaney's spawn lived, and he would kill them one by one. Because...

"Nobody steals from me! Nobody!"

A Spring of Magic

When reality turns into a nightmare, a dreamer might be their only chance.

After saving her friends in the dreamworld, Rachel sets out to live in the real world. But with the Archdemon of Greed eager to steal Greenvalley's magic, an ancient prophecy promising the end of the world, and half of her friends still hating each other, reality isn't exactly a pleasant place.
When her town starts descending into hell, and her friends lose all hope, Rachel has to find a way to make her dreams for a better future come true. Can she find her powers in time to stop greed take it all, or will her life become an endless nightmare?

A Spring of Magic is the gripping finale of the action-packed Ashuan Greed trilogy. If you liked *Buffy's* wit and snarky one-liners, the magic of *Charmed,* or the supernatural drama of the *Vampire Diaries,* you'll love this new urban fantasy series.

Buy *A Spring of Magic* now to find out what's in store for the Greenvalley Crew today!

JANNA RUTH

A SPRING OF MAGIC

ASHUAN GREED BOOK 3

A Force of Nature

I've trusted nature spirits with my life, until the storm king decided I had to die.

Did you ever wonder what living on the streets of Berlin is like? My name is Rika and I've been homeless for eight years. It's not too bad, since I've got salamanders to warm me in winter and dryads to protect me from stragglers. People say I'm crazy, because to everyone else, those nature spirits are invisible. But they're real. Real and *dangerous*, as I learn when I accidentally cross the plans of the Erlking, an ancient and hate-filled spirit. Now he and his deadly storm are after me.
My only chance are the Spirit Seekers, an elite group of soldiers trained to battle nature's wrath. Since their precious commander is missing in action, they need me to be their eyes. Signing up with the Spirit Seekers is the opposite of run and hide, but they offer me protection and the tools to fight for my survival. All I have to do is betray my old spirit friends and try not to die.

Join Rika and the Spirit Seekers in this action-packed stormy urban fantasy adventure and start your supernatural trip to Europe today!

JANNA RUTH
A FORCE OF NATURE
SPIRIT SEEKER BOOK 1

Ghosts of the Catacombs

I'm a ghost whisperer, not a catacomb crawler. But when you live in Paris, sometimes you end up being both.

Hi, I'm Alix. During the day, I'm a history student at the time-honoured Sorbonne University. After class, I hang out with the ghosts of the revolution, the many undead misunderstood Parisian artists, and adventurous scientists that glow in the dark. None of them are alive, but they come to me to solve their problems with the living. When a recently deceased catacomb tour guide asks me to retrieve a mysterious personal item from the underground, things take a turn for the weird. Suddenly, I find myself in a city of ghosts, hunted by murderous cave crawlers, and stumbling across haunting secrets. If I'm not careful now, I might end up a ghost myself.

Urban Fantasy with a French twist. If you like cave-crawling adventures, hopeless romantics, and ghosts, you'll enjoy Ghosts of the Catacombs, the first book of the Parisian Ghosts series. Travel to Paris today to embark on your catacomb adventure.

JANNA RUTH
GHOSTS OF THE CATACOMBS
PARISIAN GHOSTS 1